The Grief Syndrome

by Terry Wright

2019, TWB Press
www.twbpress.com

The Grief Syndrome
Copyright © 2011 by Terry Wright

© Cover Art by Terry Wright

ISBN 978-1-94404558-6

Chapter One

I *never should have come to Colorado.* Marco San Lucas brooded as he slouched in his seat on the speeding bus. With old and wary eyes, he watched out the oval window, uninterested in the purple mountains drawing nearer but on the lookout for bounty hunters. They could come out of nowhere and leave chaos and death in their wake. And he was one of their prime targets.

Perspiring in his long brown coat, he observed the flow of traffic gliding alongside the bus. Identical sleek-white autocars were evenly spaced and under the complete control of electronic sensors in the roadbed. Overhead, a police cruiser flew by, engine whining. Things had not always been this way. He'd lived long enough to remember a time when people actually drove cars: different makes, different models, and different colors.

But in 2235, even the bus kept automated pace with the surrounding traffic as it headed west, a nonstop afternoon express to the rundown suburb of Boulder. It was known as a haven for misfits and derelicts, and he planned to eke out a living there, collecting garbage for the power plant at St. Vrain, retrofitted to burn methane after the government banned the use of nuclear energy. He'd heard the pickings were good in Boulder.

"Excuse me," the passenger sitting next to him said. "You're one of them, aren't you."

Marco didn't answer the stranger but regarded his narrow face, slicked-back hair, and rough hands with manicured nails—similar to the hands of bounty hunters and their snitches. He wore a tan overcoat, shiny black pants, and knee-high boots, garb not definitive of his profession. Obviously, he was interested in the latest news. The Denver Star Hologram shimmered in front of him; the headlines read: *Cure For West Nile B Found.*

Marking the young man as worthy of caution, Marco returned his attention to the traffic sweeping along outside.

"You smell of garlic," the persistent man said. "I've heard that's how to spot your kind, though I've never met a Weller before."

Still looking out the window, Marco clenched his jaw. His body odor had betrayed him. Reeking of garlic was the interminable side effect of his condition. "I'm a garbage hocker," he insisted.

"You stink like a Weller."

"If you don't like it, move to another seat."

"I'm just curious, that's all."

Marco wished the man would go away.

"What's it like to live so long?"

"I don't know what you're talking about," Marco lied.

"You have a name?"

Now he faced the man, scowling. "So you can report me to the bounty hunters?"

"We're on a moving autobus, for Christ's sake."

"Snitches have their ways."

The Grief Syndrome

Smiling, the man showed perfect teeth. "So you *are* one of them. I knew it. Do you know Jerry Well?"

Marco's chest tightened at the mention of that name. He'd never met Jerry Well but cursed him daily.

"What happened back there in 2020?" the man asked.

"What do you care?"

He produced a wireless microphone. "I'm a reporter."

Marco glanced again at the young man's hands. "And I'm a belly dancer."

"You can trust me."

Turning away, Marco raised his coat collar. Unwanted memories flooded his mind. Back then, ads for Jerry Well's Everlife pills were everywhere: on billboards, radio and TV, in newspapers and magazines. The Internet was choked with spam touting his little green garlic pills that would make everyone feel better and live longer. Outrageous as the claims sounded, more than five hundred thousand people responded to the ads. No one knew that Everlife would make them immortal.

"What do you say, old man? There are so few of you left. Tell me your story." He poked the mike at him.

"Leave me alone."

The reporter retracted his mike and spoke into it. "There you have it, folks, a real live Weller on the 105 to Boulder."

Annoyed, Marco returned his gaze out the window just in time to see a black van careen across several lanes of traffic. Tires throwing smoke, the van weaved between evenly spaced autocars, gaining on the bus.

His throat seized. *Bounty hunters.*

They'd found him. The reporter was a snitch, his

microphone a link to the bounty hunters, the salutation a signal. Marco whipped around, balled a fist at the snitch. "What have you done?"

"Go easy, old man." The snitch opened his overcoat, revealing a Glock 401 particle blaster. "You don't want any of these nice people to get hurt."

Marco glanced around, saw people minding their own business, except one young man toting a sport bag. His wide eyes locked on Marco's, and he knew the man had been paying attention. The connection was intense. A trap? An ambush? Marco had to act fast. With practiced speed, he delivered an elbow to the snitch's chin, which made him keel over in the aisle and blood gush from his mouth.

Someone screamed.

Fighting panic, Marco frisked the snitch and snatched up the Glock blaster.

Passengers bolted from their seats, clambered over one another in a frantic attempt to distance themselves from the gunman.

He swiveled the blaster to aim at the attentive young man, but he'd ducked for cover. "Shit." Scrambling forward down the aisle, Marco shoved people aside, "Get out of my way," and threw his body at the door. It didn't give, just sprang back and flung him to the floor. Rising, he fired the blaster at the door. Bursts of energy shrieked from the muzzle.

Pheuw-Pheuw-Pheuw!

White-hot bolts peppered the door.

Pheuw-Pheuw...

But the locks held firm.

Fitz... fitz...

The Grief Syndrome

The particle clip was empty before he realized his efforts were futile. "Damn." He hurled the blaster at the windscreen, but it just bounced off the glass.

The black van careened up alongside the speeding bus. Van doors slid open and bounty hunters appeared. They wore black fatigues and blast jackets, helmets and goggles. Rifles were slung across their backs. One by one, they tossed grappling hooks up to the bus's roof, and using microburst boosters anchored to their belts, they propelled themselves up the ropes with amazing agility. A stampede of heavy boots thundered on the roof. Seconds later, a blast tore a hole in the ceiling. Choking smoke swirled in. Passengers screamed and crowded toward the rear of the bus. Bounty hunters spilled in and advanced down the aisle, rifles leveled at Marco, their infrared beams shining on his chest. "Hold it right there, Weller."

Terror lit fires in Marco's bloodstream. He recognized that voice. It was John Parish, the most bloodthirsty bounty hunter of all time. He was meaner than his father and his grandfather combined. During the past century, Marco had run-ins with Parish's murderous family. This time there was no way out. Marco pressed his back to the front windscreen. "Don't shoot."

A death-like silence came over the passengers. Wind shrieked through the breached roof and wheels whined on the road as the bus neared Boulder.

On the floor, the reporter snitch stirred, spitting blood. He looked up at the bounty hunters. "Kill the freak."

Parish admonished him with a swift kick in the ribs then moved to the front of the bus. "You and me been a long time comin', Weller."

Sweat beaded Marco's face. The odor of garlic exploded from his pores. His only hope to survive was to try bribing the killers. "Please...I've got some money."

"Ya don't say." Parish removed his goggles, revealing gray eyes. "Jerry Well put five million dollars on your head. Got more than that?"

"I can get more."

"He's lyin', boss." The snitch got to his feet, wiped blood from his mouth. "I say we take Jerry Well's money. It's a sure bet."

"All in favor?" Parish asked over his shoulder.

"Aye," came the bounty hunters' unanimous response.

Hands in the air, Marco pleaded, "Wait a minute—"

"You lose, Weller." Parish opened fire.

Searing pain tore through Marco's body as magnesium slugs burned through his chest and shattered the windscreen behind him. The force knocked him backward and blew him out the front of the bus. He slammed to the roadway in a shower of glass, rolling and flopping until finally he was crushed under the speeding wheels.

Passengers felt the thump-thump.

John Parish saluted thin air. "And I win." By the time the bus entered Boulder, he and his bounty hunters had fled the bus and sped away in the black van. Only then did the passengers begin moving forward, braving the rush of air coming in through the blown-out windscreen.

Scott Dunn groped for a seat, his sport bag dangling from his shoulder by the strap. His heart hammered wildly in response to what he'd just witnessed. During the ordeal, he'd ducked low and forced himself to remain calm. Now he felt sick to his stomach, his garlicky odor obvious. He could have easily been the bounty hunters' target.

The bus glided to its preprogrammed stop inside the Boulder terminal. The doors slid open. Passengers surged forward, pushing against each other as if escaping a fire. Transit security personnel converged on the scene. While a maintenance crew inspected the damaged bus, police rounded up witnesses.

Scott didn't want any part of their investigation. Keeping his head down, he made his way through the crowd.

"Bounty hunters did it," he heard a passenger telling officers.

"We've had reports of Wellers coming into the area." The officer sniffed the air. "They always bring trouble."

Veering left, Scott dodged a solicitor who shoved a printed flyer in his face. "Save Alpha Ketari."

Scott figured he'd be lucky to save himself, much less some faraway planet. He drew in a deep breath and pressed on, hoping his faded cotton jacket, bleached jeans, and soiled shoes would make him look like a local worker. As he moved, he concentrated on controlling his fear. It was the only way to reduce his perspiration, and in turn, dampen the garlicky odor that would give him away.

His medium frame was unimposing but forceful when in motion. The fact that he looked twenty-five years old helped divert suspicion away from him. Most Wellers were old, having taken Jerry Well's Everlife in a last-ditch effort to ward off the debilitating effects of old age. Back then, Scott's motivation was different: he was young, and so was his bride, and as it was with many young newlyweds, they wanted to live long and healthy lives together.

They'd turned to Everlife and lived to regret it.

Anyone who ever knew Scott Dunn would say he was lost without his family. His loved ones' deaths had made him callous and unapproachable. Long ago he'd given up caring about anyone but himself. His entire life, he'd prided himself as a fixer of broken things: mechanical things, electrical things, but there was one thing he could not fix, his grief. When he sought professional treatment, the doctors told him he suffered from a rare condition.

They'd explained that it was the late psychologist C. B. Schwartz, in a paper published by the American Psychology Association, who'd outlined the ten stages of *The Grief Syndrome*. His research into the grief experienced when a loved one died had revealed that most bereaved worked through the process within one or two years. This he called *short-term* grieving.

"Grief is something every human experiences," Schwartz had written. *"Typically, the grieving process has a beginning, a middle, and an end, starting with initial shock and denial, moving through guilt, anger and depression, and finally on to acceptance of the loss suffered and eventual healing.*

"Wellers, on the other hand, outlive everyone they love. After watching their spouses die, their children die, and grandchildren, and on and on over the centuries, long-term grieving sets in. A pattern of behavior emerges. Most Wellers become loners, mired in the guilt or depression stages of grief, rejecting everyone: no friends, no lovers, no pets. In that way, their immortal lives become bearable." Schwartz summarized by saying, *"The Grief Syndrome*

persists far into the unforeseeable future, a crippling anomaly brought on by the Weller phenomenon."

Scott Dunn couldn't foresee letting go of his grief any time soon, but the reason he had come to Boulder had nothing to do with the Grief Syndrome and everything to do with revenge.

A female voice echoed through the terminal. *"Attention passengers departing to Denver. There has been a delay."*

Hanging from the ceiling, plasma-ray monitors displayed the activity around the bus. Roving hover-cams fed images to mainframe receivers so everyone got real-time information, including video feeds along the highway, which now replayed the old man's crushing demise.

The crowd gathered in clusters, watching the monitors. Scott feared his lone retreat would draw unwanted attention, so he merged with the onlookers and mingled. Suppressing his anxiety, he glanced behind him and saw the crowd of curious faces, and floating above them, the gray disc and inverted black dome of a hover-cam. He quickly turned back to the monitor, hoping the camera operators weren't zeroing in on him.

On the screen, a black van appeared. Bounty hunters piled out and body-bagged the old Weller's remains.

John Parish supervised the retrieval operation. As automated traffic whizzed by behind him, he looked up at the hover-cam and stepped forward, the camera zooming in for a close up of his goggled face. "Wellers be warned," he growled out, his gritted teeth flashing white in the sunshine. "There's nowhere to hide in Boulder." He raised his blaster. In a flash, the image shuddered, distorted to diagonal black and white lines, and blinked out.

The image of the damaged bus reappeared. The crowd cheered John Parish and began to disperse. Hover-cams followed the action. Scott let the current sweep him along as voices resounded a familiar rhetoric. "That'll teach them Wellers to show up around here," one man said.

"They're an abomination to God," a woman cried.

Scott understood their disdain. Wellers had been the *new minority* for the last century. Most people either hated Wellers for being different, or envied them for being immortal, immune to aging and disease, but not bullets and blasters. So this inability to die from natural causes meant Wellers were condemned to die violent deaths, including Scott's wife.

"Death to the Wellers," someone shouted.

The crowd emerged from the terminal at 2200 Pearl Street Station. Electro shuttles and radar cabs descended on the masses and moments later zoomed off with their fares. Scott looked around for the person who was supposed to meet him.

A red hydrogen cycle whined up to the curb. Its helmeted rider wore shapely red leathers adorned with yellow stripes. Calf-high orange boots hit the pavement, and her black helmet came off. "Are you Scott Dunn?" Her blond hair cascaded over her shoulders.

No way...a woman? She was attractive enough, had the cutest dimple on her chin, but he'd expected a man to meet him, one of H. G. Carson's men from the Weller underground. Unsure his contact was genuine, Scott asked the code question. "When did your mother die?"

"She didn't, but my father was in the war."

It was the correct response, though deep down inside he wished she'd gotten it wrong. "In that case, I'm Scott Dunn."

She peeled off a glove, "Sue Masters," and offered her hand.

Stepping forward, he took her fingers and lifted them to his lips as if to kiss the back of her hand, but instead, he paused to smell her skin. A strong odor of garlic greeted him. Assured she was a Weller, he released her hand and threw a leg over the back of her idling cycle. "Take me to Katherine."

"You can't just bust into a cryo-lab." Sue pulled on her glove.

"I've got everything I need except the crypt number." Scott wedged the sport bag under his arm. "Jerry Well's not getting her back."

"You're going to unplug his wife," Sue whispered conspiratorially. "Sounds a lot like murder, doesn't it?"

Scott leaned forward. "West Nile B, remember? She died two hundred twenty five years ago."

"Technically." Sue donned the helmet. "But the cure has just been found. Jerry's going to reanimate her in two days."

"Not if I can help it."

"No wonder Carson picked you for the job. You're a hard man, Scott Dunn."

"Hard as stone."

"Hang on."

As the cycle tore away from the curb, a hover-cam recorded its departure.

Chapter Two

In the basement of his mansion on Diamond Back Ridge, Jerry Well pushed through a thickly insulated door. He wore a long thermal robe, silver and black, with a matching hood that draped over his head. Mink-lined boots and gloves protected him from the severe cold. The room gleamed with white tile walls, floor and ceiling, all sparkling clean and smelling of lime. This wasn't any ordinary room. He had built it especially for his wife.

Behind him, the thick door closed with a loud thump. Breath vapors wisped from Jerry's nostrils as he strode toward the center of the room. He was a handsome man, two hundred seventy-four years old, six-foot-three with sweptback black hair. There wasn't an ounce of extra body fat on his lanky frame. Those who knew him described him as a *health nut to a fault*. He'd been like that from the age of fourteen, after the neighborhood bully beat him to a pulp. In response, he regimented himself to a strict diet, multivitamins, and exercise. He got tougher, and he got meaner. Before long, nobody bullied Jerry Well anymore. Nobody liked him either, but he was in control, in control of his body, in control of his life.

Control meant everything to Jerry.

In the center of the room stood a ten-foot tall titanium

cryostat that creaked from the freezing liquid hydrogen inside. The number *34-B* had been stenciled in bold black letters on the outer shell, and a triangular-shaped logo read: *Alcor Life Extension Institute, Boulder, Colorado*. Mounted below it, a crystal-framed photograph sealed in glass revealed the once-vibrant life now suspended inside: a woman with bedroom brown eyes, flowing brown hair, and sun-kissed skin. He never tired of her smile, though the warmth of her touch had long escaped his memory. "Katherine, I bring good news," he told the picture. "We will be together again very soon."

He imagined her reply in a sensual voice. *"I miss you."*

That brought a smile to his face. "The doctors are making preparations to reanimate you. They've finally found a cure for West Nile B. You're coming home."

"Jerry, it's been so long."

"Have patience, my love. Hope has been our only ally."

"I love you, Jerry."

He touched the creaking cryostat with a gloved hand, imagined it was the sound of their bedsprings, the crumpling of crisp sheets, the moan from her throat upon their embrace. For two hundred and twenty-five years he had loved her this way. "Our love will never die, Katherine."

"I'm c-cold, Jerry."

Christ, she had to go and wreck his romantic mood. What did she have to complain about anyway? She asked for what she got. Did she expect him to be sympathetic? If she had listened to him in the first place, he wouldn't have almost lost her. Was it so hard to understand that he loved her more than anything? In an attempt to quell his rising anger, he forced her past transgressions out of his mind. "In two days, you will be warm forever."

"Only death is forever, Jerry."

"But I have defeated death," he growled out. "Haven't you heard a thing I've been telling you?"

"Will I live forever too?"

At that, he produced a vial from his robe pocket. "This is yours, Katherine. I've been saving it for you." He held it out for the picture's inspection. "It's a concentrated dose of my longevity formula, Everlife."

"It's sugar water, Jerry."

He felt another jolt of anger. Of course it was sugar water; he knew that. The real vial was in his office safe. Did she think he was stupid enough to carry it around with him? He'd worked hard to develop Everlife. In college, he experimented with allicin, the plant chemical found in garlic. The health benefits of garlic could be traced back 5,000 years, so believing that allicin was the key to good health, he set out to find a way to produce it synthetically inside the human body.

Katherine could never appreciate the work he'd put into Everlife, the sheer genius of it all. She had no clue how he'd altered the DNA of garlic and Lactobacilli Acidophilus bacteria that thrived naturally in the human digestive tract, and how a symbiotic relationship began between the garlic and the mutated bacteria, which then produced allicin, much like a spider produced silk. This wasn't only miraculous in itself, but it also resulted in the byproduct Delanthropine, a bio-toxin lethal to all other pathogenic microorganisms. On the cellular level, the combination of Delanthropine and allicin stopped chromosomes from shrinking. Cells stopped aging. He'd made the greatest discovery of all time, control over death, but Katherine didn't appreciate anything he'd done for her. Everlife could've saved her life, the dumb bitch.

Katherine sobbed. *"You hurt my feelings, Jerry."*

It was as if she'd read his mind. He held his breath, knowing he shouldn't let her emotional outburst bother him now. Her support was crucial in order for his plan to succeed. Returning the phony formula to his pocket, he said, "I'm sorry, Katherine. Won't you forgive me? I'll never call you a bitch again. I promise."

She sniffled. *"You always promise."*

"I have a surprise for you," he sang teasingly to win back her favor. "A coming home gift."

"You do? What is it, Jerry? What is it?" He pictured her clapping her hands, her eyes wide open in wonder, and her face beaming with expectation. *"Oh please tell me."*

Not wanting to hear her whining any longer, he smiled at her picture and leaned in close. "Alpha Ketari."

"Yes, yes. It would be wonderful, Jerry."

He imagined her excitement, and it warmed his heart. "But first, my love, I must deal with the Council of Elders."

"Oh, oh, Jerry. They have other plans for Alpha Ketari." He imagined hearing disdain in her voice.

"Do you think I'm stupid? I have everything under control."

"As usual, Jerry."

That was more like it. "We'll live on Alpha Ketari together, forever."

"I can't wait."

He remembered Katherine's previous refusal to take his Everlife formula and the deadly irony of that decision. She wouldn't have come down with the West Nile B virus. The Delanthropine would have protected her. Instead, she'd told him she didn't want to live with him forever. Unimaginable. With that recollection hurting his stomach, he growled, "You'd better not be lying to me, Katherine. This time you will take the formula and become an immortal like me."

"Yes, Jerry," he imagined her obedient reply. *"But we aren't the only immortals."*

"The Wellers," he spat, slamming gloved fists together.

"They could spoil our plans."

"My bounty hunters are dealing with the problem."

"And what about John Parish? He believes that vial of Everlife is his."

"I had to lie to him."

"What will he do when he finds out, Jerry?"

"Don't fret yourself over it, Katherine." God she could be so naïve. "I'll kill him first."

"Be careful, Jerry."

"I will, my love." Jerry gazed at her glassy picture, his heart beating wildly. "Now I must go. There is much to do." He turned with haste and left the room. The door closed behind him with a solid thump.

***

The titanium cryostat creaked.

Inside, Katherine was wrapped in white gauze, her

body supported by interlocking steel clamps, like fingers, and frozen in liquid hydrogen. A network of finely engraved cracks, like frost on a windowpane, etched her slate gray skin. Her eyes and mouth were sewn shut, and her fingernails had turned black, her toenails, too, split and grossly deformed. Her head was shaved, and two holes had been drilled into her skull. Sensors tipped with blinking green LEDs protruded from the holes and reported vital information to monitoring computers. Her core temperature was minus 320 degrees Fahrenheit. There was nothing beautiful in the cryostat, nothing that resembled Katherine's picture outside.

Back in 2020, she was twenty-nine and terminally ill with West Nile B, a mutated form of the 2003 virus. Meningitis had already paralyzed her central nervous system, destroyed her motor controls, and within days, encephalitis would set in as the virus attacked her brain. The virus could not be stopped. She could not be cured. And though she knew she would die, she inhaled every sweet breath greedily, clinging to life with all her might.

However, her husband had other plans for her. She was very much alive when Jerry placed her in a tub and began covering her with ice.

"I'm c-cold, Jerry," she stammered, unable to move.

He dumped another bucket of ice on her. "Sleep, my love. When you awaken, you will be cured."

"No."

"I love you."

"Let me go."

"You're not leaving me, Katherine."

"I hate you." Those were the last words she said.

A cryonics team was on hand. Jerry explained to them that the West Nile B virus had killed her. Everything had to be done with great urgency. They packed her in dry ice, lowering her temperature further, but slowly. If they'd frozen her too quickly, every cell in her body would have exploded as fluids turned to ice.

After bundling her in canvas, they rushed her to the cryo-lab. When her body temperature dropped to 5 degrees Celsius, they moved her to an embalming table. There, in the manner of morticians, they drained her blood and replaced it with a cryo-preservative solution of glycerol, toxic as automotive antifreeze. This chemical leached the water from her cells to reduce the damage that freezing would inflict on her tissues. Wrapped and sewn and hung like a side of beef, she was clamped in the steel fingers of cryostat 34-B and submerged in liquid nitrogen. The lid was closed and sealed. One hundred fifty years passed before Alcor replaced the liquid nitrogen with liquid hydrogen, which had become cheaper and more abundant. Through it all, very little ice had formed in her body, but every part of her was rigid as frosted glass.

Before Katherine met this fate, music was her life. She could sing like a songbird, hitting the high notes with thrilling perfection. At the age of three, she sang in her church choir. She soloed at five. By eight, she'd mastered the piano, and in high school, the violin, but singing was her greatest love. She worked her way through college performing in nightclubs and theaters from Cheyenne, Wyoming, to Albuquerque, New Mexico.

It was backstage at Fiddler's Green in Denver that she met Jerry Well. Fit and trim and smelling of Stetson, he handed her a huge bouquet of flowers. His smile was alluring, his words soft and filled with compliments. Later, as he wooed her, he kept showing up without calling first. He brought gifts and doted over her constantly. And he made wonderful promises. "Marry me, my love. I'll see to it that your voice graces the finest theaters in Paris and London and Moscow. The world awaits you on bended knees."

Those who knew Katherine best would have said that she sang from her heart because she longed for romance. Orphaned young, she grew up displaced and lonely. The experience made her strong, but as independent as she'd become, she still dreamed of being swept off her feet one day by a handsome knight in shining armor. So it didn't surprise anyone when she accepted Jerry Well's proposal. During their short engagement, she ended every performance with her favorite song, which she dedicated to Jerry: *I Will Always Love You* by Dolly Parton. Katherine had found romance, but soon after the wedding, she realized she'd mistaken his obsession for love. It was a bitter step into hell.

As it turned out, Jerry Well wanted her all to himself, under his control, and to that end, he accused her of cheating on him and locked her in her room. To explain her absence from the stage, he'd told everyone that she was happy now. "She has withdrawn from the limelight of her own free will," he'd lied. So there were no more performances, no trips abroad, and no world awaiting her on bended knee. Those promises were replaced with sweat and toil and despicable acts behind closed doors. When she tried to leave him, he caught her and beat her black-and-blue. She wanted to die, but unbelievably, he began pleading for her forgiveness. Weeping on his knees, he promised he'd change. And gifts poured in: sexy lingerie, fancy clothes, jewelry, and exotic perfumes. He'd acted so sincere that Katherine thought it was possible to be happy with him after all.

With high hopes, she gave him another chance, but before long, the cycle started over. Subtle at first, he began showing no regard for her feelings, interrupting her when she spoke, not listening to what she had to say, and not caring about what she needed. Then the belittling started: her hair was combed wrong, her dress inappropriate; how could a slut like her think she deserved a man like him?

When the faucet in the master bath sprang a leak, he lost his temper, blamed her for breaking it, and beat her severely. After that, the beatings became more frequent. If she fought back, she suffered twice the pain. Finally, he broke her spirit. She began to believe that his anger was her fault. If she could have been a better woman, he wouldn't have treated her so brutally. So she tried to change, to be submissive, obedient, and serving, but nothing she did was good enough to please him. She became bitterly depressed and withdrawn. In the end, a merciful mosquito infected her with West Nile B.

But even in death, she had not escaped him.

Chapter Three

Under sunny skies, Washington D.C. traffic zipped along at maximum computerized efficiency. Dar Anders, sitting in the driver's seat of his Toyota Scanstreamer, reclined the seatback, satisfied that his autocar's onboard computer had complete control over the twenty-minute journey to the Capitol in City Center. His wife, Ishar, stretched out in the passenger seat and opened the novel she'd been reading. They both wore the official scarlet robes and high black collars of the Council of Elders. Last night, they'd been summoned to attend an emergency meeting at 9:00 in the morning. Yet again, the Jerry Well Foundation had stalled development efforts on Alpha Ketari. Dar expected another lengthy legal battle, this time over the habitat of a worm.

As the autocar sped along in perfect harmony with the surrounding traffic, Dar noticed that a small group of citizens had scaled the ten-foot concrete barrier skirting the sterile roadway. They clung to the tall chain-link fence atop the barrier where they'd tied banners and signs reading: *Save the Sawtooth Worm,* and *Vote No on Alpha Ketari.* Flying police cruisers moved in on the crowd. When Dar's autocar sped past their position, the citizens began jumping and waving fists.

He frowned. "I wonder what that's all about."

"What, dear?" Ishar didn't look up from her book.

"There were some people..." He saw another group gathered on a viaduct ahead, displaying similar signs. Dissent was brewing, and he didn't want to alarm Ishar. "Never mind."

"Get your copy of the Times, dear," she said without looking up.

"Yes, of course," Dar agreed, thinking how the demonstrators had altered his routine. "Computer," he spoke into his micro-transceiver. "The New York Times Daily, please."

Intricate electronic circuits engaged. Voice recognition was confirmed. *"Right away, sir,"* the onboard computer replied. Instantly, his order went out on a microwave signal to CNSS, the Commercial News Satellite System, which simultaneously drew charges on his account, acquired the latest news from the Times, and then assembled and beamed a hologram down to him via a locator beacon fixed on his position through the Global Pinpointing System. Within seconds, Dar had the world news shimmering in front of him.

"Coffee, sir?" the computer asked him.

"Please."

Ishar didn't drink coffee, so Dar knew the computer wouldn't ask her. While waiting for his coffee, he read the headlines. *Cure for West Nile B Found.* "Look at this, dear."

"Uh, huh." She didn't look up from her book.

He touch-selected the article. A mechanical voice came through his transceiver, reciting the text that described the virus, the miraculous cure for West Nile B, and the determination of the scientists involved. *"As primary contributor,"* the voice relayed, *"the Jerry Well Foundation gets full credit for this remarkable medical achievement."*

Dar knew that this publicity would give Jerry Well a boost in the public's eye. Environmentalists had already banded with him on the Alpha Ketari issue. The Council of Elders was in for another beating, he was sure.

As the autocar zoomed along at 100 miles per hour in bumper-to-bumper traffic, Dar scanned the area for more demonstrators. He noticed how the steering wheel slightly twitched to the onboard computer's commands. Tires hummed on the smooth roadway. The hydrogen-powered ceramic engine, permanently sealed and lubed, ran silent as a whisper. Dar found pride in the fact that his Scanstreamer had won Autocar Magazine's *Best of the Year* three times running. He appreciated the aerodynamic wedge-shaped design, the butterfly doors, and the completely hidden tires, which gave the autocar the appearance of flying only inches above the roadway. And with the Council of Elders' official seal on the doors, he enjoyed the envious looks he'd receive now and then from those traveling alongside.

"Your coffee, sir." A spill-proof cup appeared in the overhead server.

"Thank you." Dar took the cup, knowing he didn't have to thank the computer. Another article grabbed his attention: *Council of Elders Called into Emergency Session.* Already privy to the information, he sipped his coffee and reflected on his position. At 109 years old, he and Ishar, at 96, were the oldest Council members. That automatically gave them the *Chair*, the highest and most respected position in the Executive branch of government, next to the President, of course. He remembered how they'd been elected to the Council ten years ago, following the expected death of a previous Councilman. Four years before, he and Ishar had sold their successful advertising firm and quickly became bored. They decided to run for a seat on the Council, which meant, if elected, they would serve for life. Should one of them die, the surviving spouse dropped out and the next oldest couple on the Council automatically transferred to the *Chair*. The resultant vacancy triggered an immediate election.

The reasoning behind the council was simple. *With age came wisdom.* Dar didn't entirely agree with that, as he'd known some pretty stupid old people. However, since the eradication of Alzheimer's a century ago and advances in medical technology, which had extended human life expectancy to 120 years, the Council had proven the adage true. Indeed, serving on the Council gave a new perspective on Senior Citizens' ability to contribute to the world, something which Dar and Ishar relished.

As Democrats and Republicans in Congress dealt with the country's domestic issues, the Council of Elders, led by the Chair, conducted their affairs in the space arena. Anything that concerned interplanetary travel, commerce, and law had to be conducted on the Council's authority. One hundred years ago, it was a comparatively simple responsibility: a couple of lunar bases, one exploratory space station cruising somewhere beyond the solar system, and a few scientists poking around on Mars, that was about all. Nowadays, space affairs were much more complicated.

The Grief Syndrome

Dar sipped his coffee. Back in the 21st century, Congress disbanded NASA in favor of a new technology, Higgs Degeneration, which replaced expensive launches and explosive propellants. The Higgs Field Teleportation Authority, HFTA, established safe and near-instantaneous space travel. As a result, new frontiers unfolded every day, most notably the planets orbiting Proxima Centauri, the nearest star to earth's sun. The fourth planet in that solar system, Alpha Ketari, had been a rare find indeed.

Even today, the New York Times Daily Hologram touted the riches to be found there. Dar selected an article entitled *Earth's Savior* and listened to the text:

"With resources dwindling on earth, the mining conglomerates welcome the challenges on Alpha Ketari. 'It's all there,' a spokesman said at the conference in Geneva. 'Gold, silver, copper, iron ore, magnesium, you name it. It's an oasis compared to the mineral desert of earth. I say production should begin at once of the huge transports needed, the drillers and scrapers and borers, the loaders and dockers. Workers must be assembled and readied. We have the full support of HFTA. Now it is left to the Council of Elders for their approval.'"

Dar nodded, fully understanding the responsibility on their shoulders. He finished his coffee as the hologram narrative continued:

"Many experts agree that heavy industry, consumer goods, technology, and communications are strained, some into bankruptcy, due to the lack of minerals and ores to supply the demand of world populations. Should the Council of Elders fail to approve this enormous venture, the quality of human life on earth will sorely suffer.

"They're really putting the pressure on us," Dar said to Ishar as he deposited his empty coffee cup into the dash-mounted trash atomizer. In a buzzing split second, the cup was gone.

Ishar closed her book. "Alpha Ketari is a paradise. It would be a shame to dig it up and ship it piece-by-piece to earth."

"Yes." Dar had seen pictures the explorers had relayed back to HFTA: tropical rainforests, blue waters, white sandy beaches, red volcanic highlands, and green river basins. The abundance of birds and animals and insects were unlike anything on earth, and better still, there were no intelligent beings to conquer or displace. Alpha Ketari was free for the taking. Knowing all this, Dar agreed with his wife, but still, his concerns for humanity's future overweighed any sentimental value she, or anyone, had placed on Alpha Ketari.

"In less than a hundred years," he said, "there'll be no minerals and ores left on earth to support the needs of the human race."

"There are other options."

"Yes, and the Council has yet to address them."

"Humans could leave the earth en mass—"

"A vastly impossible chore, you realize. It's better to bring to earth what we need to survive."

She nodded, her rolled and tucked gray hair so firmly tied it didn't waver. "Jerry Well's vision of a Fantasy Planet is very endearing to many citizens. Just think, Dar, a vacation tour on an unspoiled world, a romantic evening stroll as Proxima Centauri sets in the north, the seasons always summer."

He grumped. "I see Jerry Well's thinking has gotten to you also."

"It is in all the Council members' minds," she replied softly as the autocar slowed for its preprogrammed turn off the highway to Jefferson Parkway. "However, we know the reality, the gravity of our position. The earth should not suffer for Jerry Well's wants."

"Still..." Dar watched the scenery shift from the sterile highway grid to the tree-lined boulevard advancing toward City Center. "He has kept the mining conglomerates at bay."

"For twelve years."

"Our hands have been tied with frivolous lawsuits, environmental studies, and this last debacle—"

"The disturbance of *Sawtooth Worms* on Ketari Flats," Ishar finished for him.

"Ketari Flats is rich in Platinum Group Metals. We need those minerals more than we need the worms."

Ahead, the crystal spire of the Capitol dome became visible through the trees. Dar drew in a lungful of air, welcoming the imminent confrontation with Jerry Well on this trivial issue.

"He can't win." Ishar put her book in her satchel. "The final vote draws nearer with each defeat he suffers."

"He may change his strategy again," Dar said, thinking of the legal circus acts they'd endured. "He's done it many times before."

"He's out of arguments, Dar. The worm issue is sheer desperation."

"Perhaps he has other options..." The hologram's article about the cure for West Nile B came to mind. He knew, as everyone close to this issue knew, that Jerry Well's wife had died from West Nile B. She'd been kept in cryonic suspension ever since. Reanimation, if successful, would mean that Jerry Well and Katherine would be the oldest couple on the planet. Her reanimation could seriously change Jerry Well's tactics from legal confounding of the issues to an all-out takeover of the Council's Chair. That thought sent Dar's stomach tumbling. "My God. If Katherine comes back, Jerry Well could use her as his running-mate to seek seats on the Council."

Ishar reached over and patted Dar's arm. "There's not an opening."

"But if one becomes available, together they could tip the Council in his favor."

"This should not concern us. Even if Katherine comes back, she won't be mentally qualified to run as Jerry Well's spouse for the Council."

"Yes. You're right, of course. The virus would have destroyed her brain, as it was with all West Nile B victims."

"So you see?"

Dar knew that in all probability, Katherine would be lucky to walk much less have the mental capacity to hold such a high office.

The autocar's computer beeped. *"Sir, prepare to disengage the transportation grid in five seconds."*

Dar's seatback automatically moved to the upright position. The hologram imploded into a thin card, which he put in his breast pocket.

"Grid release is confirmed," the computer reported.

"Please drive safely."

Taking control of the steering wheel, Dar turned onto the access road to the Capitol. A heads-up display on the windshield tilted down into view. Now he could see the position, direction, and speed of every vehicle within one hundred yards around him. This confirmed activation of the crash avoidance system. The autocar's onboard computer had established communication with the computers in all the vehicles shown on the display. Because of this information, he knew that around the next bend a line of traffic had stopped at the security checkpoint, but his computer could not possibly detect the angry crowd gathered there.

Rounding the curve, Dar and Ishar were speechless as pandemonium surged toward them. Hundreds of citizens carried signs and pumped placards reading: *Save Alpha Ketari*, and *Damn the Mining Conglomerates*. A bald and long-bearded fellow's sign proclaimed: *Jerry Well is Jesus*. The demonstrators were chanting: "Jerry Well. Jerry Well."

Ishar gasped.

The unexpected distraction caused Dar to lose attention on his driving. He felt a tug on his steering wheel as the computer swerved the autocar left to avoid an overzealous demonstrator who'd run into the road. The radar brakes engaged, safely stopping the car behind the last vehicle in line at the checkpoint. A taxi screeched to a halt behind them. They were pinned in. There was no way to escape the onrushing mayhem.

Reporters lunged forward, microphones extended to the glass. "Dar Anders...can you tell us...Dar Anders...where does the Council stand? Dar Anders...why don't you speak with us? Jerry Well is a hero. Ishar...what information do you have?" They were pushing one another and shouting all at once.

Ranting citizens surrounded them, sneering and showing fists and rocking the autocar. Capitol guardsmen fell into formation, raised their riot shields, and advanced on the mob. M56 Stun Tasers crackled. Clouds of pepper gas drifted in the air.

Dar could only sit there, his jaw dropped and heart hammering. He took Ishar's trembling hand. "Somehow Jerry Well has duped them into fighting for his crazy cause."

"But certainly they must realize—"

"What do they care what happens to the world in a hundred years? They'll all be dead and gone."

"Their children's children and so on will suffer the consequences."

"But not Katherine and Jerry Well," Dar reminded her.

Chapter Four

In the anteroom outside Katherine's subterranean crypt, Jerry Well removed his mink gloves, unbuttoned the thermal robe, and stripped the hood from his head. As he damped garlicky sweat from his brow, he realized his heart was beating wildly with excitement. Katherine was coming home.

Just then, the door opened, and Parish stormed in. "We got us another Weller."

Jerry looked him up and down. The bounty hunter stood six foot seven in combat boots, broad at the shoulders and narrow at the hips. His upper arms were big as railroad ties. A scar ran the length of his left cheek, and his nose had been broken, proof that hunting Wellers was a dangerous occupation. Jerry hung his robe on a brass rack. "Where?"

"On the 105 to Boulder."

"That makes sixteen this month. I don't like it."

"It's a goddamned reunion," Parish said.

"And they were all headed to Boulder?"

"Looks like it."

Disturbed by that revelation, Jerry kicked off his boots, stepped into a pair of slippers, and donned his green high-collared cloak. He feared the sudden influx of Wellers had come at a time much too close to Katherine's return. "Do you think it has anything to do with my wife?"

"That would be suicide. They can't get to her in here."

Jerry agreed. The electronic surveillance systems along the perimeter walls were impenetrable, and his encampment of security personnel was highly trained and vigilant. However, his plans for Katherine were at stake. "Just in case, activate the security-bots."

"The Walkers or the Fliers?"

"Both." Jerry removed the vial of sugar water from the pocket of his hanging robe and held it up to the light, pretending to inspect its clarity as he would a fine wine. In his peripheral vision, he caught Parish staring at the vial. Pleased, Jerry said, "Get on with it, man."

"Is that my vial?" he asked with wide eyes.

"When all the Wellers are dead."

The wonder from his face disintegrated. "We don't even know how many are left."

Jerry didn't care about the numbers. He only wanted to muddle the issue. "According to the Bureau of Vital Statistics, last count was eighty-seven."

"The Bureau is never right."

"Less the sixteen you've killed," Jerry pressed, "leaves seventy-one."

"I don't believe it." Parish balled a fist. "You should've kept your own records."

"Do I look like a bean counter to you?"

Parish bared his teeth.

The bounty hunter's size and demeanor intimidated most men, but not Jerry Well. He had the vial; he had the control. Parish was nothing more than a leashed Doberman.

Sure, Jerry knew the bounty hunter could kill him and take the vial, but he also knew Parish wouldn't violate his family's code of honor. He'd come from a proud lineage of bounty hunters. Besides, they had a lucrative deal: five million dollars for each dead Weller and immortality as a bonus. That was enough to keep Parish in line until it was time to get rid of him. Jerry slipped the vial into his cloak pocket. "I suggest you find out why the Wellers are migrating to Boulder."

Thoughtfully, Parish ran an index finger along the scar on his face. "We may have to take one of 'em alive."

"Kind of goes against the grain, doesn't it?" Jerry grinned.

Parish didn't look amused, so Jerry got back to business. "Check the video feeds from the bus terminal. Look for anyone suspicious, anything out of place."

"All right."

"And don't forget about the security-bots."

"Of course."

Satisfied, Jerry bounded upstairs to the main level of his mansion and moved immediately to his office. The latest developments in the Washington demonstrations were on his mind. He closed the door behind him. As sophisticated electronics detected his entrance and confirmed his identification, a hyper-plasma-ray screen, which filled the entire area of one wall, flashed on. A synthesized female voice said, *"I'm happy to see you, sir. Starnet interlock confirmed."*

He approached the screen where a 3-D yellow star rotated on a blue background. "Video feed," he commanded. "Washington D.C., Capitol, Council of Elders demonstration...Activate."

The screen blinked. A video feed appeared, beamed down from satellites in geosynchronous orbit. The image zoomed in on Washington City Center, the Capitol, the manicured grounds, and finally the security checkpoint and a crowd gathered around an official car.

"Reception confirmed," the sultry voice reported.

"Yes indeed." Jerry stood before the giant screen, hands clasped behind his back, feet spread, and watched an overhead view of his constituents taking part in a full-blown riot. Smaller windows opened around the screen's perimeter, each a view from different hover-cams and news media feeds at the location.

Flying police cruisers descended on the crowd, their loudspeakers blaring. "Disperse at once or you will be arrested."

The crowd jeered.

Capitol guardsmen shot them with taser streams, and then tossed concussion bombs. Gray clouds of pepper gas drifted in the air. Demonstrators threw rocks and bottles. There was screaming and cursing and mayhem of the highest degree. Jerry took it all in with immeasurable pride. Through the efforts of his foundation, the cure for West Nile B, and by preying on the emotions of concerned citizens and environmentalists alike, he had managed to bring the public's voice into the Alpha Ketari debate.

Everything that had come before: the injunctions, title disputes, and lawsuits over trivial matters such as worm infestation, water rights and tariffs, these had all been stall tactics. He knew he had to keep the Council tied up with these legalities while the crux of his plan awaited final initiation.

As he watched the riot unfold, he thought how the timing of these events could not have been planned with any certainty, but only strived for, as the cure for West Nile B and Katherine's return could not be predicted. Now that these things were coming to fruition, the final stand would be in the streets. Violence and disruption would mask the final blow to the Council of Elders, the blow John Parish would administer without realizing the consequences. Jerry chuckled at his own cleverness. "Starnet, take a message for CNSS."

"Ready, sir."

"The Jerry Well Foundation, all its officers, administrators, and the CEO himself, are appalled at the upheaval in Washington today. We wish to remind the Council of Elders, and all the good citizens of this great country, that today's violence, though regrettable, was inevitable. The peoples' demands should not be taken lightly. Save Alpha Ketari. End."

"Message sent, sir."

"Exit," he told Starnet.

The screen blinked back to the rotating star and blue background.

Assured of victory, Jerry left his office. As he worked his way to the west veranda, he was pleased to see a security-bot treading the hall. The black Walker moved upright on stilt-like legs. Four arms ratcheted from its crescent-shaped torso, as well as several other appendages with movable antennas, camera lenses, and laser-optic sensors. It carried a Winchester 606 blaster in its three-fingered grippers. Manufactured by Honda Bionics USA, this security-bot and twenty-five others like it were controlled by a mainframe computer. Another dozen were equipped with hover technology. They all reinforced his highly trained security personnel. Indeed, Katherine was well protected.

As he stepped outside, a gentle breeze greeted him. He looked out across his Hylander estate, a green valley of swaying grass and stands of aspen and pine all enclosed within towering concrete walls. He could see his private bike paths and hiking trails here and there, cutting through the woods. Deer grazed in the meadows, fish rings dotted the ponds, and an eagle soared overhead. Beyond his valley below Diamond Back Ridge, rolling foothills rose to the snowcapped Rocky Mountains.

He preferred this view to the scene from the eastside picture windows: the Platte River Valley sprawl, Denver's jagged skyline in the distance, surrounded by housing developments that swelled outward in every direction. There wasn't a vacant parcel of land for two hundred miles. The whole affair sickened him.

Inhaling the mountain air deeply, he thought about how he'd witnessed the rapid growth along the Front Range, the destruction of open space, and the end of that feeling of living *Out West*. It had begun a hundred years ago when a 9.2 magnitude earthquake leveled San Francisco, killing millions. After that, Californians flocked to Colorado; the LA basin emptied like a dirty sink. The influx forced him to build a twenty-foot concrete wall around Hylander to hold back the tide of immigrants and preserve a piece of the old world for Katherine. But as the decades passed and earth's resources dwindled to dangerously low levels, he knew his sanctuary would be worthless on a dead planet. He had to devise another plan, or his immortal life would be worth no more than the rest of humanity.

As he watched the eagle soar, he considered how longevity had taught him something. Since he would live forever, he knew he'd have to be a good steward of his environment. However, he was only one in twelve billion inhabitants of this stripped land. He had no control over them, no control over Earth's future. In a few decades, all his efforts would have been wasted.

When HFTA explorers discovered Alpha Ketari, he realized that the small pristine planet was his only hope to live his immortal life and not suffer extinction along with everyone else. As the mining conglomerates courted the Council of Elders to strip the planet of its minerals and ores, he began a campaign to save Alpha Ketari. With Katherine at his side, he could take over the Council and appoint himself governor of that unspoiled world. Earth's fate would no longer concern him.

On that thought, he decided a drink would be in order and called out, "Robert."

A hovering cylinder with several moveable appendages approached, humming, its camera-lens eyes swiveled toward Jerry. Manufactured by Teledyne Robotics International, this model 630C cyber-bot was equipped with the most humanistic microprocessor technology to date, multitasked and interfaced to Hylander's mainframe and Starnet. *"What is your pleasure, sir?"* He spoke in a synthesized voice. *"Ten to one on Malagasy in the fifth heat, or perhaps you would like to pick a number between one and ten?"*

"Orange juice," Jerry replied.

The butler-bot, as Jerry preferred to call him, dispensed his request in a crystal glass, added a cherry and a little umbrella then offered it to him with a pincher hand. *"Fresh squeezed, sir. Care for a sandwich?"*

"Maybe later."

A video display on Robert's chest lit up, shuffling a deck of cards. *"Pick a card, any card."*

"No thanks." Jerry took the glass, irritated by his butler-bot's antics. Though it was sophisticated enough to hold a federal chauffeur's license, he wished the damn machine didn't have such a flare for gambling. Interlinked through Starnet, as all legal computers were, Robert was known as the Bookie of Hylander. Most of the employees and guards were indebted to him in some way. "That will be all, Robert."

"My pleasure." The cyber-bot zoomed away, his voice trailing: *"Anyone for Malagasy in the fifth?"*

Just then, John Parish rushed up to him. "Ya better take a look at this." He activated a remote hologram player. A 3-D image appeared before them, big as life, a red hydrogen cycle and two riders leaving the Boulder terminal.

Jerry sipped his juice. "So?"

"Watch." Parish ran the images backward and restarted the recording at a point where the cycle pulled up to the curb. The shapely driver removed her helmet. A man carrying a blue and white sport bag slung from his shoulder approached her. Their conversation couldn't be heard over the whine of the cycle engine, but the woman's face was clearly visible. An overlay appeared on her image, typing text deciphered from her moving lips. *"You Scott Dunn?...My father was in the war...Sue Masters...You can't just bust into a cryo-lab..."*

"Right there!" Parish paused the replay. "They're talkin' about the lab. I found that suspicious, but get the clincher." He resumed play.

"...You're going to unplug his wife. Sounds like murder, doesn't it...?" She put on her helmet, ending the transcription.

A jolt of adrenaline hit Jerry's bloodstream. "Wife? My wife? Katherine?"

"Whoever it is, they think she's in the cryonics lab at Alcor." Parish stopped the recording. "I didn't like the sound of it."

"Damn!" Jerry threw his orange juice glass at the hologram, which responded with an array of high-voltage sparks that buzzed and spit as the image shuddered. "Who the hell is Scott Dunn?"

"There are hundreds of citizens with that name on file," Parish said. "It don't matter, though. Katherine is safe."

Jerry wasn't convinced. "Did you get a shot of his face?"

"I don't know." Parish rewound the hologram. People skittered backwards, clumped together around monitors, and skittered backwards again. A bus came into view. Jerry felt as if he could reach out and touch it. Passengers backed up the steps and disappeared inside. The door, peppered with blaster holes, closed. When the bus backed out of the terminal, Jerry saw its windscreen was blown out.

"That's the 105." Parish began replaying the images. The bus pulled into the terminal; the door slid open, and passengers hurried out. A man appeared with a sport bag hanging from his shoulder, blue and white, his face angled down from the camera. "There he is."

The man kept walking, kept looking down.

Jerry balled a fist, waiting to catch a glimpse of Scott Dunn's face, the man who might have come to Boulder to kill Katherine. Questions raced through Jerry's mind: Who was this assassin? Who sent him? And why? Contempt swelled up inside Jerry. His palms began to sweat and stink of garlic.

The crowd swallowed the would-be assassin for a moment, and then he reappeared standing in front of a monitor, his back to the hover-cam.

Impatience burned in Jerry's stomach.

The man casually glanced back at the crowd then looked up at the hover-cam.

"There!"

Parish froze the image of the man's face and activated the identity recognition scanner. A grid appeared over the face. Intersecting points were flagged, and then thousands of potential matches began to overlay the image, one after another in light-speed succession. Suddenly, *NO MATCHES FOUND* flashed on the hologram.

"What?" Jerry couldn't believe it. "How's that possible?"

"He must be a Weller," Parish hissed.

"He's too young to be a Weller."

Working the remote, Parish brought up the Bureau of Vital Statistic's list of Wellers. Scott Dunn's name was there, all right, but no photo, as was usual with incomplete Bureau files.

Jerry grumped. "It might not be the same guy."

The information link revealed that Scott Dunn was a mechanic. "He's a nobody," Parish said. "But it don't say if he's dead or alive."

Jerry saw a link labeled *Military Background.* "Try that."

When Parish selected the link, the information came on immediately. A chill jumped up Jerry's backbone. The odor of garlic mushroomed in the air as he read Scott Dunn's record. He had served with Homeland Security Special Forces during the Middle East Wars, a political assassin credited with kills ranging from terrorist leaders to foreign heads of state. And there was a picture of his military ID card. The photo on the card matched the man on the hologram.

"Son of a bitch," Jerry said. "He's an assassin."

"And he was on the 105." Parish spit. "How did I miss him?"

"It's obvious. He didn't panic like the old man. Scott Dunn must have nerves of steel." Jerry indicated the shimmering hologram. "What about his accomplice?"

Angrily, Parish jabbed the control pad, fast-forwarding to the cycle driver's arrival. He applied the same treatment to the woman's face. The results came fast. *MATCH: Sue Masters, 26, English teacher - Boulder High School - ex Navy Seal - Vice President, League of Women Voters.*

Jerry flinched. "She's a goddamned saint."

Chapter Five

The red hydrogen cycle turned on Baseline Road and headed toward Highway 93. Straddling the seat, Scott pinned his sport bag against his body with his right elbow and put his left arm around Sue Master's waist. She negotiated a tight curve then veered off the ramp to a dirt frontage road that wound its way into the foothills. "Why are we going this way?" He had to shout over the whining engine and the wheels crunching dirt.

"Relax," she yelled over her shoulder, her voice muffled inside her helmet. "Enjoy the scenery."

"I'm not here for that."

"We have to stay off the main roads," she shouted. "If not, the cycle's computer will lock-on to the transportation grid's navigation sensors. That means I'll have to enter our destination coordinates. The system will know where we're going. We don't want that, now do we?"

"I know how the system works. Where's the cryo-lab?"

"The old University of Colorado campus."

Scott leaned forward. "That's the other direction."

"Carson wants to see you first." She leaned the cycle into a dirt-hurling curve.

"I'm here to do the job, in and out, finished. It's too

dangerous to hang around here like some kind of tourist."

"We're almost there." She throttled down a short straightaway and laid on the brakes for the next curve.

"Carson better have a good reason for this delay." Scott looked back and saw only dust. He knew H. G. 'The Hog' Carson was the undisputed leader of the Weller underground. His followers numbered in the thousands, though most statistics suggested there were less than a hundred Wellers still living. Over the course of two and a quarter centuries, it was easy to understand how records were lost, misplaced, or updated incorrectly. The Bureau of Vital Statistics could hardly keep up with the data they had on mortals, much less Wellers, many of whom were constantly on the move.

As the cycle shuddered over a stretch of washboard road, Scott held Sue a little tighter. She hadn't tucked her hair under her helmet, so he often caught the scent of shampoo whipping in his face, but surprisingly, not the odor of garlic. He figured she had to be sweating rivers in those riding leathers. Wondering about that, he inched his nose closer to the back of her neck.

With a bang, the cycle hit a pothole, nearly tossing him off the seat. His sport bag broke loose from under his arm, and the wind sent it whipping behind him. The strap dug into his shoulder. As he reached back to grab the bag, his feet slipped off the pegs. He lost his balance and inadvertently grabbed a handful of Sue's left breast. She yelped. The cycle veered wildly off the road, barreled down a weeded embankment, charged through a creek, bounded up the opposing slope, and skidded to a stop on a jeep trail. The crash avoidance system had saved them.

"Watch where you put your hands, buster."

"I almost fell off."

"Are you trying to get us killed?"

He clung to her waist with both hands. His heart felt as if it would burst. Miraculously, the sport bag was still hanging from his arm by the strap. The odor of garlic was so heavy in the air, he couldn't determine if any of it was coming from her.

"Are you going to sit still now?"

He couldn't move if he wanted to. "How much farther?"

"Not much, thanks to your shortcut." She tore off down the jeep trail that snaked into the forest. About a mile in, she turned into a small clearing where a weathered old shack leaned on its foundation. An ancient mine-tailings pile spilled down the far slope. She shut off the motor and dropped the kickstand.

"What are we doing here?"

Her helmet came off. "Leave your bag with the bike."

Chapter Six

During Colorado's gold rush of the 1860s, the miners called this mine *Hell Hole Number Nine*. Now, H. G. *The Hog* Carson called it *Hog Heaven*. As surveillance cameras recorded the cycle's arrival, he leaned forward in his gigantic wheelchair, hunched his enormous mass over a hyper-keyboard with giant keys ergonomically designed for his massive hands. Long ago, he'd refused to equip his computers with voice activation for one simple reason: his keyboard gave him a physical link to his computers, which were his only connection to the outside world. Technology was not going to take that away from him.

On a plasma-ray monitor, he watched Sue and Scott Dunn dismount the cycle. Carson's pet ferret scampered across the console, reared up on her hind legs, tested the air with a twitching nose, and perked her ears. She looked at him and squeaked.

"That's right, Myrtle," Carson said, amused at her antics. She could hear Sue's cycle coming a mile away. "She'll be here in a minute." Thinking she'd use the freight elevator to enter the mine, he activated the lifting struts on his wheelchair, raising his five hundred pound body another two feet higher in order to reach the elevator controls. However, when he saw Sue leading Scott toward the mine shack, he lowered his seat and smirked. It looked as if she planned on showing him the hard way down.

To track their descent into *Hog Heaven*, Carson engaged the ion motor of his wheelchair and moved to a different bank of monitors. From this position, two hundred feet beneath the surface, he could observe every part of the mine. Nothing escaped his notice.

Working the cameras, Carson ignored all the trash that littered his counters and the floor around his wheelchair: mostly candy wrappers, microwave dinner boxes, and empty ice-cream cartons. Soda pop cans lay every-which-way like dead soldiers on a battlefield. The baryon-sphere refrigerator hummed an arm's reach away, and a ham and cheese Hot Pocket sizzled on a microwave platter. He'd seen thousands of products come and go, but many things hadn't changed in two hundred twenty five years.

Back in 2010, Carson practiced corporate law. He was known as an organizer of information, meticulous with details: the facts and the numbers. He never got anything wrong. Problem was, he had an affinity for food. He was a meat and potatoes man. Gravy and more gravy, he couldn't get enough. And sweets: Snickers, M&Ms, Fruity-Tutee Bombs. Ice cream by the buckets: chocolate, vanilla, Rocky Road Express. The pounds went on: two hundred at age fifteen, three hundred at twenty-two, four hundred at thirty, five hundred at thirty-nine. By then, the weight had drained his energy; his career began to unwind. Nobody wanted to work with him anymore. Just being in the presence of *The Hog* was downright embarrassing. Eventually, his daughter made him realize that the thing he loved most was destroying him. She'd convinced him to find a healthy program that would help him lose weight and make him feel better. It was then that he'd turned to Jerry Well and Everlife.

There was an upside to what happened after that, but only one upside. He could eat all he wanted and never gain another pound. However, the downside was horrendous. Everlife maintained his body in its present form. He didn't lose an ounce. He couldn't: not then, not now, not ever. *The Hog* was condemned to live forever in a five hundred pound body, thanks to Everlife.

Hating Jerry Well had kept Carson vigilant. Through the decades, he monitored every move Jerry made, every contribution from his so-called charitable foundation, every political venue he exploited, the Council of Elders, Alcor, and Katherine. It wasn't long before Carson had found a common thread that tied everything together: Alpha Ketari. The scheme he envisioned made him sick to his stomach.

Seeing Sue and Scott Dunn enter the old mine shack, he wet his lips, chucked a Fruity-Tutee Bomb, and swore Jerry Well wasn't going to get away with it.

***

Topside, in the mine shack, sunshine knifed through slanted wallboards, cutting the darkness with slivers of light. Centered in the room, a crossbeam with a montage of pulleys and ropes hung above an opening in the floor. Dust choked the air as Scott followed Sue to the shaft and looked down into a black abyss. He swallowed hard. "We're not going down there."

"Of course."

"You've got to be kidding."

"Come on. It'll be fun." Sue took hold of one of several ropes and gave it a pull.

Assuming they were going to rappel down the shaft, Scott grabbed another rope.

She stopped him from pulling it. "That one will get you killed."

"Huh?"

"It's a dummy. Trust me."

A clanking sound belched up from the mine followed by the rattling of metal. The rope in Sue's hand slid through a pulley on the crossbeam until it became taut. Rising from the darkness, a foot plank appeared suspended from two ropes that ran through pulleys on the crossbeam, like a swing. The plank stopped level with the floor. She grabbed one of the ropes with both gloved hands and stepped on the plank, leaving room for Scott on her right. He immediately got on. The machinery set them into motion. Downward.

At first, he couldn't see a thing, his eyes not accustomed to the darkness. All around him, wood creaked and water dripped. The place smelled of dust and rock, moisture and mud. He began to wish he hadn't listened to Sue.

Soon, a crimson glow filled the shaft, easing his eyes into this subterranean world. Timbers and girders zoomed by vertically as the plank descended, picking up speed. All around them, craggy walls leaked water.

The clanking sound got louder, the descent faster. A red light bulb flashed by, then another and another. His hands began to sweat on the rope. The odor of his garlicky sweat now overpowered the mine's musty smell.

A flood lamp flashed by, its cone of light illuminating a giant gear below. Just as they dropped between the gaping cogs, the gear groaned and began to rotate, snagging the rope just above their heads.

"Hang on," Sue said.

With a jerk, the plank lurched sideways and began swaying back and forth. Scott gripped the rope so hard his knuckles turned white. Now the rock walls and support timbers flew by horizontally. Machinery clanked and rumbled and echoed all around them. Seconds later, vertical columns of multicolored lights flashed by, one after another. He felt as if he'd jumped on a carrousel ride at the county fair. Actually, he thought it was rather fun.

Suddenly, out of the darkness, a platform came at them. It had an orange railing and a step with a sign that read: *Get On Here*. Thinking they were supposed to board, he reached for the railing.

"No," Sue shouted and held his arm. The platform pivoted and swung away. "It goes under the falls. You'd be drowned."

"What?"

"Countless bounty hunters have died trying to get in here." She pointed into the darkness on the right. "Be ready to jump on the next platform."

Without warning, the giant gear creaked and began to tilt upward. Another gear appeared. Its cogs were meshed with the big gear's teeth, turning and crunching like a meat grinder. It was getting closer and closer. Blood rushed from his head. "We're going to be crushed."

"Get ready," she shouted. Another platform angled out of the dark. It wasn't within reach, but moving closer fast. "Now."

He jumped.

It was a leap of faith, but the platform slid under them, just as Sue had said it would. Smoothly, it whisked them away from the grinding gears. As it approached the end of its pendulum swing, she said, "Jump to the conveyor."

"What conveyor?" He could hear something thumping in the dark, but he couldn't see it. The air smelled like burned rubber. "Where?" he croaked, swallowing panic.

She shoved him and jumped after him.

A conveyor belt caught his fall, but he lost his footing and toppled over, skinning an elbow on the coarse and moving surface. Just as he wondered why it was so rough, the entire assembly pitched upward, and he was suddenly glad to have the added traction that kept him from sliding off. When he came to the end of the conveyor belt, it dumped him into a dimly lit tunnel full of rushing cold water. Instinctively, he held his breath but soon realized he was plunging feet-first down a water slide. Shivering, he careened left and right through a series of sharp curves. He made a special note to kill Sue when this was over.

Sliding down behind him, she shouted, "Stay to the right up here. Don't go left."

He could hardly hear her over the roaring water. "Go left?"

"No." Her voice echoed. "The water cascades into a two thousand foot fissure. We'll never find your body."

"Now there's a happy thought."

Around the next bend, a fork in the tunnel appeared. He stayed to the right, as Sue had instructed. Moments later, the tunnel emptied into a waist-deep pool. The sounds of splashing water echoed off rock walls lit with randomly placed twinkling lights. After dragging himself out of the water, he followed Sue to an old ore cart on rails. "Get in."

No way. The rickety cart looked more like a coffin on wheels. Sopping wet, he glanced around, spotted a lighted tunnel heading off to the left. "Can we go that way instead?"

"All you'll find down there is a dead-end maze and bounty hunters' bones. This is the only way."

"Why did I know that?" He'd had about enough of this thrill ride, but experiencing it showed him one thing: Carson had engineered his protection well. Scott threw a leg over the cart rim, got in, and sat on the metal bottom. Water from his soaked clothes pooled beneath him. Sue sat in front, between his spread legs. He thought they must've looked like *rub a dub dub, two kids in a tub.*

A lighted control panel appeared in front of her. She released the brake. A high-pitched squeal came first as the cart began to roll, then a rattling clatter as the cart picked up speed. Down they went, careening around curves, left and right, and plummeting with stomach-floating force only to thrash back up, lurch violently, and then plunge downward again.

Scott gripped the cart rim as his body slammed back and forth. Low-hanging crossbeams forced him to duck or lose his head. He wanted to scream like a girl on a rollercoaster.

Sue didn't even moan. She was busy punching buttons on the control panel, which operated switchbacks on the tracks. Scott was sure that one wrong turn would mean certain death. In spite of that, Sue seemed cool and focused, perhaps even enjoying the ride. And sitting behind her like this, downwind as it were, he smelled only her perfume and not the garlicky odor her body should have been exuding. As he wondered about that again, he also wondered why he had trusted her with his life. She was supposed to be a Weller, he conceded, but on the other hand, too often she didn't smell like a Weller, which had raised doubts in his mind all over again. He thought to confront her about it but quickly discarded the idea. Distracting her with questions was the last thing he wanted to do right now. She might push the wrong button.

Within moments, the heart-stopping ride decelerated. The cart coasted up to a platform and squealed to a stop. A nozzle-boom swung over their heads, and with a hiss, blasted them dry.

Sue jumped out. "We made it."

Scott tried to find his land-legs. "Haven't you people heard of elevators?"

"There's a freight elevator over there," she pointed out. "But it's no fun. Besides, I wanted you to see how dangerous it is to get in here. One wrong decision means sudden death for an intruder."

"I got the idea." Scott climbed out of the cart. A microburst booster sent it rolling back toward its starting position at the shallow pool.

Looking around, he found himself in a towering cavern cluttered with horizontal beams, diagonal girders, and vertical columns rising a hundred feet or more. Wide catwalks connected platforms interspersed within the chamber above. Tangles of wire hung down like vines in a rainforest. Glowing dimly, small lamps illuminated the massive structure. The air felt cooler than he expected for this far underground. Air-conditioned, he assumed. "Who built this place?"

"The Weller underground. Carson's extended family maintains it, keeps it stocked with food and supplies."

"Amazing."

From somewhere above, a wheezing voice said, "Thanks for coming, Scott Dunn."

"Carson?" Scott shouted, looking up. He couldn't see where the voice had come from. "I don't have time for this tour."

"You've got nothing but time. Sue will show you the way up."

Scowling, Scott thought Carson a bit blunt...and pushy, like Sue Masters. If he hadn't known better, he'd have thought the similarity was hereditary.

He followed Sue across a lush pile carpet, past the freight elevator to a black curving wall that looked much like a wall in an art gallery. There, framed holographic motion photos were displayed, some old black-and-whites, and some in full color. In one scene, a child blew out five candles on her birthday cake. She looked up and smiled, the candles ignited, then she blew them out again, then looked up and smiled, the loop repeating itself. There was a boy in another motion photo, maybe ten years old, baseball cap on backwards, swinging a bat at a ball, which he hit over and over, each time with a mighty crack. Dozens of photos showed people smiling and waving. Others rode horses, drove cars, caught fish, and on and on, dizzying Scott with all the activity and sounds. He was speechless.

"Carson's family tree," she said.

For the briefest moment, Scott wondered what his family tree would've looked like...if...then he turned away from the motion photos, suddenly sickened by a shot of heart-wrenching grief. He instantly hated Carson's display.

Sue led the way onto a vertical conveyer that took them up to the main level, a series of platforms with wide catwalks running between them. There were no walls anywhere up here, just railings and thick cables crisscrossing from the platforms to supporting girders overhead. Light fixtures illuminated each platform as if it were a stage on Broadway. Darkness surrounded each lighted stage, and each stage was furnished differently: a living room, bedroom, dining room, and kitchen. As he walked the catwalks from one platform to another, he realized something odd about the furnishings. Everything was huge...as if built for a giant. Amazed, he forgot about the motion photos.

Whining and grinding, another lift took them up to the next level, a sprawling platform packed with electronics equipment. Most of it looked old and obsolete. There were rows of humming supercomputers and consoles, several printers ejecting paper, a hundred glowing monitors, and a dozen hologram projectors running simultaneously. Images from around the world played over the media medley, the audios jumbled and befuddling.

Scott noticed something else about this room. In contrast to the rooms downstairs, which were showcase clean, this place was a total disaster. Everywhere he looked, trash littered the floor, counters, and consoles. He grimaced at the thought of the slobs that worked up here and wondered why Carson would allow his men to be so messy.

Moving with Sue to the opposite end of the platform, he came upon the back of a wheelchair the size of a Volkswagen with four big tires, a black fabric seat with multiple pouches, and a bumper sticker that read: *Honk if you love Wellers*. Scott could see a huge body sitting in it, a man, he assumed, his folds of fat spilling over the sides of the seat. An ion motor activated with a whine. The wheelchair turned around, revealing its monstrous occupant, his drooping face, puffy eyes, and bulbous nose. His head was bald as an ostrich egg. Multiple chins spilled down his chest, and his stomach poured over his knees. He wore a tent-sized pinstriped shirt, white and blue, with the sleeves cut off to make room for the flab of his massive arms. His skin was blinding white from living down in the mine for decades without sunshine. "Carson?"

"Welcome to Hog Heaven, Scott Dunn." His voice wheezed under the heavy weight of each breath. A ferret stood on his right shoulder, its beady eyes masked in silver fur. It hissed. Carson smiled fatly, jowls flopping. "Now, Myrtle, be nice to our guest."

She scampered down Carson's arm, leaped across the gap to a nearby table, and then reared up on her hind legs, probing her pointy nose toward Scott.

"What's with the rat?" He winced at the ferret's rank odor. "Your guard dog?"

Carson snorted. "Myrtle is extremely sensitive and protective. She's a silver mitt. You can tell by the color of her paws." He reached out with a massive hand and gently stroked her black fur coat. "She can sense your moods, your tone of voice, your fear. The only reason her teeth aren't in your neck right now is because you smell like me."

"An attack ferret?"

"She's benefited from 225 years of enhanced breeding," Carson explained. "Sharper teeth, quicker reflexes, better eyesight, and keener perception than her ancestors."

"Why does she smell so bad?"

"I rather like her musky aroma. She's inquisitive and smart. Her comprehension of English is astounding. I trained her myself. She's three years old, a great escape artist, and the best of thieves." He laughed. "It took me three months to find one of my hologram remotes. And she's always off exploring, getting into mischief. Fortunately, I was able to teach her the boundaries, where it's safe and where it's not down here."

"Ferrets have no concept of home," Scott said, relying on his knowledge of what ferret's were like in the 21st century. "It's a wonder she didn't get lost."

"She finds her way back to me every time." Carson's tone beamed with pride, as if he were talking about his child. "And I haven't seen a snake down here since—"

"Snakes?"

"Rattlers mostly. She finds them challenging."

"She kills them?"

"You'd be surprised what Myrtle can do."

Sue made ticking sounds with her tongue. "She's my little sweetheart." Myrtle scampered to her. Sue picked her up, let her nuzzle her neck, and giggled like a little girl.

"Cute," Scott said with as much sarcasm as he could muster. "Animals aren't babies. Why do you treat them like they are?"

"Don't tell me you've never had a pet," she said with an unattractive tweak to her lips.

"Of course." Scott huffed. "Heartbreakers, that's all they are. And a huge bother. I've got no use for pets anymore."

"He's not a nice man," Sue said to Myrtle, kissed her shiny nose, then set her on the table. She slinked off through the litter, glancing back occasionally, as if she were trying to entice everyone into a game of hide-and-seek.

Scott dismissed her, thinking good riddance, and looked around. "Is this the nerve center of your organization?"

"I *am* the organization, Scott Dunn." Carson motored the wheelchair toward the consoles and stopped. "These monitors..." he swept an obese hand, "keep me informed on what's going on in the outside world. As you can guess, I don't get out much."

"That's right." Sue moved to the wheelchair and patted Carson's shoulder. "Grandpa never leaves this place."

"What?" Scott knew that Carson couldn't be Sue's grandfather, not if she was a Weller. And Scott had his doubts about her all along, but now he needed to find out for certain. He stepped forward, took hold of her arms, pulled her neck to his face, and inhaled deeply. Perfume. She lied. "Damn!" He shoved her backward.

She peeled off a glove and offered her hand. "Is this the smell you're looking for?"

Now he didn't know what to think. He'd been careless, too trusting. He took a step back, fists clenched, eyes darting about, knowing there was nowhere to flee in this treacherous underground hell. "You tricked me."

"It was my idea," Carson said. "I couldn't meet you at the terminal." He indicated his immense body and giant wheelchair. "And you wouldn't have gone with Sue if you'd thought she wasn't one of us."

"She's a mortal. She can't be trusted."

"She's not a snitch," Carson growled, "if that's what you're suggesting."

Sue flipped her palms upright. "I rubbed garlic juice on my hands before I put on my gloves. Not to trick you, Scott, but so you'd trust me."

"With a lie. What kind of trust is that?"

She scowled, wrinkling the dimple on her chin.

"Sue is my twelfth generation granddaughter." Carson moved the wheelchair between them as if he were running interference. "My family has taken good care of me all this time, generation after generation." He leaned forward slightly. "Where's your family, Scott Dunn?"

"They have nothing to do with this."

"Most Wellers fled their families," Carson went on, wheezing. "Or were shunned by them. What happened to yours?"

Memories stabbed Scott in the heart. "I don't want to talk about it."

Carson snorted. "I can understand that."

"How could you? You weren't there. You didn't see what—"

"I know what happened," Carson interjected. "From the beginning, I've kept track of all the Wellers. Most committed suicide; others fell victim to bounty hunters.

Either way, they all met violent ends. But you, you're a survivor, Scott Dunn."

Scott shook his head. "Sometimes I wish I weren't."

"Granted." Carson's voice grew softer, more agreeable. "The Grief Syndrome is no picnic, however, I'm immune to it. Sure, I watched my kids grow old and die, my grandchildren, too. And yes, I've watched my pets come and go. It all pains me deeply."

"I don't see how you managed."

"It's my attitude."

Frowning, Scott wondered what attitude could possibly overcome the grief. "How?"

"Better them than I...cold as it may sound. I get over the grief. I go on. You know why, Scott Dunn? Jerry Well. Hating him keeps me going, gives meaning to my life. I monitor everything he does. Now I've given you the opportunity to even the score, yours and mine."

Scott shot him a narrow-eyed glare. "What made you so sure I'd agree to kill Katherine?"

"After what happened to your wife." Carson wheezed. "If anyone has motive to destroy Jerry Well, it would be you."

"Yes..." Scott wondered how much Carson knew about Liz. "She suffered horribly because of Everlife." He glanced at Sue who was biting her lower lip, and then back to Carson. "But you seem to be happily dealing with your immortal life. Why do you hate Jerry Well?"

"He made me the man that I am." Carson indicated his massive frame with a swipe of his hands. "Do you blame me?"

"Jerry Well made you eat yourself into pigdom?"

"No.," Carson grumped. "It's his fault I can't lose the weight."

Scott understood. His body hadn't changed since he was twenty-five. Nodding, he also knew Carson couldn't seek his own revenge. He couldn't go anywhere without that wheelchair much less sneak into a cryo-lab and unplug Katherine. "So why did you bring me here? I could have been done with it and gone by now."

"Information." Carson pointed to the gadgetry surrounding him. "You don't have all the facts."

"All I need is the crypt number."

Carson huffed through hoggish lips. "There's more to this than you think. That's why I had to see you first."

"So you sent Miss Daredevil here? You should've sent one of your men." Scott tilted his head toward Sue. "Instead of her."

"What's wrong with me?" she snapped.

"Don't take it personal."

Carson interrupted their squabble with a bombshell. "There are no other men."

"What?" That confused Scott to no end. "I heard you had hundreds of followers."

"Forget what you've heard," Carson spat. "You don't know the volume of information that flows around the world every day. Overloaded data systems become unreliable...*wheeze*...I know. I've monitored them from down here for over two hundred years. Your information is wrong."

Swallowing, Scott looked at Sue. Her eyes darted away from his. He didn't like her reaction, the avoidance. "You'd better give it to me straight, Carson."

His heavy eyebrows arched. "Have you seen this?" He motored to his hyper-keyboard, the fat tires crunching trash, and activated a hologram. The replay showed a bus rolling toward Boulder, a black van careening up alongside it, bounty hunters boarding with ropes and boosters.

"It's old news." Scott steeled himself to the brutality unfolding, thankful he'd escaped with his life.

The ion motor whined as Carson moved the wheelchair to a position in front of Scott. "The numbers are wrong."

"That's not hard to believe." In the background behind Carson, playing on the hologram big as life, Scott watched the old man slam to the roadway in a shower of glass, rolling and flopping until he was crushed under the bus's wheels.

"Fact is..." Carson stopped the hologram. "We are the last of the Wellers."

Scott staggered backward into a console. He thought his heart had quit. "What?"

"They're all dead."

"How...?" Scott couldn't breathe. It was impossible to believe. He and Carson were the last of their kind? Everyone else had gone the way of the dinosaurs? Extinct? "Why?"

Carson motored his wheelchair back to his keyboard. "Contrary to the Bureau of Vital Statistics, there were only seventeen Wellers left alive, besides myself. They were drifters, opportunists, unskilled for the most part." He tapped on the giant keyboard. The hologram replayed images of a bloodbath, scene after scene, bounty hunters' guns blazed; Wellers died. "I offered them jobs as garbage hockers, high pay, lucrative benefits. While the bounty hunters were zeroing in on them, you had a better chance of making it through to me alive."

"You used them as decoys—?"

"I had no choice." Carson balled a porky fist. "We are out of time, Scott. They've found a cure for West Nile B. The clock is ticking. I took every precaution for success."

"How could you sacrifice those men?"

"Not intentionally, I assure you," Carson replied, wringing his meaty hands. "There's safety in numbers. It was by their own carelessness that John Parish found them."

Scott didn't buy it. As far as he was concerned, Carson had lured them to their deaths. Choking down anger, Scott wanted to tell the fat man to find another patsy, but then again, denying Jerry Well Katherine was the reason he'd come to Boulder. After all, Katherine was already dead, but being frozen gave Jerry Well hope of having his wife back again, something he'd taken away from Scott as surely as if he'd pulled the trigger himself. Scott's heartbeat escalated; his sweat stunk of garlic anew. "What do we do now?"

Carson leaned his bulk forward in the wheelchair. "Katherine is in cryostat 34-B at the Alcor Life Extension Institute. The reanimation team has been activated. You're going in tonight under the cover of darkness."

Chapter Seven

The bounty hunters stood shoulder-to-shoulder on the hardwood floor in Jerry Well's office. After berating them for letting Scott Dunn slip through their fingers on the 105, Jerry slammed a fist on his desk. "Don't screw it up tonight."

Parish and his men stiffened, their faces hard with determination.

"Dismissed."

They filed out just as Dr. Navarro arrived. He was head physician on the *Thaw Team*, responsible for bringing Katherine back to life. Shoulder-length hair ringed his balding crown, and a concerned frown contrasted starkly with his otherwise soft facial features.

"What is it?" Jerry peeled off the wrapper of a granola bar.

Navarro waved a bound notebook, an archaic record-keeping device from the 21st Century. "I have read Katherine's report." He slammed it on the desktop. "You should reconsider reanimating her."

"I think not." Jerry tore into a chunk of crunchy granola. He'd waited two hundred twenty five years for Katherine's return. "Now get to work."

"The report indicates she died of West Nile B,"

Navarro explained. "You should know the brain damage she suffered will make it impossible to restore her to full function. She will be a vegetable. It would be cruel to do this procedure."

Jerry examined the granola bar, thinking how Navarro didn't realize the report had been fixed, as well as Katherine's death certificate falsified. He had taken precautions to ensure the virus could not have damaged her brain. Navarro's argument had merit in technical terms, but not in fact. "Proceed as planned, doctor. You may be surprised how well your technology will work for her."

"But she won't know who she is, nor will she remember you. Think about her quality of life—"

"Enough." Navarro's persistence was becoming a bore. Jerry fought back his temper. "As long as I'm paying the bill for this, you will do as I say."

"Then I suggest that you transfer her to Alcor for this procedure."

"She's not leaving here, doctor. How long will it take you to set up your machines?"

"Some are very delicate—"

"How long, doctor?"

"You do not understand the complexity of this."

Jerry lunged forward, grabbed the startled doctor by his tie. "Get this straight. We believe a Weller is planning to infiltrate Alcor tonight. He's after somebody's wife, possibly Katherine. You will reanimate her here while my bounty hunters lay in ambush for the Weller. There's going to be a lot of shooting. So I'll ask you again, doctor. How long?"

Navarro grabbed Jerry's wrist and scowled. "My

supervisors will hear about this. You will regret your disrespect and arrogance."

Jerry wasn't worried about any interference from the higher-ups at Alcor. He'd paid for their loyalty a long time ago. He released Navarro's tie and then graciously straightened his crumpled lapels, smiling wickedly. "Katherine is coming home, doctor, whether you approve or not. We have plans for our future. Take a look."

Touching a sensor pad on the desktop activated his virtual display resonator. He motioned Navarro to step aside. "You don't want to get caught in the middle of this."

A shimmering hologram rose from the floor, forming iridescent walls and glistening towers sustained by 10,000 volts of light-imaging power and 50,000 watts of 3-D graphic illumination. It was a ghostly transparent scale model of his futuristic estate on Alpha Ketari. "Welcome to Eternal Hylander," he told Navarro, savoring the astounded look on the doctor's face.

The most striking feature of Jerry's design was a one-hundred-foot crystal spire that rose from the center of an oval garden. Tree-lined walkways connected the garden to a multistory mansion constructed of smooth stone. Its crystal-domed roof and brilliant windows glimmered from internal lighting.

He strolled around the hologram's low, sleek wall that encircled his futuristic home, and stopping at one of four towers, he indicated a crystalline photocell sphere setting on top of it. "Behold the future," he said, aglow with pride.

"Your future perhaps," Navarro said, his amazement drained. "No one else's."

"No one else matters," Jerry said flatly. "Just me and

Katherine. I suggest you get busy. Oh, and doctor..." He grinned. "Do a good job."

"I'll do the best I can, but only for Katherine." Navarro walked out, slammed the door behind him.

Satisfied, Jerry watched the virtual display sink back into the floor, and then finished eating his granola bar.

Chapter Eight

Back at *Hog Heaven*, while Myrtle curled up on a stack of computer printouts, Scott Dunn bent over a table and studied a map of the old university campus. He wore baggy black pants, boots, and a loose-fitting black shirt. The sport bag sat on the floor near his feet. Earlier, Sue had brought it down on the freight elevator, along with her hydrogen cycle. Drinking a Pepsi G, the latest rage in soda pop with ginger, he could see from the map that infiltrating Alcor would not be easy.

The map had been printed from an archaic WEB server. It showed an array of campus buildings, many numbered and others crossed out with Xs, denoting they'd been demolished. Carson had colored some of the streets red. They were part of the computerized transportation grid and had to be avoided.

Balancing a plate of ham sandwiches on his knee, Carson maneuvered the wheelchair up to his keyboard terminal on the trash-cluttered console. "The cryo-lab is housed in the old student recreation center." He gulped down a sandwich. "Building 80...there."

He explained that the Alcor Life Extension Institute of Arizona had purchased the building in 2175. By then, most of the outlying buildings had been torn down, replaced with low-income housing and strip-malls. The larger core buildings: administration, arts and sciences, and geology were still standing, though they'd been abandoned for decades. Explosive growth along the Front Range had made Alcor's satellite facility a profitable adventure, a testament to mankind's propensity for hope...even after death.

"Currently, seven hundred twenty two cryonics patients are interred there," Carson said while examining the figures on his monitor. He'd already tapped into Alcor's database systems. "There are three levels. 34-B is on the ground floor." Another sandwich went down his throat.

A three-dimensional computer graphic display of the building appeared. Scott moved in for a closer look. The point of view tilted as if he were flying in through the front doors, pivoted left and right revealing a bank of elevators, office doors, a chapel entrance, and an emergency exit. A row of barred steel gates to the cryo-crypts became visible against the far wall. They were labeled A through M. Escalators moved up to the next level. Video cameras swept back and forth in ever-silent vigil.

Scott saw a stick-figure watchman patrolling the atrium. "Only one guard?"

"No more than any cemetery might employ." Carson burped and chomped on another sandwich. "Electronic security is all they really need." His huge fingers tapped the keys again. Real-time images from Alcor's security cameras came up: sixteen windows, but none of them showed views from inside the crypts. "As you can see, they allow their cryo-patients privacy."

Scott wondered about that. "Katherine died in 2010,

long before this place was built. How did she get here?"

"Jerry Well had her moved from Alcor's Arizona facility fifty years ago." Carson clicked through several live scenes from inside the building. One camera caught the lone guard lazily strolling a hall. "The transfer was well documented."

"Is that normal?"

Carson backed the wheelchair away from his keyboard. "It was a big deal to Jerry Well."

Leaning on the counter, Scott thought something was wrong with that logic. "Why do you suppose he flaunted her move?"

"He couldn't resist bragging that his wife would come back someday. His ego got the better of his common sense."

Scott didn't think so. It was unlike Jerry Well to broadcast anything about Katherine. He was always protective of her privacy. On top of that, he wanted to keep her all to himself. And he wouldn't have stored her body very far from him. Alcor's facility in Arizona was a long way off, but at the time, it was the only place he could keep her. That must've been torture for him, Scott figured, all those decades without her being near him. But when Alcor opened its Boulder facility, it made sense that he would move her there. However, he could have done it in secrecy. There had to have been another reason that he'd advertised the move, and Scott could think of only one. He relayed his suspicions to Carson. "Perhaps he left a false paper trail so everyone *thought* they knew where she was stored."

At that, Carson chucked another sandwich then returned to his keyboard, hunkered down and began typing.

He rechecked all the data from 2175 regarding Katherine's transfer.

Over Carson's shoulder, Scott watched graphs appear that recorded temperature readings within the cryostat while it was detached and crated. There were dates and times and signatures. Release and shipping documents came next, then the actual transfer papers to Alcor's Boulder cryo-lab: crypt number 34-B. Technicians verified the draining of liquid nitrogen, the attachment of liquid hydrogen lines, and the refilling of the cryostat. Computer links and stabilization were confirmed.

"Everything is in order," Carson assured him.

Scott slung the sport bag over his shoulder. "Why don't I feel any better?"

"My information is never wrong, Scott Dunn."

"Never say never."

Just then, Sue bounded onto the platform. "I'm ready." She was wearing all black: tight body suit, tennis shoes, and a jacket zipped up the front. Around her waist, she wore a belt with various pouches and devices attached to it. Scott recognized a microburst booster and a Regal-Wesson particle blaster, the model with the internally charged magazine. Her hair was tucked under a knit cap.

This was the last thing Scott expected to see. "Where do you think you're going?"

"With you, of course."

She must be delusional. "I work alone."

"So I've heard, tough guy." She approached, Myrtle scampering behind her, and shoved a blast jacket at him. "But this time you've got a partner, like it or not."

He dropped the jacket and his sport bag, spooking

Myrtle. "Then I'm not going." It was a bluff, he knew, but he kept a stern face.

Sue scowled. "Pick up the bag, Scott." The dimple on her chin quivered. "Don't be that way."

"This isn't your problem."

"If it's my grandpa's problem, it's my problem."

Carson raised his mighty hands. "You two had better learn to get along."

"But she lied to me."

"Get over it," she said.

"I don't need you."

"On the contrary." Carson wheezed. "I'm not letting you go alone. She's going to help you get into Alcor."

"This is beyond incredible. I suppose you had this planned all along."

"And I was sure you'd not approve."

Scott glared at Sue. He didn't want to work with a woman. "What if she gets hurt? I'm not responsible—"

"I can take care of myself," she insisted.

"What makes you think I care?"

"I'm sure you don't."

"Good. The record is straight on that."

Myrtle scampered across the floor as if it were her own personal playground. She batted a squeaky toy mouse and chased after it. Annoyed, Scott wished the ferret would play somewhere else. It was distracting him from the serious issue at hand. He turned to Carson. "Sue's not going."

He just shrugged.

Unbelievably, Sue opened a drawer on the console, removed two micro-transceivers from a box, and fitted one into her right ear, her eyes rolled upward.

"She's not listening," Scott said.

"As you know," Carson pressed, "I've already tapped into Alcor's security system. From here I'll manipulate the cameras and alarms inside the building. She'll watch your back every step of the way."

"Testing. Testing," she said into the micro-transceiver. "And I'm good in a fight."

Fight! "Who said anything about fighting? We go in, pull the plug and get out."

"It's not that easy," Carson said. "Katherine's brain must be destroyed."

"That's absurd." Scott knew the West Nile B virus had already turned her brain to pea soup.

Opening a pouch on her belt, Sue removed a magnesium disc. It was the size of a quarter. A green LED flashed from its center. "We have to attach this to her head."

Scott knew that magnesium, once ignited, burned like a welding arc and could not be extinguished, not even under water. It would destroy anything it came in contact with. But how did she think they were going to attach it to Katherine's head? "She's submerged in liquid hydrogen, for Christ's sake."

"Upside down." Carson agreed. "You'll have to blow a hole in the bottom of the cryostat."

This was getting worse by the minute. "An explosion in hydrogen...are you kidding?" He could see himself being blown to smithereens.

From another pouch on her belt, Sue offered up a putty-like substance for Scott's inspection. "It's C-6C, nonflammable and smokeless."

"They make concussion grenades out of this stuff."

Sue smiled. "I'm impressed."

"Just because I'm a mechanic doesn't mean I'm slow and dopey. What happens to the liquid hydrogen?"

"The crypt floor is grated," she said. "It's a safety precaution...in case of a spill. After the hydrogen drains out, you'll reach in through the hole and attach this to Katherine's head."

"Me?"

Sue showed him a transmitter. "I'll ignite the disc with this."

Calculating the evaporation rate of liquid hydrogen and the flash point of the gas, Scott thought of the Hindenburg. "We're going to get killed."

"The crypt's venting system will purge any hydrogen gas." Sue put her lethal toys back in their respective pouches. "Besides, we'll be outside by then."

He sneered at her. The last thing he wanted to do was compliment her expertise.

"Point is," Carson said, "the magnesium will destroy Katherine's brain, derailing Jerry Well's scheme."

"What scheme?" Scott asked. "He wants his wife back. She's probably going to be a vegetable."

Sue loaded her Regal-Wesson magazine with a digital Geiger particle charger. "Maybe not."

"Her brain is history," Scott reminded them. "I only agreed to stop Jerry Well from getting her back."

Myrtle played with her toy mouse, annoying Scott.

"Look at it logically," Carson said. "Consider the facts."

Scott folded his arms across his chest, listening with little interest. It was a waste of time.

"If the disease had damaged Katherine's brain..." Carson coughed. "Jerry Well would not have frozen her. Everyone knows the brain must be viable at the time of cryogenic freeze for any hope of a successful reanimation. He wouldn't have wasted his resources on a doomed endeavor."

Scott didn't like where this line of thinking was going. "Are you saying her brain is all right?"

"Exactly."

"Then Jerry must've killed her before the virus..." Now Scott grasped the full extent of Jerry Well's treachery. "Of course, that's the only explanation."

Carson nodded. "He froze her alive."

"Murdered her." Sue attached a fully charged blaster to her utility belt.

"The poor woman." Scott grimaced at the thought of what Katherine must've gone through during the final moments of her life. But it all made perfect sense. "All Jerry needed was a cure for West Nile B."

"Reanimate her, cure her, and there you have it." Carson groaned. "Katherine, good as new." He ate the last sandwich and set his plate aside. "And I'll bet he's even stashed away some Everlife for her."

Sue was still hung up on the murder rap. "But if he brought her back to life, would it still be murder?"

Myrtle squeaked her toy.

To Scott, the revelation had just changed everything. If she was murdered before the virus killed her, then Katherine had a chance to live a normal life again. To deny her that would be paramount to murder, and he wasn't going to have any part of destroying her brain. He stooped to pick up his sport bag, but to his astonishment, Myrtle was standing on it, showing her sharp teeth. He flinched and staggered backward. "Somebody better get that rat off my bag."

Myrtle hissed.

"Shoo," he said.

Myrtle stood her ground.

"Going somewhere?" Carson asked.

"You need to get someone else to do your dirty work."

Carson screwed up his face. "There isn't anybody else." He banged a mighty fist on the armrest of his wheelchair then motored it in front of Scott. Suspension struts hissed and lifted Carson's massive body two feet higher and tilted him forward. "You can't just waltz out of here."

For an instant Scott felt afraid but stood fast and stated his case. "You're talking about murdering Katherine."

"She's already dead."

Scott winced. "But she might make it through this. She could survive reanimation."

"What do you care?" Carson huffed. "Liz didn't survive."

"But Katherine is a victim, too."

"Don't turn soft on me now, Scott Dunn."

"I can't do it."

At that, Carson lowered his wheelchair and spun around, turning his back to Scott. In a steady voice, he said, "Then Jerry Well has already won."

Scott didn't like the sound of that. He mulled over Carson's words: *Jerry Well has already won.* Won what? Scott wanted to know. He leaned on the back of Carson's wheelchair seat and spoke calmly into his hoggish ear. "Exactly what are you trying to keep Jerry Well from winning?"

Myrtle looked up at Carson, trembled as if she sensed his fear. Then the wheelchair whipped around nearly knocking Scott off his feet. "Katherine must not be reanimated. It'll mean the end of life on earth as we know it."

"Have you gone mad?"

"I was hoping I wouldn't have to explain it to you."

"You'd better."

Carson hung his massive head, quietly sighed. "You wouldn't understand. It goes far beyond your self-indulgences. You couldn't possibly care enough."

Sue rushed to Carson's side. "It's okay, Grandpa." She patted his huge shoulder. "We don't need him. I'll do it alone."

"It's too dangerous..." He wheezed. "He's the expert at this kind of thing, assassinations."

"I'll manage...somehow."

Scott's first thought was to activate the freight elevator and leave the two of them with their secrets. However, Myrtle's behavior caught his attention. She climbed up to Carson's shoulder and looked back and forth between Sue and her master, shivering, her black beady eyes shining wet. She was obviously concerned about what these humans were feeling. It was uncanny, the way she sensed things, but when she twisted her long neck around and looked at Scott, he saw disdain in her eyes. She was leering at him. And worse, her expression made him feel about two inches tall. "Stop it," he shouted. "Just stop it right now. Why can't you people level with me?"

Sue and Carson looked at each other. "Go ahead, Grandpa. Tell him. There might be a human being behind that stone façade, after all."

"But he'll have to put aside his callous disregard for everyone else. He'll have to feel the pain of caring."

"It's a stretch, I know." She shrugged.

"You can forget the guilt trip," Scott put in. "Just give it to me straight."

Still visibly shaken, Carson turned around. "Jerry Well is a hero now...now that everybody knows he was responsible for finding the cure for West Nile B, among other things. His plans are to run for election to the Council of Elders."

Scott hadn't taken any personal interest in space affairs, but he understood how the Council worked. "There's no vacancy. Unless someone has died."

Carson nodded. "That's what I fear will happen, courtesy of Jerry Well."

Scott tried to grasp Carson's gist. "An assassination?"

"With his popularity running at record high levels..." Carson snorted, "he could easily be elected to fill a vacant seat, with Katherine at his side, of course. Being the oldest couple on the Council, they'll automatically take the Chair."

Thinking about motive, Scott came up blank. "Why would he assassinate an Elder for the Chair?"

"Alpha Ketari," Carson said, regaining his composure.

"He wants the whole fricken planet to himself."

"But we need that planet for its resources. It's been in the works for years."

"And Jerry Well has blocked every attempt to develop it," Carson added. "Environmentalists are backing him. If he gets the Chair, he'll have his way—"

"But without Katherine," Scott jumped in, "he can't run for Council." The gravity of the situation hit him like a belly punch. "She's the key to his plan. Take out the key...he doesn't get Alpha Ketari. The world gets its resources. Humanity is saved."

Sue smiled. "I think he's got it, Grandpa."

"But he won't help us," Carson said.

Myrtle went back to playing with her toy mouse, as if she knew the crisis was over.

But for Scott, the crisis was just beginning. Suddenly, he remembered the reason he'd come to Boulder. Revenge. He saw it now for what it was, a self-centered enterprise. Since his wife died, he hadn't given a rusty damn about anyone but himself. He'd carried his grief like a stone shield that protected him from caring about anyone else. If he didn't care, he didn't get hurt. Now the shield had to come down. He had to care enough to save the world. To do it, he had to destroy Katherine's chance to live again. The dilemma twisted his stomach into knots. There had to be another way. "I'd rather kill Jerry Well. I can take him out like he's any other terrorist."

Carson grunted. "He's untouchable. His personal security is top rate. His estate is impenetrable. It would take you months to get close enough to pull the trigger. Katherine is the weakest link."

Scott understood how targets were chosen, the easiest hit for the most benefit. In this case, that would be Katherine, a crucial but innocent victim. Revenge. Compassion. Grief. All of these things banged around in his brain. Many Wellers had died, their lives sacrificed so that he might have one chance to stop Jerry Well and save the world. The stakes were higher than he'd imagined, and they went far beyond his own needs...dangerous territory for him.

And just unplugging Katherine might not be enough. Doctors and their modern medicine might be able to resuscitate her. To succeed, to be absolutely sure, her brain had to be destroyed. As bizarre as the plan was, to Scott it still sounded like murder, but in fact, when he thought about it, it was no different than what he'd done as a Homeland Security Special Forces assassin. He took out targets that presented a *clear and present danger* to the United States.

Katherine was a clear and present danger to the entire world.

Gritting his teeth, Scott decided that he'd have to do it...for the future of mankind, though it would be a bitter victory at best. He pulled on the blast jacket and picked up his sport bag. "All right, Sue, let's move out."

She tossed him a micro-transceiver. "Does that mean you forgive me for lying to you?"

He shoved the transceiver in his ear. "I'm working on it."

Chapter Nine

Midnight. Sue drove the hydrogen cycle into a thicket on the hill overlooking Alcor Life Extension Institute. Scott got off the back, slung the sport bag over his shoulder, and emerged from the bushes. Below, security lights blazed around the cryogenics building. He could make out the ghostly frames of abandoned buildings situated around Alcor, which were once part of the University of Colorado campus. Beyond them, the colorful lights of a strip-mall lit the background. Traffic on one of the transportation grid's feeder roadways was light to nonexistent this time of night. He wondered if infiltrating Alcor was even possible.

Sue stalked out from the bushes and surveyed the scene. "What do you think?"

"This is crazy."

She put her hand on his shoulder as they walked toward the fence. "If it makes you feel any better, it bothers me as well...about Katherine...but we have to rise above it."

"But what if she...?" He stopped himself. This wasn't about Katherine, he knew. This was about stopping Jerry Well. "Never mind."

Sue activated the micro-transceiver in her ear. "We're approaching the gate," she said to Carson.

"Something isn't right," he radioed back. "The gate alarm has been turned off."

"Deliberately?" Scott asked.

"It's as if someone is expecting you."

"We better get out of here," Sue said.

"Wait," Carson replied. "I've just found the security guard's sign-out log. He neglected to inspect the gate alarm, leastwise it's not checked off the list."

Scott pictured Carson bent over his keyboard, his fat fingers typing search commands, breaking into systems that Alcor thought were secure. In light of the guard's oversight, it seemed entirely possible that sloppy security procedures were to blame for the inactive alarm.

"That's good enough for me." Scott knelt at the gate and opened his sport bag. He quickly found the pencil laser, a handy cutter he often used when repairing autocars. He switched on the laser. A thin beam of light shot out, six inches long and bright orange. It made a buzzing sound. He drew the beam across the gate lock. Sparks flew, and in a flash, it fell off and clanked to the ground.

Carson's voice came over Scott's micro-transceiver. "I've disabled the sensors from the gate to the front door. Don't step off the sidewalk. There are sensors in the lawn that will activate alarms and release roving spotlights."

"Okay," Sue said.

Clutching his sport bag, Scott followed her through the open gate and onto the old university grounds, his garlicky odor rising.

At Alcor's front door, he heard a click. Carson had remotely worked the locks through the security system interface. "Where's the guard?" he asked Carson, then heard the tapping of computer keys.

"Front office," Carson came back. "His feet are propped on a desk...*wheeze*... He's sleeping."

"You've got to be kidding."

Sue whispered, "It shouldn't be this easy."

"I'll take luck over skill any day." Scott warily pushed open the front door.

The atrium was dimly lit, but he could easily make out the barred cryo-crypt gates in the wall across the lobby. "Security?" he asked Carson.

"I've deactivated the video modules and motion sensors between your position and cryo-crypt B. Go ahead."

"How's the guard?"

"He hasn't budged."

At that, Scott moved forward with Sue following close behind. Each footstep produced a hollow echo. The air smelled like vinegar. His heartbeat shot up when he finally made it to gate B. Peering between the bars, he could see nothing inside but darkness.

"The gate's locked," Carson said. "I haven't been able to open it. The circuitry has been system-banned."

"I'll get it," Scott replied, not having a clue about the technical problems Carson was dealing with. Reaching into his sport bag, he retrieved a spectral analyzer, an electronic tuning fork of sorts. He used it to gauge the strength of various metals, carbon plastics, and even forged titanium. After testing the bars on the gate, he realized the cutting job was too big for his pencil laser. From the sport bag he removed a power cutter with three-inch jaws and a chainsaw-like handle. The internal ridium power-cell provided fifty tons of force to the jaws. It weighed less than a pound. When he put it to the first bar, a relay clicked.

He froze.

"What was that?" Sue whispered.

Suddenly, red lights started flashing around the gate frame and a honking alarm went off. Scott flinched. The noise was loud enough to wake the frozen dead.

"The lock's been disengaged," Carson said. "I don't understand."

"Where's the guard?" Scott shouted.

"That's odd," Carson replied. "He's still sleeping."

"Can't be—"

"We better go, Scott. This isn't right."

Carson came back, "I'm getting video but no audio from the front office. It must be soundproof. He can't hear the alarm, so finish it."

"That's crazy." Scott frowned. "Why would they make it so the guard couldn't hear an alarm in the office?"

"It's an administration office, not security. Get on with it. You can't go back now."

"Can you shut off the alarm?"

"I'm trying."

Scott bagged the power cutters and signaled Sue to move back. Carefully, he eased open the gate. The flashing red lights and blaring horn were unnerving enough, but as he stepped into the crypt, a sense of awe overwhelmed him. He felt as though he'd entered an ancient tomb. However, instead of a sarcophagus and fabulous riches, he saw only the shadowy forms of cryostats lining the crypt walls, sterile and dispassionate.

Sue handed him a flashlight. "Quit gawking."

"This is so weird." Sport bag in hand, he moved deeper into the crypt. The grated floor creaked under his boots. His breath turned to vapor in the freezing air.

By the beam of his light, he noticed that the cylinders were different sizes. Each had a blue label with a silver triangular design that read: *Alcor Life Extension Institute, Boulder, Colorado.* They were numbered in bold black digits: *54-B, 50-B, 48-B.* Scott kept moving down the line, looking for number *34-B.* He saw 41, then 40. Moving faster, he came to *35-B,* then *33-B.* A sharp pain stabbed his temples. "Carson, there's no thirty-four."

"Are you sure?"

Suddenly, the honking alarm shut off and the red lights stopped flashing. The gate slammed shut with a bang. Devilish laughter echoed through the crypt. Whipping around, he saw John Parish standing outside the bars.

"End of the line, Weller."

"Carson," Scott shouted.

Sue grabbed his arm. "They've jammed our micro-transceivers."

"Just as I planned." Parish laughed. "Ya all fell right into my trap."

"Where is Katherine?" Scott asked, feigning calm.

"She's quite safe, I assure you," Parish said evenly. Then his voice turned stone cold. "Too bad the same can't be said for you."

Just then, more bounty hunters appeared. They thrust their rifles through the crypt bars.

"Let 'em have it, boys."

Gunfire erupted in a deafening barrage of flaming magnesium rounds, which pinged and clanked around in the crypt like a fireworks display gone berserk. Before Scott could find cover, a burning magnesium slug hit him in the chest. The impact knocked him backward, hammered the air from his lungs, and sent the flashlight flying. His legs folded underneath him, but Sue stopped his fall. She pushed him between two cryostats and shielded his body with hers.

Pinned against the wall, he gasped air heavily tainted with acrid smoke that billowed from his blast jacket. The magnesium slug was burning a hole through the material and soon the hot core would reach his chest. Noxious fumes stung his eyes. Squinting fiercely, he knew he had to get the jacket off fast. However, the bounty hunters' bombardment killed all hope of that happening any time soon.

As Sue pressed into him and fiery ammunition zinged all about, one round punctured the cryostat next to them. Scott heard the resultant hiss. He clenched his jaw and forced an eyelid open. Liquid hydrogen was spewing from the damaged cylinder.

Parish shouted, "It's gonna blow."

The bounty hunters stopped firing.

"Get back, men. Get back."

Echoing footfalls retreated across the atrium.

Sue pulled Scott from their narrow refuge. He tore off his blast jacket just as the magnesium slug burned through the material, clinked on the floor, and fell through the grates. Spitting and hissing, its glow disappeared.

Sue rushed to the closed gate, tugged on the bars. "It's locked."

"Carson," Scott shouted into his micro-transceiver. He

got no response.

Sue looked back at the leaking cryostat, her eyes wide with terror. "My God."

"He's got nothing to do with this." Scott knelt at the gate and opened his sport bag.

"We've got to stop that leak."

He removed the power cutters. "Put your finger in the hole."

"I'm serious."

"Our only hope is to cut our way out of here." He put the cutter's jaws around the first bar and pulled the trigger. The ridium power-cell surged with energy, and the cutter lurched in his grasp. "We have to work fast."

"But the magnesium rounds—"

"Better hope they burn out quickly."

Sue gasped. "The ventilation system hasn't come on. Parish must've shut it off. It'll only take one spark to ignite the hydrogen. This place is going to explode."

Scott knew that was a definite possibility.

It took ten seconds before the bar snapped. He grabbed the cut end and pulled on it, figuring he could bend it up and out of the way, but it wouldn't budge.

Behind him, liquid hydrogen spewed from the damaged cryostat and flowed down through the grated floor. The grates froze and formed an insulating layer that slowed the *boil off*, but within minutes, the liquid would evaporate and rise to meet the magnesium rounds that still flickered about within the crypt. There wasn't enough time to cut both ends of every bar. It would be faster to bend them out of the way.

Again, he put the full force of his muscles to the bar.

Still it wouldn't bend.

Sue leaned in to lend a hand, but they were only in each other's way. Then he saw the microburst booster hanging from her belt. "Your booster," he shouted. "Attach it to the end of this bar."

She looked at him blankly for only a second, then as if visualizing his purpose, placed the lift ring around the cut end of the bar and activated the thruster. Using both hands to stabilize the booster and steer it, she applied full power. The thruster whined, and the bar creaked as it bent upward.

"All right," she said with a sigh of relief.

Scott went to work on the second bar. As the power cutter clamped down, he assessed the task before him. Removing three bars would not open enough space for them to escape. With four bars out of the way, Sue might make it through, but just barely.

The second bar snapped. As Sue attached the booster, he glanced back to check the spill. Already, the liquid hydrogen was evaporating. An eerie mist swirled up from the grates and crept over the floor like an encroaching fog. He knew that any contact with the mist would mean instant cryogenic *burns*. "Hurry."

Sue bent the second bar out of the way.

As the hydrogen mist crept closer, he clenched his jaw and cut the third bar, and then the forth. After Sue's microburst booster bent them out of the way, he scooted to the side and pointed to the opening. "Go."

Calmly disconnecting the booster, she said, "Two more bars and we go together."

"But you can make it out now."

"Careful, Scott, I'm beginning to think you care about

me."

"Dream on." He glanced back at the encroaching mist. It wasn't two feet from them, churning and boiling and rising up toward the remaining magnesium rounds, embedded in the walls and glowing white hot. He wanted Sue to make her escape before it was too late. Then again, he knew that arguing with her would waste precious seconds. "If you think I'm going to start liking you, you're wrong," he said as he cut the next bar.

"I've been wrong before." She attached the booster, applied full power. The bar creaked and bent up out of the way.

Already the mist had gathered around Scott's feet. He could feel the cold eating through his boots.

Sue was running out of room to work. She pressed her back to the gate, the mist inching toward her. "Scott."

Frantically, he attacked the last bar. When it snapped, he took the booster from Sue, attached it to the bar, and activated the thruster. Standing ankle deep in the mist, his boots frosted over. His feet felt numb from the cold, but he steeled himself against the possibility of frostbite and guided the booster upward until he was satisfied that the bar had moved far enough out of the way. "Ladies first."

Sue sprang to the opening. "Always the gentleman."

"Just go."

She turned and ducked out of the crypt.

Sweating garlic juice, he threw his tools into the sport bag and leaped out after her. Still on his hands and knees, he was just about ready to kiss the lobby's marble floor and savor their hard-earned freedom when a blaster bolt screeched over his head. Unbelievably, a bounty hunter had stayed behind to guard the gang's retreat. Talk about drawing the short straw, Scott thought, as he belly-flopped on the floor. Flashing energy bolts flew past him like lightning.

Drawing her blaster, Sue rolled and fired, peppering the bounty hunter full of smoking holes. He flew backward, crashed through the front door, and tumbled head over heels down the sidewalk, his limbs flailing like a tossed rag doll.

Then blaster bolts came at them from somewhere in the distance, pelting the walls and ceiling with bursts of particle energy.

Crouching, Sue ran to the front office, bashed in the door, and dove for cover under a desk. Debris was flying everywhere as Scott crawled in after her, dragging his sport bag and spitting dust. He had only a moment to catch his breath when he noticed, across the room, the guard still had his feet propped on the desk, chin on his chest, hands folded in his lap. Scott couldn't believe the man had slept through all the noise. "Hey, mister."

The guard didn't flinch.

Scott looked at Sue. She shrugged, pointed at the guard, a signal he understood to mean, *go check.*

Keeping low, he moved to the man, hoping he was just sleeping off a stupor. "Mister, are you all right?" He poked his shoulder.

The guard listed then fell out of the chair, face-first to the floor. There was a hole burned through his spinal column. Black flies had laid hatches of white eggs in the open wound. The stench turned Scott's stomach. "He's been dead for some time."

"John Parish has gone to a lot of trouble to kill you," Sue stated from her crouched position behind the desk.

"Remind me to send him a thank-you card."

Just then, office windows exploded as the bounty hunters opened fire again. Scott crabbed across the floor to rejoin Sue. He pictured John Parish's face wrenched in anger at their escape from the cryo-crypt. And Scott also knew that the bounty hunter wouldn't let them leave the building. He only needed to keep them inside for a few moments longer, until the whole place exploded.

"The emergency exit," Sue said. "Where is it?"

Scott remembered seeing it on Carson's monitor. From memory, he determined its location in relation to the front office. "This way." Under a shower of glass and screeching blaster bolts, he crawled with Sue out the office door, and once in the atrium, they got to their feet and ran down the hallway.

Suddenly, a pale blue plume of hydrogen fire erupted behind him. It made more of a whooshing sound than a boom, and being that hydrogen rose and burned quickly, the cloud radiated less heat than a gasoline explosion. But the concussion carried a knockout punch.

Now, lying on the ground outside, he remembered the heat and the roar, the emergency door coming unhinged and the feeling of being hit by a truck. His left arm felt numb, his right hand tingled, and he smelled burnt hair. That's when he became aware of Sue. She was kneeling over him, her knit cap gone, and her hair singed on one side of her head. "Come on."

Pheuw. Pheuw-Pheuw!

Blaster bolts streaked past them. She turned and fired

back. "They're coming."

"Where's my bag?"

"I've got it." She helped him to his feet. "Can you walk?"

He found his wobbly legs, stumbled. "No."

"Then you'd better run."

Blaster bursts lit up the night as he half-staggered and half-ran toward a dark building in the distance. Turning again, Sue covered their retreat, firing her blaster behind them. She picked off a bounty hunter who was running across the lawn. Security system spotlights launched into the air, hovered and swarmed over the area, their bright cones of light sweeping back and forth in search of any motion.

Fear drove Scott forward. He knew he had to make it to the building, which was just a silhouette in the darkness, backlit by a strip-mall. Suddenly he collided with a chain link fence. He looked up. It was ten feet high.

Panic set in. He tried to scramble up the fence, but his numb arm failed him, and he fell to the ground. Gulping air, he sat up, facing the fence. He remembered the old man on the bus frantically trying to escape, trapped with nowhere to go. Now he understood the terror, the futility of that Weller's desperate situation.

Dropping to her knees behind him, Sue put her back to his and slid him the sport bag. "Cut the fence."

"What's the use?" he said. "It's me they want. Save yourself."

"There you go again..." She fired at a bounty hunter suddenly illuminated under a roving spotlight. He dove for cover. Blasters responded in a hail of flashes. "I'm not going anywhere without you, Scott. Now cut the damn fence."

A blaster bolt hit the chain link above his head and rained down sparks. He turtled his neck. "Who made you the boss?"

"Grandpa."

"Of course." After ripping open the sport bag, Scott retrieved his pencil laser. "You're just like him, you know."

She fired at a hovering spotlight that was getting too close. Whining, it angled into the ground and shattered. "I'll take that as a compliment."

"Don't let it go to your head." Activating the laser beam, he cut a vertical gash in the chain link then spread the opening. At the risk of sounding like he cared, he said, "Ladies first."

She smiled. "You've been doing a lot of that lately."

Blaster bolts flashed by.

"I don't want you out of my sight."

She wriggled through the fence opening. "Getting attached to me, are you?"

"Like herpes. Go."

"Sounds like a long-term relationship."

"Shut up and cover me." He wormed his way through the fence then reached back through the opening and grabbed his sport bag. That's when he saw a horde of bounty hunters approaching at full speed. "Watch it."

Pheuw-Pheuw! She fired twice.

Just then, a bright flash tore into his left shoulder. Instant pain seared through his body. He slammed to the ground as if thrown by a bull. The odor of burning flesh ballooned in the air.

Sue shrieked, fell on him. "Scott." She shook him. "Scott."

Suddenly, a blinding spotlight hovered above them. A bounty hunter shouted, "I got ya, Weller."

Sue huddled over Scott, hiding her blaster between them. "How bad is it?"

"Bad." He moaned, squinting under the intense light.

The bounty hunter stepped up, his blaster in both hands, elbows locked. "Get up, lady. I gotta make sure he's dead."

"You don't have to kill him."

"He's ours now, all five million bucks worth."

Scott winced, looked up at Sue's face, sooty and smudged, her tearing eyes barely visible in the shadow of the humming spotlight hovering overhead. "Give me the blaster," he whispered.

"I can handle him."

"He's got the drop on you."

"I don't want you to die," she said softly, her dimpled chin trembling.

"I know."

"Shut up." The bounty hunter fired a warning shot into the ground. "I'll kill you both if I have to." He glanced over his shoulder as reinforcements neared. "I got him. Over here, boss. I got him."

She slipped Scott the blaster. He clutched it in his right hand, the tingling hand, but the best hand he had. "If I miss, you're on your own."

"Don't miss," she whispered.

"Go."

She rolled off him. Scott raised the blaster and fired.

The energy bolt knocked the surprised bounty hunter backward into the fence. Blood gushed from his mouth, and he keeled over on his face, smoke swirling from a black hole where the bolt had exited his back.

In the next second, Sue snatched up the bounty hunter's dropped blaster and shot the hovering spotlight. It exploded in a shower of sparks, returning the area to darkness.

Scott had already dragged himself to his feet, and clutching his sport bag, he lit out for the abandoned building with Sue covering his tracks.

Dodging a hail of blaster bolts, they made it to a boarded up window. He tore away the boards, boosted Sue through, and climbed in after her. Surprisingly, the place wasn't as abandoned as he'd first thought. The corridors and rooms of the old college administration building teemed with life. Homeless people. Illegals. They huddled together in family groups, the old and the young. Sparse candlelight dimly illuminated their dirty faces and terror-filled eyes.

As he and Sue approached them, some covered up with tattered blankets. Others ducked into cardboard boxes. Most didn't move, just stared, oblivious to the rats roaming among them as if they were all members of the same club, tolerant of each other and possibly dependant.

Scott grimaced. His shoulder barely bled, having been cauterized by the blaster bolt, but it burned like the fires of hell. He followed Sue down the main corridor, peering into rooms in search of a hiding place. Most every nook and cranny was occupied.

In one room, two children held up their palms in front

of an old microwave oven. A small fire flickered inside, reflecting off their filthy faces. In another room, lighted by a single candle, a naked woman cowered at the feet of a brutish man, bare-chested and sweaty. A belt dangled from his fist. He stared at the intruders with ice-cold eyes.

Sue raised her blaster.

Immediately, Scott nudged her along, thinking it was a bad time to get involved in a domestic dispute. Besides, blaster fire would give away their position to the bounty hunters.

Farther down the bleak corridor, they came to a closed door with a nameplate: *Dr. Janis Mackey*. Scott tried the doorknob. It was locked. He moved on.

The deeper into the building they went, the more foul the air became: urine and feces, vomit and rotting garbage, a sickening blend of odors that melded into a stagnant pool of forgotten humanity. His stomach turned upside down. He would have vomited if it weren't for the sounds that suddenly reverberated through the building.

Blasters.

Chapter Ten

In the basement of Hylander mansion, Jerry Well looked over the technicians and doctors preparing their equipment to reanimate Katherine. It was 1:00 AM. They were ahead of schedule, which pleased him immensely.

He'd selected an enormous room for this procedure. Normally used as his private gymnasium, the floor had been covered with plastic sheeting and the walls with draping white linens. At center court sat a stainless-steel table. It looked like the slab in a morgue, he observed, or perhaps an embalming table. Above it, a rectangular crystalline dome, the same size as the table, hung suspended from the ceiling. All around the room, medical gadgetry of mind-boggling complexity cluttered every available square foot. He recognized the tunnel-shaped magnetic imaging scanner and the transparent cylinders of a heart-lung bypass machine. Tubes and wires threaded about in every direction. The hum of machinery permeated the air, as well as the smell of disinfectant. If he hadn't known better, he would've thought the doctors were preparing to perform an autopsy.

Heat lamps came on above the table. Technicians adjusted the cones of light, nodded, and then moved on to other chores.

Just then, a line of security-bots strode in through a far door. They carried huge bouquets of flowers, green leafy planters, and baskets of fruit, which they set around the machinery in strategic positions. When it came time for Katherine to open her eyes, Jerry wanted her to see something beautiful and not just the cold, hard tools of miracle medicine.

Satisfied, he donned his thermal robe and went into Katherine's cold room. Activity was at a fever pitch. Alcor personnel wearing long white smocks, facemasks, and rubber boots gathered around her cryostat. Clipboard in hand, Dr. Navarro supervised two men standing on stepladders, examining the lid. Several other technicians walked around the cylinder, scanning the shell with handheld meters. Another man removed Katherine's glassy picture and tossed it aside. Jerry gritted his teeth to remind himself that the sanctity he and Katherine shared here had to be violated this one time.

Ventilation fans came on at full power.

"Fire marshal," Navarro called out. "Are you prepared?"

"The inspection is complete," a hooded man replied from his position at the hydrogen control valves.

Jerry knew working with hydrogen was dangerous. He didn't want any accidents and appreciated the extra safety precautions.

Navarro nodded to the men on the ladders. "Proceed."

Working padded tools with gloved hands, they wrenched the clasps free from their anchors. With a hiss, the lid rose straight up three feet on vertical struts and stopped with a clunk. Hydrogen mist boiled out and drifted to the floor, swirled, and whipped away through the vents. Suction pumps chattered and began draining the cryostat of liquid hydrogen.

Heart racing, Jerry imagined Katherine's voice calling out to him: *"I'm frightened, Jerry."* He wanted to tell her that everything would be all right.

"The light is so bright."

He bit his lower lip. Always the complainer, she had no sympathy for what he'd gone through, the expense, the waiting.

Leaning over, the men on the ladders batted away the mist with gloved hands and peered down inside the cryostat.

Katherine screamed. *"Jerry. Help me. What do they want?"*

The panic in her imagined voice sent shock waves through his chest. He knew she was terrified. She hadn't seen a living soul in 225 years. But that was no reason for her to act this way. It was downright embarrassing.

"Jerry," she cried out in his mind. *"Don't let them see me naked."*

Now she was acting ridiculous, but he said nothing, and as the garlicky heft of his body odor rose, he clenched his jaw and whished she'd calm down.

"Jerry. Do something." She screamed again. *"Don't let them touch me."* He cupped his hands over his ears. Shut up, Katherine. She was going to ruin everything.

The men inserted a mist evacuation hose into the cylinder.

"What's that thing, Jerry? It's going to hurt me. No.

Leave me alone. Jerry. Make them leave me alone."

Her outcries were more than he could stand. He rushed forward. "Katherine."

Navarro whirled around, surprise glaring from his shielded eyes. "Stay back."

But Jerry wasn't listening. "Be quiet, Katherine." He leaped on the nearest ladder, got two rungs up when forceful hands pulled him down.

"Are you out of your mind?" Navarro shouted.

Jerry blinked. Several men held his arms. He tried to understand why they were restraining him. He couldn't remember the last few moments. "I'm sorry." He was sweating profusely. "I got carried away."

Navarro winced as if repulsed by Jerry's garlicky spew. "One false move, she could shatter like a china doll."

"I just wanted to see her." Actually, he had no idea what he was thinking. In all the excitement he'd lost control. Katherine was making him look like an idiot. "I don't know..."

"Just stand back and leave us do our jobs," Navarro insisted. "I must evaluate her condition."

The men released Jerry's arms. He stuck out his chin and straightened the collar of his robe. "By all means, carry on." At that, he back-stepped to the wall. An attitude adjustment was in order. Old habits were hard to break. He had to give over control of Katherine to the professionals charged with bringing her back to life. If she interfered with them again, in any way... He clenched his fists. She'd be sorry.

By now, the mist had dissipated, and the pumps shut down. The men dismounted their ladders and moved them aside.

Navarro returned his attention to his cryonics patient. "Activate the extractor."

Whining ion motors engaged. A vertical seam appeared in the cryostat shell, which then began to spread apart as curved cylinder walls rotated away from each other. Xenon lights flickered on. A frozen body appeared, upside down, tightly wrapped in white gauze, like a mummy, and still dripping liquid hydrogen. Two probes protruded from her head.

"Katherine?" Jerry felt sick at the sight of her. A part of him wanted to turn his head away. She didn't look anything like he remembered. However, another part of him couldn't stop staring at her. After all, she wasn't a sight one saw every day.

"Bring her out," Navarro ordered.

With a clank, steel interlinking fingers moved outward, bringing Katherine forward and clear of the cylinder. The odor of molded bread wafted through the room. Automatically, the fingers rotated, moving her rigid body into a horizontal position. For support, technicians activated a levitation beam underneath her. At the same time, the steel interlinking fingers opened with a snap, leaving Katherine suspended in mid-air.

Stepping up close, and with his hands clasped behind his back so he wouldn't touch her, Navarro inspected his patient head to toe. Technicians traversed her body with bio-scanners. The results were fed into a matrix interpreter, and the data appeared on a hologram suspended in front of them. "This is going to be a tough case," he said, examining the information. "High levels of nitrogen have seeped into her tissues. There is much damage here. The manner of her preparation was archaic."

A knot formed in Jerry's stomach. "It's the best we could do in 2010."

Navarro stepped back, shaking his head. "She might not make it."

"I'm afraid, Jerry."

Jerry clenched his jaw. He wanted to run to her, to embrace her, to reassure her that everything would be all right, but the troubled look in Dr. Navarro's sullen eyes gave him cause for alarm. For the first time in 225 years, Jerry began to doubt success. He feared his control over Katherine had been just an illusion.

At that moment, the thick door opened and two men brought in a hover-gurney. "We're ready for her."

Chapter Eleven

B ounty hunters' boots thundered through the old college administration building. Parish felt as if he'd entered the armpit of human civilization. All around him, terrified squatters huddled together while his helmeted and goggled men pressed their assault, firing blasters and rifles at anyone who got in their way. A few acts of bravery were met with violent suppression.

Before giving the order to enter the building, Parish knew that time was running out on the operation. There were no contingency plans for a search, no time allotted for any delays. He had already taken into account the city's emergency team response times. Fire, police, and paramedics were stretched to the limits along the Front Range, so he'd given the operation a nine-minute timeline from first contact to withdrawal. However, ten minutes had already passed and the Weller had not been terminated. Now, they worked fast, systematically sweeping the first floor, clearing each room one at a time.

Then they came to a shut door. The nameplate read *Dr. Janis Mackey*. "It's locked," one of his men reported.

Parish grinned. He had the Weller now, but he thought Scott Dunn was foolish to believe a locked door would stop the inevitable. Endorphins of murder spilled into Parish's bloodstream. "Break it down."

Expecting blaster bolts to greet them, his men kicked in the door and immediately ducked for cover. When nothing happened, Parish stepped inside and gunned a flashlight beam around the room. A young couple, naked to their waists, cowered in a corner and clung to each other, their wide eyes ringed in white. His light illuminated a makeshift bed of cardboard and burlap, a spilled bottle of wine, and a rat nibbling on cake crumbs. Wedding cards were strewn about. But there was no Weller. His anger flared. Not to be denied a kill, he aimed the blaster at the newlyweds.

"Wait," one of his men called out. "Listen."

Hearing the faint wail of sirens, Parish gritted his teeth. He was out of time. Though he and his bounty hunters supplied a needed service to humanity, as they saw it, they worked outside the law. Often, innocent bystanders were killed. These deaths had outraged local officials who then put pressure on the authorities to end the bloodshed. It was all political rhetoric to Parish, but nonetheless, he had no desire to become embattled in a dispute. Groaning, he knew he had to retreat from the area before the police arrived. The operation hadn't gone as planned. Scott Dunn had proven to be an articulate and resourceful target.

"Move out," Parish ordered his men then shot the young couple and left.

***

Moving down a corridor not far away, Scott grimaced. His shoulder wound pounded with every beat of his heart. He couldn't move his left arm. The sport bag had become a burden. Behind him, the shriek of blasters echoed through the halls. He heard the cries of the wounded and dying. Suddenly he felt responsible for their agony; after all, he'd brought it upon them by invading their sanctuary in a desperate attempt to escape the bounty hunters.

That realization sent a paralyzing wave of grief over him. His knees buckled. Only a rush of anger kept him on his feet. He spun around abruptly, surprising Sue. "I can't let them slaughter any more of those people. We have to go back."

"Are you telling me you care about them?"

"No, no," he stammered, thinking that wasn't like him. In the heat of the moment, he'd misspoken. "Of course not." He inspected the charge-level meter on the blaster in his tingling right hand. Half the energy cell had been depleted. "I just want to stop Parish."

Her eyes lit up. "From killing those people."

"Will you get off my back about that? Let's go."

"But there are too many of them."

"Ten...maybe twelve, nothing you can't handle." He slung the sport bag across his back. "I'll take care of the rest."

"But your shoulder, your arm—"

The wail of sirens interrupted her. Then he noticed the bounty hunters' blasters had fallen silent. He knew they were fleeing like rats from a fire. "They're getting away." He started off down the hall.

Sue grabbed his shirtsleeve and spun him around. "Let them go, Scott. The police are going to roundup everyone in this building. We don't want to be here for that."

She was right, as usual. They were dressed like night

raiders and armed to the teeth. He was sure the police wouldn't be sympathetic. The sirens were getting louder. He relented. "How do we get out of here?"

"I don't know."

Just then, stampeding footsteps rumbled up from down the hall. A grimy mob appeared in the dusty gloom, sprinting toward them. He stepped aside as the horde of illegals passed by, and then he signaled Sue to fall in behind them.

At a full run, she asked, "Where are they going?"

"Fire escape." He was thinking about fleeing rats. They always had a way out. Within moments, he realized the relevance of that theory as they bounded down a cement staircase, ran across a cavernous room of leaking pipes, and funneled down a creaky stairwell into a black culvert no bigger than six feet high. His boots sunk ankle-deep in fetid water. The stench of rot hit him square between the eyes.

Undeterred, he followed Sue headlong down a dark tunnel. Gasping rancid air, he regretted every lungful. Someone up ahead yelped and fell. He stumbled over a retching body but kept his feet and continued forward, driven on by the mob's mentality for survival.

At intersecting tunnels, streetlight sliced down through grated gutters above them. He saw flashing glimpses of Sue sprinting in front of him. Soon, small groups of people veered off into tunnels going different directions.

Four or five blocks went by before he realized he and Sue were running alone. By this time, he was wheezing, his lungs fighting for every breath. His burning shoulder wound demanded that he stop and rest, but he pressed on anyway.

They'd run for a mile or more when the tunnel ended abruptly at a drop-off that dumped into a stream flowing under a bridge. Scott clung to the culvert's cement wall, gasping. He couldn't hear the police sirens any longer. Only cricket chirps and frog croaks filled the night air. A streetlight on the road above bathed the shadowy scene with an eerie glow.

Without hesitating, Sue dropped into the shallow stream. Scott jumped down after her, tripped on a submerged rock, and stumbled onto the bank, instantly silencing the crickets and frogs. He collapsed in tall grass, panting. "Wait."

"We have to circle around and get back to the cycle," she said, trying to lift him off the ground.

A flying police cruiser screamed over the bridge.

"It's too risky." He pulled the sport bag strap over his head and propped his back against a cement column. "We'll rest here until everything calms down. Besides...my arm is useless. I need to fix it."

She dropped to her knees, tore open his shirt, and inspected the wound. "It's bad. I can see the bone." Wincing, she added, "You need a doctor."

"My bag...open it..."

Inside the bag, among the tools and gadgetry, he found a first aid pouch and quickly tore into it with his teeth. Sterile pads, disinfectant, and a green tube of ointment spilled out.

Squinting, she reached for the tube. "What's this?"

"Nanocream. Military grade." He leaned his head back against the cement, fighting nausea. All this time he'd been running on adrenaline. Now it had expired from his system, leaving him exhausted. "I need you to clean the wound...apply the nanocream, but don't touch it. Squeeze it out...cover it with a gauze pad."

"I've heard of this stuff. Where did you get it?"

"Super Walgreen's," he said with a painful smirk.

"Funny man." She opened the disinfectant bottle. "This is going to hurt."

From the slight twitch in the corners of her mouth, he thought she enjoyed telling him that. "Just get it over with."

When the disinfectant hit the open wound, he clenched his jaw. Every muscle in his body stiffened. His shoulder felt as if it had exploded. He closed his eyes and moaned even though he really wanted to scream. The disinfectant, a special *primer* formula, not only cleaned the wound but prepared it for the application of nanocream.

The science of this miracle medicine wasn't anything new; the idea had been around for over two hundred years: molecular machines, called nanocytes, having specialized functions, mass-produced in the trillions per gram, and programmed to work with a common goal, in essence, as one unit.

In 2045, the first windows were produced with an exterior layer of nanocytes that perpetually cleaned the glass. Fifty years later, nanotechnology broke into the medical field with the introduction of nanotoothpaste. After one application in the morning, the nanocytes cleaned teeth of tartar all day long. These nanocytes were later redesigned to clear blocked arteries and digest cancer tumors. Another hundred and twenty five years of development brought nanocreams and nanoserums into the medical mainstream, saving millions of lives each year. He had to smirk at that. The government had banned Everlife because it would exacerbate the population explosion, but nanotechnology? No problem.

As soon as Sue applied the cream to Scott's wound, a variety of microscopic machines were tasked. Some, known as *bridges*, were programmed to bridge gaps in damaged tissue structures, on a cellular level. Then there were the *Dutchboys*. These nanocytes secreted cholesterol, the body's natural bandage, and patched leaks in cellular walls as well as vascular and lymphatic systems. Several neuron-transmitting nanocytes called *electros*, some positively charged and others negatively charged, reestablished damaged nerve pathways. Some electros were sophisticated enough to regulate internal organ functions until the body healed adequately enough to take over on its own.

The nanocream could not heal the damage the blaster had done to his shoulder. It could only make emergency repairs, thus giving his body the ability to function while it healed.

"How's that, soldier?"

He flinched, thinking he must've passed out for a moment. His shoulder tingled. He detected the fishy smell of nanocream. Sue had ripped strips of cloth from his singed black shirt and bandaged his wound. "Thanks."

"Don't mention it."

Then he focused on the immediate problem. "I wonder what they did with Katherine."

"Now there's the million dollar question." Sue activated her micro-transceiver and groaned. "They're still jamming us."

Scott squirmed, tried to get comfortable. "Somehow they got wind of what we were planning. Jerry moved her without Carson knowing it."

"She was never at Alcor in the first place," Sue said. "Did you notice there wasn't an empty space between crypts 33 and 35?"

"Now that you mention it..." Scott remembered the transfer documents Carson had showed him. She'd been moved from Arizona, all right, but her final destination had been falsified. Only Jerry Well could have had enough clout with Alcor to pull that off. "I'll bet she's at Hylander."

"If she is, you'll never get in there." Sue closed the sport bag and set it aside.

Scott was already formulating a new plan, one that he knew Carson would never agree to. "There are other ways."

She gave him a disapproving glare.

He pretended to ignore her and examined the makeshift bandage. "You'd make a fine medic."

She sat back on her heels. "I'm a school teacher, really."

Trying to relax, he settled back against the cement pylon and put the blaster on his lap. His shoulder felt cold. "A teacher, huh? You like kids?"

"Don't you?"

Memories of his wife and two daughters came to mind and made his heart ache: birthdays and homework and dance lessons...weddings...grandkids... "They're all long gone."

She sighed. "Heartbreaking."

"I've learned to live with it. I ignore it...most of the time. Besides, I function better that way...most of the time."

"And the other times?" Sue asked softly.

He didn't want to tell her that sometimes the grief was more than he could bear. It would manifest itself into a demon of mourning that raised its head and demanded complete submission, often leaving him bent in half and bawling for hours. He didn't want Sue to know that he suffered that way, besides, she could never understand. "I keep it to myself."

"Forever a loner?"

"It's how I survive."

She sat next to him and folded her legs underneath her. "You're so busy surviving, Scott, you've forgotten how to live."

"I haven't forgotten anything." He flexed his fingers, noticed the feeling had already returned to his right hand. "I choose not to get involved with anyone again."

"No more wives, no kids, no pets?"

"It's too painful to watch them die."

She shook her head. "I know what you mean, but my grandpa..."

"You can't possibly know what it felt like to watch my daughters grow old while I stayed young and healthy, guilty of some horrible crime against nature."

"It's not that bad," Sue whispered.

"It's bad, I tell you...the same with my grandsons. Each time I buried one of them I walked away...immune to their fate and wondering what gave me the right to live...and not them. It's the ultimate case of survivor's guilt."

"You can't help that."

"I've tried to get over it."

"There's no getting over grief, Scott. You have to incorporate it into your life, work around it, make adjustments."

"I handle it my way," he said, though not entirely convinced that his way worked very well at all.

"My grandpa could teach you how to cope with it better. He helped me understand what it's like to be immortal."

"It's hell."

"It's what you make of it, Scott."

Closing his eyes, he wished she'd stop harping on him. He knew all about grief. It was a disease of the heart. Mourning was its most visible symptom. The sense of loss would never abate, but over time, the symptoms would be less severe...for mortals anyway. Not him. Just because Sue was Carson's granddaughter didn't make her an expert on the subject.

The crickets and frogs were back at it again. A dog barked from somewhere. He remembered when he had a dog. His name was Ranger. They'd traveled everywhere together. They were best buddies. But when Ranger died, the loss tore his heart out. He swore he'd never be responsible for another pet.

Suddenly, there was a chill in the air he hadn't noticed before. Tires thudded over the bridge. His shoulder ached.

"You should get some rest," Sue said.

He looked at her. The dim light reflected off her sooty face, and a breeze played with a lock of her singed hair. She was intelligent, courageous, and she had a way of pushing him and making him think about things he'd rather not think about. In a way, he respected her for that. She wasn't like any woman he'd ever met. For a moment, he thought about her as his lover. Then he saw her funeral, killing the image of them together.

Funerals. He remembered Liz. A heavy weight landed on his chest. He hadn't gone to her funeral. "I wish things had turned out differently for my wife."

Sue moved closer. "What happened to her?"

That was the toughest part, trying to figure out what went wrong, where it all started, and why. It was even harder to talk about. He'd dated Liz through high school: his first kiss, his first love. She'd wanted to get married right after graduation, but he didn't. If he had to be honest with himself, he would have blamed his reluctance on Liz's father, DC homicide detective Captain Bruce Hubbard.

The Captain had spoiled her rotten. She was very difficult when she didn't get her way. Like the time she'd refused to go to the Senior Prom because her father wouldn't buy her a new dress...not just any new dress, a fifteen hundred dollar new dress. Hell hath no fury like a teenager denied. The Captain finally caved and bought her the dress.

Thinking she needed more time to grow up, Scott enlisted in the war against terrorism. Liz had thrown a royal fit—

"Earth to Scott," Sue said, touching his knee.

Jolted, he muttered, "I-I was just thinking."

"Are you going to tell me what happened?"

Chapter Twelve

S cott remembered 2010 as a year of hope. The first Middle East War was over, and after four years in the service of Homeland Security Special Forces, he received his discharge and returned to civilian life. Liz was waiting for him when the plane landed.

"Scott."

He likened their reunion to a scene from the movies, she in a summer dress running toward him with open arms, he standing there in combat fatigues, anticipating her embrace. They kissed, twirling and clutching each other with a passion he couldn't deny.

"Finally," she whispered in his ear. "You're home."

Her neck smelled of roses. It felt good to hold her again, yet alien in a way, as he hadn't had close human contact since he'd left on his last assignment to Jordan. A notorious terrorist had to be taken out. It took more than a year to get close enough to pull the trigger. Holding Liz, Scott could still smell the cordite wafting from his rifle and see the bearded man's brain splatter across the café's back wall. He squeezed her and tried to concentrate on the roses.

As military assassins went, he was among the elite. Not many combat soldiers knew what it was like to snuff out a man's life as he bounced his child on his knee or held his wife in the day's final embrace. He wasn't proud of what he'd done, his only solace coming from the fact that his targets had been some of the most ruthless men on the planet. Even that being true, he'd never told anyone what he'd done for his country because, in reality, he felt as if he'd become a terrorist himself.

"Let's get something to eat."

"My mom's making you a homecoming dinner."

"Okay." A home-cooked meal sounded good.

Liz beamed. "It was my idea."

"Funny you didn't mention it earlier." They'd emailed each other almost every day he was gone.

"It's the perfect opportunity for you to ask Daddy."

"Come on, Liz, I just got off the plane."

She pushed him away, put her hands on her hips. "Do you want to get married or not?"

"Yes...of course," he said softly, not wanting to make a scene in the airport. People were already looking at them. "I'll ask him tonight."

"Promise?"

"Okay, sure."

At that, she fell into his arms again. "I've waited a long time for you, Scott. I'm tired of being alone."

"Everything is going to be all right." He held her again, fully aware of what she was doing, yet, like her father, caving in to her wishes. After all, she'd been faithful to him through the last four difficult years. Had she grown up? That remained to be seen. Still, they'd agreed to get married after he returned home. The least he could do was buck up and ask her father for his approval.

They left the airport, walking arm-in-arm to her car, a

shiny black 2011 BMW. "Want to drive?" she asked.

"Did your dad buy you this car?"

"I insisted," she said with a smile.

Liz always got what she wanted.

Twenty minutes later, they pulled into the driveway of a modest bi-level home on Berry Street. It was like a second home to Scott. On many occasions, Liz would ask him over after school under the pretense of doing homework, when in reality, they'd spent most of their time necking in her room. It seemed like only yesterday.

As he entered the familiar foyer, her father approached. The Captain wore a gray workout suit with circles of sweat under his armpits. Smiling manly, he outstretched a beefy hand. "Welcome home, soldier."

That was a switch, Scott thought. The Captain usually called him 'lad' or 'my boy.' What a difference a uniform and a few years made. "Good to see you, Captain Hubbard. We didn't mean to interrupt your workout."

"I'm trying to knock off fifty pounds." He patted his round belly. "Doctor's orders."

Liz tossed her car keys on the hall table. "Scott has something to ask you, Daddy." She winked slyly at Scott, back-stepped toward the kitchen, and then dashed away, leaving him to fulfill his promise.

The Captain looked at Scott as if sizing him up for a fight. "What's on your mind, my boy?"

How quickly things reverted back to the norm. The aroma of roast beef wafted from the kitchen, fresh baked bread, too. "I'm starved," Scott said, procrastinating.

"Martha's fixing something special." The Captain put an arm around Scott's shoulders, ushered him toward the

Terry Wright

small den. "Won't be ready for a few minutes. What say we have us a smoke in here?"

"I don't smoke, sir."

"One cigar isn't going to kill you, lad."

Scott rolled his eyeballs. There was no arguing with him.

In the den, the Captain offered Scott a cushy chair, and once the cigars were lit, clouds of smoke encircled them. Scott blinked his watering eyes, but didn't complain.

The Captain sat behind his desk, blowing smoke. "Did you catch the Redskin's game?"

Scott hadn't seen a ballgame, drank a beer, or observed a woman's knees for thirteen months. "I've got a lot of catching up to do, sir," he replied, thinking the cigar wasn't half bad.

"Got any work lined up?"

"Sampson said he'd put me on." Sampson owned an auto repair shop downtown.

The Captain frowned. "With your military duty, I think you should go into law enforcement."

"I'd rather stay as far away from guns as possible." Mustering courage, Scott took a deep breath. "But there's something I'd like to ask you."

Chin up, the Captain leaned back in his chair. "I'm not lending you any money, if that's what you're gettin' at." Smoke curled from his lips.

"No, no, not money...it's Liz and I...well...we want to get married...with your permission, of course."

The Captain leaned forward. "Still wet behind the ears, both of you."

Flinching, Scott persisted. "We're twenty-five years

old. I love her, and she loves me."

"Takes more than love, my boy. You don't even have a job."

"I'm good with cars," Scott pointed out. "And I told you about Sampson—"

"You call that a job?" The Captain shook his head. "I had my daughter pegged for the lawyer type...or maybe a doctor." He sucked on his cigar. "Besides, Liz is high maintenance. Do yourself a favor, lad. Set your sights a bit lower."

Scott's cigar began to taste bitter. "Rest assured, sir, I'm a hard worker. We'll get by."

At that, the Captain jabbed a stiff finger at Scott. "She deserves better than just getting by. I want my daughter well cared for. A mechanic can't give her the lifestyle she deserves. Is that so hard to understand?"

Scott had enough of his insults. He crushed out the cigar and stood. "We're in love. I hope you can understand that." He stormed toward the doorway.

The Captain called out after him, "Martha and I have been married for twenty-six years. I'd spend two hundred and twenty six years with her if I could. That's love, my boy, and don't you forget it."

***

Liz dropped the plates on the kitchen table. "What do you mean, he said no?"

Leaning on the refrigerator, Scott feigned calm. "I'm not good enough for you."

"He said that?"

"In no uncertain words."

Terry Wright

Martha stood at the stove, stirring gravy. "Now Liz, dear, don't get all riled up and ruin a perfectly good evening. You know your father—"

"Scott and I are getting married, Mom." She brushed her hands together and glared at Scott. "Where is he?"

"In the den...but I wouldn't go in there if I were you."

"Dad." Liz stormed out of the kitchen.

Still stirring gravy, Martha smiled at Scott. "So tell me, when's the wedding?"

"We haven't gotten that far yet," Scott told her. "I'm thinking we should elope instead."

"Well, don't worry." She tasted the gravy. "Her father will change his mind."

With Liz on the warpath, Scott had no doubt.

***

The wedding was in November. They'd picked a little church in the suburbs. Standing at the altar, Scott curled his toes inside his shoes, waiting for the ceremony to begin. He was decked-out in a rented tuxedo and wished his parents were alive to see him all spiffed up. As afternoon sunshine blazed in through high mosaic windows, bathing the crowded chapel in a medley of colors, he smiled at Martha sitting in the front row. The seat next to her was vacant, and he thought about how the Captain would sit there after walking his daughter down the aisle. It was a wonder those two hadn't killed each other.

Promptly at 2:00, the organist began playing the wedding march. Liz appeared in the arched doorway, her arm hooked in her father's, her face veiled. She wore a lacy white gown that put her fifteen hundred dollar prom dress

~118~

to shame.

Scott inhaled with pride as he watched his bride approach. He saw her beaming smile through the thin veil. His eyes were riveted on her as if she were the only other person in the world.

At the altar, Liz and her father faced the preacher who asked, "Who would give this woman in holy matrimony?"

"I-I do," the Captain choked out.

Scott glanced at him, saw his pale and sweaty face and noticed the flabby skin of his neck bulging over his collar as if he'd tied his tie too tightly. Wheezing with each breath, there was a fierce glare of impending doom in his eyes as he gave his daughter's hand to Scott, trembling during the exchange. Scott's throat went dry. He feared the Captain was having second thoughts about allowing this marriage after all.

The preacher said something about being gathered here today, and the Captain stepped back. Concerned, Scott stood next to Liz and listened to the preacher talk about the sanctity of marriage and the union of two souls.

"If anyone here knows of just reason why these two should not be united, speak now or forever hold your peace."

Swallowing dryly, Scott squeezed his eyes shut, hoping the Captain wouldn't speak up. He didn't, thank God. Liz would have come unglued. Scott breathed a sigh of relief when the preacher continued with the ceremony. The rings were presented and the vows recited. "I now pronounce you husband and wife," the preacher said. "You may kiss the bride."

With his heart beating wildly, Scott lifted her veil.

Finally they were married, *until death do us part*. He drew her to him and kissed her.

Suddenly, a shriek tore through the chapel. Scott jerked around in time to see the Captain clutch his chest and fall out of his chair.

Onlookers gasped.

Martha dropped to her knees beside him. "Bruce. Oh my God."

Gasping, Liz rushed to his side. "Daddy." They turned him over. His mouth hung open, his eyes wide and staring. "No."

"Someone call 911." Scott peeled off his tuxedo jacket and went to work performing CPR.

"Bruce," Martha cried. "Don't leave us like this."

Alarmed friends lifted her from the floor and gathered around her. Liz joined them, her eyes filled with terror.

Scott compressed the Captain's chest and blew air into his lungs, knowing full well he was trying to save the man who thought he was unfit for Liz. *Set your sights a little lower*. The Captain's voice haunted him. *Liz is high maintenance*. Each time Scott checked for a pulse, he came up with nothing. *Knock off fifty pounds*. Scott pushed on the Captain's chest. *I'd spend two hundred twenty six years with her if I could*.

"Don't die on me, goddamnit."

That's love, my boy...

Determination grew into frustration. Then the wail of approaching sirens offered hope. When the paramedics arrived, everyone was made to move back. Scott watched the emergency team fit a respirator over the Captain's face. They ripped open his suit coat and shirt, cut off his tie, and continued CPR. A hypodermic load of adrenaline went directly into his heart. They attached leads to his chest and plugged them into a monitor and modem that sent the Captain's vitals to the hospital where a doctor stood by.

A paramedic wearing a headset communicated with the doctor. "He's in cardiogenic shock."

The heart monitor displayed a chaotic, jumbled pattern.

"Pupils fixed and dilated," the paramedic reported.

They injected a thrombolytic into the Captain's arm, a clot buster. His pallid face turned blue. His eyelids swelled. He wasn't responding.

The heart monitor flat-lined.

Immediately, the paramedics brought a defibrillator into service. "Clear." High voltage surged through the paddles and into the Captain's bare chest. His body lurched. The unmistakable smell of burned hair wafted up.

Everyone's hopeful eyes were on the monitor. It displayed a straight line and sounded a steady tone.

"Clear."

The defibrillator discharged again, but again there was no response. After several attempts, the paramedic with the headset looked up and shook his head.

"No," Martha wailed and fell to her knees. "Someone help him, please, please..." Her cries were drowned in tears.

"He suffered a massive coronary," the paramedic explained. "There'll be an autopsy, of course, to find out why." They covered him with a sheet. "Nothing more we can do."

With a blank stare, Liz backed away from her wailing mother, glanced down at her dead father, and cried out,

"My wedding is ruined." Then she ran from the chapel in a lacy dash.

***

Theirs was the bleakest honeymoon in history, Scott thought, lying in the darkened bedroom unable to sleep. Liz's muffled sobs were the only sound. She'd turned over on her stomach, her face pressed into a pillow. It had been a long and trying day for both of them. He reached out, touched her shoulder.

She shrunk away from him. "It's not fair. It's just not fair."

"I didn't know he had a heart condition."

"Don't you see?" she sobbed out. "It just happened. There's no guarantee it won't happen to you. In an instant, I could be left alone, like my mother." She rolled over and looked at him with bleary eyes. "Everything will be ruined."

"But life is unpredictable, Liz."

"It's not fair."

"Of course it's not, but we have to make the best of it."

"Look what it's done to her, Scott," Liz cried. "My mom's a wreck. I don't want that to happen to me."

"Till death do us part, remember?"

"I don't want it that way."

"Life's not a BMW, Liz."

She sat up. "I don't want to lose you, Scott. I don't want us to ever end."

He smirked. "In five years, let's see if you still feel the same way."

"Be serious. We've got to live a long time, Scott. I don't want to end up like my mother."

"She'll be all right."

"No, she'll never be the same."

"Give her time."

"We can't let this happen to us. We can't get old."

"Come on, Liz, the fountain of youth doesn't exist."

"But we can take better care of our bodies... *sniff*... better than my father took care of his. We'll exercise and take vitamins, and we'll eat only no-fat foods."

"And no sugar, no carbs, no cholesterol, yeah yeah. What does that leave us, a water diet?"

She fell silent for a moment, pouting. He understood her reaction to her father's death. Sure, it couldn't have happened at a worse time, and yes, her mother had to be sedated, she'd carried on so, but the grief would pass...in time. It wasn't a permanent condition, though there'd be hard times ahead for them all. He decided to be especially supportive. "I'm sorry, Liz. I didn't mean to be negative. We'll start tomorrow."

A flicker of hope glimmered in her eyes. "I'm going to get some Everlife."

"What?" He couldn't believe she'd waste money on that junk. "You can't be serious."

"You've heard the commercials. We'll feel better and live longer."

"It's all a bunch of hype."

"I've already decided." She leaned over him, and for the first time since the wedding, he saw her smile. It was one of her famous *I-always-get-what-I-want* smiles. "What can it hurt?"

"It's five hundred dollars a bottle. Jerry Well is a crook."

"He's a brilliant bio-chemist. And everybody knows the benefits of garlic for good health."

Scott winced. "Doesn't garlic ward off vampires?"

She withdrew and tossed back her hair. "There you go again."

"I'm sorry. Okay. We'll exercise, we'll eat right, and we'll take Everlife...if that'll make you happy."

"Yes," she chirped and hugged him. "We're going to live together a long, long time."

***

A bird fluttered between the bridge girders. Scott huddled into Sue to ward off the night's cold air. All around them, frogs croaked and crickets chirped. An occasional car thudded over the bridge above.

"So that's how you became a Weller," Sue said. "You did it for love."

"For peace," Scott replied. "Liz wouldn't take no for an answer." He tested his shoulder, stretched his arm a little. It ached as the nanocytes labored to restore circulation to the damaged tissues.

"How is it?"

"I'll live."

"Then you have time to tell me what happened to Liz."

He leaned his head back against the concrete. It had been a long time since he'd dredged up the past. "We were doing well when Lisa was born. Lilly came a year later."

"Lisa and Lilly?"

"Liz had a thing for Ls."

"Sounds like you had a beautiful family."

"Martha died ten years later," he went on, trying not to think about what he'd lost. "After the funeral, the preacher took us off to the side, told us we hadn't changed a bit since he'd married us. Of course, we didn't believe him, so he got out a scrapbook and opened it to our wedding picture. We looked the same as always, but he looked like a different man. The years had thinned his hair, and his face was all blotchy with age spots. That was the first time we realized that Everlife had stopped us from aging. Around that time, other Everlife customers began noticing the same thing."

Sue said, "Jerry Well should have kept his discovery for himself and Katherine."

"She didn't want any part of it," Scott reminded Sue. "She refused to take Everlife, but if she had, she wouldn't have contracted West Nile B."

"Hindsight's 20-20." Sue fidgeted.

"When Katherine died, Jerry Well decided to go public with his invention. He needed the money to support Katherine's internment at Alcor, her reanimation, and their future."

"But Grandpa told me the FDA stepped in."

"The controversy was big news. The FDA feared the world would be doomed to overpopulation if everyone took Everlife. That's when Jerry Well found himself in a conundrum. If he brought Katherine back to an overpopulated world, they wouldn't have much of a future."

Sue agreed. "Famine, disease, environmental collapse,

anarchy, war: you name it. Overpopulation, the plague of all plagues."

"That's why he agreed not to fight the FDA's ban on Everlife, and they promised to jail him if he ever made any more. He knew it was in his best interest, long term, and Katherine's. Every bit of it was recalled and destroyed. After that, we figured we were going to start aging again, but instead, our skin began reeking of garlic. We couldn't get rid of the smell...no matter how much we bathed. It took scientists a while to figure out that Everlife was regenerating itself inside our bodies."

"Jerry Well's mutated bacteria caused it."

Scott swallowed. "That's when Liz and I realized we were going to live forever, and there was nothing we could do about it...short of killing ourselves. We were going to outlive Lisa and Lilly...my God...every parents' worst nightmare, burying their own children. Liz went crazy just thinking about it. She looked for Everlife everywhere, on the Internet, the black market."

"Why?"

"For the kids."

"If she had given it to them, they'd have stayed children forever."

"Or worse, teenagers."

A moment of reflection passed, the trickling creek the only sound. Sue plucked out a blade of grass and started chewing on the soft nub.

Scott moved his shoulder. It felt warmer.

"How did you feel about the prospect of living forever?"

Now there was a question he'd pondered a few times.

"Everybody wants to live a long time. I was dumbfounded, at first, optimistic...even intrigued. I would live to see the future."

"Is it what you expected?"

Nothing turned out the way he'd expected. "I thought we'd have destroyed the world by now."

Chilled, Sue rubbed her arms. "By nuclear war?"

"Carbon dioxide poisoning. Cars, power plants, and factories, they all burned fossil fuel. The air was so saturated with carbon dioxide, it was like breathing in a bag."

"But a hundred years ago they developed hydrogen fuel and the greenhouse effect was abated. The oil companies disappeared, along with the pollution."

"I'm glad Pepsi and Coke and Lay's Potato Chips are still around. The Internet is now Starnet. Government is still corrupt and inefficient. But I always thought there'd be cities of towering glass spires and cars zooming between them on designated flyways."

"I wonder about the future, what it's going to be like, but I won't be around to see it."

Scott thought she should be thankful for that.

She chewed on the stub of grass thoughtfully then asked, "What did Liz think about the future?"

His heart sank. "She couldn't accept the fact that she would outlive her children."

"That's it?"

"She feared the grief, even if it was only impending grief, it was still inevitable grief. She would suffer like her mother had."

Sue frowned. "Didn't she wonder what the world

would be like?"

"She couldn't care less. Everything was always about Liz. She blamed Jerry Well for ruining her life."

"But she was the one who insisted you take Everlife."

"That was eating at her too, but I'd agreed with her. Jerry Well ruined my wife. Before long, her spoiled nature mutated into clinical depression. She became a miserable person, needy and clingy and whiny. She wasn't any fun to be around."

"What happened to your daughters?"

"Liz smothered the girls, doted over them constantly. Pretty soon, they couldn't stand her. As they got older, they rebelled, which made Liz furious. Things weren't going her way. Her daddy wasn't around to spoil her. The more attention she demanded, the more the kids shunned her."

"But they eventually had families of their own, right?"

"And Liz always interfered. It was as if she were already mourning their deaths, including the grandkids. I tried to reason with her. We fought about her meddling constantly. Finally, the girls couldn't take it anymore. They packed up and moved away." He sighed. "Life with Liz was hell. She'd alienated our children from us. Then the inevitable happened."

"What?"

"Lilly died."

"Oh no."

"It's okay," Scott assured her. "She was eighty, lived a full, productive life. Then Lisa died two years later, at eighty-four. Liz and I still looked like newlyweds standing over their graves."

"It's hard to put that into perspective." Sue tossed the

blade of grass into the creek and watched it float away.

"I had a hard time with it, all right, but Liz...she hung on a thin thread of sanity, trapped in the depths of the grief syndrome, often drinking heavily, not sleeping, bawling in the middle of the night."

"Didn't they have drugs for that?"

"Nothing helped. She'd stay up at night writing letters to our dead daughters...sorrowful affairs. Wads of paper littered the floor around her. She gave misery a whole new perspective."

"You still haven't told me what happened to her."

Scott found it difficult to talk about what happened next, though it seemed a little easier with Sue being a good listener. For some reason, he felt better talking to her. "Our third grandchild, Levi, died of old age. His funeral was the final blow for Liz. She committed suicide."

Sue groaned. "I'm sorry."

Remembering how it happened, he squeezed his eyes shut. "Her death was the final blow for me, too. I left. I walked away. I never looked back. In the end, Jerry Well's Everlife had completely destroyed my family."

"So you came to Boulder to destroy Jerry's family, starting with Katherine, and in a sense, assassinating every child they would ever have."

"I hadn't thought of it that way." He looked into Sue's sympathetic eyes. "Jerry took my wife from me long before she died. I just wanted to keep him from getting his wife back."

"An eye for an eye?"

"You could say that...until Carson dropped the Council bomb in my lap. Now look at the mess we're in."

Sue bowed her head. "There's no stopping Jerry Well now. Katherine is coming back. He's going to assassinate a Councilman, and using Katherine, he'll take over the Chair. Alpha Ketari's resources will not be developed, and mankind will suffer the consequences." She took a deep breath. "We've failed."

He closed his eyes and wished she hadn't been so blunt about it.

Chapter Thirteen

Anyone who would have witnessed the events unfolding in the basement of Jerry Well's mansion would not have believed their eyes. Amidst the whir of machines and the smell of antiseptic, Katherine lay face-up on the embalming table. Wires traversed from her head probes to a control panel of gauges, dials, and flashing red lights. The heart monitor nearby displayed a solid flat line. Above, a battery of heat lamps glared down, and technicians of every imaginable specialty surrounded her, sometimes so closely packed together that Jerry couldn't see her from his position on the glass-enclosed observation platform. The team wore white hoods with clear facemasks, long white lab coats, and black rubber boots. Their first task was to thaw her body.

Working with haste and precision, they attached hoses from sterilized water faucets to shunts in her femoral arteries. These had been left in place after she was prepped for cryonic freeze in 2010. Warm water, introduced under light pressure, began to flush out the glycerol, which Jerry saw ooze from the femoral vein taps like some kind of god-awful goo. The techs continued this operation until only clean water came out.

Then the technicians removed the water hoses and

attached the transparent tubes from the heart-lung machine. He saw the tubes turn red as warm, oxygenated blood was fed to her body. The flow was just a trickle at first, but within minutes the six-chambered pumping cylinders were gorged with circulating blood. Jerry noticed that the blood coming out of her femoral vein remained red, which meant that her cells were not yet consuming the offered oxygen.

Dr. Navarro glanced up from the huddled pack of white lab coats. His eyes scanned the control panel beside the table. One flashing red light went off. A green light blinked on. He gave the okay sign to his team and hunched over Katherine again.

Just then, the observation platform jiggled. Jerry looked to the scaffolding ladder where he saw Parish ascending, still wearing his combat fatigues and blackened face. Sweating, he seemed in a rush. "How's she doin'?" he asked, looking over the scene.

Jerry stifled anger at Parish's ill-timed interruption. "Did you get Scott Dunn?"

Another flashing red light turned green.

"This had better work," Parish said.

"What do you care?"

"I lost three good men tonight." The bounty hunter gave Jerry one of those *I'd just as soon kill you* looks.

"And what about Scott Dunn?"

As if resigned to some somber fate, Parish shook his head. "I'm out five million bucks, thanks to Sue Masters."

Everything inside Jerry screamed *kill the bounty hunter right now.* "Don't you dare tell me Dunn got away."

"Blame the Hog, Carson. He was backing her."

"My guess is they're all holed up in that old

mineshaft." Jerry glowered at Parish. "I suggest you go in and get them out."

Parish took a step back. "Impossible. My father tried. My grandfather tried. Better than fifty bounty hunters died tryin'. That mine is a death trap."

"I don't give a damn if it's a sewer with rats the size of Brahma bulls—"

"Wait a minute," Parish cut in. "A long time ago, we decided Carson was contained in the old mine. We can't get to him, and he can't get out."

"He's a Weller." Jerry removed the phony vial of Everlife from his pocket to remind the bounty hunter of what was at stake. "Every Weller, Parish. You know the deal."

"That fat bastard can't do you any harm."

Jerry shook the vial then put it away. "You've underestimated him. He orchestrated the infiltration of Alcor, so don't tell me he's no threat. Get your men together."

"It's too dangerous."

"Try a different approach. Don't use his contrivances. Rappel, dig, and blast your way down. Kill Carson and send me a holograph of his corpse. I don't expect you to recover five hundred pounds of dead meat."

"How thoughtful of you," Parish shot back.

"And bring Scott Dunn to me, alive."

"But he's Weller scum."

"He tried to murder my wife. I want to know why."

Parish grimaced. "Sparin' Dunn is a bad tactical move."

"Don't you bend a hair on his head."

Parish huffed. "Make up your mind. You want him dead. You want him alive. What about my five mill?"

"Don't worry." Jerry grinned. "The Weller won't live for long."

A chime echoed through the room. It came from Katherine's core temperature probe. The monitoring gauge began rising. Two more green lights flickered on. Hope again rose within Jerry's heart. "Get on with it," he told Parish. "I've got more important things on my mind." He turned his back to the bounty hunter, his attention again riveted on the activity below.

Parish stepped up behind him and whispered into Jerry's ear. "One of these days you're gonna push me too far." Then the platform lurched as the bounty hunter stormed down the ladder and stalked away.

"Idiot," Jerry murmured. The real vial of Everlife was for Katherine, but he would use its influence over Parish one more time. His target would be the Council of Elders, the Chair, Dar Anders. When that was finished, Parish would be given his precious vial, all right: a vial of strychnine.

Slowly, from the ceiling, the crystalline dome came down. Technicians fitted it over the table edges and secured the seals. When they stepped back, Katherine's form was barely discernable through the kaleidoscopic angles of her crystal cover. The dome filled with mist, a special gas composed of nanocytes, mitochondria activators, and warmed oxygen. As Navarro had explained earlier, this would help Katherine's lungs function when she took her first breath. Anticipation of that moment pounded through Jerry's veins with every beat of his heart.

The Grief Syndrome

Inside the dome, strobe lights began to pulse, first bright white, then blistering red and yellow, orange and green. The intensity of the photon bombardment was aimed into Katherine's gray face. Sensors in her brain probes would detect any neuron response to the stimuli and report that information to monitoring computers.

Immediately after the strobes began, a droning tone began to reverberate through the room. It was an audio stimulus that the computers also monitored. The volume rose with each passing second. Navarro moved to the control panel and examined the stream of data scrolling across the plasma-ray screen. He flipped switches, inspected a red light, gave it a tap with his index finger. Then he shook his head.

Jerry looked at the heart-lung machine hoses; both fluids inside were still red. The line on the heart monitor remained flat. Artificial systolic blood pressure showed 120 with no diastolic reading whatsoever. Worse, nothing appeared to be changing, and for several minutes, the technicians busied themselves with checking their equipment.

Katherine's core temperature had already risen to 5 degrees Celsius. She was no longer frozen, but still just as dead. Then a buzzing alarm sounded. Her systolic pressure read 100, dropped to 95, and then 90.

Hot panic raced through Jerry's chest. "What's happening?"

"I told you she was in bad shape," Navarro said. "She is leaking internally from tiny fractures caused by the freezing."

"We're losing her," a technician shouted. "85."

The droning audio stimulator and the buzzing alarms were like the screaming of demons announcing doomsday. "Do something," Jerry ordered.

"Override the automatic procedure," Navarro told his team. "I will inject the nanoserum manually." He grabbed a large syringe already prepared with an emergency dose of nanocytes.

"80," the technician announced. "Nitrogen levels rising in her blood."

Navarro injected the serum directly into a fitting on the heart-lung machine's blood supply tube. Immediately, trillions of molecular *Dutchboys* went to work with their cholesterol patches, seeking out and plugging microscopic leaks in Katherine's circulatory and lymphatic systems.

"75."

"Like freezing a fresh strawberry," Navarro said as he monitored the control panel. "When you thaw it out, it is mushy because the frozen water damaged the cells. Glycerol greatly reduces this damage in a human body, but nothing can eliminate it entirely."

"80," the technician reported. "85."

Jerry thought he would faint from relief. He'd seen many advancements in medical technology over the last two hundred years. Most cancers had been eradicated; heart disease was no longer the number-one killer. However, the development and application of nanotechnology had far exceeded everyone's expectations. For the moment, it seemed to Jerry that this technology had just saved Katherine.

"100." The buzzing alarms shut off. "120...core temperature is 93 degrees Fahrenheit."

"Turn off the heaters," Navarro instructed.

Seconds later, something beeped. Jerry's attention shifted to the heart monitor. The flat line wavered like a ripple in a pond. Now everyone's eyes were on the heart monitor's screen, everyone except Navarro. Checking the control panel, he said, "It is time," and energized the heart defibrillator.

Suddenly, the flat line spiked. The monitor beeped again, then a second time, and a third, and it kept on spiking and sputtering until it settled in to a perfect rhythm. It was the symphony of life.

A feeling of wonder came over Jerry. Katherine's heart was beating again. His dreams of Eternal Hylander were becoming a reality.

Then Katherine's chest lurched, and she began to breathe.

Navarro turned away from the control panel, a wide smile on his face. Behind him, the plasma-ray screen displayed Katherine's brain waves in a sudden flurry of activity. He bent over the crystalline dome, touched it with both hands. "She's alive. She's alive."

Blue blood began flowing from her femoral vein and into the heart-lung machine, which automatically adjusted its pressure to compensate for Katherine's beating heart. Her blood pressure was 120 over 60.

Technicians applauded.

"We are not out of the woods yet," Navarro said, removing his face shield. "Every cell in her body is extremely dehydrated. Start a saline IV and shoot her with ten CCs of adrenaline. Let's move it, people." He turned off the audio and visual stimulators, then, for the first time, looked up at Jerry on the platform. "This was too easy for a brain-damaged patient."

Smiling, Jerry nodded, thinking the doctor should be delighted over Katherine's reanimation. But instead of celebrating his success, Navarro was frowning suspiciously, which Jerry found rude and condescending.

The crystalline dome rose from the table, spilling the mist out and down to the floor. Even before it cleared away, technicians crowded around Katherine. Jerry forgot about Navarro's attitude as he watched them cut the gauze from her body and remove the stitches from her eyelids and lips. With the skill of master surgeons, they removed the shunts from her legs, sutured the arteries closed, then extracted the probes from her skull, applied nanocream, and bandaged her head. When they finished, they backed away.

For the first time, Jerry saw her clearly. Unable to look at her bald and bandaged head, he focused on her slender body and savored the sights that had escaped him for more than two hundred years: every curve, the fullness of her breasts, the dimple of her belly button, her soft mound of pubic hair. He remembered the last time he'd seen her naked, the night he put her in the tub and covered her with ice. She was angry with him then, but now, he was sure she'd be grateful. He longed to hold her and kiss her, and there was so much to tell her. His heart beat wildly with anticipation.

Navarro approached the table, eyeglasses in place, and inspected Katherine's body. He lifted her eyelids one at a time and nodded. Then tapping a knee, he watched her leg jump. Gently, he felt her neck, put his palm over her heart, and touched her stomach. He seemed satisfied with the rich color of her skin, her gentle breathing. A technician handed him a syringe filled with the newly developed antibodies that would cure her of West Nile B. He found a vein in her arm and gave her the injection.

Katherine was cured, finally, just as Jerry had promised her.

The technicians covered her with a white sheet and wheeled the table around to the magnetic imaging scanner. Within seconds, they began the scan. Images appeared on plasma-ray screens, cross-sections of Katherine's body. The computers flagged thousands of areas damaged by her frozen internment, worst of which were her kidneys. Her spinal cord was also damaged due to the West Nile B virus. Jerry knew this would be corrected with electro nanocytes and a few days of rehab. On the good side, the soft tissues of her brain were in perfect condition.

"I don't understand," Navarro said as he looked over the results. "If she had died from West Nile B, as the record indicates, her brain should be Swiss cheese."

"It's a miracle." Jerry scrambled down from the observation platform and joined Navarro at the console. "She should be perfectly normal."

"She should be a vegetable," Navarro replied. "I don't like the implications here."

"What are you saying, doctor?"

"The virus did not kill this poor woman."

"Of course it did. I was there."

"Precisely my point." Navarro peeled the glasses from his face and glared at Jerry. "There is no statute of limitations on murder."

"You can't prove I did anything."

"Perhaps Katherine can set us straight on this."

"Katherine?"

"Yes," Navarro said. "She was there too."

Jerry had never considered that Katherine could be a witness to her own murder. He didn't think she'd dare speak out against him; after all, he'd given her a new life. He'd saved her, for Christ's sake. She'd never tell anyone what he'd done to her that night. "You've drawn the wrong conclusion, doctor."

"We will save that for Katherine to decide."

The technicians wheeled her back to the center of the room. As Jerry looked down at her, still fuming over Navarro's speculative accusation, he forced himself to look at Katherine's unsightly head. He didn't want to be seen with her looking like that, so he decided to get her a nice wig to wear until her hair grew out. In time, he knew the vibrant luster would return to her lips. Only then could he picture himself walking with her, hand in hand, around Hylander, through the woods and to the trout ponds. Guests would visit from all around, bidding her welcome back and bringing gifts and well-wishes for their journey to Alpha Ketari. She would be thankful that he had restored her life and health. In turn, she wouldn't bear witness against him, but instead, fulfill his every desire willingly. Accusations of murder would never be sustained.

Navarro nudged Jerry aside and injected a syringe of *electros* directly into Katherine's spinal column. They would restore the nerve pathways that the virus had damaged.

Moments later, her eyelids flew open. Her pupils shrunk under the bright lights and stared into space. As the injected *electros* caused neurons in her spinal cord to rapid-fire, she arched her back and sat upright, zombie-like.

Jerry stepped forward in awe-filled expectation of their first reunion.

Mechanically, Katherine moved her arms, first one, then the other, and then she felt her chest. Without showing any emotion, she lifted the sheet from her breasts, inhaled, then looked down the length of her body and wiggled her toes. She dropped the sheet and swiveled her head around, her blank expression shifting from technician to technician until finally stopping on Jerry.

"Hello, Katherine," he said, heart racing.

But in her eyes, there wasn't the slightest glint of recognition.

***

Katherine had been ripped from her eternal sleep and slammed back into life, cold and naked, surrounded by strange beings, sights she could not comprehend, spoken words she did not understand. Like an infant expelled from the womb, she had no conscious thought, but she had a stark realization that something had changed. She didn't know her name nor that she should have one. Looking again at her arms, at her hands, not knowing what to do with them, she curled her fingers...and screamed.

The beings reached out, grabbed her, and forced her down on her back, her vision again blinded by the brightness above her. Only an impulse of some unknown origin made her kick and holler and fight back. But soon she discovered she could no longer move her limbs. They were somehow restrained, a condition that caused a great deal of pain. Struggling became futile. She relaxed her body, but her lungs gulped air in frantic desperation.

Then a shadow fell on her, blocking the light. The silhouette of a being loomed over her. Instinctively, she tried to get away but couldn't move. "Katherine," she heard a harsh voice say but did not understand the word. "You're going to be all right...Katherine." The being looked up. "She doesn't recognize me, doctor."

"Give the *electros* more time to do their work," a softer voice said without meaning. "Everything is in her subconscious mind. It will take time for her to remember. First we must bathe her and dress her."

"Can she walk?" the harsh voice asked.

"Not yet," the soft voice replied. "We must work the atrophy from her muscles. A time of physical therapy is necessary, and then we shall see."

Katherine felt comfort in the soft voice but terror in the harsher voice. She didn't know why she felt that way. Perhaps it came from the same impulse that had made her kick and holler and fight back.

Chapter Fourteen

D aybreak threw spears of light between the bridge pylons where, the night before, frogs had croaked and crickets chirped. Scott Dunn stirred. His back felt as stiff as a tire-iron. Groggily, he blinked, saw the glistening stream and smelled the dew-slick grass. Sometime during the night, Sue had curled up against him and fallen asleep. This morning he was thankful for her warmth.

His shoulder wound scarcely bothered him. He lifted the bandage and inspected the nanocream's work, which had caused the gash to close during the night. Satisfied, he became suddenly aware of his hunger and heard traffic thudding over the bridge above. It was time to move out. He gave Sue a nudge. "Wake up."

She yawned and stretched and got to her feet. "How's your shoulder?"

"My stomach hurts worse." He stood stiffly, tucked the blaster under his belt, and grabbed his sport bag. "Let's get something to eat."

"I'm famished."

They made their way down Baylor Avenue, once the pride of Boulder a hundred years ago, but now a dirty strip of row houses and cheap motels. In the alleys, homeless men peered out from under their cardboard shelters, unshaven and filthy. A woman with two children dressed in rags sifted through a dumpster behind Benny's Café in search of their breakfast.

Inside the café, Scott directed Sue to a booth in the back. The place smelled of grease and soiled rags.

"I never thought I'd set foot in this dive," she said, brushing crumbs from the table with her sleeve.

"I've seen worse."

"I can't imagine what the lady's room looks like."

"It's down the hall."

"No thanks. I can wait."

"Suit yourself." Scott summoned the waitress, ordered coffee and eggs for two, and after she left to fill the order, he peered out the front window at the brightening day. "You suppose the cycle is still where we left it?"

Sue shrugged. "It's well hidden. Have you got a plan?"

The waitress delivered coffee without as much as a smile. Scott stirred in sugar. "We have to get back to the mine. The rest isn't going to be easy."

"What's that supposed to mean?"

Sipping coffee, he looked at her over the brim of his cup, sensed her concern, and knew she wasn't going to like what he had to say next. "Once you're safely back with Carson, I'm on my own."

"You can't do it alone," she said, not blinking.

"You've stuck your neck out far enough already."

"Why Scott, are you worried for me?"

"Of course not."

"Still hard as stone?"

He pursed his lips and studied Sue's knowing eyes. Perhaps he'd told her too much last night, accidentally revealing his weaker side. But he hadn't told her everything. The part about Liz lying on the floor in a pool of blood, he'd left out. He hadn't told Sue about the photos Liz had placed around her, the candles, and the stacks of letters she'd written to her dead daughters. She'd built a shrine to her grief upon which she'd performed the ultimate sacrifice.

"Scott?"

"Huh? Oh. I'm sorry...what?"

"Your eggs are getting cold."

Remembering the pop of the gun, he shook his head. Suddenly, he wasn't hungry. He recalled standing in the kitchen, preparing dinner that night. Liz had locked herself in the library, something she'd done many times before, writing and weeping. The gunshot startled him. In a panic, he ran down the hall, kicked open the library door, and found her lying on the floor. Sickened with fright, he rushed to her and knew right away there was nothing he could do. He didn't touch the gun lying at her side.

The paramedics arrived, and then the police. They said the bullet blew out the back of her throat, shattered her spinal cord at the base of her skull, and exited the back of her neck.

There were the usual questions under a lie-detector scan. When he was free to go, he left the house and never returned...never...not for the funeral, not to retrieve his property, not to sell the house, not ever.

Last night, telling Sue about his past had rekindled the grief. He'd spent most of his life wandering from town to town, working here and there, trying to forget what had happened. Now it was out again, in the front of his mind, the grief demon rising up. He had to think about something else. "Katherine is probably alive by now."

"Got a soft spot for her, Scott Dunn?"

It seemed to him that Sue was fishing, probing for a crack in his stone. "I don't have a soft spot for anyone." Well...that wasn't entirely true, as he'd become uncomfortably close to Sue, something she didn't need to know. "I can't kill Katherine because I'm not a murderer. Not because I care about her. But I can still kidnap her away from Jerry Well. That should be enough to screw up his plans."

Sue scowled. "You're going to Hylander, aren't you."

"It's the only way."

"You must have a death wish."

"Why don't you go back to teaching English?"

Sue forked her eggs. "It's summer break."

"Then go home."

"I live with my grandpa."

Scott frowned. "Don't you mean great-times-twelve grandfather?"

"I've always called him Grandpa, even when I was little."

"Where are your parents?"

She studied her coffee cup for a moment. A strand of dirty blond hair hung down over her left eye. "Wichita," she said finally. "I hate it there, boring."

"I don't picture you for boring. Have you ever been married?"

"No." She said it with conviction.

"Why not?"

"I haven't found a man I'd be willing to co-own property with. What's mine is mine. I like it that way."

Scott understood. She wasn't an Amendment 77 woman: the amendment that gave equal property rights to each spouse, not half like it was two hundred years ago. "Are you looking for the right man?"

She gave him a sideways glance. "Maybe."

"Don't look at me like that. I won't let anyone get that close to call me *the right man*."

"Maybe means I'm not looking," she affirmed, and smiling added, "But I'm open to the possibility one might come along. Meanwhile, I live with my grandpa. I know him better than anyone. Like I know he's not going to let you go to Hylander."

"We'll see about that."

"Right." She pointed to Scott's breakfast. "Better eat."

The eggs were cold, and when he finished, he tossed down a ten-dollar bill for the waitress. A smile could have gotten her twenty. He paid the check with a Visa bank chip. "Let's go find your bike."

Nearing the abandoned University of Colorado campus, Scott became concerned over the intense police presence. Roadblocks kept traffic and sightseers out of the area. Flying police cruisers patrolled the perimeter. A coroner's van, white with black letters, hovered in front of the Alcor building. Workmen stood on floating scaffolds and boarded up blown-out windows. All around the grounds, investigators milled about, collecting evidence and marking places with small yellow flags. News trucks, photographers, and hover-cams zoomed about everywhere.

"Looks like John Parish created quite a stir," Sue said.

"Let's just get out of here."

She went directly to the hydrogen cycle that she'd hidden in the bushes. A moment later, they sped off toward Hog Heaven, a hover-cam in hot pursuit.

***

"We've got video," a bounty hunter reported. Parish and his men had been holed up in their black van, a sweatbox full of surveillance equipment lining the walls. The air smelled of hot electronics and rank perspiration. "Good call, boss."

After Scott Dunn and Sue Masters had gotten away the night before, Parish discovered their hidden cycle and decided to stake it out on the assumption they'd return for it sooner or later. It proved to be a brilliant call. He examined the monitor receiving the hover-cam feed. The cycle with two riders leaned into a curve. "Which way are they going?"

"West...just off Highway 93 on the Baseline cut."

"They're headed for Carson's mine," Parish said. "Driver, move out."

"They can outrun us on that cycle."

"Intercept them at Flagstaff Road." Parish knew it was a long shot, but if he could capture them and use them as leverage to coax Carson out of the mine, it would save his men the perils of going in to get him out. "We have to take them alive."

"How we gonna do that, boss?"

"Disable the cycle. Shoot at the engine, the tires."

"If they wreck it, they could be killed," another man

said.

"Idiot. You're forgettin' about the crash avoidance system." Sometimes his bounty hunters weren't too bright. A built-in gyro would keep the bike from spilling. He had to spell out everything for them. "It's the only way we'll get Carson to come out of that mine. If you guys have to go in after him, some of you are gonna get killed."

"Step on it," someone shouted.

"Take the Ninth Street grid."

"Got it." The driver disengaged the computer that would have automatically locked them onto the transportation grid. It was highly illegal, of course, but necessary.

On Ninth Street, Parish gritted his teeth as the driver careened through traffic. Horns honked, but there was nothing the other drivers could do about the bounty hunter's reckless driving. Central computers had control of all the other vehicles. Their radar brakes and steering were rendered inoperable. Nothing stopped the grid.

The van squeezed between an autocar and the ten-foot concrete barrier that kept out wayward deer, stray dogs, and pedestrians. Tires screeching, the van careened behind a taxi and then shot into the next lane where it passed a truck and swung over to another lane and back again, darting around another autocar.

Parish glanced up at the airway above the corridor, looking for flying police cruisers. Sensors in the roadbed had already alerted the authorities to their unauthorized presence on the grid. As it was with the earlier strike on the 105 to Boulder, they had to be gone before the police could intercept them.

"Flagstaff Road coming up, boss."

In a cloud of smoke, the black van careened off the grid. On the hover-cam monitor he'd been watching, Parish saw the cycle a half-mile downrange, due to pass Flagstaff Road in thirty seconds. The van's speedometer showed sixty miles per hour. Parish felt confident they'd make the intersection in time. "Sharpshooters. Get ready."

A sliding hatch in the ceiling opened. Three bounty hunters climbed on the roof, the wind whipping at their black fatigues, and took prone positions along the suicide rails.

"Fifteen seconds."

The wind rushed in through the open hatch as the van barreled toward the intersection. "We've only got one chance at this," Parish said into his transceiver. "If Sue hits the throttle, they'll get away."

"Ten seconds."

Tires screeched through a curve. Parish braced himself as the van sideswiped a slower car, forcing it into the ditch. Out the front windscreen, he could see the stop sign ahead and the dirt road crossing. The whole scene rocked violently to the motion of the speeding van.

The cycle came into view.

"There it is," the driver shouted.

From the swaying rooftop, streams of blaster bolts shot forward, sheering off the stop sign, raking the pavement, and raising geysers of dust from the intersecting dirt road. The cycle screamed past, both riders ducking low.

"Damn!" Parish couldn't believe they'd missed. "Go after them."

The van skidded sideways, nearly tipping over,

careened right, and raced down the dirt road in the cycle's trail of dust. The ride was so rough that Parish had all he could do just to stay in his seat.

On the monitor, the pursuing hover-cam had a clear view of their target, both riders hunkered down, their hair blowing in the wind, the cycle in an all-out sprint, leaning and skidding.

"Keep firin', men." When he didn't see any blaster bolts ring out at his command, he popped his head up through the ceiling hatch. One man was hanging onto a suicide rail, white as a ghost, his weapon gone. The other men had vanished. "What the hell?"

"They fell off, boss. The driver's a maniac."

"Get back in here." Christ, he needed every man at his disposal. He called out on his transceiver, "You guys okay?"

There was no answer. Idiots. He'd expected to lose a few men on this sortie, but not this soon.

"The cycle's getting away," the driver shouted.

"Keep after them." The van rocked and pitched. Parish studied the monitor. He saw Scott Dunn turn around, blaster in hand, and fire at the hover-cam. With a flash, the monitor went blank.

"What now, boss?"

"Head for Carson's mine," Parish said, a knot of dread tightening in his stomach, knowing he was about to follow in his father's failed footsteps. "Now we're gonna have to do this the hard way."

Chapter Fifteen

Myrtle went into a tizzy, scampered back and forth on Carson's console, nose probing the air, ears perked. Right away, he knew she'd heard Sue's cycle outside. He hadn't been able to raise her on the transceiver all night. Having feared the worse, Myrtle's sudden behavior gave him a welcome rush of relief.

Sue was alive.

He motored the wheelchair to his monitor and saw the cycle approach at high speed, Sue without her helmet and Scott hanging on behind her. Though Carson was happy to see them, trepidation gripped him, the panic in their eyes unmistakable.

As the cycle slid to a stop at the shack, he activated the external intercom. "Get on the elevator."

"No, Grandpa," Sue said, looking up to a tree-mounted camera. "We're getting you out of here."

"I'm not going anywhere, young lady."

"We've been followed," she cried. "The bounty hunters are coming for you."

"They've come for me before. I'm not concerned...but do hurry."

Scott jumped from the cycle. "I'll hold them off here." He dropped his sport bag and inserted a fresh energy clip into his blaster.

"No need," Carson replied, impressed with Scott's resolve. "Let them find their own deaths. Now come." He activated the elevator and swiveled the camera to observe its operation. There was a rumble as twenty square feet of earth surged upward on four hydraulic cylinders made of chromium steel. Grass, wildflowers, and shrubbery rose until a platform appeared underneath. Sue wheeled her cycle onto the elevator. Scott grabbed his sport bag and followed, mouth agape.

With the flip of a switch, the entire assembly retracted. Within seconds, the area looked as natural as before.

"Come on, Myrtle. Shall we greet our guests?" The ferret jumped onto Carson's shoulder and sniffed his earlobe, whiskers tickling. "All right, I'll hurry." He engaged the ion-powered wheelchair and headed down a ramp that would take him to the elevator landing.

Above him, among the speckle of lights, the black platform descended. A rotating red beacon on its belly warned of its downward approach. When it reached the bottom, it clunked to a stop. The wheelchair whined up to the landing, and as Carson set the brakes, Sue jumped off the platform and threw her arms around his massive neck. "We failed. I'm sorry."

"They were on to you from the beginning," Carson explained, happy to have Sue back safe and sound. "You did the best you could."

"I know...but Katherine—"

"Her reanimation has been successful. We'll have to forget about her."

"No way, Carson." Scott stormed toward him, threw the sport bag on the floor. "We're not forgetting about any of this."

Myrtle reared up on her hind legs and hissed at Scott, showing razor-sharp teeth.

"That's all right, girl." Carson stroked her silver bib with a porcine finger. He noticed a distinct rise in her musky odor, which warned him of her highly agitated state. "Scott's just a bit riled right now. There's no need to be protective."

"That rodent doesn't scare me."

Carson glowered at Scott. How quickly he'd forgotten the things he'd been told about Myrtle. "I'd be careful if I were you. She'll rip a hole in your jugular before you can say peek-a-boo. Can't you see that she senses your anger?"

"You bet I'm angry. We walked into a trap."

Carson changed the subject, fully aware of his failure at Alcor. "Look at you both. You're a mess. Did you sleep under a truck?"

"Something like that," Sue said.

"Change your clothes and get Scott a clean shirt. In the meantime, I'll come up with another plan."

"Your plans don't work," Scott growled out.

Sue opened a closet. "Calm down, Scott." She tossed him a fresh black shirt several sizes too big for him. "He did the best he could."

"We damn near got killed."

She smiled. "You're still kicking, aren't you?"

"You only defend him because he's your grandpa."

Now she frowned. "He's the only family I have, and don't you forget it."

Carson jumped in. "Scott's right." He wished they'd stop arguing. "Point is...what are we going to do now?"

Sue shot Scott a disapproving glare. "Just wait until you hear what he's got planned, Grandpa."

"What?"

"I'm going up to check the monitors," she said. "You guys had better settle this before the bounty hunters get here." She jumped on the conveyer lift to the main level.

Carson watched her go and then turned to Scott. "What's she talking about?"

"I have a plan to get inside Hylander." Scott peeled off his tattered shirt.

The makeshift bandage caught Carson's attention. He wondered how Scott got wounded. "That bandage needs changing," he said, not wanting to hear any cockamamie plan about getting inside Hylander.

Donning the clean shirt, Scott said, "I'm going to surrender to the bounty hunters." He yanked the blaster from behind his belt and tossed it on the console. "With any luck, they'll take me to Hylander."

"They'll kill you." Carson found it hard to believe that Scott would even consider such a dangerous option. "We're not wanted dead or alive," he reminded him. "The bounty hunters prefer dead."

As Scott buttoned his shirt, he bent over and went nose-to-nose with Carson. "It's a risk I have to take."

Not intimidated, Carson stared back into Scott's raging blue eyes. The Weller had more guts than brains. "You're no good to me dead."

"For two hundred twenty five years Katherine's been dead. But now, she's alive again." Scott backed away from the wheelchair, frowning. "Life was once precious and unpredictable. Now it's a reusable commodity."

One hundred years ago, Carson could've argued that point, but determined to change Scott's mind about surrendering to the bounty hunters, he feigned indifference, retrieved a kibble treat from his pocket and gave it to Myrtle. While she munched on her snack, Carson decided to give Scott something to think about. "Life is full of choices. You must admit, there are many people out there who have made miserable choices, including your wife."

"You're blaming her?" Scott tucked the long tails of the oversized shirt into his pants. "She couldn't take the grief."

"She wouldn't accept it. That was her choice." Carson saw Scott stiffen at that accusation, but he went on, jabbing the air with a plump finger. "And look at you now, the choices you have made, unable to take solace in another human being, callous and unapproachable. You have no heart, not even for my little Myrtle here. Do you know why that is?"

"Enlighten me, oh wise one."

Though Carson didn't appreciate Scott's sarcasm, he pressed on. "Happiness comes from accepting your fate, making the best of it. You don't have to like it, but acceptance brings an end to the grief syndrome. But no, you're unable to accept your wife's sorrowful life, her gruesome death, or the loss of your extended family. It is you who is unhappy now, doomed to the grief of everyday living. And it'll always be that way until you learn to accept your immortality. Accept the loss of your loved ones. Set aside your survivor's guilt. Only then will you find happiness." He spread his tremendous arms. "As I have...even in this spectacular body." Carson laughed, his flab jiggling.

Scott stepped back as if surprised at the jolly outburst. He seemed thoughtful for a moment, even puzzled, and then he asked, "What about Katherine?"

"Her situation is unfortunate." Carson's eyes watered in the wake of his laughter. "But your talk of surrender is a bad choice on your part."

"Nothing has changed." Scott extended his arms, the baggy shirt billowing around his frame. "Jerry still needs her to take over the Council's Chair. If I can get into Hylander, I might be able to get her out before he can succeed."

"Kidnap her?" Any residual humor drained from Carson's body. "Hylander is a fortress. It's heavily guarded. To get in or out is suicidal."

"You brought me here to do a job. It's not finished. Now I'm going to do it my way. Besides, if you're right, if Jerry Well murdered Katherine in 2010, he doesn't deserve to have her back."

Carson raised an eyebrow, watched Scott fold down his shirt collar and jam the blaster behind his belt. His comment seemed completely out of character...for a Weller. Carson decided to press the issue. "And then what, Scott Dunn? You free her from the big bad wolf, and then will she love you for saving her? Will you then love her?"

Scott threw back his shoulders. "This has nothing to do with love." He glared at Carson as if warning him not to go on.

That's when it occurred to him that Scott cared about

Katherine. Something else had happened last night, something more than escaping a trap at Alcor and a blaster wound to his shoulder. Something had softened his heart, and Carson wondered if Sue had anything to do with it.

Suddenly, she called out, "We've got company."

"How many?" Carson asked, not that it mattered.

"Six that I can see."

"John Parish will call for backup, as his father did, but we are quite safe."

An explosion racked the mineshaft. Dirt and rock rained down.

Myrtle took off running.

"They've destroyed the shack," Sue reported.

Carson became immediately concerned. Never before had the bounty hunters resorted to the use of explosives. The resultant cave-ins and flooding would make any incursion extremely dangerous.

"They've tossed rappelling ropes down the mineshaft."

"They can't get down here," Scott said. "Can they?"

Carson spun his wheelchair around, saw Scott looking up at the rock ceiling warily. "It's time to choose, Scott Dunn. Are you going to fight or surrender?"

Chapter Sixteen

John Parish ordered his men to destroy the shack over the mineshaft. A concussion grenade made easy work of it. Wood planks and roof tiles sailed through the air. He lowered goggles over his eyes and observed six mini heads-up displays along the top edge of the lens. There he saw video feeds from the helmet-mounted cameras worn by his fellow bounty hunters. He would be in constant contact with them as they initiated their attack. Everything was in perfect working order.

Camera one showed a coil of rope spiraling down the mineshaft. Cameras two and three relayed similar images. Camera four displayed the work involved to secure the rigging to what remained of the original crossbeam anchors. Only the men's breathing came over the audio transmitters, a testament to their teamwork skills and training as they went about their assigned duties without speaking.

Parish, like any good general, had elected to stay topside until his men found a safe way for his descent. From his father and grandfather's experiences, he knew the penalty for carelessly blundering into these depths. Booby traps had killed most previous bounty hunters during the first stages of their assaults. Survivors told stories of moving platforms and churning rapids, but he had no solid information on what perils awaited his men. "Be careful," he told them. "Use your safety lines. Don't take anything for granted."

"We're going in," a bounty hunter replied.

The displays went black as each bounty hunter rappelled into the shaft's darkness. Parish felt relieved when his displays lit up again as his men activated their helmet-mounted lamps. Now he saw everything each of his men encountered.

At the bottom of the shaft, they came to a lighted chamber where camera two revealed a giant wooden gear standing on end. A ledge above it appeared to be the only way out of the chamber.

"I'll go up first." The man wearing camera three tossed a grappling hook up to the ledge and activated his microburst booster. Unexpectedly, the gear groaned and began to rotate.

"Look out."

Before he could disengage the booster, his rope tangled in the moving cogs and dragged him into the meshed teeth of an oncoming gear. He barely had time to scream before his chest was crushed. Both gears stalled momentarily, then crunched forward, spitting out the man's gruesome remains, which hit the chamber's rock floor with a splat.

One of his men screamed. "We gotta get out of here."

Fearing they would retreat in panic, Parish ordered, "Keep movin', men. Remember we got two Wellers down there, ten million dollars worth."

Camera one moved in to inspect the dead man's body.

His head was still chin-strapped inside the helmet, his face twisted in frozen agony, eyeballs bugged-out and crying rivulets of blood.

That was enough to summon Parish's lunch. Swallowing bile, he knew he would lose a few men, but seeing the first one die didn't make it any easier to accept. The upside was one less man to split the money with.

His men destroyed the moving gear with their blasters then snared rocks along the ledge and climbed up. That's when camera four captured the image of a platform knifing out of the surrounding darkness. A sign on the orange railing read: *Get On Here.*

"Don't," Parish said, and watched the platform swing away. The bounty hunters searched the ledge but found no other way off it. Then the platform reappeared.

"I'll check it out," cameraman four said and tossed his safety line to a nearby man who tied it around a rock.

On Parish's heads-up display, he watched a gloved hand reach up and grab the railing. The platform teetered as the man jumped aboard then swung forward in a smooth arc. Cameras one and two showed the bounty hunter fade into the darkness.

Instantly, the view from camera four turned pitch black. Then roaring came over the audio, getting louder and louder until Parish recognized it as the sound of a waterfall. "Jump," he ordered his man.

But it was too late. A torrent of water engulfed the camera lens, turning the scene on Parish's heads-up display into a tumbling rush of bubbles. The hot helmet-mounted lamps reacted violently under water and shorted out in a spectacular spray of sparks. A garbled scream came next, and then choking, gagging and thrashing. Within seconds, the camera gave out. Static splashed across number four's display inside Parish's goggles. Then the safety line lurched, strained, and snapped.

Parish's insides knotted, not with remorse for the loss of his man, but in anger. He couldn't afford any more mistakes. He needed every man for the final battle with Carson. "Find another way down, men." Then he activated his micro-transceiver. "Team two, what's your E-T-A?"

"Twenty minutes."

"I'll give you ten. Step on it."

He sat on the wooden platform, all that remained of the destroyed shack's flooring, and tore off his goggles. The mountain air felt cool on his sweating face. A slight breeze rustled the pine trees overhead. Despite the beautiful scenery that surrounded him, he felt only contempt, and the more he felt it, the more he thought he could hear Carson laughing at him. His wheezing snickers seemed to ride on the breeze, circle and echo through the forest all around him, now cackling from every direction until the cacophony exploded in his brain, forcing him to shut it out with cupped hands over his ears.

"What's the matter, John?"

Parish stiffened. Carson's voice echoed all around him. He felt like Moses at the burning bush. Bolting to his feet, he drew his blaster and pivoted around, searching for the source of the voice.

"You can't possibly win," Carson said. "Go home and live."

"I'll get you, Weller."

Now the response came from his left. "No you

won't."

Wheeling, Parish focused on the swaying trees around him. His blaster followed every move, side-to-side, tree-to-tree, between every trunk, beside every rustling bush. Nothing appeared: no man, no weapon.

Then from the right, Carson's voice came again. "Get out of here before it's too late."

He realized the Weller was toying with him. That eerie feeling of being watched made the back of his neck prickle. He thought he must've looked like a fool to the watcher. At that, Parish forced himself to stay calm. He inspected the trees, the tree trunks, the moving branches, both on his right and on his left, then spotted a large dark knot on the exposed bark of a nearby tree. It was circular in shape, too perfect to be natural, a speaker or camera, he was sure, and blasted it.

Pheuw-Pheuw!

The tree toppled over in a burning heap. Then the voice echoed again. "You're wasting your time, John Parish."

Flames jumped off the fallen tree and spread along the weeded ground, coaxed onward by the breeze.

"Now look what you've done," Carson's taunting voice said. "The authorities will see the smoke. They'll come. What will you do then?"

Parish spun right, blaster ready, but he hesitated to shoot in fear of starting another fire. He knew that if it got out of control, it would mean the end of his sortie against Carson's stronghold. Fire jumpers would descend on the surrounding forest. Air tankers would drop chemicals. Authorities would converge on the scene. Investigators.

Police. To save himself and his men from the law, he'd have to order another retreat. Then Carson would win again.

The thought of being defeated stuck in Parish's throat like a dull knife. He rushed to the small line of fire and started stomping on the flames.

Carson started laughing; his wheezing cackle echoed all around the clearing. Parish tamped the flames. Choking on smoke, he wished he had water, a blanket...then he remembered the fire extinguisher in his surveillance van. But if he ran to get it, he feared the fire he'd been stomping back might get away from him.

Carson kept laughing at Parish's desperate situation.

Team Two's black van careened into the clearing, throwing dust as it skidded to a stop. The sight of it, and the impeccable timing of its arrival, gave Parish a warm feeling of sure victory. Within seconds, several bounty hunters jumped from the van, fire extinguishers in hand. They quickly knocked down the flames. Parish spun a full circle, brandishing his blaster and now laughing at Carson. "It's time to die, fat man."

"Go home and live."

Parish signaled his armed reinforcements to rappel down the mineshaft. Moments later, he joined his men.

"We found another chamber, boss."

He followed them through a passageway to a dimly lit cavern with tunnels tracking off in different directions. Overhead, moving platforms and conveyors squealed and clanked. The damp air smelled musty, and he heard rushing water. "Good work, men." Now he had ten bounty hunters. He separated them into teams of two, each with one camera helmet. "Watch your step in here," he told them, checking their equipment. "Got your safety lines?"

One man said, "I don't like the looks of this."

"Any of you wanna chicken out?" Parish announced. "You're free to go."

"Not me," another man said. "I'm staying for the money."

"Me too," came back from the others. "Yeah."

Parish grinned. "All right. We're a team. Ten million dollars, men. Let's go get it."

At that, the teams took off in different directions. Parish planned to follow them after they discovered a safe route down.

***

Carson observed all this activity on the bank of monitors in front of him. A box of Snickers bars rested in his lap. He felt relieved that no more explosions followed the first one. Parish was obviously aware of the dangers: cave-ins and flooding. But without explosives, he'd already managed to get deeper into the mine than Carson expected.

Scott and Sue stood behind him, packing concussion grenades into the sport bag. Myrtle played with her squeaky toy on the litter-strewn floor. Still unsettled over their last conversation, Carson wondered if Scott would stay and fight, but he'd chosen to say no more on the subject. Besides, the goings-on in his mine were getting interesting. "Now get a load of these two idiots." Carson pointed at a monitor on the console. "They're poking around Shelby's cleft."

"You have names for them?" Scott asked.

Sue said, "Shelby was Parish's uncle."

"That's where he died." Carson gulped down a Snickers bar. "Only fitting to name it after him."

It wasn't long before the bounty hunters disappeared down the two thousand foot fissure.

Rumbling, a rockslide trapped two other men in an adjoining tunnel. It would take hours for them to dig their way out, if ever. The tremor caused Myrtle to stop wrestling with her squeaky toy mouse and perk her ears.

"Parish is running out of help fast." Carson chuckled.

***

Surrounded by darkness, Parish heard the clatter of falling rocks. Already two of his displays had gone blank. In only a few minutes, he was down to six men. Waiting for some good news, he used the time to contemplate his future: Florida, the fifty-nine-foot yacht, *Mary D. Light*, adventure on the high seas. He had plenty of money. Now all he needed was more time...like forever. But without proof of Carson's death, he knew Jerry Well wouldn't give him the vial of Everlife. Immortality would not be his. So if the bounty hunters failed, he decided to kill Jerry and take the vial anyway. He would have done it sooner, but the challenge of killing the mighty *HOG* was more important, to succeed where his father and grandfather had failed.

Suddenly, camera two transmitted an audio message. "We've found a water slide," the bounty hunter reported. "We're going down."

Parish saw it on his heads-up display. "Be careful."

They anchored a rope and tossed it down to the chamber floor not far from Parish's position. "In case this is the way, boss, you can climb up and follow us." Then they seated themselves, one in front of the other.

Parish didn't see their safety lines. "Wait."

They shoved off, and down they went. The camera mounted to the second man's helmet gave Parish a full view of the first man's watery plunge. Left and right. Up and down. It looked like a wild ride. Now Parish understood why they chose not to tie themselves to anything. There was no way of knowing how far down the water slide went. If they ran out of rope, they'd have been hung up in a torrent of water and drowned.

After several hair-raising curves, a fork in the tunnel appeared. The man in front went left. The cameraman went right. Seconds later, a scream came over the audio transmitter, then a thud, and then silence. "Damn." Parish had lost the man who went left.

Camera two's scene tumbled into a shallow pool, and via the heads-up display, Parish saw he'd found a chamber lit with twinkling lights. Panning the area, the camera revealed dimly lit spurs running off in several directions. Then something unexpected caught his eye. "What was that?" he radioed his man with the camera. "Scan back to your right."

"It's an old ore cart."

Parish saw it clearly on his heads-up display, illuminated by camera two's helmet-mounted lamps. The cart's brake lever was set, and a control panel blinked from inside the metal tub. For the first time, he felt as though success was at hand because he recognized the configurations on the panel. It was an old DOS-based-handler.

He summoned his remaining men. "We've found another chamber." They climbed the rope to the water tube entrance. "Stay right at the fork. I'll meet you at the bottom."

Excitement coursing through his veins, Parish took the water slide with ease. Within moments, he joined his men in the chamber. Dripping wet, he rushed to the ore cart to verify what he had suspected. Yes. The handler was equipped with memory and record functions. From a satchel on his belt, he retrieved a data scanner and inserted its serial cable into the side of the ore cart's panel.

His men gathered around, panting and shivering. One of them said, "Look at this junk," referring to the old DOS handler.

"Remember..." Parish activated the *PLAY* mode. "Carson's been down here for two hundred years. He hasn't done much upgrading."

The scanner's screen displayed the commands it had recorded to memory the last time the ore cart was used. Everything was there: course, direction, and speed, as well as all the switchback commands. He figured Carson had made contingency plans for such a security breach, probably set detonators along the tracks, activated by microwave signals from a control center somewhere. But Parish had a countermeasure for that, a *Jammer Module*, which he pulled from his satchel. Not knowing which frequency to jam, he set the dial to *ALL* and activated the device.

Then Parish smiled, knowing he'd just crippled Carson's defenses. At least he hoped he had.

***

"Damn," Carson said, watching Parish's satisfied expression on the monitor. "He's tapped into the ore cart's interface." Red lights began flashing on the consoles. "And he's blocking my transmitters."

"What's that mean?" Scott asked over Carson's shoulder.

"It means they're coming down." Carson motored the wheelchair around and told Sue, "Put your cycle on the elevator and get out of here."

"No." Sue jammed her hands on her hips. "I'm not leaving you down here."

"Listen up, young lady. Don't tell me—"

"I don't believe it," Scott cut in. "You said this place was impenetrable."

"Goes to show you what sheer determination can do."

"I'm still not going." She charged her particle blaster with a fresh magazine. "Come on, Scott."

Before Carson could utter another word, Scott grabbed his sport bag. "I'm with her."

"I thought you were going to surrender."

"Right now you guys need me more than Katherine does." They sprinted down the aft catwalk and out of sight.

Carson figured they were going to find defensive positions within the mine. He shouted after them. "Just don't get yourselves killed."

***

Parish and his five remaining men squeezed into the ore cart. One of them had to stand.

"Hang on." After releasing the brake, Parish activated the scanner's replay function. Squealing, the cart's wheels began to roll, slowly at first, then faster and faster as the cart picked up speed. It went down and around and up and down and around, lurching about and rattling with fury, the centrifugal forces and zero Gs nearly enough to make Parish puke. He held the scanner firmly in his grasp as it traced the current route over the previous route with pinpoint precision.

His attention was so riveted on tracking the cart's course that he failed to see the reason the standing man screamed. Parish looked up. They were approaching a low crossbeam at breathtaking speed. He ducked just as it sliced over his head with a whoosh, followed by a gut-wrenching thud and a shower of blood spatter. The standing bounty hunter was gone. His men froze, the fear of death in their eyes. Any one of them might be the next to go.

Grimacing, Parish stayed fast on his chore, assuring the cart maintained its memorized course. Switchbacks set the cart reeling left and right. The scanner he held detected microwave transmissions the jammer was blocking. He knew Carson was sending those signals in an attempt to stop them, either by derailing the cart or by circumvention of its controls. It was a futile endeavor. Within minutes, Parish expected a gun battle to the death.

***

Parked at his keyboard, Carson pounded on keys that should have stopped the approaching cart. It was now only three bends away from the platform below. None of the frequencies worked. John Parish had jammed them solidly.

There was no way to stop him.

Garlicky sweat oozed from Carson's pours, soaking his shirt. He couldn't remember the last time he was this pissed off. The bounty hunters had fouled the sanctity of his subterranean sanctuary. For the first time in over two hundred years, he thought dying was a definite possibility.

"Shit." He gave up on his radio-controlled booby traps to watch Myrtle playing with her toy mouse, romping and rolling across the litter-strewn floor. Meanwhile, he contemplated his chances for survival. There were only five bounty hunters left. His odds weren't too bad. Between himself, Scott, Sue, and of course Myrtle, they had a good probability of success, especially when he considered their advantage: they were familiar with the mine. And another upside occurred to him. He would have the opportunity to kill the notorious John Parish, a thought that suddenly frightened Carson greatly. Would he have the nerve to do it?

He retrieved a Glock 401 blaster from a pouch on the giant wheelchair and set a fully charged particle clip on his lap. He'd long ago removed the trigger guard so the blaster would accommodate his huge index finger. Motoring to the railing, he looked down at the platform where the ore cart would stop. Of course, his wheelchair was too big to hide behind anything, but from this position he figured he could dispatch a bounty hunter or two before they could bail out of the cart and find cover. Maybe one of them would be John Parish himself.

On the downside, he knew he would make one hell of a big target sitting up here with no protection. He wished he had a blast jacket as he pointed the blaster down through the railing and chucked another Snickers bar, hoping it wouldn't be his last.

Seconds later, he heard the rattle of the ore cart's wheels approaching at high speed. Myrtle hissed in alarm, abandoned her toy mouse, and scampered to the platform's edge where she peered down, head cocked, ears perked, and whiskers twitching.

"That's right, girl," Carson said, his heart hammering against his ribs. "We're in trouble."

She looked up at him, flicked her tail, and returned to her toy. But this time she didn't play with it. She carefully took it in her mouth and carried it away, as a mother would carry her young to safety.

A bad omen, Carson thought as the cart clattered up to the platform and squealed to a stop. Every nerve in his body caught fire. He'd never killed a man before, never thought he'd have to, but the bounty hunters had changed all that. He aimed his blaster and squeezed the trigger. Several bolts flashed from the muzzle at once, slicing through space with a *pheuw-pheuw-pheuw!* Sparks splayed off the oar cart's rim. One bounty hunter keeled over, his neck on fire.

Quickly, Carson realized that the lethal bolt had not come from his volley but from a spray of blaster fire originating below and to his left. Sue and Scott had taken up positions on the living-room platform. He couldn't see them, but he pictured them lying flat on the floor as bolts of return fire streamed up at them. The intense bombardment seemed impossible to survive.

Fearing for their lives, Carson opened fire again, more in panic than with any measurable skill. Through the flashes, he saw bounty hunters scatter, crouching and firing. They wore black fatigues, blast jackets, helmets and goggles. He was amazed at their uncanny ability to survive the hail of blaster bolts raining down on them. Already, the air stunk of ionized particles. Smoke swirled around him. A girder overhead spit a shower of molten steel.

Ducking, Carson ejected an empty clip and slapped in the fresh one. He couldn't see the bounty hunters any longer, so he fired at flashpoints, hoping to hit the shooters. Another shower of sparks sprayed him from above. A particle bolt shrieked past his left ear, so close he felt the heat. He let loose another volley, firing like a mad man.

It didn't take him long to realize that the bounty hunters had zeroed in on his position. Streams of hot energy flew up at him, an inconceivable torrent of fire, but he kept pulling the trigger wildly.

Suddenly, searing pain shot through his left arm. He smelled his flesh burning but kept shooting. A flash blinded his right eye. Then the wheelchair's left front tire exploded, pitching him forward. Flames roared up from the ion fuel cell. The blaster ran out of ammunition. Good God, he was going to die.

Retreat, he thought, dropped the empty blaster and backed the wheelchair away from the platform's edge, out of the line of fire, but right into a raging inferno. The litter on the floor had been set ablaze, crackling and popping. Then the console went up in flames. Churning black smoke choked the air. The heat was like a furnace, and if that wasn't bad enough, sparks rained down on him, sizzling on contact with his sweat-soaked skin and clothes. He hoped Sue and Scott were faring better. Even breathing, as hard as it had always been, was now frighteningly difficult.

The left side of his wheelchair was completely ablaze. Leaning away from the intense heat, he knew he had only one hope to survive. He had to get out of the chair. Normally, this was a struggle under the best of conditions, but now, with only one useful arm, he couldn't push himself to his feet. He'd have to fall out of the chair, knowing he'd not be able to stand again without assistance. Like a beached walrus, he'd have to move by undulating his fat across the floor, perhaps only inches at a time, wounded as he was. But he had no other choice. Gritting his teeth, he tipped over on his right side and let his body weight take him out of the wheelchair.

Sprawled on his back on the floor, he expected the fire to tear into him without mercy. However, his sweat-soaked clothes acted as a retardant, and the enormous area of his body covering the floor smothered the fire underneath him. And being low as he was, the smoke didn't burn his throat as badly. He'd cheated death...for now.

Somewhat relieved, he rolled over. It wasn't a simple chore, as it took massive effort just to get on his stomach. Then he managed to get on his left side, his useless arm painfully lodged underneath him, and then flopped over on his back again. He could hear his sweat sizzling, but his will to survive drove him onward until he came to a place on the platform that wasn't yet ablaze, by the railing, down a little ways from where he'd abandoned his burning wheelchair. Again, blaster bolts flashed overhead. Sparks rained down. As long as the battle raged on, he knew Sue and Scott were still alive, possibly pinned down but definitely fighting for their lives. He wished he could have been more help to them.

Undulating his flabby body a few feet farther, he found a place where he could lay somewhat concealed behind a hologram projector. He stole a look over the platform's edge just as a grappling hook streaked up at him, its rope tail whipping behind it. Instinctively, he ducked. With a clank, the barbed jaws snared the railing to his right. He looked again and saw a second grappling hook coming up. It caught the railing a few feet to his left. He was about to be outflanked.

Knowing he couldn't escape, he took the time to scrutinize the current situation below. Sue and Scott had moved down to the main floor. They were holed up behind the freight elevator. Two bounty hunters laid down cover fire while the other two launched their assault on the upper platform.

They flew up the ropes using microburst boosters. Fierce firing escalated below. A couple flashes shot up at the killers but missed. They reached the top and dove over the railing, somersaulting to their feet like Ninjas, blasters in hand.

Carson expected his life to end quickly. He'd lived two hundred and sixty four years. He was tired. John Parish had outsmarted him. His last thoughts were of Sue, Scott, and of course Myrtle. He wondered what would become of them.

***

Pinned down behind the freight elevator, Scott retrieved the last particle clip from his sport bag and slapped it into his blaster. That, and a half dozen concussion grenades were all the firepower he had left. He stole a glance at Sue, twenty feet off to his right, holed up behind a steel column that supported the infrastructure. She too was low on ammunition.

Parish and his bounty hunters had mercilessly pounded them, barrage after barrage, so intense that he couldn't keep tabs on their movements or positions. Better than half the time, he didn't dare show his head for fear of losing it.

So it surprised him when the firing stopped abruptly. He looked at Sue.

She shrugged.

"Come out, Weller."

Scott recognized John Parish's voice from the 105 to Boulder. "Never." It sounded like the right thing to say.

"Throw down your blasters. Keep your hands where we can see 'em."

"In your dreams," Sue shouted.

Scott gave her a thumbs-up, a show of solidarity if nothing else. Then he wondered why Carson hadn't thrown in his two cents. "Carson," Scott called out, hoping for a quick response.

None came.

Grabbing a quick breath, he peeked around the elevator casing and saw two ropes dangling from the upper platform shrouded in smoke. He felt a chill, ducked back again, pointed to Sue, and then up to the platform.

She looked. Her face turned white. "Oh my God. Grandpa. Are you all right?"

There was no response.

"Grandpa!"

"Surrender, Scott Dunn," Parish said. "I'm not gonna kill ya. Jerry Well has dibs on that pleasure. Sue Masters, put down your weapon. You're free to go. We got no beef with you."

"Parish," Scott shouted, his back pressed against the elevator casing, blaster in both hands pointed up. Ionized air burned his throat. "How do we know we can trust you?"

"Ya don't."

"Where's Carson?"

"He's been askin' to see his granddaughter."

Color returned to Sue's face. "What have you done to him?"

"My men got him," Parish said proudly. "He's bleedin' pretty bad. Now I'm no doctor, but I'd say he don't have much time left."

Sue's shoulders sagged. She looked at Scott, the blank look of doom in her eyes. "I've got to help him."

"There's nothing you can do."

She tossed down her blaster. "He's all I've got." She stepped out from behind the column with her hands raised in surrender. "All right, Parish. Take me to him."

Scott readied his blaster in case they started shooting. "What are you doing?"

"He doesn't have much time, Scott."

"Parish is lying—"

"Now your blaster, Scott Dunn, or we'll drop her where she's standin'."

Isn't this just peachy, Scott thought. This whole thing had taken a rotten turn, not because of Parish's brilliant combat skills, but because Sue had a weak spot for her grandfather. They could have fought it out. They might have even won. But after this, it all came down to the same thing: he shouldn't have trusted her. Clenching his jaw, Scott set the gun on the floor and kicked it out into the open then leered at Sue. "Satisfied?"

She returned a riveting glare. "He needs me, Scott, but you wouldn't understand that. You abandoned your family." Each word was a chip of ice.

"Come out, Scott Dunn," Parish ordered.

Scott spit. Sue was right. He'd been so busy thinking about himself that he'd interpreted her feelings for her grandfather as a breach of trust. Now that he thought about it, he realized he was worried about Carson's fate more than he was willing to admit. "Christ!" Hands in the air, he stepped out. He not only felt defeated; he felt like a heel. He wanted to tell her he was sorry but didn't have time. The bounty hunters surrounded him.

After stripping him of his blast jacket, they patted him down for weapons, wrenched his hands behind his back, and slapped energy cuffs on his wrists.

Sue also gave up her blast jacket, and they searched her for weapons. However, they didn't restrain her in any way. Scott thought that odd, at first, but quickly realized that if Parish had energy-cuffed her, it would show his men that he was afraid of her.

"Take me to my grandpa now," she demanded.

First, Parish made her explain how the freight elevator worked. Two of his men had already started rounding up the booty: tools, computer equipment, a hologram player. "The spoils of war," Parish bragged as they stepped on the conveyer lift to the upper platform.

"Take what you want," Sue said, engaging the lift.

She remained silent the rest of the way up, her face etched with worry. Scott couldn't find words to ease her fears. Then he was surprised at himself for feeling the need to console her. She meant a lot to him. That realization made him feel uncomfortable...vulnerable.

At the top platform, a bounty hunter standing guard smiled at Sue, showing choppy teeth as he escorted her off the lift. His bug eyes wandered up and down her body. "What say you and I have us a little fun?"

"Your breath stinks," she shot back.

Scott saw red. "Touch her, I'll kill you."

The bounty hunter showed him a middle finger. "Up yours."

"Save it," Parish barked. "I wanna see this Weller I've heard so much about."

"He ain't much to look at now, boss."

Worrying about the severity of Carson's injuries, Scott noticed that the fire had been extinguished, the smoke clearing. Someone had propped Carson's five hundred pound mass against a blast-damaged console, his legs splayed on the floor. His puffy eyes were open, his mouth gagged, obviously the reason he hadn't responded when Scott had called out to him. He seemed to be in shock, listless, his white skin sunburn-red. His clothes were scorched, and his seared left arm hung loosely at his side.

"Grandpa." Sue ran to him and untied the gag around his head. "Look what they've done to you."

"I'm tired," he replied, wheezing terribly.

"You're hurt."

"That's the least of my worries."

"Don't talk like that." The dimple on her chin

wrinkled. "You're going to make it through this."

Scott didn't know what to say to Carson. His situation looked bleak, with two blaster wounds leaking smoke from his belly. Even a small measure of encouragement would have been a lie.

The bounty hunter guarding Carson grabbed Sue's arm and yanked her to her feet. "That's enough family reunion." He flicked his tongue at her. "Now for the fun part."

She pushed him away.

"Feisty one, are ya?"

"Leave her alone," Scott shouted, wishing he could bash the bastard.

Parish did nothing to control his man, just stood there staring down at Carson with a twisted look of disgust on his face. "So you're the mighty Hog."

"I've had better days." Carson coughed.

The look of despair in Sue's eyes threatened to tear out Scott's heart. Her grandfather was near death, and as if that weren't enough stress, the bounty hunter grabbed her butt.

She yelped and spun away from him.

Adrenaline lit fires in Scott's bloodstream. He wasn't about to let the bounty hunter put his hands on Sue without paying a stiff price. Problem was, the energy cuffs. He fought to free himself, but the more he struggled the more the taser energy bit into his wrists like bee stingers.

"Come on, honey." The bounty hunter cackled.

"I'm warning you." She showed him a fist.

With lightning speed, he struck out and seized her by the throat, slammed her against a supercomputer. "So you want to do this the hard way."

"Let go of me," she choked out.

"Makes no mind to me, bitch."

She kneed him in the groin, but the bounty hunter only grinned, then he backhanded her across the face. She fell to the floor, looked up, lip bleeding, her eyes suddenly frozen to something above her attacker. "No, Myrtle, don't."

Just then, a shrill cry shrieked through the air like an incoming missile. A flash of black fur and silver paws startled Scott, the motion quick and furious as Myrtle dropped from an upper girder. She landed on the bounty hunter's right shoulder blade, claws digging into his shirt.

He spun around, flailing his arms and screaming.

Parish jumped back, his eyes wide in surprise.

With razor-sharp teeth, Myrtle bit into the bounty hunter's neck. A crimson spray erupted from his jugular. Panic-stricken, he stumbled over Carson's outstretched legs and fell over the railing.

"Oh no." Sue threw her hands over her mouth. "Myrtle."

By the time Scott moved to the railing and looked over the edge, Myrtle was nowhere in sight. He feared she'd landed under the bounty hunter who lay motionless in a pool of blood, twisted and broken. The bastard got what was coming to him, Scott decided, thanks to Myrtle. His breath hitched. *Poor Myrtle.*

"What the hell was that?" Parish shouted.

Whipping around, Scott saw the veins on Parish's temples bulge, the anger in his gruff voice alarming.

"Are there any more of them rodents around here?"

Carson managed to shake his head. "She was my pet ferret."

"You son of a bitch." Parish activated a hologram hover-sphere and tossed it into the air. "I should thank you for leaving me one less man to share the bounty on your head." He drew his blaster. "But I won't."

"No," Sue cried.

Pheuw-Pheuw!

Carson stiffened for an instant before his chest collapsed and his head lolled to the side.

"Grandpa!"

Parish held out his palm. The spherical recorder flew back to him. "Say your goodbyes. We're leavin' in ten minutes." He turned and walked away as if what he had done was nothing.

Sue dropped to her knees and hugged Carson's neck.

"I'm sorry about your grandfather," Scott said, trembling but thankful Parish hadn't shot them all. He looked around the disheveled platform and up to the rock ceiling, escape on his mind, unguarded as they were while Parish and his men looted the place. "Is there a way out of here?"

"Just the elevator, but the bounty hunters are using it."

No wonder Parish wasn't worried about leaving them alone. With hope of escape lost, he bent down to check the blaster wounds in Carson's flabby chest. He saw movement. Surprised, he wondered if Carson's fat had saved him from a fatal blow. "He's still breathing."

"Grandpa?" She patted his face. "Can you hear me?"

His eyelids fluttered, opened slightly. "Sue? I...I can't see you."

"We'll get you to a doctor."

"Too late...for that," he rasped. "Where's Scott?"

It was obvious Carson was so weak that he couldn't lift his head. Scott got on his knees and leaned to Carson's ear. "Hang in there, sir."

"I must...*wheeze*..."

"Save your strength."

"...tell you..."

His voice was barely audible. Scott put his ear close to Carson's lips, heard blood gurgling in his throat. "I'm listening."

"There is... *gasp* another..." he coughed, "another..." He exhaled with a wheeze.

Scott nudged him. "Another what?"

His mouth hung agape, jaw crooked, his eyes wide open as if his last breath had been excruciating.

"Grandpa." Sue fell on his stilled chest and sobbed.

"What was he trying to tell me?"

"I don't know."

"Another life? Another love? Another time?" Just then, Myrtle scampered up to Scott. "Another chance...?" He sat back on his heels, surprised she'd survived the fall. And he was happy to see her. After all, she'd proven herself a worthy ally. But he'd never seen a sadder-looking creature. Flopping on her belly, she looked up at him with watery eyes, her ears bent back, and her whiskers drooping. Her master was dead. Somehow she sensed it. Scott wondered if she'd be able to survive on her own. Who would feed her? Who would play with her? More alarming than that, he realized he actually cared. He couldn't leave her behind, not now, not after she'd risked her life to protect Sue.

"You'd be surprised what this ferret can do." Carson's words came back as Scott looked at Myrtle's long face. He had to smuggle her out of here. "Come here, girl."

She just looked at him with those sad, beady eyes.

Because his hands were tied behind his back, he had no way to coax her to come to him or pick her up, so he tried bobbing his head. "It's all right, come on."

She tilted her masked face at him quizzically then looked at Sue hunched over her grandfather. That's when Scott remembered how she'd called Myrtle before: she'd made ticking sounds with her tongue. He decided to try it. *"Tic-tic!"*

Myrtle's ears perked.

"Come on, girl. *Tic-tic!*"

She scampered up Scott's thigh and nosed her way in between the buttons of his baggy black shirt. He felt her soft fur on his stomach, found solace in her acceptance of him. Compassion. And his heart went out to Sue as she sobbed over her dead grandfather. On top of that, tears burned his eyes as well.

When he realized what was happening to him, panic set in. He fought to block out the grief brewing inside. Carson was dead and Sue's sorrow affected him deeply, made his feelings impossible to ignore, feelings that Myrtle had stirred in him. He wished his hands were free to embrace Sue, to comfort her, and to receive comfort from her in return. *Unbelievable.* How could he be feeling so much for these people...and for a ferret? His heart had betrayed him. That wasn't acceptable, but he couldn't shake the sorrow that engulfed him.

The Grief Syndrome

He suddenly found himself in a familiar world, a very scary place in which someone's heartbreak had broken through his stone façade and knifed into him with the force of a steel blade. Now his own sorrows spilled from the gaping wound. He saw his dying children, his dying grandchildren, and his miserable wife taking her own life. Memories filled him with that grief again. The demon reared up, salivating in its lust for misery. It pounced on him, crushing him with its mighty weight.

Balling his fists behind his back, only his stone cold tenacity kept him from crying out. He knew he had to keep the demon bottled up; he had to cage it before it beat him into a wailing idiot.

Parish returned with two men, their boots tromping across the platform, blasters drawn. "Happy Hour is over."

Chapter Seventeen

D ar Anders felt a momentary sense of relief as the doors closed behind him. The resulting thud reverberated through the empty Council chamber. Outside, he and Ishar had narrowly avoided a boisterous mob of environmentalists and reporters, all awaiting word from the Administrators, eager to hear the Council's ruling on the fate of Alpha Ketari.

With Ishar at his left elbow, he strode across the oval marble floor and looked up at the circular rows of plush stadium seating that surrounded them. He felt honored to be in this place of high authority but stressed over the tremendous responsibility Jerry Well had placed on them.

They moved past a semicircular arrangement of twelve high-backed chairs, lushly upholstered in red fabric and gold trim, and approached two similar chairs on a raised platform basking under the bright glow of ceiling lights mounted high in the superstructure. Dar allowed Ishar first seating and then sat on her left. After situating the folds of his robe, he turned to the hologram teleprompter that shimmered before him. *STANDBY* scrolled across a transparent background.

He knew the teleprompter would record and transmit their conversations to similar holograms at the other Elders' chairs so that they can review what had been asked of them and weigh their responses accordingly. In turn, their responses would appear on his teleprompter.

After receiving a nod from Ishar, Dar said, "We are ready."

The teleprompter relayed his words to a mainframe, and the Administrators set in motion the particulars to begin this emergency session of the Council of Elders. Dar understood, that during this closed meeting, they would forgo the normal formalities of a public affair.

A door to his left opened, releasing a harsh shaft of light. Silhouetted figures immediately moved through the doorway, two-by-two. Wearing long velvet robes with matching hoods folded back, the distinguished couples strode across the Council floor. When they stood before their assigned chairs, they bowed to Dar and Ishar.

"You may be seated," she said.

A time for pleasantries followed. Dar kept his manner stoic. Ishar was more cordial toward the other couples. After a few minutes, Dar raised his right hand, silencing the light chatter. "We're holding this session in private so that we can discuss the fate of Alpha Ketari without the constant interruption of spectators."

"Yes," they responded.

"As you know..." Dar looked over the elderly Council members, "we must decide if the mining conglomerates will be allowed to work on Alpha Ketari, or should the planet remain pristine, as Jerry Well and his followers are demanding? This task falls within our duty of managing our country's space assets, but the implications of this issue go much further. Our decision will ultimately determine the future of life on Earth. Your descendants and ours will suffer or prosper because of what we decide here today."

The Elders nodded.

"The first issue before us is not a simple one. Should we set forth a referendum that the mining conglomerates find some other planet to exploit? What has been discovered on this matter?"

Brac and Theta Wilson, retired geologists, took the floor. "The mining conglomerates' position is clear," Brac said. "They cannot guarantee finding equally vast mineral reserves elsewhere within a reasonable timeframe."

Theta bowed and added, "Discovery, exploration, and determination of a planet's asset potential requires many years, possibly decades."

"My wife and I have investigated these claims and found them undeniable."

Mrs. Dennison spoke next. Her expertise in environmental science had served the Council well. "Accessibility to these assets is of paramount concern. It's the atmosphere of Alpha Ketari that's most favorable. All other discovered planets showing mineral promise are molten or frozen or shrouded in poisonous gases. These hostile environments are not conducive to human survival, much less resource development. Consider Mars, for example, a difficult place to work, costing billions in life-support overhead."

Ishar asked, "Have you investigated the feasibility of developing another suitable planet, should one be found farther away?"

"Yes," Mr. Dennison replied. The burly Councilman was an ex-railroad man who'd specialized in the management of high-speed Levitation trains. "If a planet like Alpha Ketari were discovered orbiting Sirius B or another star system, logistics from those great distances would make any such endeavor cost-prohibitive. We have taken the liberty to calculate these expenses for the Council. May we submit?"

"Yes, of course."

Immediately, Dar's teleprompter displayed columns of figures, all of which illustrated an alarming fact. The conglomerates' finances would fall in the red, making bankruptcy inevitable. Dar was pleased that his fellow Council members had done their research well. "On these points, it appears the miners have presented valid issues. I move to strike any referendum requiring them to look elsewhere for our needed resources."

Ishar nodded. "I second the motion."

The Council members cast their votes via the teleprompters: five in favor, one against.

Wondering which couple was holding out, Dar said, "The second issue we must address is Jerry Well's petition to prevent the development of this planet for the sake of the Sawtooth worms on Ketari Flats. Is there any discussion on this matter?"

"Let's look at this logically," Brac said. "Humanoid future or a worm's future. Which is more important?"

"Anyone else?" Dar asked.

Brac stood, shouted, "The environmentalists have gone too far this time."

"Be seated," Dar ordered.

"Jerry Well will have our grandchildren living in caves."

Terry Wright

"Enough," Dar shouted. "This is not the Senate floor or the House of Commons. Outbursts will not be tolerated. We are more civilized than that."

Brac grumped and returned to his chair. His wife patted his arm with a doughy hand.

Hand raised, Mrs. Dennison requested the floor again.

Dar acknowledged her.

"The miners came to me for advice on this because of my experience in environmental science. We developed a plan to spare eighty percent of the worm's habitat. Jerry Well and his attorneys have no case against a survival rate that high. His petition must be denied."

"I second the motion," Brac said.

The couples voted, and the issue was put to rest, five to one.

Not surprised, Dar knew there was one remaining point to address, and he moved the session into it. "The last issue we must rule on is a referendum requiring HFTA to make preparations for a mass exodus from Earth to Alpha Ketari. The Aquariis have been charged with that investigation. What do you have to offer on this matter?"

Mr. Dwaine Aquarii stood. Dar knew the noted economist well. His wife authored many books on social order and civil law. After acknowledging her with a smile, he spoke to the Council. "The notion of humanity's mass migration to Alpha Ketari fails on three points. First, I want my honored colleagues to note that the planet is smaller than Earth. We are overcrowded here as it is."

At that, Dar held up his right hand. "There are some who have argued that we should move half the world's citizens to Alpha Ketari, thus relieving much of the pressure on our strained resources. Have you addressed this concern?"

"Yes." Dwaine reseated himself next to his wife. "If only half the populace were allowed exit visas, then the situation becomes highly explosive. Who will go...who will stay? The selection process alone would cause mass hysteria."

"Civil order would be at great risk," his wife added. "The concept of everyone in the world working together toward their common survival is beyond human expectation."

Dar nodded in agreement, as did Ishar. He knew anyone left behind would suffer in short order. During the transition, factions were sure to rise from the ranks. Looting. War. Land-grabbing, tyranny, oppression...

"The second problem is logistics," Dwaine went on. "My wife and I have consulted with HFTA engineers on this matter. We agree that the number and size of transports required to accommodate even half our population for such a journey would be a behemoth construction job requiring more material than we have left on this planet."

A stir went through the assembly. Dar raised his right hand to quell interruptions.

"Third and the most important point, who would pay the enormous cost? There's not only the transportation to consider but also the building of cities and roadways and flight terminals on Alpha Ketari. Factories must be built to produce everything needed for these construction projects as well as the arriving citizens. All this must be accomplished in minimal time. Fields must be cleared and crops planted, livestock raised, schools and shopping malls erected. These things are not impossible, we realize, but they will be much more difficult than settling the West four centuries ago."

Dar thought that was an understatement.

"On the other hand," Dwaine went on, "the mining conglomerates would profit from their work on Alpha Ketari. They won't need to build a planetary infrastructure. Any living expenses incurred would be considered an investment in their expected returns. Only by mining the materials and shipping them to Earth for resale can we be assured that mankind's future needs are met."

Well done, Dar thought. "In light of these facts presented today, have the mining conglomerates made their case?"

"Yes," Mrs. Dennison responded. "My husband and I are in complete agreement."

"We too," Mr. Aquarii said.

"But we are not," Mr. John Markab interjected. He was a famous government lawyer who'd unsuccessfully fought to outlaw telemarketers. His wife was a retired schoolteacher from Maine. "We feel that competition among the mining conglomerates would bolster their resolve to overcome the financial burden of finding and extracting resources from other planets besides Alpha Ketari. They are too comfortable...in bed with each other...as they are."

Caph Setti jumped in. He and his wife were retired bankers and stockbrokers. "Capitalism has proven itself in the past. Jerry Well is right. We should not desecrate a square mile of Alpha Ketari in the name of economics."

The resistance is mounting, Dar thought as he gave

over the floor to Kyle and Lillian Standecker, a retired farming couple from Ohio.

"My wife and I are God-fearing Christians. We believe the Lord works in mysterious ways. Mere mortals cannot understand His ultimate plan. As we see it, since mankind has laid waste to the land God gave him, then it is mankind who should suffer the consequences. Extinction is God's way of cleansing the land. In time, the earth will recover. Alpha Ketari should not be sacrificed to mend our mistakes and change God's will. My wife and I feel strongly about this and move the Council to a vote."

Dar was sure he'd found the holdouts. He glanced at Ishar. "They are impatient to put an end to this."

"Very well. Cast your votes, everyone."

The Elders went to work.

Dar watched his teleprompter as the six couples voted. The results were instantaneous: three for the development of Alpha Ketari and three against.

A murmur went through the chamber as the Elders received the same information on their teleprompters. Then the innuendoes and finger pointing began. The debate became noisy between the couples, each turning in their chairs and confronting the others. But none would budge from their positions.

Dar knew that he and Ishar would have to end the stalemate with a tie-breaking vote. The pros and cons had been convincing. It would take many hours to sort through the information presented to them. In the end, the fate of Alpha Ketari and Earth would rest squarely on their shoulders. With that realization burning holes in his stomach, he raised his right hand.

The arguing stopped.

"We shall give you our decision in two days. This session is officially concluded." Dar took Ishar's hand. They rose together.

Everyone stood, and he bid them good day.

Chapter Eighteen

To Scott Dunn, the mine once known as Hog Heaven was now a hellhole. Burnt platforms, shorted lighting, and drifting smoke were all that remained of Carson's sanctuary. His death left Scott feeling empty and numb.

Parish jabbed him with a blaster. "Get movin', Weller."

With his hands energy-cuffed behind him, only one thing seemed certain now: his execution at the hands of Jerry Well.

Scott followed Sue to the vertical conveyor that took them down to the elevator on the main floor. As he passed the blast-scarred wall of motion photos, he felt ashamed for having hated them earlier. Now Carson's entire family showcase lay in complete disarray: canted, broken, and fallen. Photos flickered. Soundtracks skipped.

Sue stopped abruptly, knelt to a glowing picture, and lifted it from the debris. When she shook off the loose shards of glass, the scorched frame came apart, leaving an incandescent image that blinked in her hand.

Parish kicked her. "Keep movin'."

She stumbled getting to her feet but quickly reclaimed her position beside Scott. "Something to remember me by."

She folded her flickering picture and put it in his shirt pocket.

"Thanks." The thought of never seeing her again hurt him more than he was willing to admit, but he was thankful that Parish planned on letting her go.

She hugged his arm as they walked, which made him feel a little better. He wondered how she could be so strong after losing her grandfather, though her tear-reddened eyes revealed her inner grief.

Just then, Myrtle poked her nose out of his shirt. Sue's eyes got big when she saw the ferret, but she didn't say anything. Myrtle sniffed the air and retreated.

Scott wanted Sue to take her. However, he hesitated to suggest it for fear of revealing Myrtle's presence to the bounty hunters. He felt certain that Parish would kill her in retribution for what she'd done to one of his men.

At the elevator gate, Sue picked up Scott's sport bag, left there during the battle. "You might need this to escape," she whispered.

Parish grabbed the bag. "What's in here?"

"My tools and things," Scott replied.

Frowning, Parish peeled back the flap and looked inside. "You won't be needin' this junk."

"You can have it," Scott said. "My compliments."

"Get on the elevator."

The other two bounty hunters crammed onto the platform with them. As they rose toward the surface, Sue pressed against Scott's side and glared at Parish. "Where are you taking him?"

"Hylander," he said with a grump. "But I'd rather just kill him right here."

"Let him go," she said. "He'll leave Colorado. Isn't that right, Scott?"

"Of course," he replied, but he didn't mean it. He would get inside Hylander, after all, exactly what he'd wanted. "I'll never come back."

Parish laughed.

"I take that as a no." Scott thought his plan to kidnap Katherine might now be possible, though he wasn't sure how he would stay alive long enough to pull it off.

"Your ass belongs to Jerry Well," Parish said. "Personally, I don't give a damn as long as I get my money."

"How much is my life worth?"

"Not a plug nickel to you," Parish spat.

"I've got to be worth something." Scott hoped to inflate his value to Jerry Well and buy enough time to get Katherine out of Hylander. "I'm the last Weller."

Parish stiffened. "What are you talkin' about?"

Sue said, "Don't tell him, Scott."

"Shut up," Parish shouted.

"It's no secret," Scott said. "Carson kept immaculate records. Thanks to you, I'm the only one left."

"Ya don't say." Parish's scarred face lit up with a smile. The last Weller meant something important to him, Scott realized, but he didn't know what it was or how it could help his doleful situation...or make things worse. Maybe he should've listened to Sue and kept his mouth shut.

With a clang, the rising elevator broke through the surface and jerked to a stop. Scott squinted against the bright afternoon sunshine. Inhaling fresh mountain air, he noticed the bite of recently burnt wood. To his right, a fallen tree and a small area of brush had been scorched black. Splintered wooden planks lay scattered about the clearing. Parish and his men had made a mess of the place.

"Move it."

The bounty hunters grabbed Scott's arms and muscled him toward a black van. Parish shoved Sue along, blaster in hand as if he expected an escape attempt. At the van's open back door, the procession stopped.

"Get in," Parish ordered Scott then turned to Sue. "We don't need you." He swiveled his blaster.

"No," Scott shouted.

Pheuw!

Sue flew backward. Her body slammed to the ground, bounced and slid a few feet, kicking up dust, before she came to rest on her back, arms spread and legs contorted one over the other. Smoke swirled from a black wound in her chest, the odor of burned flesh unmistakable.

"Son of a bitch." Scott tried to tear loose from the two men clamped to his arms. "You said she was free to go."

"I lied."

"Sue!"

Scott hoped she was only wounded, but to his horror, she lay there still as death. His heart sank in despair, and then an insane rage came over him. He lurched and tugged against his captors. "You didn't have to kill her."

Parish paced the few steps to her body. "She's worthless to us." He spit. "Besides, I don't wanna be lookin' over my shoulder for her to show up again." He dropped the sport bag on her stomach and looked at Scott, a crooked grin now warping the bounty hunter's face. "My only regret is that we don't have time to send her off properly." He grabbed his crotch and pumped his hips.

Scott couldn't see straight. "I'll kill you." Fighting to get free of the bounty hunters, he head-butted one and kneed the other in the groin. They responded with swinging fists. In spite of his best efforts, he couldn't fend off both men. They beat him half senseless and threw him into the van.

Parish cackled. "It's the end of the line for you, Weller." The door slammed shut with a bang.

Lying on his back, Scott ached and bled, but that was nothing compared to the anguish he felt for Sue. The shock. The grief. The demon rising. He doubled over, felt a lump under his shirt and remembered Myrtle. A chill gripped him.

She wasn't moving.

Chapter Nineteen

These were the darkest days of Hylander. Katherine had finally come home, but for Jerry Well, the victory felt empty. He realized her very presence represented the epitome of his technological prowess, his will over God's will, his control over all things physical and spiritual. But in reality, Katherine was an abomination.

As he reclined in his hover-lounge on the west veranda with a *Time* hologram on his lap, he donned his sunglasses and watched Katherine move about the sunlit garden below. Dressed in a flowing white gown, her arms hung limp at her sides, and her blank eyes always stared forward. She didn't stoop to smell the flowers. She didn't reach out to touch the fruit on the trees. It was the same earlier when she strolled the lavish mansion halls. She'd drifted from room to room like a ghost, a bald, pale woman without expression or voice.

Her condition was unacceptable. Being this way, Jerry had no control over her. He couldn't coax her to do anything, force her to react to him or submit to his will. She was a walking vegetable. For that he blamed Dr. Navarro whom he'd summoned an hour ago to rectify the situation or suffer the consequences. Impatient, Jerry wondered why the doctor hadn't yet arrived.

Just then, Robert whizzed by as if on a mission.

"Wait," Jerry called out.

The cyber-bot swung around and zipped back to the floating recliner. *"May I be of assistance, sir? Perhaps the Powerball numbers for tonight's game. They are sure winners..."*

"Where is Dr. Navarro?"

"One moment, sir." Robert made a series of beeping sounds and extended cone-shaped antennas that rotated. Blinking lights on his control panel indicated that an attendant server nearby had established communication with Starnet, which gathered information about Dr. Navarro's whereabouts. In less than five seconds, Robert responded. *"Grid sector 566K, Highway 93 outbound. ETA twenty minutes, sir."*

"Hell. Does he have an excuse for being late?"

"It is not recorded."

"You're worthless." Jerry threw the *Time* hologram at Robert. It bounced off the cyber-bot's shell and fell to the floor, shimmering.

Beeping wildly, Robert zigzagged a hasty retreat.

"You stupid machine," Jerry shouted.

That's when he noticed Katherine. She was looking up at him from the garden as if she'd suddenly become aware of his presence. A glower creased her ghostly face.

"What are you lookin' at, bitch?"

***

Pain told Sue she was still alive. Sprawled on her back in the dirt, she didn't dare breathe. She didn't dare move, not a muscle, not a twitch, even though her chest felt like it was on fire. Mind over body, she thought. *Concentrate.* She had to suppress the flight or fight instinct. She had to play dead. If she showed any sign of life, Parish would surely finish her off.

Lying with her eyes closed and her head wrenched painfully to the right, disbelief and denial warped her sense of reality. It had happened so fast: Parish's blaster turning, the flash. She'd flinched, cranked herself sideways enough to angle her body to the particle bolt's main thrust. Even so, the impact had knocked her backward. She must've blacked out, at least for a moment, because she didn't remember hitting the ground.

You didn't have to kill her. She heard Scott cursing and Parish's demonic laughter. And then came the sounds of knuckles cracking, moans and thuds. Unbelievably, Scott was fighting for her. He cared. There was a crack in his stone after all. The warm spot she found for that thought quickly dissolved when she realized the bounty hunters were beating the hell out of him. She couldn't help him, so she used the men's distraction to steal a painful sip of air.

The van doors slammed, engines roared, and tires churned dirt. As the mechanical din faded away, she gulped air, though the price for doing so was chest-stabbing pain. The stench of burned flesh made her stomach revolt.

"Oh God!" She spit bile and thought she would die.

A jay screeched from somewhere. Not another sound came to her. She opened her eyes and scanned the area. She was alone. On one hand, that was a good thing. On the other, she was in the middle of nowhere, badly hurt, and there was no one around to help her.

The extent of her injury became her next concern, but

she was afraid to look at the wound. Steeling herself, she turned her head. The first thing she saw was Scott's sport bag on her stomach. Then she felt its weight and wondered how it had gotten there. Gritting her teeth, she told her toes to wiggle. They obeyed. She moved her legs, her fingers and her wrists, testing each part, relieved that they still worked.

But moving her arms gave her a jolt of searing pain, especially her left shoulder, which caused her chest muscles to spasm and burn. In spite of the pain, she pushed the sport bag off her stomach, and then turned her attention to the blaster wound. Her black shirt was burnt and smoldering. Beneath that, she saw a charred gash in her flesh, about four inches long, just above her left breast. Blood leaked from tissues the energy bolt hadn't cauterized, and she saw a rib bone.

Stomach clutching, she wrenched her eyes from the wound. "Goddamn you, John Parish." Cursing made her feel better. But she was lucky, she knew; she could have been killed outright. Then again, if she didn't get help soon, she would surely suffer a slow and torturous death. Already, flies buzzed about the wound, and every breath came with stinging retribution.

Death would be a welcomed relief.

Jeeze. She couldn't believe she'd thought that. She needed a doctor. Get up. Get moving, she ordered herself. *Don't just lay here and die.*

At that, she worked her body onto her right side, propped herself up on her elbow, and then pulled her knees up to where she could roll over on top of them. Any strain on her left arm and shoulder felt like a thousand knives stabbing her chest. But that wasn't going to stop her. She'd crawl back to Boulder if she had to.

It took that kind of determination for her to rise up on her knees and struggle to her feet. That wasn't so bad, she thought, until her vision blurred and her head started spinning. She staggered, tripped over something, and hurtled back to the ground.

Pain.

She swore she wouldn't cry. She demanded that much of herself. An ex-Navy Seal, she was too tough for that, though she wasn't against wishing for a miracle.

And suddenly, there it was: the sport bag she'd just tripped over. She remembered Scott's shoulder wound, the military-grade nanocream he kept in the bag. It had to be there.

Clawing dirt, she dragged herself to the sport bag and tore into it.

***

The gates of hell, Scott thought.

He stood before Hylander's great wall as the steel gates ratcheted upward, clanking and banging. Myrtle flinched at the noise. She was still hiding in the folds of his baggy shirt and had stirred very little during the trip from the mine. Now Scott hoped she wouldn't bolt.

Seconds later, the rising gate opened fully. Energy-cuffed, with a bounty hunter on each arm and the murderous John Parish leading the way, he entered Jerry Well's estate.

Expecting fire and brimstone, he was unprepared for what he encountered. He'd entered an alien world of green landscapes and forested hills. The air simmered with the fragrance of mowed grass, and chirping birds fluttered about gardens brimming with flowers, vegetables, and fruit trees. Adorned with rainbows, magnificent fountains sprayed water over the flora. Scott thought it was the most beautiful place he'd ever seen.

"Quit gawking," a bounty hunter ordered, shoving Scott forward.

They approached a stone mansion that stood majestically in the sunshine, its towering walls reminding Scott of a castle with windows and balconies that overlooked the lavish grounds. Parish led him up a flight of marble steps to a massive porch leading to a pair of dark wooden doors.

"*Halt,*" a mechanical voice ordered.

The bounty hunters jerked Scott to a stop. A spherical plasma-ray scanner hovered above them, humming, its highly sensitive detectors examining them thoroughly.

Alarms suddenly rang out.

"*Do not proceed,*" bellowed a gruff voice from the scanner's speakers.

Parish shouted, "What's the meaning of this?"

Security-bots surrounded them, some hovering, some striding on mechanical struts, like skeletal legs. They carried blasters in their three-fingered grippers. Seconds later, a scanner-bot flew directly to Scott, its probe extended and beeping like mad.

Frozen with fear, he was unsure of the machine's intentions. Perhaps it didn't recognize his heat signature; after all, he'd never been here before. Or had it detected his altered biochemistry and his garlicky odor?

"Do not move," the voice demanded. Starting at Scott's head, the scanner-bot descended with its beeping probe. A hologram materialized in front of him. The bot's optic sensors scrutinized the image that formed, an x-ray projection of Scott's skull, jaw, neck bones, and ribs. Moving downward over his abdomen, something else became visible: a pointy skull, curved backbone, ribcage, and a long tail.

John Parish saw it too and rushed forward. "I'll kill the little shit."

With a hiss, Myrtle tore out of Scott's shirt, clawing skid marks on his stomach. She leaped to the ground and took off running across the lawn.

Spooked, the bounty hunters flinched and hesitated to open fire.

"Run, Myrtle, run," Scott shouted.

But the security-bots didn't hesitate. Their screeching blasters hurled energy bolts at the ferret as she hightailed it, dodging the fiery onslaught to and fro. Flaming divots flew up all around her, but she made it to the garden and disappeared in the foliage.

"She got away. She got away." But Scott's elation was short-lived as burly hands grabbed his throat with bone-crushing force.

"I'll kill ya myself, Weller."

"Don't do it, boss," someone said.

With his hands cuffed behind his back, Scott was powerless to defend himself against Parish. The towering bounty hunter bent over him, growling and squeezing. His lungs burned, begging for air, and his head felt as if it were going to pop off his shoulders. He started thinking about

Sue and how he would soon join her.

"Parish," a demanding voice shouted.

"Keep your lousy five million bucks, Jerry." Parish kept squeezing. "This one's on me."

Scott's vision blurred. He knew he was going to die.

"He's mine," Jerry insisted, his hand hovering over his holstered blaster. "Or are you forgetting something?"

"I don't care anymore."

"Immortality, John. Florida. Your yacht—"

"This Weller thinks he's so damn smart sneakin' that ferret in here. Carson trained it to kill."

"My bots will take care of the ferret," Jerry said flatly. "Meanwhile, don't throw your future away because your pride is hurt."

"Christ." Parish shoved Scott to the ground. "You shouldn't have made me bring him here."

Jerry looked over the group. "Where's Sue Masters?"

"I shot her dead, the dumb bitch, like I should'a done him. He's trouble, I tell ya."

"You let me worry about him," Jerry said.

Gasping, Scott curled into a fetal position, nearly retching. He looked up, focused on the two men standing face-to-face, shouting at each other.

"You should let me kill him. Right now."

"I have other plans for him."

Parish grabbed Jerry's cloak lapels. "But he's the last Weller."

Jerry stood firm, his voice level and cold. "Let go of me."

Scott fought for air.

"I want the vial now," Parish hissed. "I've earned it."

"I need proof that he's the last Weller."

"Carson kept good records."

"I don't believe it," Jerry shot back.

"Give me my vial."

"Get your hands off me."

Scott started coughing. He gave up trying to make sense of their argument. Besides, with needlelike pains poking his throat, he feared his windpipe was crushed. Then he felt something strange, unexpected: a soft touch on his shoulder.

The men suddenly stopped arguing.

Swallowing hard, Scott slowly turned his head. He flinched. His first instinct was to get away from the thing kneeling next to him. It was the angel of death, he was sure, in a flowing white gown, its skin ghostly pale. But he didn't move. Something about this apparition struck him with awe. Perhaps it was the forlorn face of this being that entranced him, the pinholes around its eyelids and mouth, its lusterless lips, feminine in shape but dry and cracked. Its head was bald, and the eyes of this creature stared at him curiously, as if *he* were the oddity.

"Katherine," Jerry Well shouted the name as if it were a curse. But she didn't respond, just kept looking at Scott. And he couldn't stop staring at her...at Katherine. Mesmerized by her presence, he could hardly believe that she was back from the dead.

"Get in the house, Katherine."

She didn't comply.

Jerry grabbed her hand from Scott's shoulder and yanked her to her feet. "You'd better start listening to me."

She said nothing, as if he weren't there, her head bent

down and her gaze still on Scott.

Jerry slapped her.

Wheeling, her eyes widened and her mouth opened in shock, and as if suddenly terrified, she shrunk away from him. Already, a red welt began to form on the side of her face.

Jerry shook her shoulders. "Now look what you made me do."

She looked at Scott again with confused and pleading eyes. Jerry started dragging her toward the open mansion doors. She kept looking back at Scott. Her eyes never left his, and his never left hers. He saw her terror, felt her pain. The woman was living again...in hell. Her husband was the devil himself.

A smoldering rage tore through Scott. He wished he could do something to save her.

Growling, Parish jerked him to his feet. "What's the matter, Weller? Never seen a ghost before?"

"Are you so cold that you don't see what's going on around here?"

"All I see is a dead Weller."

How ironic, Scott thought. He couldn't even save himself, much less Katherine.

Chapter Twenty

J erry knocked Katherine to her bedroom floor. "You wanted him, didn't you. I've reanimated a tramp." He turned his back to her. Every nerve in his body screamed out to strike her. He crossed his arms and ground his molars to keep from beating her to death. "Haven't I given you everything?"

Katherine remained mute, sprawled on the floor.

"Look around. Your own room. The flowers, the sunshine coming in, beautiful clothes, and this...this wig." He stormed to the dresser, grabbed it: long, brown, and flowing, like her hair used to be. "I told you to wear this." He bent over and shoved it at her. "Cover your ugly head."

She pushed it away and turned her face down.

"You disgust me." He threw the wig at her and picked up a framed photo of her once beautiful face. "This is you, Katherine. This is what you looked like two hundred twenty five years ago."

She didn't look, just stared at the floor.

Jerry grabbed her chin, forced her head up, and jammed the picture in front of her face. "I saved you. I saved your brain. Why won't you remember me?"

She said nothing.

"Snap out of it, Katherine," he shouted, hoping the

sheer volume of his voice would bring her around. "We're running out of time. The Council meets again in two days. There'll be an election. You must be ready."

Still, there was no response.

At that, he lifted her from the floor and set her upright on the edge of the bed. She sat limp like a rag doll. He had to hold her up. "Look at me."

She stared past him.

He shook her. "You looked at me on the veranda. You looked at Scott Dunn. What's the matter with you now?"

Suddenly, a beep came from behind him. Startled, he turned and saw Robert hovering in the doorway with Navarro at his side.

"I warned you this would happen," the doctor said.

"This is *your* fault." Jerry let go of Katherine. She slumped to the bedcovers, her bare legs dangling over the edge of the bed.

"May I come in?" Navarro asked. "Or should we discuss this from the hallway?"

"Look at her. She's worthless."

"To you, perhaps." Navarro stepped into the room.

Robert swiveled his camera-lens eyes to Jerry, pitched them up, and with an electronic *"humph,"* turned and zoomed off.

"I'll deal with you later," Jerry shouted. The last thing he'd tolerate was a disrespectful butler-bot. Then he turned to Navarro. "Robert shows more emotion than Katherine. She's a damn freak."

"You should be kind," Navarro said, moving to the bed. "Even your cyber-bot has turned against you."

"It's just a goddamned machine. I can de-energize it

anytime I want."

Navarro bent over Katherine, examined her eyes then gently touched the swelling on her face. "How did this happen?"

"She fell down," Jerry said. Navarro's glare looked doubtful, but before he could press the issue, Jerry added, "I want Katherine back, doctor, the way she was before."

Navarro lifted her legs and gently placed them on the bed then arranged her gown modestly. "She is very weak."

"Give her a shot of Dicryptone." Jerry knew that drug had cured Alzheimer's.

"It will do no good," Navarro said, standing. "Her condition is fragile. If she does not get proper injections of nanoserum, she will suffer CR."

"Cryonic Relapse?"

"Yes."

Jerry had read about the condition: nitrogen contamination of the mitochondria, leaking cellular walls, internal bleeding. He knew CR was fatal if not treated quickly, but her current mental problems outweighed Dr. Navarro's disturbing prognosis. "When is she going to remember me?"

"For that, I have an idea that may bring results."

Just then, Robert whirred in, followed by several bounty hunters operating hover-lifters piled high with boxes. *"Where do you want this junk?"* Robert asked.

Jerry frowned. "What is it?"

"I've brought materials I've received from the Bureau of Archives," Navarro explained. "Movies, television shows, and music from the 20th century. Perhaps something here will jog her memory."

"Where do you want this junk?"

"Where do you want this junk, *SIR*?" Jerry snarled. "Are you forgetting your place here?"

"I forget nothing."

"You're acting like a maid-bot."

"Flattery will get you nowhere."

Jerry balled his fists. "Flattery will get you nowhere, *SIR*."

Navarro jumped in. "Will you two stop it?" He turned to the bounty hunters. "Put the boxes in the corner and unpack the machines."

Beeping, Robert whirled around and zipped out the door.

The bounty hunters went to work. They unboxed an old television set, a four-track video machine, DVD player, and extension speakers. Jerry hadn't seen the likes of these things for nearly two hundred years. The machines were set up on an old folding table and plugged into a power adapter. Wires and cords ran every-which-way. Then Navarro pulled a video cartridge from a box. "These tapes have been refurbished every twenty-five years. Thanks to the efforts of the Bureau of Archives, they are in perfect working order."

"No holographic reproductions?" Jerry asked, wondering why these antiques were necessary.

"Think about it," Navarro said. "Seeing these old machines might help Katherine remember her past. Her subconscious won't recognize the technology we have today."

"Of course," Jerry said, feeling bitten by Navarro's foresight.

With a clink, the machine accepted the video cartridge. Navarro activated the old vacuum-tube television, which flickered on. Eerie music suddenly blared from the speakers. He adjusted the volume. Jerry figured the doctor had studied the machines' manuals before his arrival.

The movie began with the swaying and cracking of jungle vegetation and the snorting of a wild beast. Headlights illuminated the scene as a forklift broke through the foliage, hauling a huge steel crate. It approached a group of heavily armed men waiting beside a massive gate. They wore red helmets and stern faces. One man nervously chewed gum.

"What's this?" a bounty hunter asked.

"I remember..." Jerry scowled at Navarro. "Why do you want Katherine to see *this* movie?"

"Shock value," Navarro replied. "Back then, nearly everyone on the planet saw Jurassic Park."

"Sure," Jerry agreed. "Now if we can just get Katherine interested in it." As he spoke, he turned toward the bed, and to his surprise, Katherine was sitting upright and staring at the TV, a glint of recognition in her eyes.

"See?" Navarro said, pointing at his temple. "Deep inside her subconscious cortex, she remembers."

On the screen, the forklift lowered the crate in front of the gate. Inside, an unseen beast squealed. The men readied their weapons. A man wearing a bushman's hat said, *"Loading team, move in. I want tasers on full charge."*

Katherine smiled brightly, like a child watching a cartoon.

"She likes it," Jerry said to Navarro.

"However, she has no comprehension of what she is seeing. She thinks it's fun."

"But a reaction, nonetheless." Jerry felt a glimmer of hope. His future, his plans for Alpha Ketari seemed suddenly possible, thanks to Navarro's efforts. "You've gone to a lot of trouble for me, doctor. I appreciate that."

Frowning, Navarro said, "You assume too much."

"What's that supposed to mean?"

"Gatekeeper," the man on TV shouted. *"Open the gate."*

Navarro turned to the door. "What I have done, I've done for Katherine, not you. I want her to remember her former life, yes, but mostly, I want her to remember how she died."

"West Nile B," Jerry spat. "You read the medical report."

"But her brain shows no signs of meningitis. Your account of her death is not possible."

Jerry flinched. "You talk like a traitor."

"My loyalty lies with Katherine."

"As well it should," Jerry replied. "But don't bite the hand that feeds you."

"We shall see." Navarro walked out.

"Is that a threat?" Jerry shouted. *I should have killed him.*

Meanwhile, everyone's attention was riveted to the movie. A man standing on top of the crate bent down and lifted the heavy gate. Suddenly, the beast lunged forward, screeching. The crate slid back. The gatekeeper fell, and still unseen, the beast within grabbed the screaming man's feet and started pulling him into the crate. The man with the bushman's hat took hold of the gatekeeper's arms, but squealing wildly, the beast refused to release him.

Jerry felt the sting of annoyance that the bounty hunters were still hanging around. "Did you guys get that ferret?"

"Parish is after it," one man replied, not looking away from the tug-of-war between man and beast.

"Get out there and help him before that rodent digs holes in my garden."

"But..."

Jerry felt like a parent trying to get the kids to do their chores instead of watching TV. "Now, I said."

At that, they left the room.

Then Jerry turned his attention to Katherine. She was sitting on the edge of the bed, hands clasped in her lap, staring wide-eyed at the TV...and smiling.

The man with the bushman's hat gritted his teeth as he desperately held on to the gatekeeper. Squealing and snorting, the beast appeared to be winning.

"Katherine, my love," Jerry sang, hoping to distract her from the movie. Her intense gaze on the man's muscular arms sent a pang of jealousy through his stomach. "Katherine?"

She stared at the TV.

The man shouted to his heavily armed men: *"Shoot her!"*

"Katherine."

Still smiling, she didn't look at him.

"Shoot her!"

Chapter Twenty-One

O ne place in Hylander wasn't beautiful, a dim and musty cellar with a dirt floor and walls of mortared stone. Only a sliver of light seeped in from under a wooden door. Scott moved about the room, his hands still restrained behind his back with the energy cuffs.

Hunger gnawed at his stomach. He paced six steps from the door to the piss pot, and then four to a wooden cot with a single folded blanket. He wondered about dinner, if he'd get anything to eat or not.

Then he thought about Katherine, the hell she was living, a victim of Jerry Well's repeated abuse. Slumping on the cot, Scott leaned against the rough wall and closed his eyes. His mind worked through the incredible chain of events that brought him to this horrible place. Carson was dead, Sue brutally murdered. Thinking of her reminded him of the blinking picture in his pocket. He wished he could take it out...look at it...if his hands were free. God, he missed her smile, the dimple on her chin, the way she stood up to him and the banter they shared. Now she was gone.

Tears stung his eyes.

His heart ached with loss...and worse, guilt. He blamed himself for letting her get involved. How could he have been so damn stupid? Though he'd only known her for a few days, she'd done more for him than anyone else in the past hundred years. She'd made him feel alive again. She'd made him care. Why God...why had it cost her her life? Grief began tearing at his heart. She was dead, and for what? He sniffled.

The big picture, he knew, included Alpha Ketari, its vast resources, and the fate of humanity on a barren planet stifled by global warming. These problems were huge to him, far more than he could grasp. The smaller picture, however, seemed equally unmanageable: Katherine, Jerry Well, John Parish...and a vial. He remembered them fighting over a vial, but a vial of what? Everlife?

If that were true, if in fact there was a vial of formula left on Earth, John Parish obviously wanted it, and Jerry dangled it in front of him like bait. Scott recalled Carson's speculation that Jerry Well had saved a vial for Katherine. That made two possible recipients of one vial. The mix meant trouble. Then again, perhaps that vial could provide the leverage he needed to further pit his adversaries against each other.

He wished he knew what happened to Myrtle.

An electronic lock buzzed, and the door swung open. Harsh light poured in around John Parish's massive frame. Scott blinked away tears and sat up. Every nerve in his body went on full alert. "What do you want?"

The murderer entered carrying a domed tray. "Your supper, Weller. I hope ya choke on it." He set the tray on the cot.

Scott wanted to dive in but... "What about my hands?" He turned sideways to show Parish the energy cuffs.

Parish removed a deactivation chip from his shirt pocket and pointed it at Scott. The energy cuffs dissolved.

Rubbing his wrists, Scott looked at the food tray, unsure of its safety. "You don't expect me to eat that."

"You can piss on it for all I care."

"It's probably poisoned."

Parish chuckled. "You should be so lucky. Jerry Well's got somethin' else in mind for you, Weller."

"Dead is still dead."

"You'll wish."

"Then it's got to be something worse..." Scott glanced at the tray. Having lived almost two hundred fifty years, he recognized the smell of mutton stew, sheepherder's cakes, and onion soup. Ferrets loved mutton. He wondered if Myrtle could smell it, if the aroma would lead her to him, if Parish hadn't already killed her. Scott wanted to ask him, but he was sure the bounty hunter wouldn't give him a straight answer, so he thought of a way to trick him into revealing Myrtle's fate. "What is it?" he asked, pointing at the tray.

"Just eat it," Parish barked.

"It's Myrtle isn't it...you sick bastard. You killed Sue and now you're going to make me eat her ferret."

"Good idea." Parish growled. "When I catch it, I'm gonna strangle it before I stuff it down your throat."

"She," Scott said. "It's a she."

"It's road-kill when I'm done with it."

Relieved that Myrtle was still alive, Scott thought about eating, but he wondered why Parish had brought the meal himself, as opposed to sending one of his henchmen or a security-bot. "You've had your fun, now leave me eat in peace."

"I'm not going anywhere."

"Then what's on your mind?"

Parish grinned manically. "Nothin' that seein' you dead won't fix."

"You can't be civil for one minute, can you?"

"Eat, asshole. I don't have all night to baby-sit you."

Setting the tray on his lap, Scott lifted the dome and looked at the plate of food. Parish's mere presence was killing Scott's appetite. "Why do you hate Wellers so much?"

"I hate everybody. Shut up and eat."

Scott picked up the spoon, gulped. Could it be poisoned? He began to think not. Parish wouldn't go against Jerry Well, at least not until the bounty hunter got what he wanted. The vial. But still, the possibility of a double-cross lingered in Scott's mind. Procrastinating over the food, he decided to press Parish harder. "The last time you tried to kill me, Jerry stopped you. Why?"

"Your lucky day, I guess."

"You were arguing with him."

"That's nothing new."

"Something about a vial?"

"My Everlife." Parish spat on the floor.

"Let me get this straight. You want to be immortal so you can hate everybody forever?"

"I've got plans, yeah."

Scott seized the opportunity to throw a wrench into the works. "But there's only one vial."

Parish leaned against the open doorway, folded his lumberjack arms on his chest. "It's all I need."

"Are you forgetting Katherine?" Scott injected it like venom. "Jerry's gone to a lot of trouble to bring her back. If you ask me, I'd say he saved that vial for her."

"She don't want it."

Scott huffed. "When's that ever stopped Jerry from getting his way with her?"

Parish stiffened. "He wouldn't dare give it to her."

"I wouldn't put it past him." Scott scooped up a spoonful of stew. "But then again...I'm not you."

"You think I ain't thought of that?"

"He's walking all over you." Scott put the spoon to his lips. "You're just too dumb to see it."

"You son of a bitch."

Scott tossed the stew into his mouth, expecting the belt of cyanide. He chewed and swallowed quickly, relieved he was still breathing. "I'm just saying you'd better protect your interests."

Parish winced. "You have no idea how it pains me to say this, but you're right. Jerry's been playing me like a fish on a line. It's time I yanked him out of the boat." Parish pivoted on his boot heels. "Don't try anything stupid, Weller. I'll be back with my blaster drawn."

"Leaving so soon?" Scott said, another spoonful of stew loaded. "We were bonding so nicely."

Sneering, Parish reset the electronic lock. He didn't see Myrtle dart between his legs. Scott flinched in surprise at her sudden appearance. The door shut with a bang, plunging the room into semi-darkness.

Myrtle jumped up on the cot and sniffed the food.

Reaching out, Scott smiled, stroked her smooth fur, and savored her musky odor. "Here you go, girl." He slid the bowl of stew toward her. "Help yourself."

She selected a juicy chunk of mutton then rolled on her back, and while holding it in her front paws, she ate it noisily, one lip-smacking bite at a time.

Joining her in the feast, Scott picked up the onion soup and drank it straight from the cup. He was beginning to feel better, not only for the meal and Myrtle's safe return, but for the angry doubt he'd planted in John Parish's one-track mind.

***

Sitting behind his office desk, Jerry heard loud bootsteps approaching from down the hall. He knew it was John Parish storming through the mansion. *Now what?* He double-checked the Derringer 840 mini-blaster he kept in his top drawer. The gold and silver gun was fully charged. By the time the bounty hunter appeared in the doorway, Jerry had closed the drawer and returned his attention to an electronic file on his desk.

"I've come for my vial, Jerry."

Jerry didn't appreciate the demanding tone in Parish's voice. "Have a seat," he said, not looking up. "I'll be with you in a moment."

"Quit stallin'," Parish growled out. "Let's have it."

"I've been studying this file." Jerry flipped through the projected holographic data pages. "The Bureau of Vital Statistics supplied me with the latest inventory of living Wellers."

"I've delivered the last Weller."

"Sorry, John, the record doesn't agree."

"It's wrong. I've done my end of the deal."

"Prove it." Jerry swiveled the projector so Parish could see the hologram. "Show me death certificates for all these Wellers and I'll believe you."

"Fork over the vial or they'll be signing your death certificate."

"Look at this list."

Instead, Parish walked to the wall safe and drew his blaster. "Open it."

Though the sight of the blaster's muzzle sent a pang of fear through him, Jerry feigned calm. "You're resorting to armed robbery?"

"Call it what you like. I want my vial. Now."

"What's the rush?"

Parish scowled. "I want to make sure I get it before you give it to Katherine."

Very perceptive. Jerry inched his hand toward the top drawer. He figured he could get to his blaster unnoticed due to Parish's inadequate line of sight over the projected hologram. "What makes you think I'd give her the vial?"

"I'm not stupid," Parish hissed. "Quit wastin' my time."

"Katherine never wanted Everlife," Jerry reminded him, fingertips touching the drawer handle. "She doesn't want to live forever."

"She doesn't want to live forever with *you*, Jerry. Can't say I blame her."

"Katherine loves me. I should kill you for saying that."

"I'm shakin' all over. Now open this safe."

Jerry grasped the drawer handle, fighting back his temper. "Look at you, John." He slowly pulled the drawer open a crack. "What would your father say if he could see you now?"

"If a Weller hadn't killed him, he'd be standin' next to me, his blaster drawn along with mine."

"I don't agree." By now, Jerry had opened the drawer fully. The last thing he wanted was a shootout, but he had to protect that vial. "Your father wasn't as hotheaded as you, John. He would never go against the Parish family code."

"Screw the code."

"Shame on you." Jerry now realized the extent of Parish's resolve. "I hired your grandfather. I watched your father grow up. I hired him—"

"Screw you too."

It would come down to killing him, Jerry knew, his hand now on the mini-blaster. He'd have to deal with Dar Anders and the Council some other way. Or...? An idea dissuaded him from grabbing the blaster. He leaned back in his chair instead. "I'll tell you what," he said, thinking he'd found a way to end the stalemate. "We are in disagreement on the Weller situation, correct?"

Parish waved his blaster. "It's not up for debate."

"I'm willing to concede."

"Only with a gun to your head." Parish wagged the muzzle back and forth.

"Let's assume that Scott Dunn is the last Weller."

"He is. Open the safe."

"You won't shoot me, John, we both know that. If you do, you'll never get that safe open. It's made of titrainium amalgahyde, ten times stronger than titanium. You can't pick the locks. You can't blow it. Even a C-Dox laser won't cut it."

"Get to the point."

"Kill me and you'll never get the vial. You'll die, John, just like every other mortal."

"But you'll be dead first. I can take that to my grave."

Jerry knew Parish was bluffing. "Immortality, John. You'll have unlimited time to enjoy your yacht, cruise the world, spend the millions I've paid you for killing Wellers. Don't throw it all away now. Put the blaster down."

Parish aimed the gun at him, straight-armed. "I'm sick of your bullshit."

Swallowing hard, Jerry reassessed the mini blaster's position in the drawer, only an arm's length away. It was good as a mile. "Hear me out."

"All I want is the vial."

"There's another way to settle this disagreement, to both our satisfaction."

"Open the safe. It's the only way—"

"No." Jerry folded his arms across his chest. "You're just going to have to kill me."

Parish looked at his blaster, shook his head, dropped the useless threat to his side. "All right. I'm listening...but if I don't like what I hear, the last thing you'll see is a bright flash of light."

"We'll square all accounts on the Wellers if you do one more killing for me...personally."

Parish frowned. "Not a Weller?"

"No."

"I only kill Wellers."

Jerry knew that was a lie. "You killed Sue Masters."

Parish didn't flinch.

"Interested?"

"And after I do this killin' for you, the vial is mine, no matter how many Wellers turn up?"

Jerry nodded. "Unconditionally." Of course, that was a lie, too.

"Who's the target?"

"Dar Anders."

"On the Council of Elders?"

"Yes."

For the next few moments, Parish remained silent, traced the scar on his cheek with a manicured fingernail.

Jerry's impatience surfaced. "You have two days to accomplish the mission. He must die before he rules on the Alpha Ketari issue."

"Why do you want him killed?"

Jerry stood, leaned forward, his hands flat on the desk. "You're a hired gun, John. You don't need to know. Just do the job you're paid for."

"What are you gonna do after I kill him?"

Jerry smiled. "Give you the vial, of course."

"Good answer." Parish holstered his blaster.

Jerry had him right where he wanted him. "Just be sure you make a clean getaway."

"I never get caught," Parish said.

"I'm not implying that you're incompetent, after all, your successful attack on Carson's mine convinces me that you can pull this off."

"It's not the same thing. There's a security force at the Capitol."

"Well...if it's too much for you..."

"I can get around them."

"Of course you can." Jerry extended his hand. "Then we have a deal?"

Approaching the desk, Parish accepted Jerry's handshake. "Screw me this time, I'll kill you." His grip tightened around Jerry's hand with knuckle-crushing force.

Without wincing, Jerry glared at the bounty hunter. "I take that as a yes."

"I'll be back for the vial." Parish released Jerry's hand and stormed out of the office.

Wiggling his fingers to work out a painful cramp, Jerry retook his seat and smiled. He knew that Parish would soon be a most-wanted criminal. After the assassination, Jerry would have to rise to his patriotic duty, kill Parish, and turn his body over to the authorities. Jerry would become a national hero, which would boost his status among the citizens even higher, his election to the Council of Elders guaranteed. Alpha Ketari would soon be his new paradise...with Katherine.

***

By now, Katherine had the gist of the VCR and DVD player, the TV, and the remote control, which felt familiar in her hand though she didn't know why. Robert was a big help. He'd zoom to the machines and change the tapes and discs for her. Earlier she'd watched Navarro scan the instructions into Robert's central processor, whatever that was. The results were a wealth of information coming at her, all of which she took in greedily.

From her seat on the bed, she could fast forward, pause, and rewind the shows as she watched them. She especially liked the first movie. She'd replayed the beginning several times.

"I cannot bear to watch this again," Robert said, antennas trembling.

"Shoot her," she said, then suddenly felt a jolt of dread but didn't understand why. The more she watched, the more she realized that the movie frightened her, made her heart jump when the beast squealed. Then a chill made her shudder. The sense of fear became overwhelming. She switched to another movie.

"Smokin'." The man in the mask was funny, his girlfriend in the short dress, beautiful. She was singing on stage at the Coco Bongo Club. In Katherine's awakening mind, the scene struck a familiar chord, but she didn't know why.

Robert inserted a tape of an old TV show. *"Bad boys, bad boys, whatcha gonna do?"*

She sang along, enjoying the sound of her voice. Incredibly, as she listened to the words coming from the machine, she began to remember them. It wasn't the same thing as learning words from scratch, as a child would have to, but only dredging them up from the back of her mind. She especially liked the music. The notes, the tunes, and the strains of musical instruments seemed natural to her.

Another movie: *"I was born a coal miner's daughter."*

Katherine's mind was no longer an empty slate, but an exploding rush of information. First she'd remembered the basic things: she was a human, a female. She had fingers and toes, arms and legs. She should've had hair on her head, but she'd lost it somehow.

And her name was Katherine.

That was a big revelation, but there were a lot of blanks in her memories of who she was: her life, her education, her loves. Was she a coal miner's daughter? What was a coal miner? And she had no memory of how she'd come to Hylander. Jerry, the man who imprisoned her here, frightened her like the beast in the first movie.

"Show me the money," a man said in the movie Jerry McGuire.

What's money? Katherine wondered.

For several hours, Robert changed the tapes and discs so she could watch snippets of the movies.

"Houston, we have a problem."

"Go ahead, punk, make my day."

Soon Katherine realized she was having fun. She liked Robert, though she didn't understand how the robot could fly. He made drinks and sandwiches, and was about to serve them when heavy boots thumped down the hallway. Robert's antenna swiveled toward the door. Her heart pumped hard, like it did when she watched the first movie. "What is it, Robert?"

He zipped to the door, and with a pincher hand, opened it a crack then rushed back to the bed. *"John Parish,"* he reported. *"He looks mad."*

"Mad?"

"Angry," Robert explained. *"Make my day."*

"Angry." Katherine pressed the remote button that paused *Dirty Harry*, slid off the bed, and stalked to the open door in her bare feet.

"Katherine," Robert said. *"You must not leave the room."*

She slipped out anyway.

"Houston, we have a problem!" Robert whizzed out the door after her. *"Please, Katherine. We must go back. The odds of being undetected are..."*

"Shhh."

The big man stomped down the hallway and went into an office. Loud voices erupted from inside. Katherine moved closer to the door. She could hear their words now:

"Who's the target?" Parish's gruff voice asked.

"Dar Anders," Jerry Well said.

"On the Council of Elders?"

"Yes," Jerry replied.

Robert tugged Katherine's gown with a pincher hand. *"Please,"* he said in an electronic whisper. *"Bad boys, bad boys."*

Parish asked: "Why do you want him killed?"

"What's killed?" Katherine whispered to Robert.

"Shoot her," he said with a shudder.

She didn't understand, but she could see that the words upset Robert a great deal.

Then footsteps came toward the door.

The robot floated backwards. *"Hurry."*

She scurried after Robert, back to her room, closed the door, and immediately restarted the *Dirty Harry* movie. Sitting cross-legged on the bed, she'd barely caught her breath when the door opened. She froze.

John Parish poked his head inside. "What are you two doin'?"

"Nothing," she muttered.

"I saw you in the hall, damn it."

Hovering next to Katherine, Robert said, *"I'll give you the Broncos by eight points."*

Parish sneered. "And I'll give you a blaster bolt between your antennas."

Temples throbbing, Katherine kept her eyes on the movie. Dirty Harry pulled a gun and shot a bad boy. Blood spurted from his chest. He grimaced and fell.

"Shoot her! Shoot her! Shoot her!"

Suddenly she remembered the meaning of *killed*.

Chapter Twenty-Two

Scott awoke with a start. Lying on the wooden cot in the cellar below Hylander mansion, he felt a bone-grinding chill. Myrtle was gone. She'd been curled up on his chest when he'd fallen asleep. He feared something had spooked her.

Listening intently, he determined everything was quiet in the hallway. He sat up, tossed the blanket aside, and rubbed his shoulder. The blaster wound was healing nicely, thanks to the nanocream...and Sue.

That thought brought back her memory. From his pocket, he retrieved the incandescent picture she'd given him. He touched her face and the dimple on her chin. His heart felt like an empty oil drum, each beat a hollow thud. He clenched a fist, cursing himself for letting her get close to him. Now he missed her. The demon of grief was on the loose again, bearing down heavy on his chest. It would never let him accept Sue's death. He'd survived. She hadn't. *Guilty*, the demon snarled.

She didn't die for nothing, Scott swore in his defense. Without her, he wouldn't have gotten this close to Katherine. Now it was up to him to derail Jerry's plans to take over the Council of Elders, if he could ever get out of this damn cellar.

Just then, a scratching sound came from under the cot. Scott blinked. "Myrtle?"

More scratching.

He pocketed Sue's picture, bent over, and saw the ferret digging dirt under the cot. She held a silver object in her mouth. He reached down to take it from her.

She hissed and scooted backwards.

"What do you have there, girl?" Curiosity drove him to his knees on the dirt floor. Wondering where she'd found the item, he scrunched down and tried reaching for her. He recalled Carson saying that ferrets were great escape artists. They were able to squeeze through unbelievably small openings. And ferrets were notorious thieves. They liked to hide their booty.

"Come on, Myrtle. *Tic-tic!*"

Dirt flew in his face.

"Don't bury it." He moved the cot aside, revealing Myrtle's energetic digging. Before she realized she'd been exposed, he grabbed her by the scruff. "Gotcha." He brought her masked face up to his eyelevel. She hung there, kicking her little legs, the curious object clenched in her teeth. He seized it with his free hand and gave it a tug, but like a spoiled child, she refused to give it up. Jerking it back and forth, he was surprised at the nimbleness of her long neck. Right now he wanted to wring it.

That left him with only one alternative. Force. He released the object and put his thumb and index finger at the back of her jaws. Feeling her teeth, he gently squeezed. The constant pressure finally forced her to open her mouth and drop the object.

It was a key.

He stroked Myrtle, set her down, and picked up the key. It was lightweight, poly-carbon cast, barrel-shaped, and code-inscribed for an onboard computer. Stooping to the light seeping in from under the door, he examined it closer. It read *Ford Flyer* on the thumb-plate. He knew that meant the key fit a civilian version of the police department's flying cruisers.

There weren't many flying cars available to the general public, and for good reason. Flying them required extensive training. And though most wealthy citizens hired professional pilots, the already-jammed flight corridors couldn't handle the added traffic if everyone owned flying cars. Besides, there were huge risks involved. Gravity was unforgiving, human error a certainty. The carnage would have been greater than twentieth-century automobiles had unleashed on the highways.

Looking at the key, it didn't surprise Scott that Jerry Well owned a flying car. Problem was, having the key didn't give Scott any particular advantage. He didn't know how to fly a car. Perhaps Jerry had a professional pilot on his payroll. But who was he? And could this pilot be persuaded to help him escape?

He pocketed the key.

Myrtle went back to digging. As with most ferrets, digging was one of her favorite pastimes. Meanwhile, Scott reclined on the cot, closed his eyes, and wondered how he could escape this cellar and find Katherine.

Just then, the door lock buzzed and disengaged. Feigning sleep, he opened his eyelids a narrow bit and wondered why the door was still closed. Had someone unlocked it and left, an ally to his escape perhaps? Such was the hope of the condemned, he thought, and noticed something else. Strangely, Myrtle had curled up on the blanket, unconcerned about the intruder. He wondered if she'd lost her uncanny ability to sense danger.

Slowly, the door creaked open. A humming sound came next. Bright light beaming in through the doorway made it impossible for him to identify who was entering, so he squeezed his eyes shut, his heart racing, every nerve in his body on full alert.

The humming grew louder.

Suddenly, Myrtle lit out for the open door.

In that split second, Scott leaped up, hurled the blanket over the figure entering the room, and then dove for his legs. Unbelievably, he landed in the hallway flat on his back. Looking up, he saw the blanket hanging in mid air, draped over a hovering robot. Beeping like crazy, it was trying to cast off the blanket with pincher hands.

Scott didn't waste a second. He scrambled to his feet, turned to run, but tripped and fell. His elbow hit the tile floor. Pain shot through his body, but not from his elbow, from his ankles. They felt like they were on fire.

He rolled over, tried to kick, and then saw the device that had prevented his escape. Sparking and crackling, a taser stream was wrapped around his ankles, hogtying him with energy and biting into his flesh. The other end of the taser stream came from an appendage on the hovering robot.

"Let me go."

"Make my day," the robot said.

It was no use, Scott decided. "I give up."

By now, the robot had managed to remove the blanket

covering its camera-lens eyes, which swiveled to Scott, sprawled on the floor. *"The odds of escape are 3,000 to 1 against you."*

"I was going to the bathroom," he lied. "Let me up."

"You will not run?"

"Not while you're looking."

The taser stream blinked out. His ankles burned. He sat up and rubbed them vigorously. "What do you want?"

"Return to your room at once."

Scott found his feet, rose unsteadily. Hands in the air like a criminal, he staggered past the robot. "I don't want any trouble."

"I do not trust you."

"Feeling's mutual."

"Then how about a game? Pick a card, any card."

Scott examined the robot. It was a strange-looking unit with a cylindrical body, multiple appendages, and a chest-mounted display depicting a fanned-out deck of cards. "You came here to play card games?"

"I brought your breakfast. You must be hungry."

"Yes." He sat on the cot, wondering where Myrtle had gone. She was probably hungry too.

A steaming food tray ejected from a port on the robot, which extended it to him with three pincher hands on telescopic arms. *"Eggs marloff, pork stew, and apricots. I hope you like your coffee black."*

Taking the tray, Scott wondered, *What are eggs marloff?* Then he wondered why a robot was guarding him instead of the bounty hunter. If he'd left Hylander, then Scott's chances for escape had improved. "Where's John Parish?"

"Would you like to play a quick game of 21?"

"I asked you a direct question, robot."

"I am not a robot. I am a cyber-bot. My name is Robert."

Scott didn't know the difference, didn't care. "Just tell me where he is, Robert."

"Perhaps a roll of the dice?"

Obviously, the cyber-bot had a gambling problem. Scott considered that observation for a moment then decided he wasn't getting through to Robert any other way. "Sure. Why not?"

"Thumb print, please."

After licking his thumb, he pressed it to a square field on Robert's chest display. It recorded his fingerprint and DNA for Starnet's bank-drafting system, same as all electronic financial transactions were handled. The *ker-ching* sound of a cash register followed. Then two tumbling dice appeared, a three-dimensional holograph projected from a gem-port centered in the robot's chest, plus a round button labeled *TOSS*. *"Press the button to play."*

Scott leaned back. "First, tell me where John Parish went."

"The game is in progress," Robert announced flatly.

The dice kept tumbling.

"John Parish, Robert."

"Press the button to play," he demanded.

"If you don't tell me, I won't play."

"My circuits will run in a loop until you press the button."

"You don't say," Scott said, thinking he'd found Robert's Achilles heel.

"You must finish the game in progress," Robert shrieked. *"It takes priority over all other functions."*

The dice tumbled. Scott glanced at the open cellar door, thought about bolting, but changed his mind when he remembered the odds stacked against him: three thousand to one. He decided information about Parish's whereabouts was more important, especially if he planned to rescue Katherine and escape Hylander. Leaning forward, he pressed Robert harder. "Tell me what John Parish is up to, or your gambling days are over."

Robert responded with an electronic shout. *"All right. He went to Washington."*

"Why?"

"I have a recording that will explain," Robert said. *"But the game is running. I cannot play it."*

Scott hadn't heard panic in an electronic voice before. Obviously, Robert had been programmed with emotional responses. He wasn't just a run-of-the-mill cyber-bot, he was something special, but even so, Scott wasn't going to let him off easy. "How much is the wager?"

"One hundred dollars."

"Make it five dollars."

"I cannot pay Starnet's processing fee with that."

"Too bad."

"All right, five it is. Press the button."

Scott pressed *TOSS*. The electronic dice clattered, bounced, and stopped.

"Seven," Robert sang. *"You lose."*

Scott didn't take Robert's glee personally. He knew the cyber-bot's response to the dice was preprogrammed. But he did take offense when Robert said, *"Well, I must be going now,"* and whirled around.

"Oh no you don't." Scott kicked the cellar door shut.

Robert emitted a shrieking beep. *"You have locked us in."*

"You haven't answered my question."

"I cannot work the door's keypad remotely."

"Why did John Parish go to Washington?"

Robert's camera-lens eyes swiveled back and forth between Scott and the closed door. *"Very well,"* he said with a tone of defeat in his voice. *"I did not think you should see this. It is very disturbing. You have enough to worry about."*

"Thanks a lot," Scott said, noting that Robert showed empathy for his situation, definitely not a robotic trait.

Another hologram projection shot out from the gemport and angled to the ground. Images of Jerry Well and John Parish appeared in miniature.

Jerry said: "We'll square all accounts on the Wellers if you do one more killing for me...personally."

Parish: "Who's the target?"

Jerry: "Dar Anders."

The hologram flickered off.

Scott could hardly breathe. Now he knew how Jerry Well planned on vacating a Council seat. "I have to get out of here."

"I will help you."

Sure you will, Scott thought, still feeling the sting of Robert's taser lasso. He couldn't see any reason to trust the cyber-bot. Besides, Jerry Well could have sent him in as a spy. He was probably monitoring their conversation right now. "You aren't programmed to turn against your owner."

"You do not know me. I am programmed to think, make judgments, weigh the odds, decide, and act."

"You're a gambling machine."

"You are right, but I am also the only friend you have."

"We are not friends," Scott said, thinking the notion impossible. A cyber-bot...his friend? Sue was his friend...his heart sank...was his friend. "You're Jerry Well's servant."

"We have had a falling-out. My loyalty program is no longer running."

"You're not concerned that Jerry might hear you say that?"

"I am only afraid of data-fragmentation."

Scott doubted the cyber-bot could be afraid of anything. Fear was much too primal a human emotion to be programmed into a machine. But as long as the cyber-bot was feeling brave, Scott decided to ask him a question that was sure to get a response from Jerry Well, if he were listening in. "Where can I find Katherine?"

Robert's antennas tilted forward. *"Katherine?"*

Expecting alarms to go off, Scott pressed the issue. "I need to get her out of here too."

Robert said, *"I recorded this last night."* Again the hologram flickered on. Jerry Well's image appeared, this time with fists balled and standing over Katherine. She lay crumpled at his feet, weeping.

Scott jumped up, knocked over his breakfast tray. "Why are you showing me this?"

"So you will know her terrible situation."

It was worse than Scott imagined. The fact that Robert

showed him Katherine's plight proved the cyber-bot had her best interests at heart. And though it sounded ridiculous, Scott believed Robert actually had a heart. He cared. Feeling a bit awkward, Scott offered his hand to the cyber-bot. "I was wrong about you."

Robert beeped happily, extended a telescopic arm and shook Scott's hand. *"Friend?"*

The connection between man and machine had never been more profound, Scott thought, carbon alloy and human flesh, bonded. "How are we going to get out of here, my friend?"

"I know where Katherine is."

Bam, Bam, Bam!

"What's going on in there?"

Scott's heart seized. Jerry Well was pounding on the door. He'd been monitoring his cyber-bot, all right, just as Scott had suspected. Now they were in big trouble.

The lock released, and the door swung open. Jerry stormed in with three heavily armed security-bots. "You're not touching Katherine, you hear me?"

"How could you beat her like that?" Scott shouted.

"Shut up, Weller."

"You don't deserve her."

The security-bots surrounded Scott, brandishing their weapons, their optic-lens eyes glowing red. He didn't dare move.

Glaring at Robert, Jerry looked as if he would explode, his face mottled with rage. Scott saw the reason why. Robert hadn't turned off the hologram. Katherine's battered image was still sobbing on the floor at Jerry's feet.

"You double-crossing bastard." Jerry shoved Robert

backwards. The hologram stuttered and shut off, but the audio continued, Katherine's cries still resonating in the air. From a pocket, Jerry withdrew a silver chip, pointed it at Robert like a gun. "Turn it off."

Robert beeped frantically, vibrated and clattered. His circuits were under so much stress that he was incapable of responding.

"Turn it off."

Scott saw the cyber-bot's fear, felt helpless to save him.

"I warned you." Jerry squeezed the chip. It made a zapping sound. With an oscillating whine, Robert sank to the floor. All his lights went out, his display blinked off, and Katherine's weeping faded away.

Scott backed against the wall, feeling as if he'd just witnessed a murder.

Whirling around, Jerry pointed a manicured finger at Scott. "Tomorrow at noon, you are going to meet your fate." He stalked out, his mechanical goons in tow. The door slammed shut.

Numb with shock, Scott slumped to the cot and stared at his dead friend, Robert, the last friend he had left in the world.

Chapter Twenty-Three

I n the foothills west of Boulder, dawn came with a chill, the buzzing of insects and the occasional screech of a jay. Sue tested the movement of her left arm, pulled back the makeshift bandage, and inspected the wound to her chest. Last night, she had treated it with nanocream, propped herself against a tree, and fallen asleep.

This morning, the four-inch swath of disintegrated flesh had already begun to fill in. Color had returned to the surrounding skin: from charred black and gray to red and pink. This told her the nanocytes had restored circulation to the damaged tissue. It didn't hurt much. She assumed the *Electros* had rerouted the damaged nerve pathways. Other than a raging hunger, she felt good.

Getting to her feet, she moved to the wrecked mineshaft. She had to get inside to properly take care of her grandfather's body. There was no time to grieve for him, not now, not with Scott's life in peril, and Katherine's, and likely the future of mankind. She knew the risks of getting inside Hylander. She feared what would happen if she failed: Scott would die at the hands of Jerry Well. With those concerns pressing on her mind, she grabbed a rappelling rope and began the treacherous descent into the mine.

Twenty minutes passed before she made it to the main floor and the freight elevator. There, she found a hover-lifter and rode it up to the platform where Carson's body lay sprawled on the floor. Batting away flies, she engaged the grappling straps around his five hundred pound body. Groaning, the lifter lowered him to the main floor. She did everything in accordance to his last wishes, simple and fast: no flowers, no prayers, no tears. The latter she'd never promised him.

As she stood over his body, she remembered his laughter, his kindness, and his words of wisdom. She knelt beside him, fighting back tears. "I'm sorry, Grandpa. I'm sorry we couldn't protect you from John Parish." She swallowed. "We're not going to let him win, I promise. Scott and I..." A strange feeling drifted through her, talking to grandpa this way. Death had closed his eyes, but she believed he was listening. "I love Scott, Grandpa...and I love you too...always." She sniffled and stood. "Gotta go now." It was hard to leave him, but she had no choice.

After changing into her red riding leathers, she found a Snickers bar and pushed her cycle onto the elevator platform. One last look around, one last inventory: Myrtle was with Scott, the few clothes she had here she didn't need, most anything else of value the bounty hunters had looted or destroyed. There was nothing left for her here, no reason to ever return. Sadly, she punched a special code on the keypad then pressed the UP button.

Topside, she retrieved Scott's sport bag, straddled the cycle, and started the engine. Speeding away under full power, she heard the mine explode behind her, a mighty blast that shook the ground and belched smoke from the resulting crater. The hillside above the mineshaft collapsed and filled in the hole.

"Goodbye, Grandpa." She couldn't get away fast enough. Stinging tears clouded her vision of the road ahead. She wished she could accelerate to a million miles an hour and disintegrate into infinity. But instead, she gritted her teeth and eased back on the throttle. Her grandfather had taught her to make her choices wisely and accept her fate, whatever it might be. Now she had to go on without him. There was nothing she could do to change that. But Scott needed her now. She couldn't let him die. Not without a fight.

Chapter Twenty-Four

On the television screen in Katherine's room, a girl in pigtails sat on a fence and sang: *Somewhere over the rainbow...* Angry storm clouds gathered in the background, the wind rising.

"You'll do as I say," Jerry shouted.

Katherine cowered at his feet. Again, the sanctity of her room had been brutally invaded. Her dress was torn and her lip dripped blood onto the back of her trembling hand. And for what, Alpha Ketari, Eternal Hylander, the Council of Elders? These things meant nothing to her. Why should she agree to help him? "I don't want anything to do with you."

He struck her again, an open-handed blow to the back of her head. "Show some respect for your husband."

"Why are you doing this to me?" she sobbed out.

"You've turned Robert against me."

The spew from his pores stunk...of garlic she now remembered.

"And Scott Dunn is here to interfere with my plans."

Tears blurred her vision. "That's not my fault. I don't even know him."

"You lie. I saw the look in your eyes. You wanted him, didn't you."

Hauntingly, she suddenly understood his words, his accusations of infidelity. Like a nightmare, everything came back in a rush: the badgering, the beatings, and Jerry's incessant obsession with having complete control over her, control over everything. And she remembered the penalty for talking back to him, but even that pain didn't hold her tongue. "He was hurt, that's all. I just wanted to help him."

"And look at the trouble you've caused." The angrier he got, the more he stunk. He struck her again.

Horrid memories of pain and humiliation flooded her mind. She remembered being locked in a dark room. Alone. Crying. Then bright lights surrounded her, and cheering crowds, and then a voice came to her, a singing voice: it was her voice. She was standing on a stage...like the Coco Bongo Club. A microphone appeared in her hand. She was singing, *"I will always love you..."*

Applause.

He kicked her. "Now you're going to pay for cheating on me."

Pain.

She couldn't draw a breath, felt bitter cold, and recalled the image of Jerry Well's snarling face looming above her. Fighting for air, she couldn't move. She remembered lying on her back in a tub. Jerry was covering her with ice. Encroaching darkness covered her like a thick blanket, the will to live seeping from her consciousness. She remembered how she'd died, her helplessness, her anger.

"No." A bolt of rage surged through her. She rolled over, started kicking and screaming.

"Stop it, Katherine." He grabbed one of her feet.

"Leave me alone."

"You don't understand how much I love you."

Love? His love sickened her. She kicked him.

"Cooperate, Katherine. You'll be much happier."

"I hate you."

"Don't make me hit you again. You know how much it hurts me."

"Liar. Losing control, now that's what hurts you. Even when I was dying of West Nile B, you refused to let me go. And look at you now, trying to control me again. It's not going to work this time—"

He dropped down on her, put a heavy knee on her belly. "Listen to me, you little slut." His snarling face came close to hers, that murderous face. His garlicky stench was too putrid to be near. "You're the only reason I haven't killed Scott Dunn."

Gasping under his weight, she managed, "What...?"

"It's simple, really. Cooperate with me, he lives. Cross me, he dies. His blood will be on your hands, not mine. Do you understand?"

"You can't...mean that."

"You're powerless to stop me."

"Robert," she called out. "Help me."

Jerry laughed, produced a silver chip from his pocket, and displayed it to her pinched between his fingers. "I've de-energized him."

"He was my only friend." She swung a clenched fist, struck his hand. The chip flew across the room and slid under the bed.

"You bitch." He slugged her. "That chip is fragile."

Pain, but she still fought back. "I hope I broke it."

He grabbed both her wrists and pinned them to the floor. "There's no one left to save you."

She turned her head, arched her back, and tried to throw him off.

"It's your destiny, Katherine. Face it. Together, we will hold the Chair on the Council of Elders. Soon, we will leave this sick planet for Alpha Ketari, live and prosper forever at Eternal Hylander. When this is over, you will thank me."

She spit on him.

Spittle dripped off his cheek. "That will get Scott Dunn killed."

"What did he ever do to you?"

"He tried to take you away from me."

Take me away? She couldn't understand why a stranger would do that...unless... "He came to rescue me?"

"You stupid whore. He was going to kill you."

That made no sense. "I was already dead." She squirmed harder. "Get off me."

"Promise to cooperate first."

"I won't."

"Then Scott Dunn will die."

She remembered his face, that look of astonishment when he first saw her. His hands were bound, and he was coughing. She'd felt the urge to kneel beside him, to touch him, but she didn't know why. Now the last thing she wanted was to cause his death. "All right," she whispered.

"I didn't hear you promise, Katherine."

"I promise," she shouted, nearly gagging on his garlicky spew. "I'll do whatever you want...as long as you don't hurt Scott Dunn."

"Kiss me." His lips came nearer to hers.

She turned her head away. "Promise me he won't be harmed in any way."

Mute, he came closer.

Again, she bucked and squirmed. Her arms were pinned solidly.

His hot breath brushed her cheek.

She felt the sting of tears in her eyes. Oh God, please don't let him do this.

His lips moved in.

"No."

He mashed his mouth on hers.

Writhing underneath him, she wished Scott Dunn had succeeded in saving her from this hellish life.

***

This time, a real security-bot, armed to the electrodes, brought Scott's dinner to the cellar. Scott lifted the domed lid, saw the porterhouse steak he'd requested, baked potato, and chocolate cake: his last meal.

Thinking about that moment of death, when his final breath was drawn, his appetite left him. He'd lived two hundred forty eight years, some good...but mostly bad. In less than twenty-four hours, his battle with the grief demon would be over.

The security-bot left the room in semi-darkness. In the corner, Robert's stiff form was but a motionless shadow. Myrtle hadn't been around all day. He wondered where she was, what trouble she'd gotten into. He set aside the tray, lay on his back, and thought about her, his only link to his recent past, to Sue and her grandfather. Myrtle was all he had left of them. Then Carson's last words haunted him again: *"There is another..."* Another what? Another life? Another love? The dying man made no sense.

Suddenly, a tinny crash shattered the silence, launching Scott to his feet. The dome that once covered his food tray was rolling in circles on the floor, like a thrown hubcap. His heart did summersaults until he saw Myrtle dragging the porterhouse steak across the cot.

"You little thief." He chuckled. "Let me help you with that."

A tug-of-war ensued. Hissing, she managed to tear off a small portion of meat. In sheer ecstasy, she rolled over and gnashed away at her meal with razor-sharp teeth.

Scott sighed. It was good to have her back. His spirits lightened, he bit off a chunk of steak for himself. That's when he saw a glint of silver on the blanket. Myrtle had found something else. When he picked it up, he recognized the device immediately. It was the electronic chip Jerry Well had used to silence Robert. Where did Myrtle find it?

Flipping it over in his hand, he felt the smooth surface, the convex button in the center, and wondered if the chip worked in reverse. *It's worth a try.* He aimed it at the stilled robot and hoped the device wasn't programmed with a *DESTRUCT* command. Holding his breath, he pushed the button.

Robert's lights blinked on. His display glowed dimly, flickered. He muttered a beep. *"What happened?"*

Scott rushed forward, amazed. "Are you all right?"

Robert's hover engine whined to life, and he sprang into the air, his brilliant energy illuminating the room with the colors of Christmas. *"I'm alive. I'm alive."* He spun like a top, snapped pincher hands, and wagged his antennas. *"Show me the money."*

"Calm down, will you?" Scott said. "You're going to bring the bots down on us."

"Pick a card, any card." His display showed cards flying everywhere. *"How about a number from one to ten?"*

"How about getting us out of here?"

"The odds of escape are a 3,000 to 1, an unacceptable wager."

At that, Scott showed him the flyer key. "Does this mean anything to you?"

Robert's camera-lens eyes extended to zoom. He made a whistling sound. *"Ford Thunderclap 9000. Where did you get the key?"*

"Myrtle found it. Now all I need is the car and a pilot."

Robert hovered upright, his appendages bent in pincher-hand salutes. *"At your service, sir."*

"You? You're a pilot?"

"I am programmed and certified to operate over seventy models of autocars and flyers. Professional chauffeur number 4411-B12." His display began scrolling a list of credentials. *"I was once a valuable asset to Jerry Well. I am currently seeking new employment."*

After the way Jerry had treated him, Scott understood why. But still, as pilots went, he preferred humans to robots. Machines, no matter how sophisticated, could never be programmed to handle every situation. "Don't look at me for a job."

"I can pilot the flyer."

"I don't have a flyer."

"You have the key to Beta-Alpha-Twelve...Jerry Well's flying car."

"Do you know where it is?"

"Of course, but the odds are 34-1 that we do not make it to the garage."

Holding the key out to Robert, Scott frowned. "Without this, the odds were 3,000 to 1 against us. What's the matter, Robert? I thought you were a gambler."

Robert backed up. *"Only when the risks are acceptable."*

"What are the chances of getting out of this cellar?"

"We cannot."

Myrtle sprang to her hind legs. She tested the air with a probing nose, her whiskers bristling, her ears perked. Frantically, she scampered to the edge of the bed, reared up again, sniffed and ran back the other way. There was something outside, something she sensed. She skittered back and forth, her excitement palpable.

Alarms went off in Scott's head. "What is it, girl?"

She looked directly at him, squeaked, and sprang for the wedge of light under the door. It happened so fast: she flattened her body, squeezed through the impossibly small crack, and was gone.

Chapter Twenty-Five

Scampering along the hallway baseboard, Myrtle felt the slippery tile beneath her paws and the rush of air over the fur on her face. She had a good feel for the place already. She'd spent her time away from Scott wisely, exploring the house, the garden, and the vast plain of grass that stretched out to the great wall. Her mind was on the wall. She had to get there. The familiar whining sound was coming from beyond it. She didn't understand what caused the sound, but she knew that whenever she heard it, Sue would soon appear.

Myrtle stopped at the bottom of the stairs, heard voices, and sniffed the air warily. The humans weren't hard to avoid, but the fire-spitting robots worried her. They had sensors that humans didn't have. It was harder to sneak past them. She had to be extra careful when they were around.

In spite of the danger, she scampered up the stairs and skittered across a carpeted floor, dashing between the furniture funhouses and on toward the kitchen with its wonderful aromas. In a relatively short time, she had mentally mapped out her new territory. She now considered this her home. And there had been good reason for her urgency in settling in. Disorientation. It was the downfall of being a ferret.

The Grief Syndrome

Instinctively, she liked to roam and explore, as all ferrets do. It was fun. But like all ferrets, she could easily become lost. Most dogs and cats knew their way home, but she could easily forget where she'd come from, end up exploring aimlessly, and never return. Her last owner had taught her to investigate her territory, establish her boundaries, and stay within them. It was a matter of survival in the mine.

Squeezing under a kitchen cabinet, she pressed on toward her new boundary, the great wall. She'd been there several times, poked around inside it, and found some interesting holes and cracks to explore. But she never went any farther. Beyond the wall, it was noisy with moving machines and the bustle of humans, something scary and unfamiliar.

She slinked through a mouse hole, dashed across the concrete flat, the whine driving her onward. After bounding down the stone steps, she darted into the garden. Nothing could persuade her to stop and play, not the hose coiled on the nearby lawn, not all the soft dirt she loved to dig, nothing. Her focus was concentrated on that familiar sound.

In her haste, she didn't sense the danger slithering through the garden in search of a meal.

***

Hylander looked like an impenetrable fortress. Sue sat on her idling cycle fifty feet from the main entrance and contemplated the impossible task before her: the fourteen-foot-tall iron gates and twenty-foot-high walls. She thought she'd have better luck jumping over the moon. But somehow, she had to get inside. She had to rescue Scott

Dunn.

City squalor had grown up to the base of the wall. Rundown tenement buildings, strip-malls, and hydrogen dispensing terminals cluttered the area. Dense traffic clogged the streets. As she scanned the scene, the sun beat down on her helmet. Sweat leaked over her brows and stung her eyes. Her chest wound ached. She felt mentally and physically exhausted.

Engaging the cycle drive, she accelerated around a line of slow-moving cars, their occupants gawking at the formidable landmark before them. Jerry Well was more famous than ever now. People flocked to Hylander in hopes of getting a glimpse of him. They were all in her way.

She turned down a side street that paralleled the wall, careful to keep Scott's sport bag from slipping off the hydrogen fuel cell. Dodging vehicles and pedestrians, she motored down a hundred yard length of the wall. Its footing was landscaped with small evergreens, waist-high bushes, and riverbed rock. She looked for a place to breach the wall, but it shot straight up, smooth as glass. A thick cap hung over the upper edge, extending outward a good five feet. Coils of electrified barbed wire lined the protrusion. Above the cap, parapets and guard towers were evenly spaced along the upper rim. These fortifications were duplicated as far down the wall as she could see.

Dismayed, she turned the cycle around, ran a second pass, stopped, idled the whining engine, and observed the guards patrolling on top of the wall. They were heavily armed with rifles and blasters. Security-bots hovered among the guards, and Honda Walkers too, black and menacing. Everything looked exactly as she'd expected.

She recalled telling Scott that he couldn't get into Hylander. Now, here she was hoping to do the thing she'd said was impossible. The more she looked, the less hope she held. Perhaps the only way in was to knock on the front door.

She killed the engine, tore off her helmet, and welcomed the fresh air on her sweating face. Her chest wound throbbed, but she was thankful it didn't interfere with her movement.

As traffic inched around her, an impatient man blew his horn. She decided to get out of traffic, pushed the cycle off the road, and wedged it between a tree and a bush. Sport bag strap over her shoulder, she emerged and headed for the front gates, her future uncertain.

Just then, a darting movement in the bushes caught her attention: long and sleek, black and silver. It was Myrtle. Sue couldn't believe it. She bent down. "Come here, girl. *Tic-tic!*"

The ferret was a bundle of energy, jumping up and down, running circles around her. It was heartwarming the way Myrtle reacted to her.

Sue gathered her up and wondered how Myrtle knew she was out here. It must've been the familiar sound of the hydrogen cycle, she surmised.

Nuzzling Sue's neck, Myrtle squirmed and chattered. She was almost impossible to hold. "What is it, sweetheart?" Sue had never seen her act this way. "It's all right. Settle down." Something had her in a tizzy. Perhaps it was Scott.

At that, she tucked Myrtle under her arm, opened the sport bag, and rummaged through it until she found the micro-transceivers. She put one in her ear and heard static. The frequency was clear. She showed the other transceiver to Myrtle. "What's that?" she teased.

Interested, Myrtle sniffed the offered prize.

"Do you want it?"

Myrtle opened her mouth to snatch it, but Sue moved it out of her reach. "It's mine." She knew that Myrtle loved to steal things. She preferred electronic devices and anything shiny. Remotes were her specialty, both handhelds and chips. She'd usually hide them, but sometimes she'd entice grandpa or her to play keep-away. Sue hoped that Myrtle would take the transceiver to Scott.

"You want it?" The more she teased her, the more Myrtle wanted the transceiver. Worked into a frenzy, she started clawing at Sue's arm to get at it. Finally, Sue let her take it.

Myrtle hissed and hit the ground running. Sue watched her scamper behind a bush and dart into a small crack at the base of the wall.

Listening to static in her ear, Sue closed the sport bag and waited.

***

Myrtle squeezed through a dark crevice in the great wall and made it to daylight on the other side. She relished the new prize clamped between her teeth, and she couldn't wait to bury it. In an all-out sprint, she had her mind set on the room with the dirt floor.

Dashing into the garden, she skittered left and right, dodging leafy plants and corn stalks. The loose dirt gave way under her hurried feet. She yearned to dig into it, bury her prize right away. The only reason she didn't was her fear of not finding it again in this vast jungle of rowed vegetation. Her prize was too valuable to lose. It was from Sue.

Blinding bursts of sunlight shot down through a leafy canopy. She scampered along a valley of soft dirt, her direction set for the mouse hole that would take her inside the house. Breathing rapidly, she heard the air whistle as it rushed past the prize locked in her teeth. She was getting thirsty and tired. A nap would be in order after this—

The motion came out of nowhere. If she'd had to think to react, it would have been too late. Instinct made her jump. She screeched and dropped the prize. The flash of fangs, she'd seen it. The hiss of viper's breath, she'd felt it. But quick on her feet, she'd escaped being bitten.

Her first reaction was to run. But the prize had flown off into the dirt. She couldn't leave it behind. It was much too valuable. She stopped, whirled around, and moved side-to-side, sniffing the dirt, keeping one wary eye on the troublesome snake.

Tongue flicking, it rolled forward on tense coils of scale and muscle, its tail rattling, is broad head cocked above its diamondback body.

In spite of the menace, she searched for the prize. Rattlesnakes were nothing new to Myrtle. She'd run across them in the mine on many occasions, though those snakes had been much smaller than the monster coiled before her now. She wasn't afraid, just cautious. Nosing the dirt, she felt bold and a little crazy, especially now, desperately searching for her dropped prize...from Sue.

The snake struck. She saw its open mouth coming at

her, white throat and ivory fangs. But the big snake was no match for her agile frame and lightning reflexes. The fangs missed her by a mile.

Frantically, she kept scouring the dirt, to-and-fro, searching. Her fur stood on end. Her tail was a bottlebrush. The snake struck again. Myrtle bolted back.

The prize. The prize. She had to find the prize.

Coiling and moving sideways, the rattler pressed its attack again and again.

Myrtle circled the snake, still searching.

Swiveling, the viper's head followed her every move, tail rattle rattling.

Then she saw her prize. It was half buried under the snake's coiled body. It struck. She jumped straight up off the ground. Dust leaped into the air. With her little heart drumming, she landed on all fours and lunged forward with a toothy mock attack, chattering madly.

But the snake held its ground, struck again.

Leaping sideways, she escaped the fangs then dashed in to snatch the prize even as the snake's long body unfurled. But the motion of her charge caused the snake to twist. Suddenly her prize disappeared under the snake's coils. She was forced to veer away.

In an instant, the snake recoiled like a finely tuned killing machine.

Now Myrtle knew there was only one way to recover her prize. She'd have to kill the snake. But the risks were high. She was no mongoose, and this was no cobra. The rattler's venom was twelve times more powerful. Worse, the snake had ten pounds over her two. Oblivious to all this, she bared her teeth and attacked, pounced on its monstrous coils and retreated, again and again, circling, attacking, nipping and scratching. Rattling with fury, the snake struck, more in self-defense than with intent to procure a meal.

By now, a cloud of dust choked the kill zone. In the chaos, the snake panicked. Every strike left it weaker, its recoil time slower. Around and around Myrtle ran, hissing, assaulting, retreating, a continuous barrage of fur, teeth and claws. Blood oozed from the snake here and there, but the monster stood its ground atop the prize, swiveling and reeling, rattling and striking.

It wasn't long before disorientation set in. Myrtle ran in front of the snake; the snake looked behind. She ran behind; the snake looked in front. By the time it whipped around, she was gone. Now the confused snake looked left and right, unaware that Myrtle was poised to attack from behind. In an instant, she sprung for the snake's neck.

Her jaws clamped down. Teeth crushed bone.

The snake went into fits, rolling and thrashing its long body about, and flinging Myrtle around like a rag in the dirt. But she wouldn't let go, not until the snake lay still, and even then, not until the dust had settled. She gulped air hard and fast between clenched teeth. Every muscle in her body ached.

After a few minutes of calm, she released the snake's broken neck, sniffed the length of its limp body and sneezed. This was the biggest snake she'd ever killed. As she pawed blood from her face, she remembered the prize.

Nosing around, she found it in the dirt. Without another thought for the snake, she again bounded off toward the house.

***

In the shadow of Hylander's wall, Sue leaned against her cycle and watched the traffic go by. A half hour had passed. Cooler now, she wondered if Myrtle had found Scott or if she'd gotten sidetracked by something to play with.

Then the transceiver crackled in her ear. "Sue, are you there?"

"Scott." She cupped her hand over her ears to block out the traffic noise. "You're alive." Her heart raced, excited at the sound of his voice.

"I thought you were dead."

"You're not that lucky."

"But I saw Parish shoot you."

"He missed," she lied. "Are you all right?"

"Now I am."

He sounded breathless with relief. That was proof enough that he cared about her, another crack in his stone. She heard a beep. "What's that noise?"

"Robert. He's a cyber-bot."

"Have you seen Katherine?"

"She's not doing well. I need my laser pen to get out of here. Do you have it?"

Quickly, Sue pawed through the sport bag. "I've got it."

"Call Myrtle back."

Sue pictured Scott holding the transceiver to Myrtle's ear. "Come on, girl. *Tic-tic!*"

"She's just lying here all tuckered out."

"I've got an idea." Sue started the cycle engine,

revved it up, and let it idle. "What's she doing now?"

"She's gone."

A few minutes later, Myrtle appeared. She looked as if she'd been rolling in dirt. "She's here, Scott."

"Hurry."

Sue showed Myrtle the laser pen. It was bigger than the micro-transceiver but smaller than a hologram remote. Myrtle could manage it, Sue thought, but not without difficulty.

Myrtle chomped down on the laser pen and ran off.

Sue called back to Scott. "She's on her way."

Chapter Twenty-Six

This time, Sue's gift was harder to get through the jagged crack in the great wall. Myrtle had dropped it several times. Dashing through the garden now, she was especially on the lookout for snakes. What she found was much worse.

Security-bots.

"Spread out," a guard ordered them. They'd found the dead snake. "Search the grounds. That ferret has to be around here somewhere."

Security-bots took off in every direction.

Myrtle pressed on.

Suddenly, shrieking fireballs rained from the sky. Greenery caught fire. Geysers of dirt sprayed up behind her. Nearly blinded by fear, she abandoned the relative safety of the garden in favor of the fastest route to the house. At top speed, she cut a zigzag path across the open lawn. Fiery divots flew up all around her. She felt the heat of a blast that knocked her hind legs out from under her. Rolling out of control, she was determined not to drop the prize. Regaining her feet, she ran, expending every bit of energy she could muster. The house was dead ahead.

But when she reached the mouse hole, she had to stop because she couldn't wriggle through it with the prize clamped lengthways in her mouth. Complicating the dilemma, shrieking bolts of heat again exploded all around her. She set down the prize from Sue, ducked inside the hole, turned around under the cabinet and returned to the opening to grab it endwise...when disaster struck.

"What do we have here?"

She saw a human bend down and pick up the prize. Instinctively, she scooted backward.

"A laser pen? Where the hell would a ferret get one of these things...unless..." He spun around. "Search the perimeter. Someone is out there helping Scott Dunn."

Security-bots sped off.

"And somebody plug this hole."

She lunged forward to attack the thieving human, but just then the opening went dark. Mud splatter hit her in the face. The hole was blocked. She didn't have time to dig out the mud. There was only one thing left to do. Run around the other way.

She came out from under a cupboard and dashed across the kitchen floor. Voices yelped in alarm. By the time she made it halfway across the carpeted room, the human who'd stolen her prize rushed in. "There it is."

She tore toward him, fully intent on drawing blood until security-bots rushed in with raised weapons.

The human shouted, "No shooting in the house."

Fearing the rain of fire, she abruptly reversed direction and headed for the stairs.

Dashing down the steps, she heard security-bot joints clicking behind her.

"Get it, you fools."

She hit the tile floor running, slipping and sliding,

clawing for traction. They were almost on her. There was no time to make it down the hall to the room with the dirt floor. In a flash, she scooted under the nearest door she came to. It was a room full of furniture and boxes. *What a lovely playground.*

Suddenly, the door flew open.

She found a place to hide.

***

"Now we've got you," Jerry Well shouted and turned to his squad of security-bots. "Find it. I want that ferret dead."

The mechanical mob set down their weapons and went to work unloading the closet. They communicated in tones, coordinating their efforts. Hovering bots flew out of the closet with boxes grasped in their grippers. Four Honda Walkers lifted a desk and walked it out on stilt-like legs. A parade of chairs, panels, and spare displays went by. Then a roll of carpet came next and an old stationary bike Jerry had forgotten he owned...and then a couch and more boxes.

***

Scott heard a commotion in the hall outside his room. It sounded like a wrecking crew at work. He got up from the cot, and pressing his ear to the door, he wished he had his laser pen to cut out the locking mechanism. "Myrtle should have been back by now."

Robert made a forlorn buzzing sound. *"Your little friend is in big trouble,"* he reported, hovering behind him.

Alarmed, he turned around. "How do you know?"

"The security-bots are talking to each other in tones.

They are looking for your ferret. Seems she is trapped in a closet."

"We've got to help her." But Scott didn't know how. In desperation, he started pounding on the door. "Jerry Well, you son of a bitch. Leave my ferret alone." He kept pounding. "Jerry, do you hear me?"

Beeping hysterically, Robert backed into the corner and vibrated with fear.

"Jerry, you chicken-shit bastard." More pounding. "I'll kill you."

***

Junk from the closet piled up in the hallway. "Hurry," Jerry shouted at his mechanical assassins. "I want that little rat."

Over the clamor, he heard pounding on the cellar door. "I'll kill you," Scott Dunn shouted. "Do you hear me?"

Jerry smirked as he supervised the closet's excavation. The Weller was talking tough for a man in his position. Come noon, Scott would be out of the way for good, Jerry mused, in spite of what he'd told Katherine. As long as she thought Scott was alive, Jerry figured he'd have some measure of control over her.

"Put that old hover mattress down there," he instructed two of his security-bots. Several minutes passed. More tables and chairs were thrown into the heap.

Scott Dunn kept pounding on the door, screaming threats that Jerry thought ludicrous.

Suddenly, the security-bots stopped their work, stood around and hovered nearby, dumbly.

Jerry moved to the doorway and looked inside. There was nothing but bare walls and an empty floor. The ferret was gone. Rage tore through his body. He'd lost control of the situation. The ferret had made him look like a fool. It was Scott Dunn's fault for bringing that rat to Hylander.

**

Scott heard heavy footsteps approaching the door.

"Jerry is coming," Robert said.

Scott whirled around with the silver deactivation chip pinched in his fingers and pointed at Robert. "Sorry, pal, but I don't want him to see you reactivated."

BEEP.

He pushed the button. Robert blacked out and settled to the floor.

At the same time, the lock clicked and the door flew open, knocking Scott backwards. He dropped the chip. Jerry was on him like a wild bear. They slammed into the wall and fell onto the wooden cot, smashing it to splinters.

"I've had enough of your interference," Jerry growled, his sinewy hands clamped around Scott's throat. "And that rat of a ferret you brought here."

Gagging, Scott tried to wrench himself free. He began to see spots. Clenching his jaw, he jammed a knee into Jerry's stomach. It had no affect on his extremely fit body. Then Scott hammered Jerry's ribs with a fist. The man didn't even flinch. Straining his eyes sideways, Scott reached out, looked for a scrap of wood from the broken cot, anything he could use as a weapon. A glint of silver in the dirt caught his eye. It was the deactivation chip. He stretched out to reach it...to get Robert's help.

"So that's where it went," Jerry said, his attention on the chip also. "Have you two been plotting behind my back again?"

Scott's outstretched fingers were only an inch from the chip. His vision was blurring.

"Oh no you don't." Jerry released one hand from Scott's throat, leaned over and reached for the chip.

That gave Scott the leverage he needed to twist sideways. He almost touched it.

Jerry dove for the chip, but Scott managed to hit his hand. The chip flipped across the dirt floor. Jerry crawled after it. Scott pounced on his back, bashing his head with a fist. It was like hitting a rock with bare knuckles. Pain shot up his arm.

But Jerry's momentum had carried him to the chip. Just as his hand was about to cover it, Myrtle dashed in and snatched it in her teeth. It made a zapping sound.

Robert beeped weakly.

Hissing, Myrtle scampered out the door with her prize.

The sudden turn of events caused Scott to hesitate, and Jerry too. They looked at each other in stark disbelief. The respite lasted one second. Jerry jabbed an elbow into Scott's belly. He keeled over. Then Jerry got up and kicked him in the ribs. "You stupid Weller."

Fighting for air, Scott tried to get up.

Jerry kicked him again. "You can't win."

Scott curled into a fetal position, gasping.

Again, Jerry kicked him. "I'm in control here."

Just then, Robert zoomed out of the corner, beeping like mad. The taser probe ejected. A stream of sparkling energy whipped around Jerry's ankles and yanked his feet out from under him. He hit the dirt hard.

Scott clawed his way to his feet, half buckled over, hugging his ribs as Jerry writhed on the floor.

"Go. I will hold him here."

Jerry shouted, "Guards."

Staggering into the hallway, Scott expected a welcoming committee of security-bots. Instead, he saw their blasters leaning against the wall, the guards nowhere to be seen, and he quickly realized why. Their last orders were to capture the ferret. Myrtle had led them off somewhere...on a wild ferret chase.

He picked up a blaster, checked the charge meter: *FULL.* For the first time, he began to believe escape was possible. But there was something he had to do first. Blaster in hand, he returned to the cellar.

Robert's electronic voice shrieked. *"Why are you here?"*

"Saving the planet," Scott said. He aimed the blaster at Jerry Well's face. It would be the easiest assassination he'd ever pulled off.

"Guards." Jerry raised his arms defensively.

Scott's finger settled on the trigger. The blaster bolt would burn right through Jerry's arms and into his head with ease. "You're not going to hurt anyone ever again...especially Katherine."

Jerry bared his teeth. "She deserved what she got."

"Like hell." Scott pulled the trigger.

Unbelievably, the blaster shot a hole through the ceiling. It happened so fast that it was beyond comprehension. A pincher hand had clamped around his wrist. A telescopic arm had thrust his hand upward. "Robert?"

"He is not worth it."

"You don't know what you're saying." Scott tried jerking the gun back down, but Robert's arm wouldn't let him.

"Do not kill Jerry Well."

"What do you think you are, an angel of mercy?"

"The odds of getting away with murder cannot be calculated."

"But he's a clear and present danger."

"Every dog has his day."

It felt humiliating to be morally one-upped by a cyber-bot. Scott sighed. "I suppose you're right."

Robert's pincher hand released Scott's wrist, and the telescopic arm retracted. *"Now we must rescue Katherine."*

"Don't touch her," Jerry shouted through clenched teeth. "She's mine."

"She doesn't belong to you," Scott said. " Besides, we know she didn't die from West Nile B."

"You don't know anything."

"You killed her."

Accusingly, Robert's camera-lens eyes rotated down to Jerry. *"There's no statute of limitations on murder."*

"All talk, no proof," Jerry spat. "You and Dr. Navarro sound like a broken record."

Robert scanned his data banks. *"What is a broken record?"*

"Never mind." Scott knew what the old cliché meant. "What do we do with him?"

"Lock him in here," Robert said and released the taser

stream.

"But the security-bots can unlock the door. He'll change their orders to go after us instead of Myrtle."

A sparkling band of taser energy appeared around Jerry's ankles. *"That will hold him for ten minutes."*

"Traitor," Jerry barked.

"But I cannot stop him from changing the bots' orders."

"Can you shut them down?"

Robert beeped as he checked Hylander's mainframe. *"Changes locked out."*

"Then let's hope they don't find him sooner." Scott backed toward the door, blaster ready in case Jerry Well made a false move. Though he looked helpless lying on the floor, his cloak dusty and stained with garlicky sweat, the menace in his glaring eyes was still powerful. Scott hoped he hadn't made a mistake by sparing his life.

"Follow me." Robert hovered off down the hall.

They had ten minutes to escape Hylander.

Chapter Twenty-Seven

Sue saw a flurry of activity erupt on top of Hylander's perimeter wall. Security-bots raced along the parapets, peered over the edge at the jam-packed streets below. Hover-cams launched at an alarming rate, zoomed back and forth. Fearing something had gone wrong, she ducked into the crowd.

"Sue, we're on the move." Scott's voice came through her transceiver. "We need a diversion. Are the concussion grenades still in my bag?"

"Yes." It was strapped to the cycle's fuel cell. She had to get back to it, but already, security-bots were patrolling the street. "What do you need me to do?"

"Set one off at the main gate and get the hell out of here."

"Just one? I have six."

"You won't have time to use them all. Blast the gate and run."

One concussion grenade wouldn't cause enough commotion to cover Scott's escape. She knew he needed all hell to break loose. "I've got a better idea."

"Don't do anything stupid," Scott said. "I don't want to lose you again."

"I know." She dashed to the cycle, hoping she'd live

long enough to see him again.

A security-bot spotted her. *"Halt!"*

She jumped on the seat, started the engine. Blaster bolts streaked by as she spun the cycle around, the back tire hurling rocks. The security-bot didn't react fast enough and was pelted to the ground.

Panicked, the crowd parted, scrambling and screaming. She accelerated through the newly formed gap. Steering with her right hand, she used her left to open the sport bag and pull out a concussion grenade. A blaster bolt shrieked past her head. She pressed a red button on the grenade and lobbed it over the wall.

Blaster bolts screeched down at her. Sparks sprayed from the front wheel. The grenade exploded. Security-bots tumbled over the edge.

Just then, a formation of seven flying bots fell in behind her, firing their weapons. Dodging terrified pedestrians and stopped vehicles, she took out another grenade and lobbed it over the wall. A thundering boom followed. Rubble and bots rained down.

The next grenade bounced off the overhang and fell behind her. The pursuing security-bots darted about wildly in an attempt to evade it, but the explosion destroyed two of them. The others regrouped and continued their murderous pursuit.

***

Scott peered out a window, saw heavily armed security-bots streaming toward the wall. "Can you stop them?" he asked Robert.

"They have switched to defense mode," Robert said,

reading Hylander's mainframe. *"Changes locked out."*

"Damn!" Sue had put her life in grave danger. Now he had to find Katherine and make a clean getaway.

"Nine minutes," Robert reported.

Scott turned from the window. "Where's Katherine?"

"This way."

Blaster ready, he followed Robert through the mansion. It wasn't long before a security-bot challenged them from a door down the hallway. *"Stop."*

Scott shot it right between the optic lenses. Its microprocessors spewed sparks, and it fell over backwards. He jumped the smoldering remains and came to the door the security-bot had been guarding.

"She is here."

"Katherine."

No answer. He kicked open the door. Nothing could have prepared him for what he saw.

Wild-eyed, Katherine lay on her back on the bed, writhing against ropes that bound her wrists and ankles to the bedposts. Her mouth was gagged, her white gown torn in places that revealed more than she would have wanted him to see. Worse, she was in no condition to travel.

Robert flew across the room. *"Seven minutes."* He went directly to her feet, began cutting the ropes with his pinchers.

Scott stood rooted to the floor, repulsed by Jerry Well's cruelty. Looking around, he saw DVDs scattered about the floor, an old TV, clothes strewn around, and a wig.

Already, Robert had freed her feet and now zoomed up to her tied hands. *"Six minutes."*

Katherine squirmed and squealed.

Booming, another concussion grenade exploded outside, propelling Scott to action. He rushed to her bedside and quickly removed the gag from her mouth.

"Get out of my room," she cried, her face wrenched with fear.

"We're going to rescue you."

Her right hand came free of the ropes. She grabbed Scott's wrist. "You're going to get me killed."

"Relax."

Robert went to work on her other tied hand.

"Jerry will kill me if he finds us together."

"Don't worry. You're getting out of here."

Her eyes were fierce. "I'm not your problem, Scott Dunn."

That caught him by surprise. "How do you know my name?"

"Jerry beat me for just looking at you."

Scott recalled the hologram Robert had showed him. He felt a pang in his heart. "I'm really sorry."

Katherine released his wrist. "I didn't ask for your help."

She was right. She didn't ask for any of this, but no matter how sympathetic he was to her situation, he had to be firm. "Like it or not, you're coming with us."

Seconds later, she was freed from the ropes. Dragging the sheets with her, she scooted across the bed on her knees, covered herself and rubbed her wrists. "I don't want you to rescue me."

"You don't have a choice." He gathered up pink shorts, a white lacy top, socks and shoes and tossed them on the bed. "Get dressed."

She shook her head. "I'm not going to be responsible for your death."

"Jerry was going to kill me anyway."

She gritted her teeth. "He will find me. He'll kill you for this. I don't want that on my conscience."

"It's not all about you, Katherine. A Councilman's life is at stake. Now hurry up."

The shriek of blasters echoed outside, and the bang of rifles. Another concussion grenade exploded. What the hell was Sue doing out there?

"Five minutes," Robert said. *"The security-bots have found Jerry Well."*

"How do you know?"

"The cellar door is open."

"Damn." Scott knew it wouldn't be long before the bots received new orders. *Kill Scott Dunn.* He looked at Katherine. "We've got to go. Now."

"Save yourself," she said.

"I haven't come all this way to leave you behind." He picked up the wig and held it out to her. "When you're done dressing, put this on."

She looked at it with tortured eyes. "No."

"Why not?"

"You think I'm ugly."

"It's not that."

"Jerry says I'm ugly."

Scott leaned on the bed, locked eyes with her, and spoke softly. "Forget him. Out there in the real world, you'll stand out like a ball in a box factory. Wearing the wig will help us blend in." He hardened his voice. "Now put it on."

"Katherine, you must hurry. Four minutes. Bad boys, bad boys."

Her eyes shifted to Robert. "Can I trust him?"

"I do."

At that, she took the wig and shot up from the bed. "I hope you don't regret this." Just as she was about to drop her gown, she twirled a finger at Scott. "Do you mind?"

"Oh brother." Scott turned his back, listened to the rustling of cloth behind him and the *pheuwing* of blasters outside. Sue was stirring up a hornet's nest. Somehow, they were going to have to get around it.

"Ready," Katherine said.

"Let's move." Scott turned. "We got..." He saw her and staggered, unprepared for the transformation that had taken place behind him. Every curve, every line, the flow of hair over her shoulders, the rise in her bust, even the suture scars on her eyelids and lips were gone. Katherine was a beautiful woman.

Just then, the blasters stopped firing outside. Alarmed by the silence, Scott activated his transceiver. "Sue, are you there?"

No response.

"Sue?"

Static.

She was either captured or dead. The realization made his knees go weak.

Katherine grabbed his arm. "Is something wrong?"

"Something's always wrong." Scott felt as if the air had been kicked from his lungs. "Let's go."

"Three minutes." Robert led them down the hallway

to an open office door.

Scott knew it wasn't the way out. "What are we doing here?"

"You will need this."

"Need what?" Holding Katherine's arm, he followed Robert inside. A Starnet screen blinked on, failed to identify the intruders, and sounded a gyrating alarm.

Now the whole damn place knew where they were. An alarm was sure to draw more security-bots. No way Scott needed that. "You're going to get us killed."

Immediately, Robert zoomed to a wall safe. He beamed a laser-optic probe into a lens on the door. With a click, the lock released, and the thick door opened.

Scott couldn't believe it. They were taking time for a robbery? "Forget the money," he shouted over the shrieking alarm.

Mute, Robert reached a pincher hand into the safe, extracted a glass vial and examined it with camera-lens eyes.

"What is it?" Katherine asked.

"Everlife."

Scott moved in for a closer look. The liquid was crystal clear. There was so little of it. He found it hard to believe that this stuff had caused so much misery.

Katherine's eyes were white around the rims. "Break it."

"Never throw away your ace," Robert replied.

"Like hell." Without warning, Katherine batted the bottom of Robert's pincher, sending the vial straight up in the air.

Time stood still. *Never throw away your ace*, Scott

thought. Robert was right. John Parish and Jerry Well would do anything for that vial. As it tumbled toward the floor, Scott caught it in mid air.

"What are you doing?" Katherine shouted.

"We may need this for leverage."

"It'll cause you more trouble than you can imagine."

"More trouble than this?" He couldn't see how that was possible. He put the vial in his pocket with the key Myrtle had found.

"One minute."

"Show us the way out of here."

In the hallway, he encountered stiff resistance from two security-bots responding to the alarm. A hail of particle energy peppered the walls as Scott ducked around a corner, keeping Katherine and Robert behind him. He waited for the bombardment to wane, then jumped out and destroyed the bots with his blaster.

"Hurry," Robert squeaked out. *"The security-bots have been ordered to stop us. I cannot shut them down."*

"Great." Scott figured they were scattered all around the perimeter, thanks to Sue. Running and stumbling, he followed Robert outside and then sprinted across the lawn. Katherine ran alongside him. A flat-roofed outbuilding sat forty yards away, which seemed to be Robert's destination.

Already, security-bots were responding from the perimeter wall. One of them spotted the escapees. It fired its blaster.

Fitz-Fitz...

The muzzle made spitting sounds. It was fully discharged.

Fitz-Fitz...

And the same condition afflicted the other arriving security-bots, having exhausted their particle energy in defense of the wall.

Scott worried over Sue's fate. She must've been subjected to an intense barrage. It didn't seem possible that she could have survived. He wanted to find out what happened to her, but there wasn't time. His heart ached for her.

In an all out sprint, he led Katherine toward the building. Robert arrived first and opened an exterior panel. They dove into a dark room. The panel slid shut and locked electronically. Robert made the lights come on.

Gulping air, Scott realized they were in a garage, lit like a stadium and smelling of ozone. In the center of a Zodiac design on the floor sat a Ford Thunderclap 9000, sleek as a falcon, glimmering white with intricate designs made of blue and red pinstriping. It was a four-door model with a bubbletop dome. It sat on struts instead of tires, and the entire body was shaped like an airfoil. Chrome thruster-chutes protruded from the tail and stabilizers.

Katherine gasped.

Mechanisms whined as Robert raised the dome and the doors opened. *"Get in."*

Hesitating, Scott looked at Robert, so formal and preprogrammed, the mechanical pilot of this complicated machine. Scott feared the cyber-bot would be incapable of handling an emergency. "Maybe this isn't such a good idea."

Katherine stepped back, trepidation growing in her widening eyes. "Are you saying it's not safe?"

Holding out a pincher hand, Robert said, *"Give me the*

key, sir."

Still, Scott balked. If only he could find a real pilot.

Suddenly, the panel started shaking, banging. *"They are in here,"* a security-bot's electronic voice reported.

"Blast it," Jerry Well ordered.

Pheuw-pheuw-pheuw.

Blaster bolts pounded the panel, which lurched and screeched with every blow. The security-bots had been rearmed. It was too late for a case of cold feet, Scott decided, dug the key from his pocket, and gave it to Robert. "Our lives are in your hands, my friend."

Robert beeped. *"Thank you, friend."*

After helping Katherine into a rear bucket seat, Scott jumped in next to her. Orange straps of glowing energy came on around his waist and chest, and Katherine's, too. She shrank from them in terror.

Robert flew in behind the wheel and anchored himself to the control panel. He inserted the key into the starter port. The engine whined to life.

As the dome came down and the doors began to close, Scott saw Myrtle bounding across the garage floor. "Come on. Come on. *Tic-tic!*"

She leaped through the narrowing gap, and just as the doors closed, jumped up on his lap. He stroked her back and inhaled her musky odor, happy to see her and smell her.

Suddenly, screaming blaster bolts penetrated the panel, ricocheted and flashed around inside the garage. Robert operated the controls with three pincher hands and a laser-optic probe. Whining, the Thunderclap rose straight up, retracted its struts, and rotated. Scott saw no way out of the garage. Everything was noisy and shaking. Then sunshine burst through as the roof panels slid open. The flying car climbed into daylight.

Bolts of particle energy streaked past the bubbletop dome. Looking down, Scott saw reinforcements arriving, their weapons tilted up at the rising Thunderclap.

Katherine screamed. "They're going to shoot us down."

The engine whined louder. The flying car rose faster.

Another wave of blaster bolts shrieked up at them. Sparks blew from the tail and stabilizer. Shuddering violently, the Ford pitched down and yawed left. Robert fought the controls. The engine coughed. Scott felt a hitch in his stomach. He held Myrtle protectively, glanced at Katherine, saw terror in her eyes. They were going down.

Just then, Robert pulled the nose up and applied full throttle. In a chest-crushing instant, Hylander was just a spot on the ground.

Scott sucked air between clenched teeth and swore he'd never doubt Robert's piloting skills again.

"Where are we going?" Katherine asked.

"Washington." Scott was unable to mask the venom in his voice. "We have to stop John Parish."

Chapter Twenty-Eight

Dumbfounded, Jerry stood in front of his blast-damaged garage and watched the flying car zoom up and away. His security-bots had scored one hit to the tail section, but the damage wasn't severe enough to force the car down. Probably just as well. Katherine might have been killed.

"Get back to your posts," he ordered his security-bots. That's when he noticed the front gate opening. Several security men carried in a limp body, a blond he recognized: Sue Masters.

"Is she dead?"

"Doesn't look good, boss."

He saw scorched spots on her abdomen and arm and blood leaking through holes in her riding leathers. The stupid bitch had to get involved in this, a mistake she would soon regret. "Take her inside."

The security men took her to the cellar. Jerry summoned the resident physician. He was more of a medic than a full-blown doctor. When he saw her, his face turned mournful. He opened a silver hover-bag and removed gauze pads and a tube of nanocream.

Jerry left them and rushed to his office to check on the wailing intruder alarm.

The Grief Syndrome

"I'm happy to see you, sir. Starnet interlock confirmed."

He slammed the door. His computer's cheery voice did nothing to ease his rage. "Shut off the alarm and report."

"Yes, sir."

As the wailing ended, he scanned the room for anything out of place, his insides filled with dread and a terrible feeling of being violated. Goddamned Scott Dunn had kidnapped Katherine. Jerry kicked a chair. He'd lost her. Parish was about to trigger an election to the Council of Elders and Jerry couldn't run without Katherine. How much worse could it get?

That's when he spotted the open safe door. Anger drained out of him, replaced by cold shock. He'd been robbed. He rushed to the safe and looked inside. The vial...the goddamned vial of Everlife was gone. But how...? He inspected the door and the lock. It hadn't been forced. "Computer, video surveillance."

"Replay running, sir."

The plasma-ray screen revealed the culprit. "Robert." Jerry had just lost everything that meant anything to him. Scott Dunn had to be stopped...at all costs. "Starnet, tracking, Code: One-Zero-Three-J-Well."

Instantly, the video shut off and the Global Pinpointing System came up in a window labeled *TRACKING*. *"Code One-Zero-Three-J-Well is headed for Washington, sir."*

A flight path showed the car's course, confirmed by Air Traffic Control.

"Damn." Jerry slammed his fist on the desk. Scott

Dunn was going to thwart the assassination. There was no way to warn Parish, as the mission was so clandestine that no transceiver communications could be risked. Jerry's only option was to keep Scott Dunn from reaching Washington. "Starnet, report that code as stolen."

"Right away, sir."

At that, Jerry slumped into his desk chair. He knew he'd just signed Scott's death warrant, and Katherine's. Two hundred years of waiting, planning, wasted. It was unavoidable. ATC would not allow a stolen aircraft to continue on course. If they didn't surrender to the authorities, they'd be shot down.

Now he had to proceed on the assumption that Scott wouldn't surrender and Katherine would die. He needed to start over. He had to find another woman as his running mate to the Council of Elders, an old woman, old enough to ensure they'd be the oldest couple and take the Chair, and yet naïve enough to go along with his wishes. Perhaps there was a female Weller still living somewhere. "Starnet, list names, female Wellers."

A data search processor engaged. The 3-D yellow star blinked on, rotating on the light blue background. Seconds later, the results came up on the monitor. *NO MATCHES FOUND.*

"Damn." Then he thought about the inaccuracies in the Bureau of Vital Statistic's records. Parish had told him that Carson kept immaculate records on all the Wellers. But to tap into those records, he'd have to get into Carson's network. For that he had just the right tool, a hacker module, which he manually activated from his keyboard. A red window appeared on his plasma-ray screen. "Starnet.

Network. H.G. Carson's files. List names, female Wellers."

Again, the 3-D star rotated until a message displayed: *NETWORK DOWN.*

Jerry figured Carson's mineshaft and everything in it had been destroyed. But all was not lost. He knew that Starnet was just one gigantic computer, and like all computers, files could be lost or destroyed. Thus, all computers maintained external backup systems in the cloud. Carson's computer network would be no different.

"Starnet, search, female Wellers, cloud network."

Within seconds, a list of female Wellers scrolled down the screen. Right away, Jerry realized that John Parish was right about Carson's record keeping. It was meticulous, including names, birth dates, addresses, occupations, and obituaries. Everything was there, but every woman was listed as either buried, cremated, or atomized...except one. She was interred at Alcor...cryo-crypt 55-M. The name damn near stopped his heart.

Elizabeth Dunn.

"Son of a bitch." He couldn't believe it: Scott Dunn's wife. "Starnet, get me Dr. Navarro."

Chapter Twenty-Nine

At Washington City Center, John Parish drove a sleek gliding step-van up to the Capitol's security checkpoint. Two of his best men were with him, one sitting in the passenger seat, the other on a toolbox in back. They wore dirty brown coveralls with fictitious nametags and greasy baseball caps. *Just Toilets* and a picture of a leaking sewer pipe adorned the side of the van.

"It's an emergency," Parish told the Capitol guardsman and presented him with false ID chips he'd produced on an illegal computer. The van was stolen, of course, the original driver murdered.

As the guard examined the chips in a reader, Parish observed the man's uniform: silver trousers, matching shirt, a black belt, and a black ball cap. Satisfied the uniform he wore under his coveralls matched perfectly, Parish glanced at the bounty hunter sitting in the passenger seat. An hour ago, the man had been dressed much differently. Disguised as a tourist, he'd mingled with a group from Ohio, used the men's room outside the Council chamber, and flushed a small time-delayed concussion bomb down the toilet. To the untrained eye, the result was no more suspicious than a busted sewer pipe. "I hear you boys got quite a mess in there," Parish drawled out.

"Let's see a work order."

"What's going on?" Parish asked, handing the guard a hologram work order he'd hacked from *Just Toilets'* Starnet interface. "I've never seen such a ruckus around here."

"The Council is going to decide on the Alpha Ketari issue today."

"I'm not into politics." Parish thumbed the van's marquee. "Just toilets."

Not amused, the guard laser-scanned the hologram and verified its authenticity. "The Council chamber is in the west wing, fourth floor." He returned the ID chips and hologram work order.

"Thanks."

The van peeled off.

***

In the skies over Kansas, the Thunderclap 9000 flew like a wounded duck, shuddering and yawing left. Robert fought the controls. Scott looked back through the bubbletop dome, saw chunks missing from the smoldering tail and stabilizer. He feared it would take a miracle to make it to Washington.

With white knuckles, Katherine clung to the armrests of her bucket seat.

The radio crackled. "Beta Alpha Twelve, contact Air Traffic Control on 124.3 without delay."

Robert responded, *"Beta Alpha Twelve with you."*

"We're receiving your chauffeur number and vehicle ID. Also, your transmitted flight plan to Washington is confirmed. You are on course and altitude. However, your telemetry is unstable. We're showing you have mechanical problems."

The Thunderclap shuddered relentlessly.

"I can hold it," Robert said, the strain on his mechanical arms obvious.

"Return to your base for repairs," ATC instructed.

Concerned for their safety, Scott leaned forward and tapped Robert's cylindrical body in a place he construed to be his shoulder. "Are we going to be all right?"

"The odds are fifty-fifty."

"Some rescue," Katherine said.

"Beta Alpha Twelve," ATC radioed. "Your vehicle has been reported stolen. You must terminate your flight in Kansas City and surrender to the authorities there."

"What if we don't?" Scott asked.

"ATC will scramble the Air National Guard," Robert squeaked out. *"They will shoot us down."* He fed a code into the onboard computer. *"I hope this will override the theft report as a hoax."*

"Beta Alpha Twelve," ATC came back. "Your code is no longer valid. You are hereby instructed to engage your autopilot and prepare to be remotely landed."

"What's that mean?"

"They are going to bring us down on a laser beam. We will be arrested and imprisoned."

Scott's stomach felt sick. "There's no time for this delay. Let me talk to them."

"The radio is only activated by my voice," Robert said. *"What do you want me to say?"*

"Just do what they want," Katherine demanded. "This thing is a flying coffin."

For a moment, he regarded Katherine's creased expression and thought Robert should take her advice, but on the floor between their seats, Myrtle lay curled in a ball, unconcerned. Her lack of fear told him he was doing the right thing.

"Robert..." He looked into Katherine's eyes and hoped she'd understand why they had to risk their lives. "Tell ATC that Jerry Well has sent an assassin to Washington. John Parish is going to kill Dar Anders. We are on our way to stop him and must not be delayed."

While Robert relayed the message, Katherine's features hardened. "We can't let him get away with it."

"We won't," Scott assured her.

The air traffic controller came back. "Engage your autopilot or we'll send up the fighters."

"First," Robert said. *"Forward these transmissions to the Secret Service in Washington."*

"Negative," ATC radioed back. "Tell it to the judge. Engage now."

"Damn." Scott slapped his armrest.

"We are going to have company," Robert said, his camera-lens eyes scanning the horizon. *"Odds are they will not be friendly."*

"Do something," Katherine shouted. "You guys are so damn smart, going off half-cocked, stealing my husband's flying car. What's the matter...?"

"That's it," Scott said. "This is your husband's car. Amendment 77 makes it your car, equally. You're legally entitled to use it, so it can't be stolen."

"Amendment 77. Spousal rights are equal in all respects."

Katherine looked at Scott Dunn incredulously.

"Things have changed since you died," Scott explained. "What's his is yours...and vice versa, of course."

"That means I own this car?"

"Exactly."

She looked at Robert. "Tell them."

Robert beeped. *"ATC, Beta Alpha Twelve."*

"The fighters have been scrambled, Beta Alpha Twelve."

"Mrs. Katherine Well is aboard. She wonders why you are interfering with her 77th Amendment right to own this car."

ATC fell silent.

The Thunderclap streaked over Missouri at twice the speed of sound.

Fighters were in the air.

***

Dar Anders stood before his bedroom mirror and buttoned his formal robe. He was ready for the return trip to Washington City Center and a special session of the Council.

Ishar strode in. Every hair in place, tied back and twisted tightly behind her head, she looked regal in her long robe and sparkling jewels. "We should walk the garden before we leave. It's such a beautiful day."

"Of course." He turned from the mirror, and they strolled outside. Flanked by junipers and blossoming azaleas, they walked together. He thought about the good fortunes of his life, his beautiful wife, their children and grandchildren, the way they'd made him proud, as did his high position on the Council of Elders. "This day will go down in history," he told her.

"Save the earth at the expense of Alpha Ketari?"

"Future generations will know that we did what had to be done."

"Yes." She glanced around the garden. "The roses are beautiful." Morning dew dripped from the petals, reds and yellows. The white ones had died of a mite infection.

Dar could tell she didn't want to talk about the decision they'd come to during the night. "It's a fine year for roses."

A squirrel dashed up the bark of an old oak and chattered. Chirping birds bathed in the fountain, fluttering about. How ignorant Earth's creatures were to the blight to be set upon Alpha Ketari.

"We should take a vacation after this," Ishar said. "Bermuda or Brazil perhaps. You choose this time."

"Not Alpha Ketari?"

"We've already decided to strip mine it. Why would we want to go there?"

"Just checking." Dar had given her one more chance to change her mind. They followed the path to the driveway where the Scanstreamer gleamed in the sunshine. He opened the doors, they got in, and within moments they were off toward Washington...to save the world.

***

Security at the Capitol was tight. Crowds had gathered. There were posters and signs and placards everywhere. *Save Alpha Ketari.* John Parish drove the van up a winding drive that ended at the security entrance to an underground freight dock. As armed Capitol guardsmen approached, Parish's head itched under his reversible baseball cap.

"You the plumbers?" a guard asked through the open window.

Parish nodded.

"It's about time." The guard looked inside the van and eyed Parish's men. "Takes three of you to fix a leaky sewer pipe?"

"I'd rather be home tossin' ball with my boy," Parish said.

"This won't take long." The guard whistled.

Two German Shepherds came out of the shadowed entrance, straining against their hover-leashes.

"You carry any explosives in there?"

Parish made a face. "Of course not."

"Anything else I should know about...like a little weed in the old lunch pails?"

"Don't touch the stuff."

"We'll see," the guard said.

Parish wasn't worried as the dogs sniffed around and under the van. He'd already inspected it for contraband. And the toolbox they'd be taking inside had been specially prepared for the toughest scrutiny. His biggest worry was the escorts that would show them to the broken sewer pipe. He didn't want to leave a trail of dead bodies lying around to be discovered. "Who's taking us in?" Parish asked the guard.

"You see the problems we've got around here?" the guard griped. "Must be a hundred thousand demonstrators. Our security people are swamped. You're on your own in there."

Problem solved, Parish thought.

Less than a minute went by before the dogs sat at the guard's heels, tongues lolling. He waved the killers in.

***

Traveling at twice the speed of sound, an unstable aircraft could easily spin out of control and break apart. No human pilot had the physical endurance required to continue a flight under such severe conditions. Robert, however, had a tight rein on the controls, though the Thunderclap 9000 shuddered violently. Scott's nerves were frayed to the limit.

And if that weren't bad enough, two F-97 fighters appeared on the dash-mounted scope, their delta-shaped images flying an intercept course. ATC came on the radio. *"Beta Alpha Twelve, transmit Mrs. Well's security code."*

"What security code?" Katherine asked.

"I don't know," Scott said. "Robert?"

Beeping, Robert had already busied himself with the task of finding it. His diagnostic circuits interlinked with the Thunderclap's onboard computer. *"Jerry Well considered Katherine in all his plans. He included her code in all his computers. I should be able to find it."*

On the scope, the fighters were getting closer. Scott looked out but still couldn't see them. "You'd better hurry up."

"It might be here."

A window opened on the monitor, displaying the results of Robert's search. The code appeared, flashing in red. Immediately, Robert responded to ATC.

"Katherine's code is One-Zero-Three-K-Well."

The fighters appeared out of nowhere, announcing their arrival by firing proton bolts across the Thunderclap's nose. Scott winced at the bright balls of light flashing by. Stomach seizing, he feared the next volley would bring them down.

"Beta Alpha Twelve," a fighter pilot radioed. *"Engage your autopilot."* Several more jets flanked the shaking Thunderclap. They were slim flying wings powered by pulse-light thrusters that glowed bright as welding arcs, impossible to look at directly. The helmeted pilots were clearly visible under their bubble canopies. *"Follow us to base or you will be destroyed."*

"You jets are interfering with a legal flight," Robert radioed back. *"ATC, call them off."*

ATC didn't respond.

Scott felt a terrible sense of dread. Instead of saving Katherine, he'd brought her to the brink of death.

"You have been warned." The pilot ended his transmission, and the fighters pulled back. On the scope, Scott saw them flying a wedge formation several hundred yards back.

Katherine gasped, her eyes on the scope screen. "What are they doing?"

"Particle beam lock detected," Robert reported.

"They're going to shoot us down," Scott shouted. "Engage the autopilot, Robert. We'll straighten this out on the ground."

"Yes, sir." Robert began engagement.

"What about John Parish?" Katherine asked, her voice raspy. "No one else can stop him."

The wind went out of Scott. "We tried."

"Beta Alpha Twelve," ATC radioed. *"Katherine's security code is an old one, but it checks out. You may proceed on course."*

Roaring, the fighters again flew up alongside the Thunderclap. Katherine waved at them. The pilots saluted her and peeled away.

***

Outside the Capitol, demonstrators were chanting: *Save Alpha Ketari.* Inside, invited attendees of the council meeting jammed the corridors, pushing and shoving each other in heated debate. John Parish understood this chaos was Jerry Well's intended plan, though he was sure the Council Administrators were determined to proceed with as much normalcy as possible. But as expected, Capitol guardsmen again subjected the phony plumbers to another security search. This time, the equipment in the toolbox had been laid out on a table.

"What do you need three flashlights for?" the Capitol guardsman asked, sliding the switch on one of them. The bright baryon-gas light beam came on.

"There's three of us," Parish replied, his men standing behind him. He was confident the guard wouldn't disassemble the flashlights because they were functional. If he had, their ruse would have been discovered.

Shrugging, the guard set aside the flashlights and sifted through an assortment of strange-shaped tools, wrenches and drivers, not the least bit suspicious that these too had been modified for a special purpose.

Another guard inspected several small boxes marked

Stant and *Rogan*, a puzzled expression on his face. "What are these?"

"Spare parts," Parish explained. "That's a device-elector valve for a pressure regulator, and the others are tank captivators."

"What are they for?"

"Your toilets, or have you forgotten why we're here?"

The guard screwed up his face. "It's a stinking mess up there." He returned the disguised blaster resonators and particle charges to their respective boxes. "I'm glad I don't have to fix it."

"Come on," one of Parish's men said. "I wanna get home in time for my daughter's birthday party."

"All right," the first guard said. "Put this junk back in your toolbox."

"Which way to the broken pipe?" Parish asked.

"On the other side of the loading dock, take the freight lift to the fourth floor...but mind you, the place is packed with people waiting to get into the Council chamber."

"Is that right?" While Parish's men packed everything away, he worried about all the witnesses up there. "You got a maintenance entrance?" he asked the guard.

"Sixth floor, but you'll have to double back down the stairs. I'd just fight the crowd, if I were you."

"Sure." They got in the elevator that would take them up to the Council chamber on the fourth floor. When the doors slid shut, Parish hit the button for the sixth floor instead.

***

Dar and Ishar arrived at the Capitol, passed through

the security checkpoint and drove toward the underground parking garage, the entire route lined with riotous demonstrators. A taser field kept them back from the roadway. Walking Secret Service bots patrolled the narrow corridor. As Dar drove along, an angry roar rose from the crowd.

"I can't wait for this to be over," Ishar said. "Jerry Well brings out the worst in people."

"Our decision is not going to set well with them."

"Environmentalists against Capitalists, the next civil war."

"Brewing right before our eyes."

Ishar exhaled.

At the garage, the attendant recognized them immediately and opened the steel gate. Dar drove into a shadowy interior and parked the car in his reserved space. The Scanstreamer's doors whined as they opened, and the steering wheel retracted. Before getting out, he turned to his wife, saw the dire look in her eyes. "We'll be out of here in an hour."

"I've got a bad feeling about this."

"Security has everything under control."

"Of course." She didn't say it with conviction.

On the elevator to the fourth floor, he stood next to her in silence. He wanted to hold her hand, or her elbow, and he even thought about putting his arm around her. But he didn't. They'd been together over seventy years. They were strong for each other without physical contact. It's just the way it was.

They arrived at the Council chamber's anteroom and stepped into a rush of activity. Administrators and attendants cut short their conversations and jockeyed for position in a line forming along the far wall. Lush scarlet and velvet draperies, plush carpeting, and claw-footed furniture of red and gold, got barely a passing notice from Dar as he headed directly to the massive desk centered in the room. Once Ishar was seated next to him, he waved the Chief Administrator to come forward. The pre-meeting business had begun. In one hour it would all be over.

***

John Parish and his men stalked down a curving hallway on the sixth floor and came to a door marked *Maintenance*. He checked the area for hover-cams, and because he didn't see any, he figured the security people had tasked them to watching over the crowd. Satisfied, he removed a hammer from his toolbox, unscrewed the capped handle, and extracted a digital lock pick. His men stood guard as he bent down to the crystal encoder and pressed a seek button. The electronic pick sent random codes to the lock, searching for a match.

A minute passed. Sweat dripped down his cheek. The LED on the display glowed red.

"Hurry up, boss."

His men were getting nervous.

Two minutes. Still red.

"Come on," Parish muttered to the lock picker.

Just then, voices echoed from down the hall. Footsteps.

"Someone's comin', boss."

The LED blinked green. Parish pressed the unlock button, and the door came ajar. "We're in."

They scrambled inside. Parish shut the door quietly behind them and listened as the voices passed by.

Then he turned his attention to the maze of railed gantries that crisscrossed high above the Council chamber and intersected at a center platform. "That way." As he followed his men, he worried over their footsteps, the creaking sounds from the narrow catwalks and the hollow echoes that followed. They passed over ceiling lights that glowed down on plush stadium seating, which surrounded an oval floor and the Council members' chairs. The place was empty and eerily quiet, but by the time he reached the center platform, he felt sure they were well concealed above the glaring lights.

Without instruction, his men opened the toolbox and began assembling their blasters. The barrels were hidden inside the flashlights, and the rest of the blasters were assembled from components disguised as hand tools. The toilet parts were disassembled, revealing the vital blaster resonators and particle charges, which his men assembled with practiced precision. Within three minutes, they were armed.

"Over there," Parish whispered, directing one of his men toward the other side of the structure to an air-conditioning duct about a hundred feet away. He told the man standing with him to stay on the center platform. "You might get a clean shot straight down."

Satisfied, he moved along a gantry that traversed over an array of ceiling lights and a set of doors that opened to the oval floor below. From here, he believed he would have the best angle of fire. And he hadn't gotten into position too soon. With echoing bangs, all the doors around the Council chamber's outer ring opened at the same time.

People began pouring in, media personnel first with their camera equipment, handhelds and hover-cams, crystal Teleprompters, and sharply dressed reporters. They jammed the front rows, chattering loudly. The next wave was let in, suited and cloaked men and women, all of whom he figured had a stake in Alpha Ketari, either monetary or moral. Seemed they were each trying to out-shout the other.

Then several groups of demonstrators entered last. Chanting and clapping, they took up standing positions around the chamber ring, each group identified with a placard: *The Jerry Well Foundation, The Alpha Ketari Liberation Front, and Environmentalists Against Capitalization* were a few he could read from his perch above the fray. The Council chamber filled quickly. Then the doors below him opened. Two figures, side-by-side, stepped into the doorway and stopped. They wore long robes. One was taller than the other. Dar Anders.

A knot of determination grew in Parish's stomach. He clutched the blaster, looked across at his fellow assassins, and clenched his jaw.

***

Somewhere over Maryland, the Thunderclap 9000 decelerated to subsonic speed. The flying car shuddered and boomed. Robert gripped the controls firmly, though the incessant shaking had subsided enough to stop rattling Scott's teeth.

"Beta Alpha Twelve," ATC said over the radio. *"Welcome to Washington. You are cleared to enter City Center airspace. Be advised, you are now VFR."*

"What's that?" Scott asked Robert.

"Visual flight rules. Look for the Capitol dome spire. It should be up ahead shortly." Robert switched on the GPS screen. A map of City Center appeared, overlaid with evenly spaced concentric rings. An icon representing the Thunderclap's position appeared on the outer ring. Other blips indicated air traffic in the vicinity.

The Thunderclap moved swiftly across the city. Within moments, the Capitol came into view.

"There it is."

"It looks different than I remember," Katherine said.

Scott turned to her, noticed her pallid skin, probably from the rough flight. "It won't be long now. Robert, land on the lawn. We'll notify the Secret Service right away."

"Yes, sir."

But when they approached the Capitol, Scott saw no place to land. A writhing sea of humanity covered the grounds, spilled into the streets, and stretched out as far as he could see, clear to the Washington Monument.

"What are we going to do?" Katherine asked weakly.

Cars jammed the parking lots and access roads.

"Over by the steps, Robert, set her down slowly, on the lawn. People will move out of the way."

Robert started the landing sequence.

***

Dar stood next to Ishar in the open doorway to the Council chamber's oval marble floor, waiting for the crowd to settle down before making a formal entrance. This was the fullest he'd seen this room in recent memory. Looking at Ishar, he noticed a tremble in her lips.

"There are so many of them," she said.

"Makes me wish we were back at the advertising firm."

"How were we to know this job would turn so ugly?"

"It's important what we do."

She took his elbow, surprising Dar. "Let's get this over with."

They stepped through the doorway and into the Council chamber.

***

Parish saw the couple enter. Wetting his lips, he raised the blaster. This would be easy.

Just then, attendants took positions around the couple, blocking his shot. He swallowed. The procession walked directly beneath him, now shielded by the gantry he stood on. Swiveling around, he moved the blaster and aimed at a spot where he thought his target would reappear. When it did, the attendants again kept him from getting off a clear shot. He ground his molars, lowered the blaster.

The bounty hunter on the center platform peered down, aimed, hesitated, and then shuffled to a different position. The gantry squeaked under his weight, but the sound was barely audible over the applause now clamoring through the chamber.

Below, the elderly couple moved like royalty to the throne chairs, stepped up on the raised platform, and turned to the spectators, waving. The exuberant crowd was so noisy Parish could hardly think straight. From this angle, cables and ducting interfered with his line of sight. Even stretching out over the gantry railing, he still couldn't line up a good shot. His two men repositioned themselves again.

He waited.

***

As Scott had expected, the crowd below parted when the Thunderclap descended vertically to the lawn. Some demonstrators were curious about the landing, but most carried on with their ranting, trying to sway the system that would determine Alpha Ketari's fate.

However, the flying car's arrival attracted security's attention right away. Capitol guardsmen and a contingent of Secret Service bots forged a channel through the crowd to reach the landed car. Just as they swarmed around, Robert raised the bubbletop, and the doors opened. Myrtle jumped on Scott's lap as the glowing safety harness blinked out. Picking her up, he tucked her under his left arm and got out. Immediately, he found himself on the business end of a dozen blasters. Right hand in the air, he said. "This is an emergency."

"You're under arrest," a guard said.

Myrtle hissed.

One of the guards spoke into his transceiver. "We need a prisoner extraction team out here."

"Listen to us," Katherine said, her hands in the air behind Scott. "Everybody, listen. There's an assassin inside."

"Don't move, lady."

Robert began toning with nearby Secret Service bots. They in turn relayed Robert's startling news to their mainframe, which promptly notified human superiors.

"Attention all personnel," came over the guardsmen's transceivers. "Code Red. There's been a security breach."

"The Council chamber," Scott declared, thankful Robert had intervened on their behalf. As the guardsmen and Secret Service bots took off in the council's direction, he set Myrtle on the car seat. That's when he noticed Katherine. Her face was sickly gray...from the excitement, he assumed: the guards, the guns, and the riotous crowd. "You don't look well."

"I feel dizzy."

"You'd better stay here."

"Hurry back." She slumped into the car.

Dashing after the Capitol guardsmen, Scott hoped Katherine would be all right.

***

A muscle in John Parish's back started cramping. He'd been crouched on the gantry too long. It was hot, and he was sweating. He worried over the guard uniform he wore under his coveralls. It would be soaked.

He and his men hadn't been able to draw a sure bead on Dar Anders. No wonder, with all the surrounding attendants and dignitaries. They were making presentations to the honored couple as they sat pompously on their almighty thrones. The ceremonious start to the Council meeting dragged on. Impatience burned in Parish's gut. He thought about blasting everyone standing in the way, but decided against it. This was an assassination, not a massacre.

While waiting, he rethought the steps of his planned escape: shoot, strip off coveralls, reverse ball cap, and walk out the front doors. Once the killing was done, his men knew that it would be every man for himself. What they didn't know was that he planned to kill them anyway. A secret between three men was safe only if two were dead.

The Council chamber doors closed.

"Order." An administrator's voice echoed above the din. "This special meeting is now in session."

Like the receding clatter of a train, the crowd settled down. Every nerve in Parish's body went on full alert. He had to kill Dar Anders before he uttered his ruling on Alpha Ketari.

"The Council of Elders welcomes you," echoed over the intercom.

In double file, six elderly couples strode in. They wore long robes, their hoods folded back, revealing gray hair and doughy skin. The Council members were about to be seated. Time was running out.

***

Dar Anders sat next to Ishar and acknowledged the arriving Council members with dignified nods. The ceiling lights seemed especially bright, the spectators overcharged. While he attended to the formalities of greeting his counterparts, his mind was elsewhere, swimming in the crystal clear waters of the Bahamas with Ishar, a Corona for him and a margarita for her, waiting for them on a beachside table.

She reached out to him, patted his sleeve, and smiled. "The Bahamas?"

"I was just thinking..."

"I know. We deserve the rest."

The administrator addressed the crowd. "Before us this day, we have the final vote on the Alpha Ketari issue."

***

Scott couldn't believe how many people had jammed into the Capitol's corridors. It was a sweaty, smelly mob, consumed by their own purposes. In urgency, pushing and shoving, the Capitol guardsmen cut a swath through the throng, ever onward toward the Council chamber. Scott pressed along with them, swept up in the confusion of the moment. He fought for calm in hopes his garlicky spew would go unnoticed.

By the time they arrived, they found the doors had already been closed. Secret Service agents converged on the scene, shouting into their transceivers, trying to get the Administrators to open the doors.

"What's the problem?" Scott asked the guard he'd followed in.

"Once the Council's in session, the doors are shut. Nobody gets in or out."

Scott knew Parish wouldn't allow himself to be locked in the room with his target. It made no sense. He probably wasn't even in there.

Just then, the administrators opened the doors, and guardsmen rushed in. "Everybody get down."

Someone screamed.

Instant and complete chaos erupted in a stampede for the doors. The news people turned their cameras on the panicked spectators. Hover-cams zipped to and fro.

"Get on the ground."

Guardsmen surged down the aisles, guns leveled,

blasters charged, sweeping back and forth in search of the assassin.

Scott's mind flashed back to a time when he was an assassin. With knowing eyes, he surveyed the room, the stadium seating, the doors, the walls, the raised platform, and the lighted superstructure above. He was looking for the best vantage point to sight from, the clearest shot, the most clandestine position with the fewest possible witnesses and a sure escape route. He knew the assassin had not mingled with the spectators. It was a good way to get caught, or worse, stopped. Behind the spectators, maybe, Scott rationalized, but not with a wall to his back. And the guard had said that once the doors were shut, nobody could get in or out. Parish had to have known that. He had to be above the room...but where?

Scott followed the guard down the sloping aisle toward the Council floor where elderly men and women wearing long robes had risen from their chairs. "Which one is Dar Anders?"

"There on the platform."

Scott saw the old man standing at his chair, his eyes round with disbelief over the interruption. Tracing possible trajectory paths to Dar, Scott looked up, left and right, the glaring lights nearly blinding him. He heard the creaking of a gantry and spotted the glint of a blaster poised just beyond a bright ceiling lamp. "Up there."

The guard braced himself and fired a volley of blaster bolts up to the gantries, a sweeping pattern without aiming. "I don't see him."

Scott lost sight of him too. "Keep his head down." He stole a glance to the raised platform, saw Dar Anders sprawled on the floor, covering his wife with his body. Already, Administrators and Secret Service agents were converging on them and the other prone Council members as well.

Blasters shrieked.

Screaming in crazed panic, the crowd surged toward the open doors, clawing and trampling each other.

Administrators reached the oval floor, began helping the elderly couples to their feet and herding them toward the exit. Secret Service agents covered Dar and Ishar's retreat.

The guard with Scott kept firing up to the ceiling. Then a blaster bolt shot down from a spot clear across the room, searing a hole through the guard's chest, slamming him to the floor.

Scott squatted at the dead guard's side, grabbed his blaster, and fired at the spot where he'd seen the lethal particle bolt originate. A scream, a stagger, and a body fell, landing on the marble floor with a solid thump. Scott saw his face. It wasn't John Parish. How many assassins were up there?

The other guards started spraying the superstructure with particle energy. Ceiling fixtures exploded, and sparks rained down.

Mobbed together, the Council members kept moving toward the exit. Dar and Ishar lagged behind. Two Secret Service agents covered them.

Scott was forced to hurdle a row of seats as the aisle had become jammed with people trying to get out. He studied the target and the angles. Everything was in motion, constantly changing, confusing him, but on a hunch, he blasted a ceiling lamp so he could see beyond its glare. There he spotted a man in brown coveralls, aiming a blaster down.

Scott fired.

In a blinding flash, the man slammed backward, flipped over the gantry railing, and tumbled to the floor.

But this time Scott hadn't seen the assassin's face. He had to find out if it was Parish. Scrambling over the seats, falling, rolling, leaping, he made it to the Council floor and to the dead man's side. "Damn." It wasn't John Parish. Scott noticed the man's brown coveralls were ripped open, revealing a silver uniform underneath. A ball cap lay upside down next to the body. The inside was black. The cap was reversible. Scott bared his teeth, realizing the assassins planned to escape disguised as Capitol guardsmen.

Pheuw-Pheuw! Pheuw!

Wheeling around, he saw a volley of energy bolts flash down on the retreating Council members, first leveling the agents protecting them, and then blasting a hole through an Elder's back. A woman's scream tore through the air. She toppled to the floor. Dar Anders fell to his knees and hunched over her. "Ishar. My God. Ishar."

Above, a shadow retreated into darkness beyond the lights. Scott recognized John Parish's brutish form. Soon he would be disguised as a Capitol guardsman. "How do I get up there?" he shouted to a wounded Secret Service agent lying nearby.

"Sixth floor...maintenance."

Blaster in hand, Scott muscled his way through the thinning crowd, made it to the hallway, found the staircase, and started up, running hard, taking two and three steps at a time. He thought about how long it would take Parish to chameleon: less than twenty seconds. Scott knew he was cutting it close as he burst through the door on the sixth floor.

He couldn't believe his eyes. A sea of black ball caps bobbed down the corridor, moving along, Capitol guardsmen systematically clearing the halls and offices. There must've been a hundred of them.

Chapter Thirty

F eeling defeated, Scott made his way back to the Thunderclap 9000. He wasn't surprised to see the crowd still pressed around the flying car. As he neared, Robert rose from the pilot seat, beeping frantically. Myrtle was there too, but Katherine was gone. Scott's stomach dropped. "Where is she?"

Robert hovered up to him. *"It came on suddenly,"* he said in a squeaky electronic voice, obviously strained by what his optic sensors had witnessed. *"She passed out."*

Myrtle leaped into Scott's arms, shivering.

"Medics arrived and summoned an air ambulance." In all Robert's excitement, he activated a hologram recording, which beamed out a replay of the events that had taken place while Scott was inside. Capitol guardsmen forced the crowd back as a red and white hover-copter came down. It read *Presidents' Memorial Hospital* on the sliding doors. A medical team disembarked, rushed to the car, and removed Katherine's limp body. They placed her on a hover-stretcher, one arm hanging over the side, and took her away.

"We've got to get to the hospital." He jumped into the front passenger seat and put Myrtle in back.

"But the Secret Service may want to question you..."

"We don't have time for that." Scott stashed the dead guard's blaster under the seat. "Katherine is more important to me than seeing Parish face justice. Let's move it."

"Whatever you say." Robert fired up the engine. The bubbletop came down, and they took off.

While Robert piloted the Thunderclap toward Presidents' Memorial, Scott recalled the sickly look on Katherine's face, how she'd spoken weakly before he left her in the car. He'd thought she was just stressed after the rough flight and all the excitement. Now he knew it was something more severe. "Is there any word on her condition?"

Robert checked Starnet. *"There is no record of Katherine Well at President's Memorial."*

Swallowing, Scott feared he'd lost her. "Could they have taken her somewhere else?"

"The hover-copter has landed."

"Then she has to be there." Scott looked down at the Potomac River, felt an icy dread wash over him. It was his fault Katherine had fallen ill. He should have known she needed special medical care following her reanimation. Her body's natural immune system was probably destroyed during cryonic suspension. Even the most harmless of bacteria could poison her. He should've left her at Hylander. Now he feared he'd have to accept the responsibility of causing her death. And what about Sue and Carson? Everyone close to him was dead or dying. Survivor's guilt piled up on him. The demon roared. He started caving in to its crippling demands. His body began to tremble. Tears welled in his eyes.

Just as he was about to succumb to the grief, the

Thunderclap landed at Presidents' Memorial. Gulping air, he knew he had to get a grip on himself, for Katherine's sake. As the glowing seat harness dimmed out, the bubbletop dome whined open. He glanced in the back seat, saw Myrtle napping, as usual, decided to leave her there and pulled himself out of the flyer. Robert secured the car then hovered behind him as he dashed up the steps and pushed his way into the hospital lobby.

If opulence and extravagance were ever evident in architecture, this hospital was the epitome of overindulgence, a testament to corporate profits fueled by insurance company payoffs. No finer hotel or office complex had ever been built, towering gold columns and lavish motifs, Greek statues and plush furniture all around. But the hired help left a lot to be desired, Scott decided as he waited in line at the information counter. Katherine could have died and been atomized in the amount of time it took to get waited on.

"I'm sorry," the soapy-smelling clerk finally said. "We have no Katherine Well admitted to this hospital."

"But the hover-copter just brought her in."

"No," the woman reassured him. "No Katherine Well...however...we do have a Katherine Dunn...yes...just came in on LifeFlight...she's in room 4715."

"Katherine Dunn?" he whispered to himself, perplexed at the way their names sounded together. Then he glared at Robert. "How'd they get that name?"

Robert inched closer to Scott. *It was all I could think of to keep her real name off the record.*

"Of course," Scott said, realizing Jerry Well could have found her over Starnet. "Her maiden name is Well," he lied to the clerk.

She frowned. "Are you family?"

"Her husband...newlyweds."

"Got any ID?"

Scott showed her his mechanic's union chip.

"You can go up...but," she pointed to the cyber-bot, "you'll have to leave your toys outside."

Leaning on the counter, Scott asked, "How is she?"

The clerk looked at her screen. "Critical."

"Come on, Robert." Scott sprinted for the elevator, Robert right behind him and the sound of the clerk's sharp voice promising eviction for disobeying hospital rules. Her threats were forgotten by the time the door opened on level forty-seven. Nurses standing at the substation eyed him suspiciously as he approached, in a hurry, as if every second counted. "I'm here to see Katherine Dunn."

One nurse stepped forward. "She's barely hanging on."

"What happened?"

"We don't know. She's bleeding internally, as if every cell in her body is leaking."

Robert beeped. *"I am contacting Dr. Navarro."* He extended his antennas. The display panel on his chest became a flurry of colorful activity. *STARNET COMMUNICATIONS ONLINE.*

"Who's Dr. Navarro?" Scott asked Robert.

"He reanimated her."

The nurse stepped back, mouth agape. "She's a cryo-patient?"

"A few days ago," Scott said, hoping this information would be of some help.

"Dr. Demone, stat," the nurse said into her transceiver.

Robert sent a digitized message to Navarro's computer at Alcor in Boulder. *RECEIVING* paraded across his chest monitor. A moment later, the response came in. Robert decoded it and played a recording of Dr. Navarro's voice. "Treat Katherine for CR, cryonic relapse, 100 milligrams nanoserum. I'm in the middle of an emergency reanimation right now. Will arrive there in four hours." *TRANSMISSION TERMINATED.*

The nurse said, "You may wait with her if you like."

"Yes...please." Scott swallowed dryly. "Thank you."

"This way."

"Robert too?" Scott asked.

She walked up to Robert, touched him under the rim of his speaker mouth. "Cute little guy."

Robert beeped. *"Pick a card, any card."*

"A real hustler," she quipped. "Of course he can go in with you."

"I just happen to have Melanie Blue in the sixth heat at Dover, eight to one for only—"

"Will you stop?" Scott snapped.

"I was just trying to be friendly."

"Come on."

In the room, Scott felt a jolt when he saw Katherine. Her body hung suspended inside three elliptical force fields glowing orange, yellow, and red, a sort of levitation bed. A doctor was with her, administering the nanoserum treatment. His nametag read: *Demone.*

"Have a seat." He indicated a bedside chair.

Scott sat, feeling lost and helpless and overwhelmed

by the technology. "What is this contraption?"

"This levitator prevents fluids from pooling inside the young lady's lungs and abdomen, and it keeps leaking blood from settling in her tissues. No ugly bruises and bedsores this way."

Amazed, Scott noticed that no part of her body touched any part of the glowing levitation bed. There were no sheets, no blankets. The force fields maintained her comfort, he assumed. She wore a thin strap of white material over her breasts and white shorts. Her arms were extended and her feet slightly spread. Someone had removed her wig, revealing a pale scalp that shined with perspiration. She looked like a mannequin waiting to be dressed for a department store window display. Her eyes were closed, and he wondered if she could hear the cacophony of sounds emitted from the machines along the wall.

Whirring up to Katherine, Robert examined her with swiveling camera-lens eyes and made a whistling sound. *"Houston, we have a problem."*

"Is she going to be all right?" Scott asked the doctor as he stepped back from his patient.

The levitator tilted two degrees right.

"I'm waiting for Dr. Navarro to arrive." He consulted one of the machines along the wall. "How long have you two been married?"

"Me...us...?" Scott stumbled. "Not very long."

"How long was she frozen?"

"I'd rather not talk about it." Actually, Scott didn't know how to explain it. He didn't think the doctor would believe him anyway.

Demone turned from his machines, looked Scott up and down. "Something's not right about this."

"My father-in-law said the same thing. Please, may I be alone with my wife?"

"She's very sick, but okay. I'll return in ten minutes." He left the room.

The levitator swiveled four degrees left and pitched four degrees down.

"I thought he'd never leave," Katherine said.

Scott shot up from his chair, his heart stuck in his throat. "Katherine."

Her eyes were open, and her skin was beginning to look a little pinker. "What are we going to do now that we're alone...my husband?" She winked.

"Robert told them we were married."

She smiled, the radiant arcs glowing in her eyes. "Wouldn't this bed be fun to make love in...or on...or whatever?"

Make love? Scott couldn't believe it. She was sicker than he thought. "I'd better go."

"No, please stay. I'm sorry. It's just that you really are my hero."

"You're married to Jerry Well," Scott reminded her.

"That can be rectified."

He understood why she would want to be rid of him. "You need to rest."

"Did you save Dar Anders?"

Scott fell back into the chair as Katherine rotated five degrees up. "Parish shot Ishar."

"Who?"

"Dar Anders' wife."

"Is she dead?"

Nodding, he knew the consequences of her assassination. Dar would lose his high position on the Council. Elections to replace the elderly couple would begin right away. It was all handled over Starnet. There'd be no campaign trails, no conventions, caucuses or speeches. Candidates presented themselves on Starnet, detractors and supporters gave their testimony, and citizens voted from the convenience of their homes. It would all be over in forty-eight hours. For Jerry to succeed with his plan, he needed Katherine, now more than ever.

"Jerry will stop at nothing to get you back," he told her. "If not, he'll have to drop out of the election."

"Or get another wife."

"An old woman, maybe," Scott said, but he didn't think Jerry would do that, even if he could. It wouldn't guarantee him the Council Chair.

"What about John Parish?"

One failure after another. "He got away."

"He'll come after the vial, you know." Katherine's bed tipped up three degrees.

Scott looked at her feet, her polished toenails, her legs, and her curves. Even without a wig, she was beautiful. Worse, she was vulnerable. "You're not safe here."

"I can't just walk out." She indicated the glowing bed. "Is there any way we can find out what Jerry is up to?"

"Sure, Robert can."

Beeping, the cyber-bot went to work, interfacing with Starnet's election links. The candidates were easy to find. He accessed Jerry Well's entry and displayed the information on his chest monitor. What Scott saw blew him out of his chair.

"Liz?"

It was a picture of Liz, all right, posing with Jerry Well, arm-in-arm. No way, no way, he kept thinking. Liz was dead and buried...or...or was she? He couldn't be positive about that. After she shot herself, he'd left...walked out. He didn't have the stomach for another funeral. And he was angry with her. No, he was downright fuming mad. He'd tolerated a lot from her over the years, but not that. She didn't have the right to kill herself. But obviously she was alive, this sadly pathetic woman who hated life so much. How was that possible?

No. It couldn't be. He studied the photo on Robert's monitor more closely. The image had to have been doctored. She and Jerry Well had never met. They couldn't have posed for this picture. Someone had dubbed her in. And she looked terrible. Her bleary eyes stared out of deep skull sockets, zombie-like, those same sad eyes that held no hope. He saw pinpricks around her eyelids...and around her mouth, and something else wasn't right. She'd never worn her hair long like that. It was a wig, the hair draping over a white bandage around her neck. Surgery. Someone had repaired the damage the bullet had done. "My God," he whispered. "It looks like she's been reanimated."

"Who is she?" Katherine asked.

"My wife." He didn't want to believe she was back from the dead. Then he remembered Carson's last words: *"There is another."* He'd meant there was another Weller. Carson had known all along that someone had suspended Liz in cryonic freeze.

But who would have done that...and why?

Chapter Thirty-One

There was a new woman at Hylander.

Jerry locked her in the same room Katherine once occupied. It was time to initiate Liz into his scheme to take over the Council of Elders. Entering her room, he shut the door behind him.

At first, he didn't see her, his attention immediately drawn to the disheveled room: the old television tipped and smashed, the vanity broken, drawers pulled out and clothes thrown helter-skelter. The mattresses were askew, and the sheets had been ripped to shreds. He clenched his fists and scanned the carnage warily. "Elizabeth? What have you done?"

"Leave me alone." Her sharp and sobbing voice came from behind the upturned mattress.

"You're going to pull the stitches in your neck."

"I don't care."

Jerry inched toward the mattress. "The doctors worked very hard to repair the damage you did to yourself."

"Fuck 'em."

"That's no way to talk."

"I'd rather be dead."

Moving closer to her, he tried to keep his voice calm.

The Grief Syndrome

"I've given you a second chance—"

"Fuck you."

That was it. "You disrespectful bitch." Jerry lunged over the mattress, grabbed Liz by the arm and yanked her out of her hiding place. Fist balled, he held it over her like a club, only holding back his wrath when he saw she'd ripped the bandages from her neck, revealing the sutured incisions from her post-reanimation surgery.

"Go ahead," Liz spat out. "Hit me. Kill me."

He shoved her to the floor. "All in good time." He wanted to kill her right now, but that would mean Liz was in control of him. Then he thought about how he'd lost control of Robert, Katherine, and Scott Dunn. It wasn't going to happen again. "You're no better than your husband."

Rising up on her hands, she choked out, "Husband?"

"Scott Dunn."

An amazed look came over her face, as if she had suddenly remembered him. "You know Scott?"

"I know you had two children."

"Yes. I remember now. Lisa and Lilly. Oh my God, they're dead." She keeled over and started bawling. "I killed myself because I couldn't live without them."

"You took the easy way out."

"What happened?" she cried, crumpled on the floor. "Why am I alive again?"

"You put the gun in your mouth, but the angle was wrong. The bullet missed your brain. Lucky for me, you can't do anything right."

"Who are you?"

"Your savior."

"No." Liz reached out, grabbed a wedge of broken vanity mirror, held it to the stitches on her throat. "What do you want with me?"

Jerry felt a stab of terror, held out his open hand. "Give it to me." He couldn't risk her killing herself again, not this close to the election. "Liz?"

Her grip tightened on the glass until blood leaked from her fist. "I'll do it. I swear."

"I need you alive."

"What for?"

"It's a long story." He stepped closer. "Give me the glass. I'll explain."

Gritting her teeth, she pressed the sharp edge into her throat hard enough to draw a thin line of blood. "Stay back."

"All right." Jerry had lost control of the situation. He took a step back. "I need you for my running mate in an upcoming election, to take Katherine's place."

"Who?"

"My wife. You're wearing her gown."

She looked down. Her eyes traced the wrinkled and bloodstained gown. "It's mine now."

Blood dripped from her clenched fist.

"Yes." Jerry hoped for a way to regain control. "It's yours now."

Her eyes were fixed on the blood spots. "But it's ruined."

Seeing her distraction, he jumped on her, knocked her over and pinned her arms to the floor. "Drop it, Liz."

"Let me go." She fought like a wild beast.

He held on, squeezed her arm.

"You're hurting me."

"Drop the glass."

"All right." She opened her fist, but the mirror didn't drop. It was embedded in her palm.

Jerry shook it loose. He got up and kicked the bloody shard out of her reach. "You damn fool."

Curled up on the floor, she clutched her bleeding hand and wept. Jerry looked down on the most miserable person he'd ever seen. He couldn't imagine spending his immortal life with this wretched woman. Alpha Ketari wouldn't be paradise. It would be hell. He had to get Katherine back.

But for now, Liz would have to suffice. The election would commence in less than forty hours. He was running out of time to get her on board, but watching Liz carry on, he felt a knot in his stomach grow. With Katherine gone, he'd been forced to photograph Liz, even before her reanimation was completed, and paste her image over Katherine's on the photo he'd prepared for Starnet's election network. He'd barely got it posted in time. Now at least, he was confident he'd win the election, and once he attained the council's Chair, he'd rule on Alpha Ketari in his favor and break the stalemate left when Ishar was assassinated. After claiming stewardship of the planet, he'd step down from the Council, find Katherine, and move to Alpha Ketari. He wouldn't need miserable Liz anymore. Her death wish would be granted.

The security system intercom announced, "John Parish has returned from Washington."

"I'll see him at once. In my office." Jerry bent over weeping Liz. "Before I go, you should know that your husband left you the night you shot yourself."

Liz cupped her hands over her ears, smearing blood on her shaved head. "I can't blame him."

"Your grandchildren didn't know what to do with your body. They figured Scott would return to make the arrangements, so they had you frozen at Alcor. But Scott never came back, and only your life insurance policy kept you from being thawed and buried in a pauper's grave."

She looked up with swollen eyes. "I don't want to see him." She got on her knees, clasped her bloody hands together. "I couldn't face him. Please."

He smiled, delighted with her pleading. "Will you cooperate with me?"

Bowing her head she whimpered, "Anything...as long as you promise he'll never see me this way."

"That's more like it." He stepped up to her, relished the sight of her cowering at his feet. "Don't worry, Liz honey. I'm going to take care of you now." He slapped her upside the head. "And don't you forget it."

"I wish I was dead," she cried and slumped to the floor.

"Christ." The woman was going to drive him crazy. But wouldn't it be ironic if she and Scott were reunited? Talk about a just reward. *And when I kill her in front of him, he'll start the grief process all over again.* Jerry chuckled at the thought.

***

Five minutes later, Jerry entered his office, saw John Parish pacing, dressed in his usual combat fatigues. "You made it out okay?"

"No thanks to you. Scott Dunn was there."

"You shot Ishar. That's good enough." Jerry brushed past him, opened the humidor on the desk, and plucked out a granola bar.

"I almost got caught. You let him get away, Jerry, what happened?"

Peeling back the wrapper, Jerry shot Parish a stern look. "He kidnapped Katherine, too."

Parish frowned. "That's not my problem."

"I want her back."

"Hey. I've done my part of the deal. Give me the vial."

Jerry swallowed. "That's easier said than done."

"What?"

"He stole your vial of Everlife, too."

Parish's face turned pale. "How did he do that?"

"Robert opened the safe for him."

A dagger-sharp look of murder shot from Parish's eyes. "Where are they?"

Jerry bit into his granola bar, feigning calm. "They're still in Washington."

Parish stiffened. "I ain't goin' back there."

"You have to." Jerry stared at him. "That is, if you want your vial back. May as well get Katherine while you're at it."

"It's too risky," Parish said. "I barely got away."

"I'll throw in a little bonus and let you kill Scott Dunn."

"Temptin'," Parish said. "But we've gotta get him to come to us."

"You're right," Jerry said. "Besides, he's probably already given the Everlife to Katherine."

"Don't even think it," Parish shouted, pointing a stiff finger at Jerry. "No Everlife, you're dead."

Jerry had thought about that. Katherine never wanted the Everlife, but if she had taken it for Scott, one problem would be solved. Jerry pitched the granola bar wrapper into the trash atomizer. "I've got an election to worry about." He moved around behind his desk.

"But you can't run without Katherine."

"I've got a substitute."

"Who...?"

"Scott Dunn's wife," Jerry replied. *A brilliant move on my part.*

"She's here?"

"In Katherine's room."

Leaning on the desk, Parish sneered. "Then I'll use her as bait. That'll get Scott Dunn to come to us."

"I have someone better in mind."

"Who?"

"Sue Masters."

Disbelief washed over Parish's face. "But I shot her."

Chuckling, Jerry turned to the plasma-ray monitor on the wall behind him. "Starnet, internal video feed, Sue Masters."

The monitor blinked, revealing a dimly lit room, a woman bound to the wall, and three security-bots administering taser lashes to her bare back.

Parish beamed as Sue's bloodcurdling screams shrieked from the sound system. "I'll be damned."

Laughing, Jerry was thankful he didn't have to endure the smell of her burning flesh. "This will motivate Scott Dunn to bring back what he has stolen from me."

Chapter Thirty-Two

D r. Navarro arrived at Presidents' Memorial Hospital in a rush. He hadn't enjoyed one minute of his supersonic jet ride from Colorado. Katherine's medical condition could deteriorate at any time, leaving him without her version of the events surrounding her death in 2010.

The attending physician, Dr. Demone, led him into a small office to debrief him before seeing his patient. "The nanoserum treatment has stabilized the condition," Demone told him. "Cigarette?"

"No thanks." Navarro saw a rotating hologram on the desk, a transparent figure of a man, his internal organs visible. "You shouldn't smoke."

"Yeah, yeah." Lighting up, Demone leaned against his desk in front of the anatomical display. "I believe the levitator has reduced the chances of congesting, though these things are only temporary."

"But she is coherent, correct?"

"Not when she arrived, but she's better now."

Stepping beside the desk, Navarro picked up the hologram, thinking he should have one of these in his office. "I need to see her right away."

Demone crossed his arms. "Are you going to tell

her?"

At that, Navarro felt a pang of regret. "She doesn't need to know."

"But, doctor, surely you know this treatment can't go on indefinitely."

He set the hologram down. "It's all I have to work with."

"This complication is typical, yes?" Demone inspected his smoldering cigarette.

"In 2010 they did a sloppy job of prepping her for cryonic freeze, and worse, they froze her in liquid nitrogen."

"Common practice back then," Demone noted.

A picture on the desk caught Navarro's attention, a plump woman dressed in a lacy dress. "But when Alcor switched Katherine to liquid hydrogen, they were unable to expel the nitrogen that saturated her body. Now she suffers the cryonic equivalent of the bends."

"Cryonic Relapse is very painful."

"But unlike scuba divers with the bends, a hyperbolic chamber has no effect." He lifted the picture from the desk. "Your wife?"

"She died."

"Sorry." Navarro set the picture down gently. "Nitrogen saturation from outdated cryonics technology, we know so little about it."

"Except that it's fatal." Demone snuffed out his unfinished cigarette and moved to the door. "I think you should tell her."

"I don't want to ruin the time she has left."

"It's your duty as her doctor. She may need to get her

affairs in order."

Navarro glanced at the visible man hologram. "Her husband has taken care of everything."

"You know this for a fact?"

"Alcor requires the proper paperwork, marriage certificates, financial statements, wills...we have it all on file."

"Then what's so important that you must see her before her next relapse?"

"It is a long story...goes back 225 years."

The intercom squawked: *"Paging Dr. Demone. Level forty-nine, stat."*

"Ah. It appears that I don't have time to hear it. Mrs. Evanston's pancreas is acting up again. I must attend to her. Come, I'll show you to Katherine on level forty-seven. It's on the way."

***

Scott stood vigil over Katherine in her hospital room. He'd spent the hours telling her about the grief syndrome, how he could never get close to anyone again for fear of watching them die, as he had watched his daughters grow old and die, and then his grandchildren. He told her about the Wellers, how they were all dead now, except for him...and now Liz, even after she'd committed suicide.

"Do you want her back?" Katherine asked.

"Dying was the only way she could find peace. I can't imagine living through that misery with Liz again."

"What are you going to do?"

"Stay as far away from her as I can."

Worried that John Parish could appear at any time to

finish them off, he moved to the door and checked the hallway. Robert hovered behind him. Scott feared that the bounty hunter could be wearing a doctor's smock, a janitor's coveralls, or a technician's white lab coat. He'd attack without warning. About now, Scott wished he hadn't left the dead guard's blaster in the Thunderclap. He paced back and forth, Robert mimicking his every turn.

"Sit down," Katherine said. "You guys are making me nervous."

The levitation bed tilted five degrees left.

"I should check on Myrtle in the car," Scott said, thinking he'd smuggle in the blaster on his way back. "She's probably thirsty."

"I gave her some water, sir," Robert said. *"Can I get you anything?"*

"How about a beer?"

"Sorry, sir. I am not programmed to serve alcohol."

"Good for you, Robert," Katherine said. "Scott's got enough problems...with his wife being back and all."

"She's been dead for 110 years," Scott stood by the levitator's elliptical force fields.

"I was frozen twice as long."

"Unbelievable...I mean, what cryonics can do."

"Things have changed a lot." Katherine's floating body ticked right four degrees. "I hardly recognize the world, just bits and pieces, I mean, look at this bed."

"Change is good."

"Jerry Well's the same."

"He's built himself an empire, a nature reserve, and now he wants an entire planet."

"Everything for himself," Katherine noted. "But

nothing he's done has made him a better person. And what about you, Scott? What have you done in the last 225 years that's made you a better person?"

"I...well...nothing, I guess. Moved around a lot...fixed cars, lived paycheck to paycheck...that's about it."

"Seems to me that a person who could live forever would be able to do a lot of good for the world. I mean, how many people have died before their life's work was complete? I wonder if Einstein were immortal, or Mother Teresa...think about Henry Ford, Alexander Graham Bell, Bill Gates. What could they have accomplished if they had lived forever?"

Scott understood what she was getting at. "And Glenn Gary."

"Who?"

Robert said, *"He invented hover technology. Ta da."*

"That's after my time." Katherine's levitator tilted again. "Don't you see, Scott? It's not how long you live...it's how you live, how well you share your life with the ones you love, the ones that love you."

She was right. He slumped back into the bedside chair. Since Liz died, he'd been running from life, from love, dueling with the demon of grief. There was never any peace, any closure, just grief, solitude, and the survivor's guilt that made him shun everyone who tried to get close to him. Now he realized he should have been sharing his life with someone special, doing something productive with his time.

Looking at Katherine, he felt the need to stop running, plant his feet, and settle down. He thought about Sue, wondered if she were dead or alive. How could he bear her funeral? He pictured himself standing over her coffin, tossing down white roses. The mental image stiffened his resolve to remain alone. He could never endure that much grief again.

Katherine's levitator pivoted two degrees left. The door creaked. A doctor came in: long smock, dark hair. Scott's anxiety level skyrocketed, fight or flight, but when he saw the doctor's face, he relaxed. It wasn't John Parish.

"Dr. Navarro," Katherine said.

"You look to be in quite a fix." He strode toward her. A small smile played at the corners of his mouth. Scott thought it looked forced.

"What are you doing here?"

"Checking on my favorite patient."

"I don't know what happened. I just woke up on this amusement park ride."

"Yes." He set a small disc on her chest, just above the white wrap that covered her breasts. A green light blinked on from the center of the disc. Scott thought it was some kind of medical gadget.

"I couldn't catch my breath," she added.

"Your alveoli have been leaking fluid into your lungs," Navarro explained. "And there is nitrogen buildup. It is very dangerous."

Scott didn't like the sound of that. "Is she going to be all right?"

"Who is your friend?" Navarro asked Katherine.

"Scott," she said. "Scott Dunn."

Navarro frowned, took off his glasses. "My last patient's name was Dunn...Elizabeth Dunn. Any relation?"

"She's my w-wife," Scott managed. "My miserable

wife. She committed suicide...over a hundred years ago."

Navarro winced. "And you have not forgiven her."

Never. "Jerry's going to use her in Katherine's place...to run for a seat on the Council."

"I work for Alcor. I am not aware of his plans."

"He sent an assassin to Washington. Ishar Anders is dead."

Navarro stepped back. "My God. Are you sure it was Jerry's doing?"

Katherine's body pitched down five degrees. "We came here to stop him. When can I get out of here?"

"One thing at a time." Navarro moved in, near one of the levitator's force fields, his profile glowing yellow and his face taut. "I have come to talk to you, Katherine, about your death."

"I'm dying?" she asked as if it were the time of day.

"Your first death."

"I don't understand."

Alarm tensed Scott's spine. "What are you saying?"

"I am suspicious of the circumstances of her death and subsequent internment at Alcor. Her brain shows no damage from the West Nile B virus." He turned to Katherine. "Do you remember how you died?"

Her face went ashen. "I don't want to talk about it."

Of course, Scott understood perfectly. Jerry wouldn't have frozen Katherine if her brain had been damaged. Scott checked his watch. *Thirty hours until the election.* He moved to the levitator opposite Dr. Navarro. "Tell him, Katherine. It might be our only hope of stopping Jerry Well. He can't run for the Council from a jail cell. Remember, there's no statute of limitations on murder."

"I have the medical evidence that contradicts his story of your death," Navarro assured her. "Your testimony is vital if I am to take this to the authorities."

Katherine closed her eyes. "It's true." She told him how Jerry had put her in the tub and covered her with ice, how he had frozen her alive.

"I knew it." Navarro snatched the disc from Katherine's chest. "It is all recorded here." He turned to Robert, stepped forward, bent down. "Easy there, little guy."

Robert backed away, beeping warily.

"It's all right," Scott told Robert.

Navarro inserted the disc into a data drive below the cyber-bot's chest monitor. "Starnet."

A rotating 3-D yellow star appeared on a blue background.

"Alcor Headquarters, priority Delta 47995, transmit."

WORKING flashed on the monitor.

Then: *TRANSMISSION SUCCESSFUL. END.*

"That should do it."

***

Across the country at Hylander, the plasma-ray monitor in Jerry Well's office flashed on. *"Starnet transmission detected."*

Jerry flew out of his chair. "Where?" He had placed an alert search on Robert's Starnet access encoding script. The system had detected it signing on and notified him directly.

"Delta 47995, originated Presidents' Memorial Hospital, Washington City Center."

"Send video feed," he instructed Starnet. "That'll get their attention." Activating the intercom, he said, "Parish, I've found them."

***

Back at the hospital, Robert started beeping like crazy, drawing Scott's attention. A hologram shot out the cyber-bot's gem-port, and floating in mid-air, the images of three security-bots appeared, black Honda USA Walkers. Their taser resonators crackled on rapid fire. "What's that, Robert?"

"Replay in progress, sir. I'm analyzing it for—"

A woman's scream suddenly shrieked through the room. The back of Scott's neck prickled. "What the hell's going on?"

In slow motion, the viewfinder tracked along the wriggling streams of energy to a woman's bare back. She was tied face-first to a wall. Blond hair flung to and fro as the woman writhed in agony. It was Sue. His heart almost stopped. She was alive. But how? He recognized the cellar under Jerry Well's mansion. She was his prisoner. The joy of seeing her again crumbled to the horror of her predicament. "I've got to go back to Hylander."

"My God," Navarro said.

Scott rushed to Katherine's side. "I thought she was dead."

"That poor woman...who is she?"

Reaching into his top pocket, he removed the blinking incandescent picture of Sue and handed it to Katherine. "Sue Masters...she saved my life."

Tasers crackling, Sue screamed again. Scott's insides

~337~

knotted. Fighting nausea, he shouted, "Turn it off, Robert."

"I'm trying, but the data feed is on a tracer beam, 47995. Jerry Well has found us."

Katherine grimaced, turned her eyes from the torture scene.

Parish's pockmarked face appeared in the hologram. "You've got somethin' of mine, Scott Dunn. Do ya wanna make a trade?"

"The vial."

"You should have destroyed it," Katherine said. "I warned you."

"I've got to get Sue out of there."

"She must be important to you...I mean, you'd go back to Hylander and risk your life for her?" She returned the picture to him.

Sue's screams ripped through the room.

Grimacing, Scott looked at Sue's smiling face, recalled when she'd given the picture to him, just before they left Hog Heaven, only minutes before John Parish shot her. He remembered how horrible he felt thinking she was dead. The grief. The guilt. But somehow she'd survived then came to his aid...risked her life again to battle the security-bots. Without her, he'd have never escaped Hylander. He couldn't help her then, but now... "Damn right I'd risk my life for her."

"Then I'm going with you."

"It's too dangerous...besides..." He indicated the levitation bed.

Finally, the morbid hologram flickered off. Robert shook so badly his antennas rattled. *"The odds of infiltrating Hylander and rescuing Sue are—"*

"Stuff it, Robert." Scott was sick of hearing how impossible the odds were. "By all rights I should be dead by now." He bent over Katherine. "You'll be all right here."

She gritted her teeth, began thrashing about. "You're not leaving me here."

Navarro jumped in. "Take it easy, Katherine."

"I'm not staying." She fought the force field.

"Stop it," Navarro said.

"Don't leave me here, Scott."

"Okay," Navarro conceded. "You can go."

"Get me out of this contraption."

"No way." Scott jumped between Navarro and Katherine. The last time he let someone get involved with his problems, she almost died. And now she was being tortured.

"You need me, Scott," Katherine pleaded, her face pinched with determination. "Jerry will open the doors for me."

"And he'll open the doors for this vial." Scott indicated his pocket. "I'm not putting you in danger."

"I thought Wellers didn't care about anyone but themselves."

He thought she understood what was going on in his head. Of course he cared, damn it. Sue mattered. Katherine mattered. Even Myrtle and the gambling cyber-bot mattered. They brought back those lost feelings of longing and compassion for someone else, feelings he'd suppressed since Liz committed suicide. It hurt, like knife blades to the heart. He didn't like the pain, but for the first time in a long time, he felt alive again. "This is different. You're not going."

"I'll reason with Jerry. He'll listen to me."

"You've never been able to stand up to your husband. He wins every time."

"I'm going anyway."

"No you're not."

Navarro cleared his throat. "Listen to me—"

"She's staying here," Scott cut him off. "Where she can get the medical attention she needs."

"I am trying to tell you...all of this medical technology is not going to save her."

Scott's lungs seized. "What?"

Navarro's eyes turned solemn. "I wasn't going to tell you this, Katherine, but in light of your discussion about leaving the hospital, it is not recommended."

"Why not? I'm better now."

"You are dying."

"No." Scott breathed. "She's fine."

"There is nothing we can do for her."

Amazingly, Katherine remained calm. "What's wrong with me?"

"CR. Cryonic Relapse. You suffered a major seizure. There will be more. They'll come faster and last longer."

"How much time do I have?"

He put his hand on her shoulder. "If you stay here, you will most likely survive the next two relapses. But out there..." he pointed to the window, "you will not survive the next one."

Her expression went flat. "When's the next one?"

"Twenty...maybe thirty hours. Do you still want to go with Scott?"

Katherine's eyes rolled up, as if she were seeking heaven or advice from a higher authority. A small tear appeared in the corner of her eye. "I'm going to die again." She said it with a sigh of relief.

Or so it seemed to Scott. For the entire time, he hadn't realized he'd been holding his breath, his mind rejecting all that came in. Katherine wasn't going to die. He couldn't accept it. He wouldn't. "Don't listen to him."

"Believe it," Navarro said. "Make the best of the time she has left." He walked out, the door closing softly behind him.

Denying it all, Scott searched her eyes, looking for any sign of hope. "He's wrong." He got on his knees. "Katherine, you've been given another chance at life."

"There's no such thing."

"But you've been through so much. You deserve to live a long and happy life." Then it hit him. The vial. Everlife would preserve her body in its present condition. An explosion of joy surged through him. "I got it." He sprang to his feet, danced in a circle, shoved his hand in his pocket and pulled out the vial. "This is the answer to the problem." Rushing back to Katherine's side, he showed her the vial. "Drink this and you will live."

Unbelievably, she looked away.

"Katherine?" He examined the vial, the crystal clear fluid inside, felt the smooth curve of the glass. Salvation was in his hand, and she didn't want it. A helpless feeling came over him, like when he was trying to save the Captain at the wedding but knowing failure was imminent. "Don't die on me."

"Dying's not so bad, Scott. People do it all the time."

That's when a stark realization hit him. She knew the truth about dying. Whatever it was, she didn't fear it. "W-what's it like?" he managed to ask her. "Death?"

Smiling, she thought a moment. "Sleep." There was a dreamy quality to her voice. "An unimaginable peace."

"Were you in heaven?"

"I don't know. It's like I woke up from a dream I can't remember. I was somewhere, I think, but wherever it was, nothing mattered there. Nothing at all."

He couldn't imagine that kind of place, but he knew he didn't want her to go back there. "Katherine, take the vial and live."

"I don't want it, Scott. Look what it's done to you."

He mulled over her inconceivable resolve, looked at the vial and then back at her stern face. "You never wanted it, did you."

"I'd have been stuck with Jerry Well forever. You saw how he treated me."

"I know, I know, but please, take it for me."

"You need it...to trade for Sue's life."

"Let me worry about Sue. You don't have to die."

"I don't want to end up like Liz."

"You won't."

"No? What makes you think I'm so strong? I could suffer from the grief syndrome, distance myself from everyone, live alone...like you. No thanks."

She was right. Reluctantly, he slipped the vial back into his pocket, but still hoping she'd change her mind before the next seizure.

"Now that that's settled, I'm going to help you rescue the woman you love."

He blinked in disbelief. "I never said that."

"Because you haven't accepted it yet. You're going to be her hero now, so let me go with you. Besides, you don't want to face Liz alone."

"Liz?" His breath hitched.

"You're going to rescue her too, right?"

"She's dead, I mean...to me, she'll always be dead."

"But she's your wife."

"Till death do us part. That was the extent of our contract. I'm free to go."

"You don't mean that."

He hung his head. Deep down, he hadn't forgiven her for leaving him like she did. The blood. The shock. The disbelief. His life became an empty, loveless slate...because of Liz. Now she was Jerry Well's problem. "I'm going back for Sue, that's all."

"Parish is counting on that, you know. You should have destroyed the vial."

Scott didn't agree. The vial was the only thing keeping Sue alive. And so what if he was in love with her? He turned to Robert. "Fire up the Thunderclap. We're going back to Hylander."

"Aye, aye, sir." He hovered to the door.

"And send Dr. Demone in here." Scott took the vial from his pocket. "I need him to do something for me."

Robert beeped and was gone.

Chapter Thirty-Three

Thunder rattled the windows in Hylander mansion. Over Starnet, Jerry watched the poll results come in, predictions for the upcoming election to the Council of Elders. He could see that he and Liz had a decisive lead over the other couples. What a depressing woman. After the Alpha Ketari issue was settled, he wouldn't need Scott Dunn's suicidal wife any longer. Jerry's phony marriage to her could then be annulled...with a blaster.

Pleased with the numbers scrolling down his wall-sized plasma-ray monitor, he leaned back in his chair and devoured a granola bar. Everything was going as planned. Scott Dunn and the last vial of Everlife had left Washington, and according to the hospital's data transmissions, Katherine remained behind in bed with pneumonia. He would retrieve her later.

"Starnet. Inquiry, ATC, One-Zero-Three-J-Well."

"ETA, twenty minutes, sir."

Yes, right on time. Scott Dunn and Sue Masters were in for a *frigid* reunion. He laughed.

"Starnet, Capitol riot, view."

The monitor blinked to a scene at the Capitol. Pepper gas mist drifted across the lawns. Environmentalists threw rocks at Secret Service bots, and guardsmen ducked behind riot shields and advanced, their taser streams set to stun. The assassination of a Council member and the subsequent delay of the final vote on Alpha Ketari had angered the mob into mayhem, exactly as Jerry had predicted.

"Starnet, Council of Elders, update."

The monitor switched to a slick-suited reporter from CNSS. "Behind the scenes, funeral preparations are underway for Ishar Anders, assassinated yesterday, thus unseating Dar Anders just before the final vote on Alpha Ketari. Elections to replace the distinguished couple will be held in twenty hours."

Just as the law required, Jerry thought.

"Starnet, investigation, assassination report."

"Authorities confirmed two dead attackers. After discovering fake travel vouchers for three men, a third suspect is being sought."

Jerry's blood pressure went up. Parish may have left a trail back to Hylander. Now he'd have to execute his plan to get rid of the bounty hunter sooner than expected.

"Exit Starnet." He opened his top desk drawer and took out his gleaming silver and gold Derringer 840 mini-blaster. After verifying the particle charge indicator was loaded with four shots, he put it in his cloak pocket and activated the intercom. "John Parish, report to my office."

The bounty hunter entered. Jerry knew his plan would have to work perfectly, his aim true. "Is everything prepared for our arriving guests?" He kept his tone businesslike.

"Alcor's people are standin' by." Parish leaned on the desk. "But they say they can't do the procedure downstairs.

Might muck it up."

"I don't care if they can do it right or not, just as long as it's done."

"All I want is my vial. Then I'm outta here."

"And that brings us to another problem."

Parish sniffed the garlicky air. "Must be serious. You're stinkin' up the place."

Trying to stay calm, Jerry folded his hand around the blaster in his pocket. "The authorities are on to you, John."

He stiffened. "That's not possible."

"Something about travel vouchers."

"I faked 'em, Jerry." He paced across the office. "They're untraceable." Pivoting on his heels, his face suddenly turned stone cold as his wide-open eyes seized on the mini-blaster Jerry pointed at him. "What..?"

"You're not going to Florida after all." Jerry aimed the small gun at Parish, hoping he would be intimidated. "I'm making a citizen's arrest for the assassination of Ishar Anders." It was a lie, of course. The bounty hunter was going to die.

"You and what army?" Parish's hand moved slowly toward the blaster holstered at his side.

Jerry stepped from behind the desk, his nerves on high alert for any sudden movement from Parish. "Life in prison without parole, John, not very appealing to a guy whose life's dream was to sail around the world."

He couldn't resist toying with the bounty hunter, savoring the control he had over him. The anger in Parish's eyes was lethal, intoxicating. Made the moment more memorable. Jerry had waited a long time for this. "You and your father and your grandfather, you're all alike, just money grubbing fools, dealing in human flesh. None of you got the big picture."

"Livin' on another planet with Katherine ain't my idea of a good time." Parish moved his hand closer to the blaster. "Just give me my vial of Everlife. I'll be gone before the cops get here."

"There is no vial, John."

Frowning, "I saw it," Parish said.

"It was sugar water."

Parish bared his teeth. "I should've known you'd screw me." He went for his blaster.

Pheuw!

Jerry shot him in the chest.

Staggering backward, the bounty hunter managed to get off a wild shot. The wall-mounted plasma-ray monitor exploded. Jerry dove behind his desk just as a blast of glass shards and sparkling plasma modules blew over his head. Two blaster bolts hit the wall behind him, punching holes. Ducking the shower of fiery particle dust, he scooted to the end of the desk, looked around it, saw Parish standing in the center of the room, firing the blaster with both hands, elbows locked. The chest wound hadn't fazed him.

Pheuw-Pheuw!

Jerry scrambled backwards just as the corner of the desk exploded in a shower of splinters. "Goddamnit, Parish."

"You're a dead man."

He was pinned down. Three shots left in the mini-blaster.

Pheuw!

Another bolt shot through the desk nearly hitting his

ear. He could feel the heat. Heart hammering, he was trapped behind a desk that offered no protection against a blaster.

Pheuw Pheuw!

Sparks and splinters flew everywhere.

The door was too far away. If he tried to make a run for it, Parish would cut him down for sure. There had to be a way to distract him. Then he remembered the virtual display. That was it. Risking a blown-off hand, he reached up and touched the sensor pad on the desktop.

With a droning sound, the hologram rose up around Parish, 10,000 volts of sustained light-imaging power and 50,000 watts of 3-D graphic illumination.

Parish screamed.

Jerry jumped up, saw Eternal Hylander sputter and hiss as forks of static electricity speared the bounty hunter's body. He went into convulsions, dropped the blaster. His bug-eyes were nearly popped out of their sockets, but in spite of the unimaginable pain, his rage drove him forward like a charging bull.

Standing his ground, Jerry raised the mini-blaster and steadied it with both hands. "Goodbye, John Parish."

Pheuw!

One shot, right between the eyes. The bounty hunter's knees buckled, but his forward momentum caused him to slam headlong over the desk and land on Jerry. They hit the floor in a heap. The Derringer went flying.

Jerry struggled to catch his breath under the bounty hunter's weight. Blood dripped from the hole singed through his skull and pooled on the floor beside Jerry's head. The stench of burned flesh caused bile to rise from

Jerry's stomach.

Swallowing hard, he rolled Parish off him, stood and glanced around for the mini-blaster. Not seeing it, he turned off the virtual display. As Eternal Hylander sank back into the floor, he looked down at the dead bounty hunter, his startled eyes staring out into empty space. The victory made Jerry feel invincible. He rifled Parish's pockets, found an energy cuff deactivation chip, keys, a handful of bills, and several bank chips. Spoils go to the victor, he thought and picked up Parish's dropped blaster. It was less than half charged.

Just then, perimeter security announced, *"The Thunderclap is approaching, sir."*

He'd have to clean up this mess later. Shortly, he'd have the vial back, and Scott Dunn would finally die. Jerry jammed the blaster behind his belt. It was going to be a great day.

Terry Wright

Chapter Thirty-Four

In a driving rainstorm, the Thunderclap 9000 descended on final approach to Hylander. Scott watched Robert fight the controls. It had been a rough flight back from Washington. They'd spent the time trying to work out a plan to free Sue Masters. It all came down to Katherine. They'd have to surrender to get inside, and then she'd have to make a deal with Jerry, her cooperation with the election in exchange for Sue's freedom, and Scott's. It was a risky plan, especially when dealing with Jerry Well. Scott didn't trust him as far as he could throw him.

Lightning flashed. Myrtle trembled in Scott's lap...a bad omen. He petted her. "It'll be all right, girl." Descending, the flying car pitched and yawed in the wind.

Katherine, energy-strapped in the seat next to him, put her hand on his thigh. Her touch tore at his heart. The thought of her impending death was unbearable. He couldn't accept it. The hospital hadn't officially discharged her. He hoped to get her back there as quickly as possible.

Below, on the sprawling lawn in front of the mansion, security-bots gathered with their weapons raised. Rain soaked their crescent black bodies and drizzled off gray sensor covers that looked like inverted bowls on their electronic heads. Scott detected a rise in his garlicky odor and tried to stay calm.

The Thunderclap settled to the ground, its engine whining down to a subtle whir. Myrtle uncurled from Scott's lap and stretched.

"The security-bots demand that you throw out your weapon first," Robert said. *"Shall I shut them down?"*

"Jerry will just reactivate them." Scott retrieved the blaster from under the seat. "Tell them I'm unarmed."

"Their scanners have detected one blaster aboard, sir. I suggest you comply."

Scott looked at Katherine. "I won't be able to protect you."

"We don't need the gun. He wants my cooperation. That'll be enough."

"Why don't I feel good about that?" Scott set Myrtle on the floor.

The bubbletop rose with a whine. Wind driven rain streaked in and stung Scott's face. Knowing he would regret it, he tossed out the blaster. The doors opened. Hands up, he and Katherine stepped out on the rain-slicked lawn. Several security-bots herded them together and prodded them toward the mansion with the barrels of their blasters. Robert beeped a lonely, left-behind tone as he rose from the flyer.

Halfway to the house, the *pheuw* of blasters erupted behind Scott. Startled, he turned in time to see hovering Robert tilt in the air and crash to the ground, smoke swirling from his body seams, sparks flying. A squad of security-bots had shot him. Scott turned to run back to him, but Katherine grabbed his arm. "They'll just shoot you too."

Terry Wright

Walking backward, he saw the mechanical assassins gather around their victim. Their attention was so firmly rooted on Robert's demise, they failed to notice Myrtle drop from the flyer and dash off toward the garden. The sight of her scurrying away made Scott feel a little better, but just a little. *Poor Robert.*

The security-bots escorting Katherine and Scott nudged him around, and as he stumbled forward, he felt the crushing weight of grief. Katherine, walking next to him, wet and shivering, would die from Cryonic Relapse. He couldn't get that out of his mind. And Sue, she was in a terrible predicament, inside the mansion cellar, bound and tortured. And then there was Liz, alive again in all her misery. On top of that, Robert had been shot down in the front yard, a cyber-bot as human to him as any machine could ever be. Scott's knees wobbled. The grief was more than he could bear, but he kept moving, kept hoping he could save them but fearing he was destined to fail again.

Inside the house, the mechanical killers split them up, two of them forcing Katherine down a retreating hallway.

"Where are you taking her?"

"I'll be all right," she called out and was gone.

There was nothing he could do to help her. The security-bots shoved him down another hallway and stopped at a closed door. Toning, the door unlocked and they pushed him inside. *"You have five minutes."*

The room looked like a war zone. "What's this?" He'd expected to be locked in the cellar...with Sue. Was she here instead? "Sue?"

He heard a whimper coming from behind an upturned mattress, a sound he'd heard before, a sound he'd never thought he'd hear again. His throat went dry. "Liz?"

"Go away."

His stomach lurched at the sound of her voice. He didn't want to see her. Turning to leave, he saw the two bots standing guard at the open door. Obviously they'd been ordered to bring him here while Jerry dealt with Katherine. The sadistic son of a bitch. But Scott wasn't going to give him the pleasure of a confrontation with Liz. "Get me out of here," he ordered the bots. But they stood stoic, mute, as if in sleep mode while blocking the door.

Five minutes. With Liz. Five minutes of pure hell.

He turned again to the upturned mattress but couldn't see her. For the moment, that was fine with him, but as he stood there, anger hit him like a ball bat. For all the times he'd cursed her, for all the times he'd blamed her for ruining his life, it all came roaring to the surface. "Liz."

Sob. "Leave me alone."

"You have some explaining to do."

"Fuck you."

"You left me—"

"What are you talking about?" A bald head appeared over the mattress. Her tear-soaked eyes were slits of rage. "I... hate...you." She gasped. "Oh no...Scott...oh my God. It's you." She started bawling. "I thought you...were that bastard Jerry."

Scott swallowed. Liz was bruised and beaten. Goddamned Jerry Well. Seeing her this way tore Scott's heart out. No matter what she'd done, she didn't deserve this abuse. Something deep inside drove him forward, kicking away strewn clothes and busted furniture to get to her. "Liz."

"Scott." She struggled to her feet.

He saw a stooped woman in a wrinkled and bloody gown. Her toenails and fingernails were still black from cryonic freeze. She looked just as bad as the picture he'd seen of her on Starnet. He threw his arms around her anyway. Tears stung his eyes. "What happened to us?"

"I couldn't take it anymore," she cried.

Her embrace felt bony and cold. "But you're back. How?"

"They froze me, Scott."

"You never gave me the chance to say goodbye."

"Look at me. I'm a mess."

He noticed stitches in her throat, the fishy smell of nanocream on her skin.

"I don't want to be here. I don't want to be alive."

"But they've fixed you up. You've been given another chance at life."

She pushed away from him. "I don't want it."

"Why?"

"Nothing's changed," she said, fists clenched. "The girls are gone, the grandkids. I can't go on without them."

"But killing yourself wasn't the answer."

"Look." She bent over, picked up a shard of glass from the floor, and with a smooth swipe, cut her wrist. Blood gushed out a severed artery.

Scott gasped in disbelief. Before he could recover from shock and move to help her, the blood flow stopped.

"They put something in me so I can't kill myself again."

"Nanoserum," Scott said, relieved in a way. "It can fix anything except a brain injury. Jerry wants you alive...and so do I."

"Doesn't anyone care what I want?"

"It's always been about what you want, Liz. What about the rest of us?"

"I don't care."

He knew she meant it. "Well, I care." He snatched the glass from her bloody hand. "I'll give you a chance to change your mind." Moving to the open door and the stoic bots, Scott stabbed the lock with the shard of glass and broke it off in the mechanism. When he turned to face her again, he wondered if this would even save her from herself. "After they take me away, you can open the door."

"Don't do me any favors."

"You'll have to hide somewhere until Jerry leaves for the elections. Where you go and what you do from there is up to you. It's your life. It's what you make of it."

"I'm not going anywhere." Liz jammed her hands on her hips. "With any luck, Jerry will beat me to death."

Scott grabbed her shoulders. "Get out while you still can. He *will* kill you."

"If not...I'll find a way to die, Scott."

He feared she would. "I'm sorry things turned out the way they did."

"I'm not."

"You made your own misery."

She scowled at him. "And I suppose you've been living happily ever after."

He lowered his head. No. Katherine was right. He'd wasted all that time. "I've been okay," he lied.

The security-bots ratcheted into motion. *"Time's up."* They strode in, grabbed Scott's arms.

"Good luck, Liz."

She only glared at him as the bots escorted him out to the hallway. The door closed, and the lock made a crunching sound. He could only hope that what he'd done and what he'd said had been enough to save her. If nothing else, he had closure now.

The bots wrestled him down the stairs, down a familiar corridor, and stopped at the cellar door. After unlocking it, they pushed him inside. He landed in the dirt, right back where he started. The door slammed shut. He couldn't see anything, his eyes not yet accustomed to the darkness, but he heard someone's scratchy breathing.

"Who's there?"

"Scott?" The voice was weak and raspy, but familiar.

He got up on his knees. "Sue?"

"I thought I smelled garlic."

Straining his eyes to find her, he groped the darkness. "What have they done to you?"

"It took you long enough to get here."

With help from the sliver of light seeping in under the door, her form began to take shape, standing upright, arms outstretched, legs spread. By the time he got to his feet, he could see she was chained to the wall, face first, wearing nothing but panties. "Oh, damn, Sue." He rushed to her.

"Don't touch me."

Stopping two feet from her, he saw taser blisters crisscrossing her back. No wonder she didn't want him to touch her. Rage boiled up inside him. "I'll kill Jerry for this."

"Can I watch?"

At least her sense of humor was intact. "I'm sure we

haven't seen the last of his brutality."

"He wants the vial," she said. "Do you have it?"

"He's going to get the vial, all right," Scott replied, reaching into his right pants pocket. "But not the one he expected." He pulled out the vial of Everlife, and remembering how Myrtle had dug a hole in the floor to hide the key, he got on his knees where the cot used to be and began scraping at the soft dirt with his fingertips.

"Are we going to tunnel our way out?" Sue asked.

"Shhh."

Footsteps.

He dug faster. The footsteps were getting closer. His hole was only two inches deep, now three.

"They're coming," Sue whispered.

Four inches. He put the vial in the hole, covered it and patted it down. The electronic lock clicked and the door swung open, flooding the room with light.

By that time, he was on his feet, brushing dirt from his hands.

Jerry Well strolled in, his cloak swaying. Two security-bots flanked him. "Sorry I couldn't greet you when you first arrived," he said with his usual arrogance. "But I had to teach Katherine a lesson." He rubbed his knuckles. "I think she now realizes that there is no escaping me."

The son of a bitch. With a right hook, Scott swung at Jerry's jaw, but tasers lashed out from the security-bots, blocking his blow. Scott gritted his teeth and brought all his strength to bear against the taser streams focused on his fist. The heat and the pressure intensified until finally, he was thrown back against the wall. "Why did you have to beat her?"

"It's your fault. You brought her back to me."

"She was going to cooperate with you."

"Sure she was. But there's still the matter of my vial." His voice was calm as if reading from his shopping list.

"I plan to give it to you." Scott squared his shoulders. "Release Sue first."

"Yes. Perhaps we can come to agreeable terms." He nodded at the security-bots. They responded by amping up the taser voltage and giving Sue a jolt that sent her into screaming spasms.

"Or perhaps not."

"Stop," Scott shouted.

"Give me the vial."

"Don't do it, Scott," Sue yelled.

Sizzling tasers hit her again. Her bloodcurdling scream echoed through Hylander mansion.

Scott couldn't stand it. "All right." He reached in his left pocket and produced a second vial, one Dr. Demone had prepared for him before they left the hospital. "Take it."

Jerry's eager eyes went to the vial. "So my terms it is." He snatched the vial from Scott's hand.

"You've got what you want. Now let us go."

Jerry grinned. "I have other plans for you."

"You bastard—" Scott had no idea what hit him, but the lights went out.

***

Myrtle found the garden fascinating, the mud puddles a joy to frolic in, the rain refreshing. But she was hungry now and headed for the mouse hole that led inside the house. Halfway across the lawn, she came across an interesting sight and stopped to investigate. The rain tapped on a cyber-bot lying on the grass. It smelled burnt. She walked around it, nosing the air, testing for any hint of activity. There was none, and no way to get inside it and explore.

Bored, she again set off for the mouse hole. That's when she heard a scream. It was Sue...in the house...hurry. But when she got to the mouse hole, she found it plugged with mud. No problem. She loved to dig and went at it with urgency.

Before long, she was scampering across the kitchen floor, leaving little muddy footprints behind her. She romped through the carpeted room, exploring every nook and cranny, some familiar, some new. She hoped to pick up Sue's scent. When she got to an open doorway, she froze.

A human was lying on the floor inside the room. She recognized its smell. Her tail hairs flared. She remembered the mineshaft when this human first appeared. Fire. Smoke. Noise.

Teeth bared, she slinked into the room and approached the thing that brought back those awful images. It wasn't moving, like the cyber-bot on the lawn. She crept around the human but sensed nothing alive. Relieved, she turned away, saw a glint of silver and gold...on the floor...by the wall. This was more than she could resist, a prize...shiny and new.

She bounded over, pounced on it, dragged it across the floor, flipped it over, picked it up and hightailed it out of there. The joy of the find, the catch, and the steal, this was something ferrets loved best: besides eating and digging and sleeping and exploring.

As she skittered down the hallway, a peculiar sound came to her...from somewhere up ahead. Could it be Sue? She kept moving toward the sound, the prize clasped firmly in her teeth. A little farther...scamper, scamper...over there. She came to a closed door. The sound was coming from the other side, a moaning sound that caused her alarm.

Sue. Sue. Sue.

But nothing in the air smelled like Sue.

Myrtle set down her prize, flattened her body, and squeezed through the two-inch crack under the door. She sniffed the air for danger. Satisfied, she turned around, stuck her head back under the door, and grabbed the prize in her teeth. Backing up, she ran into a problem. The prize didn't fit. It wouldn't come through the crack. She wrestled with it, yanking and pulling, banging and clunking.

***

Katherine curled up on a bed in the small room in which Jerry had imprisoned her. She'd been moaning: the injuries she'd sustained from the last beating painful, the mental anguish of his verbal assault eroding her sense of self-worth. "It's all your fault," he'd shouted and hit her again. "You shouldn't have run off with Scott." *BAM!* "You had sex with him, didn't you." Another blow, another blast of pain. She fought back, but he overpowered her, beat her some more. As she sobbed, he gently lifted her chin and forced her to look into his heartless eyes, touched the blood on her face with his thumb...and started to cry. "I'm so sorry." He fell to his knees, professing his love and promising never to hurt her again.

Lies. All lies.

A racket coming from the door interrupted her thoughts, an unusual combination of thumping and scraping. She wanted it to stop. She wanted to be left alone. From the sound, she knew it wasn't one of those murderous security-bots coming in...or Jerry Well returning to beat her again.

"Go away," she muttered.

The annoying clatter persisted, stimulating her curiosity. "What do you want?"

There was no answer, just frantic ruckus.

When she looked, she saw Scott's little ferret in a tug-of-war with something under the door. Surprise overcame torment. She got off the bed to investigate. A sudden wave of dizziness overwhelmed her. She toppled to the floor. Her hand went to her face. She felt a large bump, a swollen brow, and a split lip. She wished she hadn't fought back and escalated Jerry's anger.

Myrtle scampered over to her, that furry face with the silver mask, full of mischief as she darted to and fro. Or was it urgency in her beady eyes? "Okay, okay. I'm coming."

She pulled herself along the floor like a cripple. Jerry had forced her to wear a thin gown. Every muscle in her body ached. She wished the final seizure would end her suffering. Sleep. No more violent world. No more abusive husband. No pain. No sorrow. Only peace. She didn't envy Scott Dunn's immortal life one bit.

At the door, she peered underneath it, curious what all the fuss was about. Myrtle was there with her, looking too, a squeak in her throat. Katherine spotted the object of the ferret's attention, but she wasn't sure what it was. Gold and silver, it looked like a small gun, but different from any gun she'd ever seen. It had a short barrel with rings around it, a pushbutton trigger. She wondered where Myrtle had found it.

Just then, footsteps pattered up to the door. She saw bare toes with black toenails, a hand reaching down, fingers with black nails curling around the gun. "Who's there?"

The gun was gone. The feet turned. She saw someone's heels, pressed her cheek harder to the floor. "Hello?" She didn't want to shout and draw unwanted attention. "I'm Katherine." She heard sobbing. "Will you talk to me?"

The feet didn't move.

"Who are you?"

A woman's voice cried out, "I'm going to do it right this time."

"Liz, is that you?"

Pheuw!

Katherine jumped.

A body hit the floor with a thud.

Horrified, she sat up, pressed her back to the door, and squeezed her eyes shut. "Oh God, no." Fists clenched, she couldn't move, a cold blade of fear stabbing her heart.

Myrtle scooted under the door and was gone.

***

Dr. Navarro arrived in Boulder. He went directly to his office to retrieve the scanner readouts of Katherine's perfect brain, the brain that should have been destroyed by the West Nile B virus two hundred twenty five years ago.

That, along with Alcor's original internment transcripts and Katherine's recorded testimony, would prove Jerry Well had murdered her.

Navarro needed to be at a meeting with homicide detectives in thirty minutes. Turning to leave, he heard his terminal beep. A message notified him that an Alcor team was on duty at Hylander mansion. What for, he wondered, examining the data screen. There wasn't a patient's name listed for reanimation...or any specific job description. A cold sweat trickled down between his shoulder blades. What was Jerry Well up to now? Navarro sent an inquiry to the team but got no response. This stressed him deeply. Were they too busy to answer? What were they doing? He feared something bad was about to happen at Hylander. Worse, he had no time to look into the matter.

He sent a message to the team. *"RETURN TO ALCOR AT ONCE. NO DELAY."*

Then he left for the meeting with homicide detectives.

Chapter Thirty-Five

Slowly, Scott became aware of a pinprick of light approaching in the darkness, growing and glowing as it neared at breathtaking speed. The feeling of weightlessness came next, and his first reaction was pure amazement, this floating sensation of death. It was true, all the things he'd heard about the light. *Go into the light.*

It came nearer and brighter, and soon it was so overpowering that it hurt his eyes. His head throbbed, and he felt cold...freezing cold. Death was very cold, he thought, and then he suddenly realized that he was able to think. Terror grabbed his chest. He felt his heart beating wildly.

His eyes blew open, his mind swimming in confusion. He found himself floating on his back, his body wrapped like a mummy in white gauze, the air so cold he could see his breath.

My God. I'm not dead.

At first, the revelation relieved him, but as he lifted his head and looked around a bright room of white walls, a new terror gripped him. He didn't know where he was, but he realized he felt weightless because levitators were suspending his body in mid-air. And beyond his bare toes, he saw the blurry form of a tall Alcor cryostat labeled 34-

B...bold black letters...the lid open. Its outer shell seam was split and the sides were rolled back revealing an extended mechanism of steel bands...no...they were more like clawed fingers or the jaws of a trap. It looked like a mechanical monster waiting to be fed. His eyes followed a black hose that ran from a fitting on the cryostat to a tank labeled *liquid hydrogen*. He could see vapor...and there were machines lining the walls. Hazy figures wearing white hoods and gowns moved like ghosts in the bright glow.

"Hey," he called out in a hoarse voice he barely recognized. "Help me."

The ghosts turned their glass faces toward him. One stepped forward, but the others pulled him back.

"Scott."

"Sue?" He was surprised to hear her voice. "Where are you?"

"Right next to you, in trouble again, as usual."

Craning his neck left, Scott tried to focus on her floating form beside him. "What happened?"

"The bots hit you with a concussion bomb. I thought you were dead."

"Now you know how I felt when I thought *you* were dead." He strained against the tightly wrapped gauze.

"I-I was sure I'd lost you," she stammered.

He squirmed. "Something tells me you still might." His vision cleared. Every muscle in his body contracted. He saw her hovering over an embalming table. She was wrapped in gauze, and her head was shaved bald. Two black Xs had been drawn on her crown. "Oh my God, Sue. Look at you."

"You don't look any better." She tipped her head.

"What?" He twisted his shoulders and looked down. There was an embalming table underneath him, too. He could see his reflection in the chromium finish, the black Xs marked on his shaved head, and the terror in his eyes. Panic raced up his spine. "What the hell is going on?"

Thump.

Jerry Well's laughter filled the room.

Whipping his head around, Scott saw the door was closed. The madman had entered. He was dressed in a long thermal robe.

"Good of you to join us, Scott Dunn."

Katherine hobbled at his side, beaten and bloody, her eyes staring out from blackened sockets. Wearing only a thin white gown, she was shivering. "Scott—"

"I thought you were going to make a deal with him."

"It's no use," she cried.

A ghostly figure stormed up to Jerry, pointed an accusatory finger. "I cannot stand by any longer. This is highly illegal. These people are not dead. I must notify Alcor of this outrage."

Jerry pulled a blaster from under his robe and shot the detractor right between the eyes. His hood exploded, blood red, and his body collapsed to the floor with a thump.

"Anyone else?" Jerry waved the blaster at the other stoic ghosts. Suddenly, a message came over the network link: *RETURN TO ALCOR AT ONCE. NO DELAY.* But no one dared answer it.

Never before had Scott felt such loathing for another human being. Even the terrorists he'd assassinated had some redeeming qualities, a love of children or a cause they were willing to die for. But not Jerry Well, the self-centered control freak that he was. Scott writhed in his gauze cocoon. "I'll kill you."

"I think not." Jerry stood next to him, bending to speak into his face. "It is I who control your destiny," he gloated. "And in less than ten hours, I will have Alpha Ketari. Nothing can stop me now." Turning, he grabbed Katherine's arm and yanked her close to him. "And in your final moments, Scott Dunn, you will witness my sweetest victory."

"Your v-victory's an illusion, Jerry," Scott growled, shivering. "You'll never have Katherine."

Jerry grinned. "And that is where you are wrong." He produced the vial from his pocket and shoved it at Katherine. "It's time for you to join me, my dear, in immortality."

Gasping, her eyes got big. "No." She tried to pull away from him, but he wouldn't let her go.

Scott hadn't told her that the vial was a fake. He couldn't tell her it was safe to drink without arousing Jerry's suspicion, so adding to the ruse, he shouted at the ghosts standing by the machines. "Help her, goddamnit."

They didn't respond.

"You're wasting your breath." Jerry uncorked the vial. "Drink up, Katherine."

"Let them go first," she said. "I'll do whatever you want."

"Katherine, no," Scott shouted.

Jerry swiveled the blaster to Scott's temple. "It's a fair request, Scott Dunn, don't you think...her immortality for your life...and Sue's? It's a generous offer that I accept...after she drinks the Everlife. On the other hand, if she doesn't, I'll kill you right now."

"Why do you need Katherine?" Scott pressed, hoping the gun wouldn't go off. "You've got Liz."

"Liz is dead," Jerry commented matter-of-factly.

"What?"

"Your wife killed herself again, the ungrateful bitch."

Heart sinking, Scott looked at Katherine.

She bowed her head, nodded. "It's true."

"Oh no," he said. She'd found a way. "Poor Liz."

"Drink the Everlife, Katherine," Jerry insisted. "Or your boyfriend is going to join his dead wife."

"Don't do it, Katherine. You can't trust him."

She looked at Jerry with hopeful eyes. "You'll let them go, right?"

"Isn't that what I said?" He smiled slyly.

"I don't believe you. Why should I?"

He tilted his head. "I told you I was sorry, Katherine." He smiled like an innocent little boy. "Things are going to be different between us...on Alpha Ketari. I promise."

"You expect me to believe you?"

"Then you leave me no choice but to pull the trigger." His elbow came up as if to brace himself for the blaster's recoil. "Say goodbye to Scott Dunn."

Scott stiffened, expecting the flash.

"Wait." Katherine's shoulders sagged. "All right." Trembling, she took the vial from his hand and looked at Scott. "I can't let him kill you."

"Smash it," Scott shouted.

She inhaled, paused, and then threw down the sugar water in a single gulp. Wincing, she dropped the vial, shattering it on the floor. She probably didn't think it would taste so sweet.

Just then, as everyone's attention was on the tinkling shards of glass, Scott spotted Myrtle bounding into the room, something gold and silver clamped in her teeth. Silently, she scooted behind a nearby machine. He wished she'd find somewhere else to play.

Jerry looked up from the broken vial and grinned. "You see, Scott Dunn, my victory is now complete. I have everything, and all that's left for you is a frozen eternity in 34-B."

"What?" Scott said, filled with alarm.

Katherine shouted, "But you said you'd let them go."

Jerry laughed. "I lied." Brandishing the blaster, he turned to the ghosts. "Proceed."

The levitators lowered Scott to the cold embalming table. Heart hammering, he strained to look over at Sue and saw that she too must have been lowered to the table next to him. He couldn't see her anymore. This can't be happening. They couldn't die now, not after all they'd been through.

An Alcor tech appeared above him, raised a bucket and dumped ice on Scott's chest. The sudden intense cold knocked the air from his lungs. "Jerry," he rasped, flopping on the table like a fish. "What are you doing?"

Jerry grinned. "Prepping you for cryonic freeze, of course."

"You've got to be joking."

"We must lower your body temperature slowly," Jerry explained. "Freeze you too fast, your cells will explode. I assure you, it's no joke."

"With ice?"

"A thermal-freon chamber is too good for you. Besides, you'll suffer more this way, like Katherine, when I froze her to death back in 2010."

"You bastard."

"It was for her own good."

Scott kicked and squirmed. Another bucket of ice hit him in the stomach, and then another and another. It soon became impossible to move under the heavy ice. The cold bit into him like a pack of mad dogs. He began to shiver violently.

"S-Scott," Sue shrieked. "I can't breathe."

God no. They were packing her in ice, too.

Laughing, Jerry moved to her table. "Hypothermia is a sneaky killer." He leered down at her. "Oh yes, you'll fight the cold for a while, but as your core temperature falls, your internal organs begin to shut down, one at a time. Your heart slows...your brain starves for oxygen...your kidneys fail. You'll get weaker as your body expends energy in an attempt to stay warm. And then you'll get sleepy, but you won't dare close your eyes for fear you'll never wake up."

"Don't do this to her," Scott shouted. "It's me you want. You've already won. Let her go."

Jerry laughed some more.

Chapter Thirty-Six

D r. Navarro chose to ride with the police captain in a Thunderbolt Cruiser piloted by a Teledyne cyber-bot, its onboard processor in constant contact with all the other tactical vehicles converging on Hylander. The safety of the Alcor team was on Navarro's mind. They'd been incommunicado for too long. With this immediate crisis and the overwhelming evidence against Jerry Well in Katherine's murder, a task force was assembled in short order. The thought of Jerry Well in energy cuffs was only overpowered by the spectacle unfolding beyond the flyer's windscreen.

Blaster bolts shrieked by as the flying police cruiser pitched nose-down and rolled right. Two nearby cars exploded. Another angled toward the ground, smoking. Hover-copters slewed in sideways and unleashed a barrage of white-hot particle bombs that punched holes in Hylander's perimeter wall. Fireballs billowed up, and black smoke churned into a rain-soaked sky.

"Take us in low and slow," the captain said.

A knot of dread twisted in Navarro's stomach. Jerry Well wasn't going to give up without a fight.

***

Inside the tiniest microcircuits in the most complex onboard computer ever built by Teledyne Robotics International, an electron moved. It wasn't a random event or a fluke, but a deliberate command from a failsafe program embedded deep within the machine's main processor. In this synchronized world of silicon, diodes, and fitzors, this simple act set off a chain reaction. Though the total machine had no concept of the processes taking place, the computer core was well aware of its intentions: an emergency reboot in *SAFE* mode.

Subsystems came online. Drivers were analyzed, damages assessed, decisions made. Information from self-diagnostic sensors indicated most of the blaster damage was centered in the main hover engine compartment and service module where an automatic fire extinguishing system had activated, sparing vital components and contributing to the large amount of smoke that had poured from the machine at breakdown.

Having determined these facts, the main processor went to work. *Audio: on. Video: scan.* Data banks flickered; some booted up, some failed entirely. Bypass circuits engaged, rerouting electron flow. Internal functions loaded: *language, mathematics, Starnet, and games.* The total machine became aware of itself.

Robert beeped.

Output drivers energized, pincher hands moved, antenna rotated and optic lenses swiveled. The backup hover engine whined to a start.

In the pouring rain, Robert righted himself and rose from the lawn. Communication functions came online with data drives running on reserve power.

The first input he received came from Hylander's mainframe. The estate was under attack. All security-bots had automatically switched to defense mode. His audio receptors detected the distinctive *pheuw* of blasters and the bang of rifle fire. Swiveling his camera-lens eyes in the direction of the battle sounds, his internal viewer blinked and flashed crazy patterns until the processor enhanced and stabilized the images coming in. An armada of flying police cruisers and heavily armed hover-copters were approaching Hylander. The authorities had suffered heavy losses.

This information meant nothing to the still-awakening machine until the main processor accessed its memory banks. Robert's awareness module became bombarded with data and sensory images of the goings-on prior to being shot down. Scott and Katherine were in trouble. Robert digitally rationalized that the police were trying to help, but the security-bots had been tasked to stop them.

By now, his logic module had interlinked with his main processor, which allowed him to decide on a response to this data.

Shut down the security-bots.

Beeping with urgency, he interfaced Hylander's mainframe and discovered Jerry hadn't locked in the automatic defense program. Why would he? His rogue cyber-bot had been shot down. Put out of commission. But not for long.

Sensors indicated Jerry was down in the white room...with Scott...Katherine...and Sue. Robert's emotion module took a surge of electrons, which he interpreted as dread. He was too late. *Beep.* He aborted the program running in the mainframe. Instantly, the blasters stopped firing, and the security-bots stood around awaiting further instructions.

The police moved in.

Having lost their backup force, human security guards dropped their weapons and raised their hands in surrender. In the midst of the incursion, Robert zoomed to and fro, dodging the incoming police cars and hover-copters that landed on the lawn in front of Hylander mansion.

"This way," he rallied the officers.

They all headed for the front door, weapons charged and ready.

Chapter Thirty-Seven

D own in the white room, Scott fought for each breath, his chest muscles tight as barrel bands. He was cold, flesh biting cold, like a million pins stabbing his skin, over and over cold. His body erupted in goosebumps and he quaked with teeth-chattering shivers. His feet felt stiff, and his muscles cramped. But this agony was nothing compared to the torment of knowing that Sue was going through the same ordeal. He looked at Katherine standing behind Jerry, saw the wrench of her mouth, her eyes ringed in white. "K-Kath-Katherine. Do something."

Laughing, Jerry tucked his blaster under his thermal robe. "She can't save you, Scott Dunn." With bare hands, he scooped the ice and piled it up higher on Scott's chest. "I bet you thought Katherine was quite the find, didn't you...sharp looking woman...but look at her real close." He patted the ice. "She's got a fat ass and less sense than God gave a piss ant." Then Jerry leaned closer to Scott's face. "But she's a damn good whore in bed, don't you think?"

Katherine glared at him and stepped back.

Uncontrollable shivering gripped Scott's body. "You d-don't d-deserve her."

"That's not for you to decide."

Scott felt his body going numb, the cold seeping into

every pore, boring down through his muscles like maggots in carrion. It had to be just as painful for Sue. "Sue?"

She didn't answer.

He tried to look over at her, but he couldn't raise his head high enough to see over the table lip. And he couldn't see Katherine either. Where did she go? And why wasn't Sue answering him? "Sue," he called out louder.

Jerry piled on more ice. "She seems to be sleeping."

"No, p-please," he pleaded, his speech slurring like a drunkard. "Wake her up-p."

"I'd rather not," Jerry said and went on about Katherine. "She'll be the mistress of Eternal Hylander, Alpha Ketari's queen, at my beck and call. Oh yes, Scott Dunn, she'll be much better off without you."

"S-Sue." He tried shouting to wake her, but his voice was weak.

"They're both better off without you," Jerry added, patting the pile of ice. "You're a Weller. Remember? You don't care about anyone but yourself."

"That's n-not true..." Sleep, he thought. Unimaginable calm. Katherine had told him death wasn't so bad. It seemed so much better than this freezing hell. No. This was better. Or... His mind fought confusion. He stiffened his resolve to stay awake, forced his eyes open, and then just as quickly, closed them. Apathy set in. His body stopped shivering. He lost his will to fight the cold and began to lose consciousness. Strangely, he thought he heard Myrtle hiss. He vaguely remembered her coming into the room...with something...why did she hiss?

"Stop it," Katherine shouted. "Let them go."

It took all the energy he had left to open his eyes

again, but nothing he saw made any sense. Katherine was pointing a small blaster at Jerry...gold and silver...Where did she get it? And worse, Jerry was an arm's length away...aiming a blaster at her.

"Don't make me shoot you, my love."

Their jaws were set, eyes narrow.

"K-Katherine, don't." Scott had to force his eyes to stay open. He saw Myrtle jump on a console and scamper across a bank of machines.

"Go ahead, Jerry." Katherine's gun hand was shaking. "Kill me. You'll lose everything, the election, Alpha Ketari, Eternal Hylander, and me, Jerry." Her eyes were full of hurt and hate. "You can't have any of it without me."

"Give me the gun," he said coolly.

"Me, Jerry." The gun shook. "The woman who loved you." Her arm shook. "I took your beatings...your abuse..."

No. Delirium plowed through Scott's mind. It wasn't true...Katherine didn't take it...she fought him and lost.

"But look what you've done to me, Jerry. Look at my face. I didn't deserve this."

"It's your own damn fault," he spat, circling to his left, blaster leveled at Katherine's face. "You made me do it."

"I just wanted to please you." She followed his every move, her gun still pointed at his face. "I loved you, damn it."

Scott knew she couldn't win. "K-Katherine." He tried to move under the pile of ice. "He'll kill you." His warning was but a whisper. How could she be so reckless? Was this her last stand? She'd drank the sugar water...She thought it was Everlife...She didn't want to live with Jerry forever. Was she trying to commit suicide by Jerry? Or maybe...He saw a flash of motion. Myrtle? She jumped from a machine to the top of the cryostat. She was leaning forward, teetering on the edge, her beady eyes zeroed in on the gold and silver gun. What was she doing up there?

Circling, Katherine's eyes remained glued on Jerry's. Her gun was shaking, but her voice was stern. "I said, let them go."

"Forget it," Jerry replied with equal resolve.

"I've got nothing to lose if I pull this trigger."

"You don't have what it takes." Unbelievably, Jerry dropped his blaster on the floor, held his arms out to his sides. "Go ahead. Shoot me."

She hesitated a second too long. He grabbed her gun, yanked it out of her hand, and turned it on her, steady and true.

Myrtle leaped from the cryostat, landed on Jerry's gun-hand, and sank her teeth into his flesh.

Scott passed out.

***

Hollering, Jerry dropped the mini-blaster and staggered backward, first consumed by shock, then rage. He tried to shake the wild ferret off his hand but quickly realized it only worsened the painful bite. Holding out his clenched fist with Myrtle dangling by her jaws, he moved toward the Alcor techs shouting, "Get it off me. Get it off me."

Hissing ferociously, Myrtle hung on.

The men shrunk back, unwilling to tangle with the

ferret.

"Katherine," Jerry shouted. "Help me."

But she was already at Scott's side, frantically pushing the ice off his body. Her disloyalty and the vicious ferret had Jerry's mind reeling. He decided to kill them both. Stooping to pick up the dropped blaster, he saw a polished shoe kick it out of his reach. "What the hell?"

Only then did the ferret let go of his hand, land on all fours, and scamper off after the kicked gun. Jerry grabbed his bleeding hand and looked up, astounded at who he saw standing over him. "Navarro?"

"For God's sake, man," Navarro shouted, scanning the room. "What have you done?"

"It's none of your business." Jerry's hand felt like it was on fire. That damn ferret. "Get out of my house."

Police officers poured into the room. Robert whizzed up. *"Arrest that man,"* he said, a pincher hand pointed at Jerry. *"I always wanted to say that."*

Jerry couldn't believe his eyes. "I thought the security-bots shot you."

"They missed."

Then Jerry saw the Alcor techs sprint to Sue and start digging her out of the ice. "Get away from her."

Navarro was there, too, checking her condition.

Jerry was losing control of his future. Everything seemed surreal, Robert hovering, the police swarming, and especially Scott Dunn now sitting up on the table. Katherine had freed his arms from the gauze. Jerry's plans were ruined. "You bitch." He lunged for her, but several policemen grabbed him and pushed him face-first against the cryostat. "Spread 'em." A sergeant kicked Jerry's feet apart and patted him down.

"You'd better have a warrant. I'll sue—"

Wrenching Jerry's hands behind his back, the cop slapped on energy cuffs. "You're under arrest. You have the right to remain silent..."

"What the hell did I do?"

"For starters, you murdered your wife."

"Nonsense." Jerry poked his chin toward Katherine who was draping a thermal blanket around Scott's shoulders. "She's right there."

The sergeant shook his head. "We know what you did to her back in 2010. There's no statute of limitations on murder."

Jerry huffed. "It can't be murder if she's not dead. Look. She's alive. My lawyers will eat you for lunch."

"Tell it to the judge."

"I'll sue you for false arrest."

Robert hovered over to Scott. *"Good job."* He gave Katherine a high-five.

"And you, you little twerp," Jerry shouted at Robert. "You're scrap iron, you hear."

"Go ahead," Robert shot back. *"Make my day."*

"Why you—"

Just then, a detective walked up. "We've found another body," he told the sergeant. "An Alcor tech. The others fingered this guy as the shooter." He pointed at Jerry.

"They're disgruntled employees," Jerry said. "Liars. You'll never prove I did it."

"In cold blood," the detective added. "Here's the murder weapon." He held up Jerry's blaster, already bagged and sealed. "I'll bet his fingerprints are all over it."

"I can explain—"

"Save it for the station," the detective snapped.

As if taking inventory, the sergeant said, "Three bodies, counting the two upstairs."

"The woman shot *herself*," Jerry put in, though he doubted they'd believe him. "I shot the bounty hunter in self-defense." He didn't think they'd believe that either.

The detective nodded. "There was a gun battle up there, all right."

"Parish assassinated Ishar Anders." Jerry pressed his case. "I did you guys a favor."

"But this isn't the gun that killed him," the detective said. "Or that poor woman up there. The blast wounds are too small."

The captain arched an eyebrow. "Then there must be another weapon—"

A clunk distracted him. The ferret reappeared, dragging a small blaster across the floor, oblivious to everything going on around her.

"Ah, another gun," the sergeant finished.

"Shit," Jerry shouted. That damn ferret had caused him nothing but trouble.

The detective took the gun from the ferret. Hissing, she glared up at him as he scanned the Derringer 840 mini-blaster with a forensic spectrometer. "It's been fired, all right." He handed the gun to the sergeant. "And I'll bet Jerry Well's fingerprints are all over it."

"Of course they are," Jerry yelled. "It's my gun but that doesn't mean I used it to kill anybody."

The sergeant poked Jerry in the chest. "With guys like

you, it's always someone else's fault. You never do anything wrong. But this evidence and Katherine's murder will get you life in prison without parole, a mighty long time for you, Weller."

An eternity in prison? Jerry felt sick. The odor of garlic leaked through his thermal robe. "But the elections...?"

"Looks like you're going to abstain." He turned to the policemen gathered around. "He's stinking up the place. Get him out of my sight."

Cops muscled him to the door.

"You can't do this to me."

***

Sitting in a scattered pile of ice, happy to be shivering again, now wrapped in a warm blanket, Scott watched the police haul Jerry Well away. The sergeant stayed behind, pacing the crime scene and typing notes on a handheld report writer. Myrtle followed him, bobbing up and down, her beady eyes glued to the gold and silver gun that he'd stuck in a plastic bag and carried under his arm. Scott exhaled, feeling relieved that the authorities had intervened and that Jerry Well was in custody.

On the table next to Scott, Sue moaned. Alcor techs worked to bring her body temperature up slowly. A relieved smile played on Dr. Navarro's face. "She's coming around."

"Thank God," Scott muttered.

"You're going to be all right," Katherine told him, vigorously rubbing his arms and hands. A policeman had given her his coat.

"I-I thought it was the end for me," he stuttered, thankful for the blanket and Katherine's warm touch. Looking into her eyes, he felt humbled. "You did it. You took the Everlife to save us...Sue and I."

"That's because you care about her, Scott."

"Imagine that, a Weller caring about someone."

"It has its rewards."

"I know." Caring was a two-way street.

"So what's a little Everlife among friends?" Katherine rubbed his shoulders. "I hope there's an antidote."

In all the excitement, he'd forgotten. He took her hands and cupped them in his, each warming the other. "It was sugar water, Katherine."

"Huh?"

"Dr. Demone made a placebo for me at the hospital. I buried the real vial in the cellar."

Relief washed over her face. She hugged him, "Thank you, thank you, thank you," and showered him with kisses.

God it was good to be alive. "Help me off this table."

Quickly, she unwrapped the gauze from around his legs, leaving a modest amount of cloth to cover his groin. Stiff-legged, he climbed off the embalming table and hugged the warm blanket. The freezing floor bit his feet, but with Katherine's support, he staggered the few steps to the table where Dr. Navarro had helped Sue sit upright. When her arms were free of the gauze wrap, a technician draped a thermo-blanket over her shoulders. She breathed warmed oxygen through a facemask.

"Is that better?" Navarro asked her.

She nodded.

Scott pushed his way between the Alcor techs and

threw his arms around Sue. "Oh God, I almost lost you again."

Shivering madly, "It's okay, Scott," she muttered through the mask. "I'd do it for you all over again, and Katherine...if I had to."

The sergeant approached the table. "I'll need your statements—"

Thump!

The sound came from behind Scott. He turned, saw the thick door closed, a hunched figure, a gray blanket covering a bent-down head, just standing there. Everyone froze, taking in the strange sight. Before anyone could react, the figure reared up, cast off the blanket, and with a guttural growl raised a blaster. "Scott Dunn," Jerry Well shouted. "You're a dead man."

"He escaped," Katherine cried.

"Get down." The sergeant grabbed for his service blaster.

Jerry shot him in the arm, severing it completely and slamming the officer to the floor, wailing, writhing, and clutching his smoldering stub.

Myrtle squeaked and darted under a nearby machine.

Scott couldn't think straight. This wasn't happening. How did Jerry get away...get his blaster back? There must've been a gunfight...dead policemen upstairs. How did he get free of the energy cuffs? Then Scott realized none of that mattered. He had to protect Sue...on the table. He positioned his body between her and the blaster. Navarro and the techs were on the floor. Katherine stood next to Scott as he watched Jerry move to the fallen cop.

With teeth bared, he stomped a boot on the captain's

stomach. "There's something about me you forgot," Jerry shouted. "I always win."

Pheuw-Pheuw!

Two particle bolts stilled the sergeant.

Jerry pivoted, blaster leveled at Scott. "Your turn."

"No," Katherine screamed.

Pheuw-Fitz...

Katherine leapt in front of Scott, took the proton bolt for him, and hit the floor hard.

Scott's heart seized. "Katherine. No."

She writhed and moaned.

He didn't dare kneel down to her and leave Sue unprotected.

With two fingers of his free hand, Jerry removed a chip from his mouth, held it up and grinned. "The cops should be more careful with their energy cuff deactivators."

"When's the killing going to stop?" Scott shouted.

"Right after this one." Jerry pulled the trigger.

Fitz... fitz...

Wide-eyed, he looked at the discharged blaster. "What...?"

Scott lunged at him, felt clumsy and stiff, but determined to end this once and for all.

Looking up, Jerry stepped back and threw the empty blaster at Scott. It hit him in the arm...*pain*...bounced off, and smashed into the cryostat control panel. Sparks flew, smoke billowed, but Scott kept moving forward, fists clenched, a growl in his throat. He didn't feel cold anymore...only hot rage.

The odor of garlic ballooned in the air.

Jerry's fist came up, found Scott's jaw, and knocked

him off balance. He swung anyway, grazed Jerry's ear, backed up, and regrouped, fists up. Jerry bulled into him, slammed Scott into a machine. Something dug into his back. *Pain*. He needed help, thought of Robert.

Jerry slugged Scott in the ribs...*argh*...

"The taser, Robert. Hit him with the taser."

In the stomach... *huff*...

There was a click, a sizzle...but no taser stream.

A kidney punch...

Robert beeped. *"Security-bot blaster damage, sir, when I was shot down. My taser is malfunctioning."*

"Damn."

A head butt...*stars*...

Jerry laughed. "I had no idea killing you with my bare hands would be so much fun."

A knee in the groin...*a knock out*...

Scott felt it coming...first the bile...and then the vomit...up his throat and out his mouth in a gush, his guts wrenching the air from his lungs. The insides of his stomach emptied down the front of Jerry's robe.

The stench knocked him back...reeled him around.

Myrtle made a break for the other side of the room, dashed between Jerry's feet, tripping him up.

Jerry stumbled, staggered.

Scott cocked his fist back, rushed forward, and landed a right punch to Jerry's nose.

He flew backward and slammed into the cryostat's open steel fingers.

Snap!

They shut around him like a Venus flytrap.

Jerry screamed.

The machine began clattering. A rotating red beacon flashed on. A buzzer sounded.

Jerry fought to get free. Screamed.

Scott stood there spitting bile, astounded, yet not fully comprehending the turn of events as he watched the closed steel fingers retract, drawing Jerry's clamped body into the cryostat.

Jerry Screamed.

It was all happening automatically. Turning to the techs, Scott shouted, "Turn it off."

That's when he realized they were already at the smoking cryostat control panel, pushing buttons, turning dials, typing commands on the terminal pads. "We can't. It's short-circuited."

The cryostat's outer shell rotated inward, the crack narrowing. Only Jerry's wide eyes and wriggling feet could be seen just before the seam closed and sealed.

"Help me." Jerry's cries were muffled inside the cryostat.

Scott ran to the closed seam, tried prying it apart with his fingers, a desperate act against impossible odds. The outcome was predictable.

He failed.

Whining, the cryostat lid began to move downward, slowly at first, an inch at a time, then faster: two inches, four inches, six inches. *Thunk!*

Red lights began flashing on the liquid hydrogen tank. Pumps started rattling.

Jerry's screams were almost inaudible.

With a hiss, the black hose lurched from a surge of pressurized liquid hydrogen. In less than two seconds, the temperature inside the cryostat dropped to minus 320 degrees Fahrenheit.

Scott stepped back, trembling, rubbed his hurt knuckles, looked for Navarro, saw Sue staring at the cryostat, her wide eyes ringed in white. He rushed to her, hugged her. "It's over."

"He-he ended up...right where he put Katherine."

"Oh, no, Katherine." Releasing Sue, Scott dropped to his knees next to Katherine on the floor. Doubled up, she gasped in pain. Dr. Navarro bent over her.

"How bad is it?" Scott asked him.

"The particle bolt only grazed her. The blaster's energy was severely depleted."

"But she's in pain. What's wrong with her?"

Navarro looked at him sullen-faced. "Cryonic Relapse."

Scott's stomach seized, felt sick all over again. "You've got to do something, doc."

Turning to a tech, Navarro ordered, "Nanoserum, 100 milligrams, stat."

"No." Katherine grabbed his arm. "Please...*gasp*...let me go."

"Don't listen to her," Scott said.

The tech presented Navarro with the injection.

"Please," she rasped, her hand raised to ward off the needle. "It's my time to go."

Navarro looked at her with soft eyes. "Are you sure?"

She nodded.

He waved off the hypodermic. "You are right, of course."

"No way." Scott couldn't believe the doctor would go

along with her wishes. "You have to save her." He rested Katherine's head in his lap.

"We've been through this before," she said. "I've had my time...besides...this crazy world of the future doesn't belong to me. It belongs to you...and Sue."

"But you saved our lives...you're my friend...I care about you...I want to save your life now."

"It's all right, Scott."

Myrtle slinked up, sat next to Scott, squeaked.

Hot tears flooded his eyes. It was happening. Katherine would die, and there wasn't a thing he could do about it.

Sue got on her knees and touched Katherine's arm. "I'm so sorry."

"Hello, Sue," she said, trembling. "Finally we meet."

"I wish it didn't have to be this way."

"It doesn't." Scott grabbed on to a thin thread of hope. "Give her the shot, doctor."

Shaking his head, Navarro sighed. "It will only postpone the inevitable. Twenty hours, maybe thirty...that's all."

Hope drained from Scott's heart. He had to accept the fact that someone he cared about was going to die. He had to face the grief syndrome again, the demon, the crippling agony.

Robert hovered over them, beeping slow and steady tones.

"I'm going to miss you all," Katherine managed to say, her eyes flicking from Robert, to Sue, and to Scott. "When Jerry killed me in 2010, he took everything I owned. Now that he's dead, Hylander is mine, right?"

"Yes," Scott said, wondering what she was getting at.

"Then I give it to you and Sue...all of it...if you'll have each other..." Katherine breathed.

"Is that your final wish?" Navarro asked her.

"If they'll care for each other," Katherine said.

"Of course." Sue patted Scott's shaved head. "I think he's got it in him now."

He looked at Sue and gazed into her eyes. Carson had told him that life was all about choices. If he let go of his grief, he could find happiness again. It was his choice. Take the risk, he thought, for love. "Yes," he told Katherine. "We'll take good care of each other *and* Hylander."

"I am witness to your agreement," Navarro said.

Katherine managed a smile. With a trembling hand, she reached up, touched a tear on Scott's cheek. "Do something good with your immortal life." She coughed. "Don't waste it grieving. Accept your losses and go on." Her face was turning blue. "And remember me."

"We'll never forget you, Katherine."

"I hear music," she said, her eyes wide with wonder. "A song...I used to sing...I will always love...you." She went limp.

Scott choked. "Doc?"

With two fingers, Navarro checked for a pulse, sighed, and with the palm of his hand, brushed her eyelids closed.

Everyone in the room bowed their heads. A wracking sob burst from Scott's lungs. He held Sue and cried.

Chapter Thirty-Eight

The funerals were on Friday: Liz's in the morning and Katherine's that afternoon. Finally they'd both been put to rest, atomized to nuclear dust. Walking from the atomatorium, past rows of old tombstones, arm-in-arm with Sue, Scott knew that Katherine was happy now, peaceful in that dreamless sleep that she couldn't remember. Her death was hard to accept, at first, but he'd made it through the initial shock and was managing the stages of his grief. He would be all right.

Savoring Sue's warmth and her companionship, he accepted the fact that she too would die someday, but he didn't want to miss the time they could share together. Katherine had taught him that much.

A black hover-limo descended from a clear sky and landed in front of them with barely a hum. Myrtle's masked face bobbed in the oval door window. Scott let Sue get in first, and when he settled in next to her, Myrtle curled up in his lap. A regular little family, he thought and saluted the pilot. "Let's go home, Robert."

"Yes, sir." The limo rose smooth as an elevator. Scott leaned back, cuddled into Sue, and watched her diamond engagement ring throw sparks in the sunshine that beamed down through the bubbletop dome. They both wore ball

caps to keep the sun off their shaved heads. If it weren't for Katherine, he and Sue would have been frozen in cryostat 34-B forever. Poor Katherine. She deserved so much more from life, more than her husband ever did for her. "I wonder if Jerry will ever get out of that cryostat."

Sue patted the back of Scott's hand. "Who knows? Someday they may find a way to reverse the damage instant freezing does to the body's cells. Until then, the cryostat will be stored at Alcor."

"If he's ever reanimated, he'll have to face justice for what he's done. Too bad the death penalty was abolished."

"You think?" Sue asked. "He'll spend his reanimated immortal life in prison, everything he does controlled by someone else forever. That would be worse than death for him."

"It would serve him right." Scott looked out the window at the city streaking by below. The world was in trouble, he knew, but it had been in trouble before. Things had a way of working out. The Council of Elders, under new leadership, called for a compromise between the environmentalists and the mining conglomerates. The resolution was threefold: for every acre dug up, another would be preserved, and for every two preserved another would be developed for human settlement. And like Antarctica, no person, company, or country would ever own or govern any part of the pristine planet. Dar Anders was appointed trustee of the agreement.

"Maybe we should take a vacation on Alpha Ketari one day," Scott said, wondering what it would be like in paradise.

Sue squeezed his hand. "That won't be possible for a

long time, probably long after I'm dead and gone."

"But I don't want to go without you."

"And so the stone crumbles."

He remembered how hard he was on her when they first met. "We have to make the best of the time we have together."

She smiled. "We will."

As the limo banked west and headed for Hylander, Scott reached into his pocket and took out the vial of Everlife. "I wanted this atomized with Katherine, but the casket was sealed."

Sue looked at the vial with wonder in her eyes. "What are you going to do with it?"

"This stuff has caused a lot of trouble...for us, for Liz, Carson, for everyone who took it." He motored the oval window down, letting in the wind. "How high are we, Robert?"

"Five hundred feet," the cyber-bot reported. *"I am on final approach to Hylander."*

"That should be high enough." He held the vial up to the open window, cocked his hand back.

"Wait." Sue grabbed his wrist.

He turned to her in total disbelief. "What are you doing?"

"I want to go to Alpha Ketari with you someday."

Scott tried to get free of her grasp. "You don't know what you're saying."

"I know better than anyone. My grandpa—"

"If you take this, you'll smell like garlic."

"So what? I'm used to it."

Looking at her hand clamped on his wrist, he

understood why Sue wanted the Everlife, but he feared the problems she would have to endure. "What about the grief syndrome?"

"I'm not afraid. There's a lot of my grandpa in me. You even said so yourself. And I'm not at all like Liz. We can have a family. We can enjoy the good times and endure the bad times. Together. I can love you forever, Scott, but not if you break that vial."

Robert said, *"Never throw away your ace, sir."*

"See?" She nodded to Robert. "Even he understands."

Scott clutched the vial in his fist. They were right. He didn't have to lose her. She didn't have to die. It was her choice to take the Everlife. If he threw it out the window, he'd be making the decision for her. He couldn't do that. He loved her too much, respected her wishes. Besides, having lived with Carson, she knew what she was getting into. He handed her the vial. "When?"

She popped the cork, tilted her head back, and drank the Everlife. Then looking at the empty vial, her eyes went crossed. Her face turned red. She coughed, clung to his arm, gasped for breath.

I just poisoned her. His heart was jumping around like a ferret in a cage. "What's wrong?"

"Smooth." She smirked.

He huffed. "You scared the shit out of me."

She winked and pitched the vial out the open window. "Now I'm yours forever."

"I'm not sure my heart can take it."

She laughed.

The limo set down on Hylander's sprawling lawn. While Myrtle stretched, the bubbletop dome rose and

Robert whizzed around to the opening rear door. *"Welcome home."*

Scott helped Sue out of the car, drew her into his arms, saw the mansion gleaming in the sunshine, the garden swaying. As Myrtle romped in the grass at their feet, he looked into Sue's eyes. "Thanks for loving me."

"Thanks for letting me." She kissed him.

Robert twirled in the air. *"Pick a card, any card."*

Terry Wright

About the Author

There's nothing mundane in the writing world of **Terry Wright**. Tension, conflict and suspense propel his readers through the pages as if they were on fire. His mastery of the action thriller has also won him International acclaim as an accomplished screenplay writer. A longtime member of the Rocky Mountain Fiction Writers, he coordinated their annual Colorado Gold Writing Contest for six years, received their highest award for service, The Jasmine Award, and was nominated for the Writer of the Year, 2014.

A Vietnam Veteran USAF, retired auto repair shop owner, certified private pilot, and an avid Harley Davidson enthusiast, he now spends his time editing manuscripts for authors across the country and publishing authors from around the world at TWB Press. He lives in Centennial, Colorado, south of Denver, with his wife, Bobette, and their Chihuahua, Spyro.

Terry Wright

Dear Reader,

Thank you for reading "The Grief Syndrome." I invite you to click on the following links for my other works where you'll find more information, video trailers, and links to purchase. And while you're there, explore other TWB Press and Amore Moon Publishing e-books and novels. You're also welcome to visit my author website at www.terrywrightbooks.com.

— Terry Wright

The 13th Power Quest, Book 1

The search for the secret of the universe
Science Fiction novel, technology, action, adventure
www.twbpress.com/the13thpowerquest

The 13th Power Journey, Book 2

Mankind's first journey across the galaxy
www.twbpress.com/the13thpowerjourney

The 13th Power War, Book 3

And then came man, and war, and death
www.twbpress.com/the13thpowerwar

The Duplication Factor

Behold the first human clone
Science Fiction novel, thriller, action, adventure
www.twbpress.com/theduplicationfactor

Black Jack

A Denver detective searches for his wife's killer
Crime drama novel, thriller, action, mystery
www.twbpress.com/blackjack

The Pearl of Death
Novel based on the true story of the world's largest pearl
www.twbpress.com/thepearlofdeath

Undead in Paris (a screenplay)
Vampire wars: the old ways vs the new ways
www.twbpress.com/undeadinparis

Justin Graves
A dead detective makes a deal with the devil
A short story horror series
www.twbpress.com/justingraves

Z-motors - The Job from Hell
An unemployed master mechanic finally gets a job
Zombie short story, thriller, satire
www.twbpress.com/zmotors

Street Beat
A woman reporter matches wits with a serial killer
Crime drama short story, action-thriller, romance
www.twbpress.com/streetbeat

Return Me to Mistwillow
A dusty ghost town gets a visitor from the past
Ghost short story, Colorado history, action, thriller
www.twbpress.com/returnmetomistwillow

Wilderness Rampage
A motorhome vacation trip turns deadly
Action adventure short story, bad guys and a bear
www.twbpress.com/wildernessrampage

www.twbpress.com